S0-DZH-442

KINDRED OF THE DUST

HECTOR McKAYE WAS BRED OF AN ACQUISITIVE RACE.

KINDRED OF THE DUST

BY

PETER B. KYNE

AUTHOR OF

CAPPY RICKS,
THE VALLEY OF THE GIANTS,
WEBSTER—MAN'S MAN, ETC.

ILLUSTRATED BY

DEAN CORNWELL

NEW YORK
GROSSET & DUNLAP
PUBLISHERS

TO IRENE

MY DEAR, TYRANNICAL, PRACTICAL LITTLE
FOSTER-SISTER
WITHOUT WHOSE AID AND COMFORT, HOOTS,
CHEERS AND UNAUTHORIZED STRIKES, THE
QUANTITY AND QUALITY OF MY ALLEGED
LITERARY OUTPUT WOULD BE APPRECIABLY
DIMINISHED, THIS BOOK IS AFFECTIONATELY
DEDICATED

THE ILLUSTRATIONS

KINDRED OF THE DUST

I

IN the living-room of The Dreamerie, his home on Tyee Head, Hector McKaye, owner of the Tyee Lumber Company and familiarly known as "The Laird," was wont to sit in his hours of leisure, smoking and building castles in Spain—for his son Donald. Here he planned the acquisition of more timber and the installation of an electric-light plant to furnish light, heat, and power to his own town of Port Agnew; ever and anon he would gaze through the plate-glass windows out to sea and watch for his ships to come home. Whenever The Laird put his dreams behind him, he always looked seaward. In the course of time, his home-bound skippers, sighting the white house on the headland and knowing that The Laird was apt to be up there watching, formed the habit of doing something that pleased their owner mightily. When the northwest trades held steady and true, and while the tide was still at the flood, they would scorn the services of the tug that went out to meet them and come ramping into the bight, all their white sails set and the glory of the sun upon them; as they swept past, far below The Laird, they would dip his house-flag—a burgee, scarlet-edged, with a fir tree embroidered in green on a field of white

1

—the symbol to the world that here was a McKaye ship. And when the house-flag fluttered half-way to the deck and climbed again to the masthead, the soul of Hector McKaye would thrill.

"Guid lads! My bonny brave lads!" he would murmur aloud, with just a touch of his parents' accent, and press a button which discharged an ancient brass cannon mounted at the edge of the cliff. Whenever he saw one of his ships in the offing—and he could identify his ships as far as he could see them—he ordered the gardener to load this cannon.

Presently the masters began to dip the house-flag when outward bound, and discovered that, whether The Laird sat at his desk in the mill office or watched from the cliff, they drew an answering salute.

This was their hail and farewell.

One morning, the barkentine Hathor, towing out for Delagoa Bay, dipped her house-flag, and the watch at their stations bent their gaze upon the house on the cliff. Long they waited but no answering salute greeted the acknowledgment of their affectionate and willing service.

The mate's glance met the master's.

"The old laird must be unwell, sir," he opined.

But the master shook his head.

"He was to have had dinner aboard with us last night, but early in the afternoon he sent over word that he'd like to be excused. He's sick at heart, poor man! Daney tells me he's heard the town gossip about young Donald."

"The lad's a gentleman, sir," the mate defended. "He'll not disgrace his people."

"He's young—and youth must be served. Man, I

was young myself once—and Nan of the Sawdust Pile is not a woman a young man would look at once and go his way."

In the southwestern corner of the state of Washington, nestled in the Bight of Tyee and straddling the Skookum River, lies the little sawmill town of Port Agnew. It is a community somewhat difficult to locate, for the Bight of Tyee is not of sufficient importance as a harbor to have won consideration by the cartographers of the Coast and Geodetic Survey, and Port Agnew is not quite forty years old. Consequently, it appears only on the very latest state maps and in the smallest possible type.

When Hector McKaye first gazed upon the bight, the transcontinental lines had not yet begun to consider the thrusting of their tentacles into southwestern Washington, and, with the exception of those regions where good harbors had partially solved the problem of transportation, timber in Washington was very cheap. Consequently, since Hector McKaye was one of those hardy men who never hesitate to take that which no man denies them, he reached forth and acquired timber.

A strip of land a quarter of a mile wide and fronting the beach was barren of commercial timber. As grazing-land, Hector McKaye was enabled to file on a full section of this, and, with its acquisition, he owned the key to the outlet. While "proving up" his claim, he operated a general store for trading with the Indians and trappers, and at this he prospered. From time to time he purchased timber-claims from the trappers as fast as they "proved up," paying for these stumpageprices varying from twenty-five to fifty cents per thousand.

On his frequent trips to the outer world, McKaye extolled the opportunities for acquiring good timber-claims down on the Skookum; he advertised them in letters and in discreet interviews with the editors of little newspapers in the sawmill towns on Puget Sound and Grays Harbor; he let it be known that an honest fellow could secure credit for a winter's provisions from him, and pay for it with pelts in the spring.

The influx of homesteaders increased—single men, for the most part, and poor—men who labored six months of the year elsewhere and lived the remaining six months in rude log huts on their claims down on the Skookum. And when the requirements of the homestead laws had been complied with and a patent to their quarter-section obtained from the Land Office in Washington, the homesteaders were ready to sell and move on to other and greener pastures. So they sold to the only possible purchaser, Hector McKaye, and departed, quite satisfied with a profit which they flattered themselves had been the result of their own prudence and foresight.

Thus, in the course of ten years, Hector McKaye acquired ten thousand acres of splendid Douglas fir and white cedar. But he had not been successful in acquiring claims along the south bank of the Skookum. For some mysterious reason, he soon found claims on the north bank cheaper and easier to secure, albeit the timber showed no variance in quantity or quality. Discreet investigations brought to light the fact that he had a competitor—one Martin Darrow, who dwelt in St. Paul, Minnesota. To St. Paul, therefore, jour-

neyed Hector McKaye, and sought an audience with
Martin Darrow.

"I'm McKaye, from the Skookum River, Washington," he announced, without preamble.

"I've been expecting you, Mr. McKaye," Darrow
replied. "Got a proposition to submit?"

"Naturally, or I wouldn't have come to St. Paul. I
notice you have a weakness for the timber on the south
bank of the Skookum. You've opposed me there half
a dozen times and won. I have also observed that I
have a free hand with claims north of the river. That's
fair—and there's timber enough for two. Hereafter,
I'll keep to my own side of the river."

"I see we're going to come to an understanding, Mr.
McKaye. What will you give me to stick to my side
of the river?"

"An outlet through the bight for your product when
you commence manufacturing. I control the lower
half-mile of the river and the only available mill-sites.
I'll give you a mill-site if you'll pay half the expense
of digging a new channel for the Skookum, and chang-
ing its course so it will emerge into the still, deep water
under the lee of Tyee Head."

"We'll do business," said Martin Darrow—and they
did, although it was many years after Hector McKaye
had incorporated the Tyee Lumber Company and
founded his town of Port Agnew before Darrow began
operations.

True to his promise, McKaye deeded him a mill- and
town-site, and he founded a settlement on the eastern
edge of Port Agnew, but quite distinct from it, and
called it Darrow, after himself. It was not a community that Hector McKaye approved of, for it was

squalid and unsanitary, and its untidy, unpainted
shacks of rough lumber harbored southern European
labor, of which Hector McKaye would have none. In
Darrow, also, there were three groggeries and a gam-
bling-house, with the usual concomitant of women whose
profession is the oldest and the saddest in the world.

Following his discovery of the Bight of Tyee, a quarter of a century passed. A man may prosper much in
twenty-five years, and Hector McKaye, albeit American
born, was bred of an acquisitive race. When his Gethsemane came upon him, he was rated the richest lum-
berman in the state of Washington; his twenty-thou-
sand-board-feet-capacity-per-day sawmill had grown
to five hundred thousand, his ten thousand acres to a
hundred thousand. Two thousand persons looked to
him and his enterprise for their bread and butter; he
owned a fleet of half a dozen steam-schooners and sixteen big wind-jammers; he owned a town which he had
called Port Agnew, and he had married and been blessed
with children. And because his ambition no longer demanded it, he was no longer a miser.

In a word, he was a happy man, and in affectionate
pride and as a tribute to his might, his name and an
occasional forget-me-not of speech which clung to his
tongue, heritage of his Scotch forebears, his people
called him "The Laird of Tyee." Singularly enough,
his character fitted this cognomen rather well. Reserved, proud, independent, and sensitive, thinking
straight and talking straight, a man of brusque yet tender sentiment which was wont to manifest itself unexpectedly, it had been said of him that in a company of
a hundred of his mental, physical, and financial peers,

he would have stood forth preeminently and distinctively, like a lone tree on a hill.

Although The Laird loved his town of Port Agnew, because he had created it, he had not, nevertheless, resided in it for some years prior to the period at which this chronicle begins. At the very apex of the headland that shelters the Bight of Tyee, in a cuplike depression several acres in extent, on the northern side and ideally situated two hundred feet below the crest, thus permitting the howling southeasters to blow over it, Hector McKaye, in the fulness of time, had built for himself a not very large two-story house of white stone native to the locality. This house, in the center of beautiful and well-kept grounds, was designed in the shape of a letter T, with the combination living-room and library forming the entire leg of the T and enclosed on all three sides by heavy plate-glass French windows.

Thus, The Laird was enabled to command a view of the bight, with Port Agnew nestled far below; of the silver strip that is the Skookum River flowing down to the sea through the logged-over lands, now checkerboarded into little green farms; of the rolling back country with its dark-green mantle of fir and white cedar, fading in the distance to dark blue and black; of the yellow sandstone bluffs of the coast-line to the north, and the turquoise of the Pacific out to the horizon.

This room Hector McKaye enjoyed best of all things in life, with the exception of his family; of his family, his son Donald was nearest and dearest to him. This boy he loved with a fierce and hungry love, intensified, doubtless, because to the young Laird of Tyee, McKaye was still the greatest hero in the world. To his wife, The Laird was no longer a hero, although in the old days of the upward climb, when he had fiercely claimed her and supported her by the sweat of his brow, he had been something akin to a god. As for Elizabeth and Jane, his daughters, it must be recorded that both these young women had long since ceased to regard their father as anything except an unfailing source of revenue—an old dear who clung to Port Agnew, homely speech, and homely ways, hooting good-naturedly at the pretensions of their set, and, with characteristic Gaelic stubbornness, insisting upon living and enjoying the kind of life that appealed to him with peculiar force as the only kind worth living.

Indeed, in more than one humble home in Port Agnew, it had been said that the two McKaye girls were secretly ashamed of their father. This because frequently, in a light and debonair manner, Elizabeth and Jane apologized for their father and exhibited toward him an indulgent attitude, as is frequently the case with overeducated and supercultured young ladies who cannot recall a time when their slightest wish has not been gratified and cannot forget that the good fairy who gratified it once worked hard with his hands, spoke the language and acquired the habits of his comrades in the battle for existence.

Of course, Elizabeth and Jane would have resented this analysis of their mental attitude toward their father. Be that as it may, however, the fact remained that both girls were perfunctory in their expressions of affection for their father, but wildly extravagant in them where their mother was concerned. Hector Mc-Kaye liked it so. He was a man who never thought about himself, and he had discovered that if he gave his wife and daughters everything they desired, he was not apt to be nagged.

Only on one occasion had Hector McKaye declared himself master in his own house, and, at the risk of appearing paradoxical, this was before the house had been built. One day, while they still occupied their first home (in Port Agnew), a house with a mansard roof, two towers, jig-saw and scroll-work galore, and the usual cast-iron mastiffs and deer on the front lawn, The Laird had come gleefully home from a trip to Seattle and proudly exhibited the plans for a new house.

Ensued examination and discussion by his wife and the young ladies. Alas! The Laird's dream of a home did not correspond with that of his wife, although, as a matter of fact, the lady had no ideas on the subject beyond an insistence that the house should be "worthy of their station," and erected in a fashionable suburb of Seattle. Elizabeth and Jane aided and abetted her in clamoring for a Seattle home, although both were quick to note the advantages of a picturesque country home on the cliffs above the bight. They urged their father to build his house, but condemned his plans. They desired a house some three times larger than the blue-prints called for.

Hector McKaye said nothing. The women chattered and argued among themselves until, Elizabeth and Jane having vanquished their mother, all three moved briskly to the attack upon The Laird. When they had talked themselves out and awaited a reply, he gave it with the simple directness of his nature. It was evident that he had given his answer thought.

"I can never live in Seattle until I retire, and I cannot retire until Donald takes my place in the business. That means that Donald must live here. Consequently, I shall spend half of my time with you and the girls in Seattle, mother, and the other half with Donald here. When we built our first home, you had your way—and I've lived in this architectural horror ever since. This time, I'm going to have my own way—and you've lived with me long enough to know that when I declare for a will of my own, I'll not be denied. Well I realize you and the girls have outgrown Port Agnew. There's naught here to interest you, and I would not have woman o' mine unhappy. So plan your house in Seattle, and I'll build it and spare no expense. As for this house on the headland, you have no interest in it. Donald's approved the plans, and him only will I defer to. 'Twill be his house some day—his and his wife's, when he gets one. And there will be no more talk of it, my dears. I'll not take it kindly of ye to interfere."

II

AT a period in his upward climb to fortune, when
as yet Hector McKaye had not fulfilled his dream
of a factory for the manufacture of his waste and
short-length stock into sash, door, blinds, moldings,
and so forth, he had been wont to use about fifty per
cent. of this material for fuel to maintain steam in
the mill boilers, while the remainder passed out over
the waste-conveyor to the slab pile, where it was burned.

The sawdust, however, remained to be disposed of,
and since it was not possible to burn this in the slab
fire for the reason that the wet sawdust blanketed the
flames and resulted in a profusion of smoke that blew
back upon the mill to the annoyance of the employees,
for many years The Laird had caused this accumulated
sawdust to be hauled to the edge of the bight on the
north side of the town, and there dumped in a low,
marshy spot which formerly had bred millions of mos-
quitoes.

Subsequently, in the process of grading the streets
of Port Agnew and excavating cellars, waste dirt had
been dumped with the sawdust, and, occasionally, when
high winter tides swept over the spot, sand, small stones,
sea-shells, and kelp were added to the mixture. And
as if this were not sufficient, the citizens of Port Agnew
contributed from time to time old barrels and bottles,
yard-sweepings, tin cans, and superannuated stoves and
kitchen utensils.

Slowly this dump crept out on the beach, and in order to prevent the continuous attrition of the surf upon the outer edge of it from befouling the white-sand bathing-beach farther up the Bight of Tyee, The Laird had driven a double row of fir piling parallel with and beyond the line of breakers. This piling, driven as close together as possible and reenforced with two-inch planking between, formed a bulkhead with the flanks curving in to the beach, thus insuring practically a water-tight pen some two acres in extent; and, with the passage of years, this became about two-thirds filled with the waste from the town. Had The Laird ever decided to lay claim to the Sawdust Pile, there would have been none in Port Agnew to contest his title; since he did not claim it, the Sawdust Pile became a sort of No Man's Land.

After The Laird erected his factory and began to salvage his waste, the slab fire went out forever for lack of fuel, and the modicum of waste from the mill and factory, together with the sawdust, was utilized for fuel in an electric-light plant that furnished light, heat, and power to the town. Consequently, sawdust no longer mercifully covered the trash on the Sawdust Pile as fast as this trash arrived, and, one day, Hector McKaye, observing this, decided that it was an unsightly spot and not quite worthy of his town of Port Agnew. So he constructed a barge somewhat upon the principle of a patent dump-wagon, moored it to the river-bank, created a garbage monopoly in Port Agnew, and sold it for five thousand dollars to a pair of ambitious Italians. With the proceeds of this garbage deal, The Laird built a very pretty little public library.

Having organized his new garbage system (the garbage was to be towed twenty miles to sea and there dumped), The Laird forbade further dumping on the Sawdust Pile. When the necessity for more dredger-work developed, in order to keep the deep channel of the Skookum from filling, he had the pipes from the dredger run out to the Sawdust Pile and covered the unsightly spot with six feet of rich river-silt up to the level of the piling.

"And now," said Hector McKaye to Andrew Daney, his general manager, "when that settles, we'll run a light track out here and use the Sawdust Pile for a drying-yard."

The silt settled and dried, and almost immediately thereafter a squatter took possession of the Saw-dust Pile. Across the neck of the little promontory, and in line with extreme high-water mark on each side, he erected a driftwood fence; he had a canvas, drift-wood, and corrugated-iron shanty well under way when Hector McKaye appeared on the scene and bade him a pleasant good-morning.

The squatter turned from his labor and bent upon his visitor an appraising glance. His scrutiny appear-ing to satisfy him as to the identity of the latter, he straightened suddenly and touched his forelock in a queer little salute that left one in doubt whether he was a former member of the United States navy or the British mercantile marine. He was a threadbare little man, possibly sixty years old, with a russet, kindly countenance and mild blue eyes; apart from his salute, there was about him an intangible hint of the sea. He was being assisted in his labors by a ragamuffin girl of perhaps thirteen years.

"Thinking of settling in Port Agnew?" The Laird inquired.

"Why, yes, sir. I thought this might make a good safe anchorage for Nan and me. My name is Caleb Brent. You're Mr. McKaye, aren't you?"

The Laird nodded.

"I had an idea, when I filled this spot in and built that bulkhead, Mr. Brent, that some day this would make a safe anchorage for some of my lumber. I planned a drying-yard here. What's that you're building, Brent? A hen-house?"

Caleb Brent flushed.

"Why, no, sir. I'm making shift to build a home here for Nan and me."

"Is this little one Nan?"

The ragamuffin girl, her head slightly to one side, had been regarding Hector McKaye with alert curiosity mingled with furtive apprehension. As he glanced at her now, she remembered her manners and dropped him a courtesy—an electric, half-defiant jerk that reminded The Laird of a similar greeting customarily extended by squinch-owls.

Nan was not particularly clean, and her one-piece dress, of heavy blue navy-uniform cloth was old and worn and spotted. Over this dress she wore a boy's coarse red-worsted sweater with white-pearl buttons. The skin of her thin neck was fine and creamy; the calves, of her bare brown legs were shapely, her feet small, her ankles dainty.

With the quick eye of the student of character, this man, proud of his own ancient lineage for all his humble beginning, noted that her hands, though brown and uncared-for, were small and dimpled, with long, delicate fingers. She had sea-blue eyes like Caleb Brent's, and, like his, they were sad and wistful; a frowsy wilderness of golden hair, very fine and held in confinement at the nape of her neck by the simple expedient of a piece of twine, showed all too plainly the lack of a mother's care.

The Laird returned Nan's courtesy with a patronizing inclination of his head.

"Your granddaughter, I presume?" he addressed Caleb Brent.

"No; my daughter, sir. I was forty when I married, and Nan came ten years later. She's thirteen now, and her mother's been dead ten years."

Hector McKaye had an idea that the departed mother was probably just as well, if not better, off, free of the battle for existence which appeared to confront this futile old man and his elf of a daughter. He glanced at the embryo shack under construction and, comparing it with his own beautiful home on Tyee Head, he turned toward the bight. A short distance off the bulkhead, he observed a staunch forty-foot motor-cruiser at anchor. She would have been the better for a coat of paint; undeniably she was of a piece with Caleb Brent and Nan, for, like them, The Laird had never seen her before.

"Yours?" he queried.

"Yes, sir."

"You arrived in her, then?"

"I did, sir. Nan and I came down from Bremerton in her, sir."

The Laird owned many ships, and he noted the slurring of the "sir" as only an old sailor can slur it. And there was a naval base at Bremerton.

"You're an old sailor, aren't you, Brent?" he pursued.

"Yes, sir. I was retired a chief petty officer, sir. Thirty years' continuous service, sir—and I was in the mercantile marine at sixteen. I've served my time as a shipwright. Am—am I intruding here, sir?"

The Laird smiled, and followed the smile with a brief chuckle.

"Well—yes and no. I haven't any title to this land you've elected to occupy, although I created it. You see, I'm sort of lord of creation around here. My people call me 'The Laird of Tyee,' and nobody but a stranger would have had the courage to squat on the Sawdust Pile without consulting me. What's your idea about it, Brent?"

"I'll go if you want me to, sir."

"I mean what's your idea if you stay? What do you expect to do for a living?"

"You will observe, sir, that I have fenced off only that portion of the dump beyond high-water mark. That takes in about half of it—about an acre and a half. Well, I thought I'd keep some chickens and raise some garden truck. This silt will grow anything. And I have my launch, and can do some towing, maybe, or take fishing parties out. I might supply the town with fish. I understand you import your fish from Seattle —and with the sea right here at your door."

"I see. And you have your three-quarters pay as a retired chief petty officer?"

"Yes, sir."

"Anything in bank? I do not ask these personal questions, Brent, out of mere idle curiosity. This is my town, you know, and there is no poverty in it. I'm rather proud of that, so I——"

"I understand, sir. That's why I came to Port Agnew. I saw your son yesterday, and he said I could stay."

"Oh! Well, that's all right, then. If Donald told you to stay, stay you shall. Did he give you the Saw-dust Pile?"

"Yes, sir; he did!"

"Well, I had other plans for it, Brent; but since you're here, I'll offer no objection."

Nan now piped up.

"We haven't any money in bank, Mr. Laird, but we have some saved up."

"Indeed! That's encouraging. Where do you keep it?"

"In the brown teapot in the galley. We've got a hundred and ten dollars."

"Well, my little lady, I think you might do well to take your hundred and ten dollars out of the brown teapot in the galley and deposit it in the Port Agnew bank. Suppose that motor-cruiser should spring a leak and sink?"

Nan smiled and shook her golden head in negation. They had beaten round Cape Flattery in that boat, and she had confidence in it.

"Would you know my boy if you should see him again, Nan?" The Laird demanded suddenly.

"Oh, yes, indeed, sir! He's such a nice boy."

"I think, Nan, that if you asked him, he might help your father build this house."

"I'll see him this afternoon when he comes out of high school," Nan declared.

"You might call on Andrew Daney, my general manager," The Laird continued, turning to Caleb Brent, "and make a dicker with him for hauling our garbage-scow out to sea and dumping it. I observe that your motor-boat is fitted with towing-bitts. We dump twice a week. And you may have a monopoly on fresh fish if you desire it. We have no fishermen here, because I do not care for Greeks and Sicilians in Port Agnew. And they're about the only fishermen on this coast."

"Thank you, Mr. McKaye."

"Mind you don't abuse your monopoly. If you do, I'll take it away from you."

"You are very kind, sir. And I can have the Sawdust Pile, sir?"

"Yes; since Donald gave it to you. However, I wish you'd tear down that patchwork fence and replace it with a decent job the instant you can afford it."

"Ah, just wait," old Brent promised. "I know how to make things neat and pretty and keep them ship-shape. You just keep your eye on the Sawdust Pile, sir." The old wind-bitten face flushed with pride; the faded sea-blue eyes shone with joyous anticipation. "I've observed your pride in your town, sir, and before I get through, I'll have a prettier place than the best of them."

A few days later, The Laird looked across the Bight of Tyee from his home on Tyee Head, and through his marine glasses studied the Sawdust Pile. He chuckled as he observed that the ramshackle shanty had disappeared almost as soon as it had been started and in its place a small cottage was being erected. There was a pile of lumber in the yard—bright lumber, fresh from the saws—and old Caleb Brent and the motherless Nan

were being assisted by two carpenters on the Tyee
Lumber Company's pay-roll.

When Donald came home from school that night,
The Laird asked him about the inhabitants of the Sawdust Pile with relation to the lumber and the two carpenters.

"Oh, I made a trade with Mr. Brent and Nan. I'm to
furnish the lumber and furniture for the house, and
those two carpenters weren't very busy, so Mr. Daney
told me I could have them to help out. In return, Mr.
Brent is going to build me a sloop and teach me how to
sail it."

The Laird nodded.

"When his little home is completed, Donald," he suggested presently, "you might take old Brent and his
girl over to our old house in town and let them have
what furniture they require. See if you cannot manage to saw off some of your mother's antiques on them,"
he added whimsically. "By the way, what kind of
shanty is old Brent going to build?"

"A square house with five rooms and a cupola fitted
up like a pilot-house. There's to be a flagpole on the
cupola, and Nan says they'll have colors every night
and morning. That means that you hoist the flag in
the morning and salute it, and when you haul it down at
night, you salute it again. They do that up at the
Bremerton navy-yard."

"That's rather a nice, sentimental idea," Hector Mc-
Kaye replied. "I rather like old Brent and his girl for
that. We Americans are too prone to take our flag and
what it stands for rather lightly."

"Nan wants me to have colors up here, too," Donald

continued. "Then she can see our flag, and we can see theirs across the bight."

"All right," The Laird answered heartily, for he was always profoundly interested in anything that interested his boy. "I'll have the woods boss get out a nice young cedar with, say, a twelve-inch butt, and we'll make it into a flagpole."

"If we're going to do the job navy-fashion, we ought to fire a sunrise and sunset gun," Donald suggested with all the enthusiasm of his sixteen years.

"Well, I think we can afford that, too, Donald."

Thus it came about that the little brass cannon was installed on its concrete base on the cliff. And when the flagpole had been erected, old Caleb Brent came up one day, built a little mound of smooth, sea-washed cobblestones round the base, and whitewashed them. Evidently he was a prideful little man, and liked to see things done in a seamanlike manner. And presently it became a habit with The Laird to watch night and morning, for the little pin-prick of color to flutter forth from the house on the Sawdust Pile, and if his own colors did not break forth on the instant and the little cannon boom from the cliff, he was annoyed and demanded an explanation.

III

HECTOR McKAYE and his close-mouthed general manager, Andrew Daney, were the only persons who knew the extent of The Laird's fortune. Even their knowledge was approximate, however, for The Laird disliked to delude himself, and carried on his books at their cost-price properties which had appreciated tremendously in value since their purchase. The knowledge of his wealth brought to McKaye a goodly measure of happiness—not because he was of Scottish ancestry and had inherited a love for his baubees, but because he was descended from a fierce, proud Scottish clan, and wealth spelled independence to him and his.

The Laird would have filled his cup of happiness to overflowing had he married a less mediocre woman or had he raised his daughters as he had his son. The girls' upbringing had been left entirely in their mother's hands. Not so with young Donald, however—wherefore it was a byword in Port Agnew that Donald was his father's son, a veritable chip of the old block.

By some uncanny alchemy, hard cash appears to soften the heads and relax the muscles of rich men's sons—at least, such had been old Hector's observation, and on the instant that he first gazed upon the face of his son, there had been born in him a mighty resolve that, come what might, he would not have it said of him that he had made a fool of his boy. And throughout the glad years of his fatherhood, with the stern piety of his race and his faith, he had knelt night and morning beside his bed and prayed his God to help him not to make a fool of Donald—to keep Donald from making a fool of himself.

When Donald entered Princeton, his father decided upon an experiment. He had raised his boy right, and trained him for the race of life, and now The Laird felt that, like a thoroughbred horse, his son faced the barrier. Would he make the run, or would he, in the parlance of the sporting world, "dog it?" Would his four years at a great American university make of him a better man, or would he degenerate into a snob and a drone?

With characteristic courage, The Laird decided to give him ample opportunity to become either, for, as old Hector remarked to Andrew Daney: "If the lad's the McKaye I think he is, nothing can harm him. On the other hand, if I'm mistaken, I want to know it in time, for my money and my Port Agnew Lumber Company is a trust, and if he can't handle it, I'll leave it to the men who can—who've helped me create it—and Donald shall earn his bread by the sweat of his brow. Tools," he added, "belong to the men that can use them."

When Donald started East for college, old Hector accompanied him as far as Seattle. On the way up, there was some man-talk between them. In his youth, old Hector had not been an angel, which is to state that he had been a lumberjack. He knew men and the passions that beset them—particularly when they are young and lusty—and he was far from being a prude. He expected his son to raise a certain amount of wild oats; nay, he desired it, for full well he knew that when the fires of youth are quenched, they are liable to flare disgracefully in middle life or old age.

"Never pig it, my son," was his final admonition. "Raise hell if you must, but if you love your old father, be a gentleman about it. You've sprung from a clan o' men, not mollycoddles."

"Hence the expression: 'When Hector was a pup,' " Donald replied laughingly. "Well, I'll do my best, father—only, if I stub my toe, you mustn't be too hard on me. Remember, please, that I'm only half Scotch."

At parting, The Laird handed his son a check for twenty-five thousand dollars.

"This is the first year's allowance, Donald," he informed the boy gravely. "It should not require more than a hundred thousand dollars to educate a son of mine, and you must finish in four years. I would not care to think you dull or lazy."

"Do you wish an accounting, father?"

The Laird shook his head.

"Keeping books was ever a sorry trade, my son. I'll read the accounting in your eye when you come back to Port Agnew."

"Oh!" said young Donald.

At the end of four years, Donald graduated, an honor-man in all his studies, and in the lobby of the gymnasium, where the athletic heroes of Princeton leave their record to posterity, Hector McKaye read his son's name, for, of course, he was there for commencement. Then they spent a week together in New York, following which old Hector announced that one week of New York was about all he could stand. The tall timber was calling for him.

"Hoot, mon!" Donald protested gaily. He was a

perfect mimic of Sir Harry Lauder at his broadest. "Y'eve nae had a bit holiday in all yer life. Wha' spier ye, Hector McKaye, to a trip aroond the worl', wi' a wee visit tae the auld clan in the Hielands?"

"Will you come with me, son?" The Laird inquired eagerly.

"Certainly not! You shall come with me. This is to be my party."

"Can you stand the pressure? I'm liable to prove an expensive traveling companion."

"Well, there's something radically wrong with both of us if we can't get by on two hundred thousand dollars, dad."

The Laird started, and then his Scotch sense of humor—and, for all the famed wit of the Irish, no humor on earth is so unctuous as that of the Scotch—commenced to bubble up. He suspected a joke on himself and was prepared to meet it.

"Will you demand an accounting, my son?"

Donald shook his head.

"Keeping books was ever a sorry trade, father. I'll read the accounting in your eye when you get back to Port Agnew."

"You braw big scoundrel! You've been up to something. Tell it me, man, or I'll die wi' the suspense of it."

"Well," Donald replied, "I lived on twenty-five hundred a year in college and led a happy life. I had a heap of fun, and nothing went by me so fast that I didn't at least get a tail-feather. My college education, therefore, cost me ten thousand dollars, and I managed to squeeze a roadster automobile into that, also. With the remaining ninety thousand, I took a flier in thirty-nine hundred acres of red cedar up the Wiskah River. I paid for it on the instalment plan —yearly payments secured by first mortgage at six per cent., and——"

"Who cruised it for you?" The Laird almost shouted. "I'll trust no cruiser but my own David McGregor."

"I realized that, so I engaged Dave for the job. You will recall that he and I took a two months' camping-trip after my first year in Princeton. It cruised eighty thousand feet to the acre, and I paid two dollars and a half per thousand for it. Of course, we didn't succeed in cruising half of it, but we rode through the remainder, and it all averaged up very nicely. And I saw a former cruise of it made by a disinterested cruiser——"

The Laird had been doing mental arithmetic.

"It cost you seven hundred and eighty thousand dollars—and you've paid ninety thousand, principal and interest, on account. Why, you didn't have the customary ten per cent. of the purchase-price as an initial payment!"

"The owner was anxious to sell. Besides, he knew I was your son, and I suppose he concluded that, after getting ninety thousand dollars out of me at the end of three years, you'd have to come to my rescue when the balance fell due—in a lump. If you didn't, of course he could foreclose."

"I'll save you, my son. It was a good deal—a splendid deal!"

"You do not have to, dad. I've sold it—at a profit of an even two hundred thousand dollars!"

"Lad, why did you do it? Why didn't you take me

into your confidence? That cedar is worth three and a half. In a few years, 'twill be worth five."

"I realized that, father, but—a bird in the hand is worth two in the bush—and I'm a proud sort of devil. I didn't want to run to you for help on my first deal, even though I knew you'd come to my rescue and ask no questions. You've always told me to beware of asking favors, you know. Moreover, I had a very friendly feeling toward the man I sold my red cedar to; I hated to stick him too deeply."

"You were entitled to your profit, Donald. 'Twas business. You should have taken it. Ah, lad, if you only knew the terrible four years I've paid for yon red-cedar!"

"You mean the suspense of not knowing how I was spending my allowance?"

The Laird nodded.

"Curiosity killed a cat, my son, and I'm not as young as I used to be."

"I had thought you'd have read the accounting in my eye. Take another look, Hector McKaye." And Donald thrust his smiling countenance close to his father's.

"I see naught in your eye but deviltry and jokes."

"None are so blind as they that will not see. If you see a joke, dad, it's on you."

Old Hector blinked, then suddenly he sprang at his son, grasped him by the shoulders, and backed him against the wall.

"Did you sell me that red cedar?" he demanded incredulously.

"Aye, mon; through an agent," Donald burred Scottishly. "A' did nae ha' the heart tae stick my faither

sae deep for a bit skulin'. A'm a prood man, Hector
McKaye; a'll nae take a grrand eeducashun at sic a
price. 'Tis nae Christian."

"Ah, my bonny bairn!" old Hector murmured happily, and drew his fine son to his heart. "What a grand
joke to play on your puir old father! Och, mon, was
there ever a lad like mine?"

"I knew you'd buy that timber for an investment if
I offered it cheap enough," Donald explained. "Besides, I owed you a poke. You wanted to be certain
you hadn't reared a jackass instead of a man, so you
gave me a hundred thousand dollars and stood by to see
what I'd do with it—didn't you, old Scotty?" Hector
nodded a trifle guiltily. "Andrew Daney wrote me you
swore by all your Highland clan that the man who
sold you that red cedar was ripe for the fool-killer."

"Tush, tush!" The Laird protested. "You're getting
personal now. I dislike to appear inquisitive, but
might I ask what you've done with your two hundred
thousand profit?"

"Well, you see, dad, I would have felt a trifle guilty
had I kept it, so I blew it all in on good, conservative
United States bonds, registered them in your name, and
sent them to Daney to hide in your vault at Port
Agnew."

"Ah, well, red cedar or bonds, 'twill all come back
to you some day, sonny. The real profit's in the
fun——"

"And the knowledge that I'm not a fool—eh,
father?"

Father love supernal gleamed in The Laird's fine
gray eyes.

"Were you a fool, my son, and all that I have in the

world would cure you if thrown into the Bight of Tyee, I'd gladly throw it and take up my life where I began it—with pike-pole and peavy, double-bitted ax, and cross-cut saw. However, since you're not a fool, I intend to continue to enjoy my son. We'll go around the world together."

Thus did the experiment end. At least, Donald thought so. But when he left the hotel a few minutes later to book two passages to Europe, The Laird of Tyee suddenly remembered that thanks were due his Presbyterian God. So he slid to his old knees beside his bed and murmured:

"Lord, I thank thee! For the sake of thine own martyred Son, set angels to guard him and lead him in the path of manly honor that comes at last to thy kingdom. Amen."

Then he wired Andrew Daney a long telegram of instructions and a stiff raise in salary.

"The boy has a head like a tar-bucket," he concluded. "Everything I ever put into it has stuck. We are going to frolic round the world together, and we will be home when we get back."

IV

DONALD was twenty-four and The Laird fifty-
eight when the pair returned from their frolic
round the world—Donald to take up this father's labors, The Laird to lay them aside and retire to The
Dreamerie and the books he had accumulated against
this happy afterglow of a busy and fruitful life.

Donald's mother and sisters were at The Dreamerie
the night the father and son arrived. Of late years,
they had spent less and less of their time there. The
Laird had never protested, for he could not blame them
for wearying of a little backwoods sawmill town like
Port Agnew.

With his ability to think calmly, clearly, and unsel-
fishly, he had long since realized that eventually his
girls must marry; now Elizabeth was twenty-six and
Jane twenty-eight, and Mrs. McKaye was beginning to
be greatly concerned for their future. Since The Laird
had built The Dreamerie in opposition to their wishes,
they had spent less than six months in each year at
Port Agnew. And these visits had been scattered
throughout the year. They had traveled much, and,
when not traveling, they lived in the Seattle house and
were rather busy socially. Despite his devotion to his
business, however, The Laird found time to spend at
least one week in each month with them in Seattle,
in addition to the frequent business trips which took
him there.

That night of his home-coming was the happiest The Laird had ever known, for it marked the culmination of his lifetime of labor and dreams. Long after his wife and the girls had retired, he and Donald sat in the comfortable living-room, smoking and discussing plans for the future, until presently, these matters having been discussed fully, there fell a silence between them, to be broken presently by The Laird.

"I'm wondering, Donald, if you haven't met some bonny lass you'd like to bring home to Port Agnew. You realize, of course, that there's room on Tyee Head for another Dreamerie, although I built this one for you—and her."

"There'll be no other house on Tyee Head, father," Donald answered, "unless you care to build one for mother and the girls. The wife that I'll bring home to Port Agnew will not object to my father in my house." He smiled and added, "You're not at all hard to get along with, you know."

The Laird's eyes glistened.

"Have you found her yet, my son?"

Donald shook his head in negation.

"Then look for her," old Hector ordered. "I have no doubt that, when you find her, she'll be worthy of you. I'm at an age now when a man looks no longer into the future but dwells in the past, and it's hard for me to think of you, big man that you are, as anything save a wee laddie trotting at my side. Now, if I had a grandson——"

When, presently, Donald bade him good-night, Hector McKaye turned off the lights and sat in the dark, gazing down across the moonlit Bight of Tyee to the sparks that flew upward from the stacks of his saw-

mill in Port Agnew, for they were running a night
shift. And, as he gazed, he thrilled, with a fierce pride
and a joy that was almost pain, in the knowledge that
he had reared a merchant prince for this, his principality of Tyee.

HECTOR McKAYE had always leaned toward the notion that he could run Port Agnew better than a mayor and a town council, in addition to deriving some fun out of it; consequently, Port Agnew had never been incorporated. And this was an issue it was not deemed wise to press, for The Tyee Lumber Company owned every house and lot in town, and Hector McKaye owned every share of stock in the Tyee Lumber Company.

If he was a sort of feudal baron, he was a gentle and kindly one; large building-plots, pretty little bungalows, cheap rentals, and no taxation constituted a social condition that few desired to change. As these few developed and The Laird discovered them, their positions in his employ, were forfeited, their rents raised, or their leases canceled, and presently Port Agnew knew them no more. He paid fair wages, worked his men nine hours, and employed none but naturalized Americans, with a noticeable predilection for those of Scotch nativity or ancestry.

Strikes or lockouts were unknown in Port Agnew— likewise saloons. Unlike most sawmill towns of that period, Port Agnew had no street in which children were forbidden to play or which mothers taught their daughters to avoid. Once an I. W. W. organizer came to town, and upon being ordered out and refusing to go, The Laird, then past fifty, had ducked him in the Skookum until he changed his mind.

The Tyee Lumber Company owned and operated the local telephone company, the butcher shop, the general store, the hotel, a motion-picture theater, a town hall, the bank, and the electric-light-and-power plant, and with the profits from these enterprises, Port Agnew had paved streets, sidewalks lined with handsome electroliers, and a sewer system. It was an admirable little sawmill town, and if the expenses of maintaining it exceeded the income, The Laird met the deficit and assumed all the worry, for he wanted his people to be happy and prosperous beyond all others.

It pleased Hector McKaye to make an occasion of his abdication and Donald's accession to the presidency of the Tyee Lumber Company. The Dreamerie was not sufficiently large for his purpose, however, for he planned to entertain all of his subjects at a dinner and make formal announcement of the change. So he gave a barbecue in a grove of maples on the edge of the town. His people received in silence the little speech he made them, for they were loath to lose The Laird. They knew him, while Donald they had not known for five years, and there were many who feared that the East might have changed him. Consequently, when his father called him up to the little platform from which he spoke, they received the young laird in silence also.

"Folks—my own home folks," Donald began, "today I formally take up the task that was ordained for me at birth. I am going to be very happy doing for you and for myself. I shall never be the man my father is; but if you will take me to your hearts and trust me as you have trusted him, I'll never go back on you, for I expect to live and to die in Port Agnew, and, while I live, I want to be happy with you. I would have you say of me, when I am gone, that I was the worthy son of a worthy sire." He paused and looked out over the eager, upturned faces of the men, women, and children whose destinies he held in the hollow of his hand. "My dear friends, there aren't going to be any changes," he finished, and stepped down off the platform.

From the heart of the crowd a lumberjack cried, "Ya-hoo-o-o-o-o!" as only a lusty lumberjack can cry it. "He's a chip of the old block!" cried another, and there were cheers and some tears and a general rush forward to greet the new master, to shake his hand, and pledge allegiance to him.

When the reception was over, old Hector took charge of the homely games and athletic contests, and the day's delights culminated in a log-burling contest in the Skookum, in which the young laird participated. When, eventually, he fell in the river and was counted out, old Hector donned his son's calked boots and, with a whoop such as he had not emitted in forty years, entered the lists against the young fellows. In the old days in the Michigan woods, when burling was considered a magnificent art of the lumberjack, he had been a champion, and for five minutes he spun his log until the water foamed, crossing and recrossing the river and winning the contest unanimously. From the bank, Mrs. McKaye and his daughters watched him with well-bred amusement and secret disapproval. They could never forget, as he could, that he was The Laird of Tyee; they preferred more dignity in the head of the house.

The McKaye family drove home along the cliff road at sunset. Young Donald paused on the terrace before entering the house, and, stirred by some half-forgotten memory, he glanced across the bight to the little white house far below on the Sawdust Pile. The flag was floating from the cupola, but even as he looked, it came fluttering down.

Donald turned toward the McKaye flag. It was still floating. "The old order changeth," he soliloquized, and hauled it down, at the same time shouting to his father within the house:

"Hey, dad; fire the sunset gun!"

The Laird pressed the button and the cannon boomed.

"We've neglected that little ceremony since you've been away," he remarked, as Donald entered the room. "'Other times, other customs,' I dare say."

He hurried up-stairs to dress for dinner (a formality which he disliked, but which appeared to please his wife and daughters), and Donald took his father's binoculars and went out on the terrace. It had occurred to him that he had not seen old Caleb Brent and Nan at the barbecue, and he wondered why. Through the glasses, he could make out the figure of a woman in the cupola window, and she was watching him through a long marine telescope.

"There's my old friend Nan, grown to womanhood," Donald soliloquized, and waved his arm at her. Through the glasses, he saw her wave back at him.

VI

THE morning after the barbecue, Donald McKaye reported at eight o'clock to his father's faithful old general manager, Andrew Daney. Daney had grown gray in his father's service, and it was no part of Donald's plans to assign him to a back seat.

"Well, Mr. Daney," he inquired affably, "what are your plans for the new hired man?"

Old Daney looked up quizzically.

"You do the planning here, Don," he replied.

"You heard me say yesterday that there would be no changes, Mr. Daney. Of course, I haven't grown up in Port Agnew without learning something of my heritage, but, in view of the fact that I still have considerable to learn, suppose you indicate just where I ought to start."

Daney was pleased at a deference he had not anticipated.

"Start in the woods," he replied. "That's where your daddy started. Felling timber and handling it is rather a fine art, Don. I'd wrestle logs for a month and follow them down the Skookum to the log boom. Then I'd put in six months in the mill and six more in the factory, following it with three months on the dock, tallying, and three months of a hand-shaking tour out among the trade. After that, you may sit in at your father's desk, and I'll gradually break you in to his job."

"That's a grand idea, and I'll act on it," Donald declared.

"Well, it's too late to act on it to-day, Don. The up-river launch to the logging-camp left at seven o'clock. However, I have a job for you. We really need the Sawdust Pile for an extension of our drying-yard. Our present yard lies right under the lee of that ridge of which Tyee Head is an extension, and it's practically noon before the sun gets a fair chance at it. The Sawdust Pile gets the sun all day long, and the winds have an uninterrupted sweep across it. We can dry our cedar decking there in half the time it requires now."

"But the Sawdust Pile is——"

"A rat's nest, Don. There are a number of other shacks there now—some Greek fishermen, a negro, and a couple of women from the overflow of Tyee. It ought to be cleaned out."

"I noticed those shacks last night, Mr. Daney, and I agree with you that they should go. But I haven't the heart to run old Caleb Brent off the Sawdust Pile. I gave it to him, you know."

"Well, let Brent stay there. He's too old and crippled with rheumatism to attend to his truck-garden any more; so if you leave him the space for his house and a chicken-yard, he'll be satisfied. In fact, I have discussed the proposition with him, and he is agreeable."

"Why did dad permit those other people to crowd him, Mr. Daney?"

"While your father was in Europe with you, they horned in, claimed a squatter's right, and stood pat. Old Brent was defenseless, and while the boys from the mill would have cleaned them out if I had given the word, the Greeks and the negro were defiant, and it meant bloodshed. So I have permitted the matter to rest until your father's return."

Donald reached for his hat.

"Caleb Brent's squatter-right to that Sawdust Pile is going to be upheld," he declared. "I'll clean that colony out before sunset, or they'll clean me."

"I'd proceed cautiously if I were you, Don. They have a host of friends up in Darrow, and we mustn't precipitate a feud."

"I'm going over now and serve notice on them to vacate immediately." He grinned at old Daney. "A negro, a handful of Greeks, and those unfortunate women can't bluff the boss of Port Agnew, Mr. Daney."

"They tell me there's a blind pig down there, also."

"It will not be there after to-day," Donald answered lightly, and departed for the Sawdust Pile.

As he came up to the gate in the neat fence Caleb Brent had built across the Sawdust Pile nine years before, a baby boy, of perhaps three years of age, rose out of the weeds in which he had been playing and regarded the visitor expectantly.

"Hello, bub!" the young laird of Tyee greeted the child.

"Hello!" came the piping answer. "Are you my daddy?"

"Why, no, Snickelfritz." He ran his fingers through the tot's golden hair. "Don't you know your own daddy?"

"I haven't any daddy," the child drawled.

"No? Well, that's unfortunate." Donald stooped and lifted the tike to his shoulder, marveling the while that such a cherub could be the product of any of the denizens of the Sawdust Pile. At once, the boy's arms went round his neck and a velvet cheek was laid close to his. "You're an affectionate little snooks, aren't you?" Donald commented. "Do you live here?"

"Yes, sir."

"Somebody's been teaching you manners. Whose little boy are you?"

"Muvver's."

"And who might mother be?"

"Nan Brent."

"Yo-ho! So you're Nan Brent's boy! What's your name?"

"Donald Brent."

"No; that isn't it, son. Brent is your mother's name. Tell me your father's name."

"Ain't got no farver."

"Well then, run along to your mother."

He kissed the child and set him down just as a young woman came down the sadly neglected shell walk from Caleb Brent's little white house. Donald opened the gate and advanced to meet her.

"I'm sure you must be Nan," he said, "although I can't be certain. I haven't seen Nan in six years."

She extended her hand.

"Yes; I'm Nan," she replied, "and you're Donald Mc-Kaye. You're a man now, but somehow you haven't changed greatly."

"It's fine to meet you again, Nan." He shook her hand enthusiastically.

She smiled a little sadly.

"I saw you at colors last night, Donald. When your

flag came down and the gun was fired, I knew you'd remembered."

"Were you glad?" he demanded, and immediately wondered why he had asked such a childish question.

"Yes, I was, Donald. It has been a long time since —since—the gun has been fired—for me. So long since we were children, Donald."

"You weren't at the barbecue yesterday. I missed you and Caleb. You two are very old friends of mine, Nan. Was it quite loyal of you to stay home?"

"You're the only person that missed us, Donald," she answered, with just the suspicion of a tremor in her sweet voice. "But, then, we are accustomed to being left out of things."

He made no effort to formulate an answer to this. Truth does not require an answer. Yet he was sensible of a distinct feeling of sympathy for her, and, manlike, he decided to change the topic of conversation.

"You have neighbors on the Sawdust Pile, Nan."

"Yes. They came when The Laird was in Europe."

"They would never have dared it had he been in Port Agnew. I'm surprised that Andrew Daney permitted it. I had thought of him as a man of courage, but, strange to say, these people outgamed him."

"They didn't outgame him, Donald. He just didn't care. I—I—fancy he concluded they would make agreeable neighbors—for me."

"I'm sorry, Nan. However, I'm the new laird of Tyee, and I've come down to stage an eviction. I didn't know of this state of affairs until this morning."

She smiled a little wistfully and bitterly.

"I had flattered myself, Donald, you had called to visit your old friends instead. When you waved at me last night, I—oh, you can't realize how happy it made me to know that *you* had noticed me—that you really were big enough to be the big man of Port Agnew. And I thought perhaps you would come because of that."

He smiled tolerantly upon her.

"Something has occurred to make you bitter, Nan. You're not like the girl I used to know before I went away to school. If it will help to restore me to your previous good opinion, however, please believe that when I waved at you last night, simultaneously I made up my mind to make an early visit to the Sawdust Pile. The discovery that these cattle have intruded upon you and your old father, because you were unable to defend yourselves and no one in Port Agnew would defend you, merely hastened my visit. I couldn't in decency come any earlier; could I, Nan? It's just half after eight. And if you're going to keep me standing at the gate, as if I were a sewing-machine agent instead of a very old friend, I *may* conclude to take offense and regret that I called."

"Oh, I'm sorry! Please forgive me, Donald. I'm so much alone—so very lonely—I suppose I grow suspicious of people and their motives."

"Say no more about it, Nan. May I come in, then, to greet Caleb and your husband?"

"Father is in the house. I'll call him out, Donald. As for my husband—" She hesitated, glanced out across the bight, and then resolutely faced him. "You cannot have heard all of the town gossip, then?"

"I hadn't even heard of your marriage. The first I knew of it was when his little nibs here hailed me, and asked me if I was his father. Then he informed me he was your boy. He's a lovely child, Nan, and I have been the recipient of some of his extremely moist kisses."

She realized that he was too courteous to ask whether her husband was dead or if there had been a divorce.

"I'm rather glad you haven't heard, Donald," she replied evenly. "I much prefer to tell you myself; then you will understand why I cannot invite you into our house, and why you must not be seen talking to me here at the gate. I am not married. I have never been married. My baby's name is—Brent, and I call him Donald, after the only male human being that has ever been truly kind to my father and me."

"Ah," said Donald quietly, "so that's why he misses his father and appears to want one so very much."

She gazed forlornly out to sea and answered with a brief nod. Seemingly she had long since ceased to be tragic over her pitiful tragedy.

"Well," he replied philosophically, "life is quite filled with a number of things, and some of them make for great unhappiness." He stooped and lifted the baby in his great arms. "You're named after me, sonny; so I think I'll try to fill the gap and make you happy. Do you mind, Nan, if I try my hand at foster-fathering? I like children. This little man starts life under a handicap, but I'll see to it that he gets his chance in life—far from Port Agnew, if you desire." She closed her eyes in sudden pain and did not answer. "And whatever your opinion on the matter may be, Nan," he went on, "even had I known yesterday of your sorrow, I should have called to-day just the same."

"You call it my 'sorrow!'" she burst forth passionately. "Others call it my trouble—my sin—my disgrace."

"And what does Caleb call it, Nan?"

"He doesn't call it, Donald. It hasn't appeared to make any difference with him. I'm still—his little girl."

"Well, I cannot regard you as anything but a little girl—the same little girl that used to help Caleb and me sail the sloop. I don't wish to know anything about your sorrow, or your trouble, or your disgrace, or your sin, or whatever folks may choose to call it. I just want you to know that I know that you're a good woman, and when the spirit moves me—which will be frequently, now that I have this young man to look after—I shall converse with you at your front gate and visit you and your decent old father in this little house, and be damned to those that decry it. I am the young laird of Tyee. My father raised me to be a gentleman, and, by the gods, I'll be one! Now, Nan, take the boy and go in the house, because I see a rascally negro in the doorway of that shack yonder, and I have a matter to discuss with him. Is that white woman his consort?"

Nan nodded again. She could not trust herself to speak, for her heart was full to overflowing.

"Come here—you!" Donald called to the negro. The fellow slouched forth defiantly. He was a giant mulatto, and his freckled face wore an evil and contemptuous grin.

"I'm Donald McKaye," Donald informed him. "I'm the new laird of Tyee. I want you and that woman to pack up and leave."

"How soon, boss?"

"Immediately." Anticipating a refusal, Donald stepped closer to the mulatto and looked him sternly in the eye.

"We-ll, is dat so?" the yellow rascal drawled. "So youh-all's de new la'rd, eh? Well, ah'm de king o' de Sawdust Pile, an' mah house is mah castle. Git dat, Mistah La'rd?"

Donald turned toward Nan.

"I'm going to have trouble here, Nan. Please go in the house."

"Proceed," she replied simply. "I have a most un-womanly and unladylike desire to see that beast man-handled."

Donald turned, in time to go under a sizzling right-hand blow from the mulatto and come up with a right uppercut to the ugly, freckled face and a left rip to the mulatto's midriff. The fellow grunted, and a spasm of pain crossed his countenance. "You yellow dog!" Donald muttered, and flattened his nose far flatter than his mammy had ever wiped it. The enemy promptly backed away and covered; a hearty thump in the solar plexus made him uncover, and under a rain of blows on the chin and jaw, he sprawled unconscious on the ground.

Donald left him lying there and stepped to the door of the shack. The frightened drab within spat curses at him.

"Pack and go!" he ordered. "Within the hour, I'm going to purge the Sawdust Pile with fire; if you stay in the house, you'll burn with it."

She was ready in ten minutes. Three more of her kind occupying an adjacent shack begged to be allowed time in which to load their personal possessions in an express-wagon. The four Greeks were just about to set out for a day's fishing, but, having witnessed the defeat of the mulatto bully, the fever of the hegira seized them also. They loaded their effects in the fishing-launch, and chugged away up river to Darrow, crying curses upon the young laird of Tyee and promising reprisal.

Donald waited until the last of the refugees had departed before setting fire to the shacks. Then he stood by old Caleb Brent's house, a circle of filled buckets around him, and watched in case the wind should suddenly shift and shower sparks upon the roof. In half an hour the Sawdust Pile had reverted to its old status and a throng of curious townspeople who, attracted by the flames and smoke, had clustered outside Caleb Brent's gate to watch Donald at work, finally despaired of particulars and scattered when they saw Donald and Nan Brent enter the house.

Caleb Brent, loking twenty years older than when Donald had seen him last, sat in an easy chair by the window, gazing with lack-luster eyes out across the bight. He was hopelessly crippled with rheumatism, and his sea-blue eyes still held the same lost-dog wistfulness.

"Hello, Caleb!" Donald greeted him cordially. "I've just cleaned up the Sawdust Pile for you. You're back in undisputed possession again."

He shook hands with old Caleb and sat down in a chair which Nan drew up for him.

"It's good of you to call, Mr. Donald," the old man piped. "But isn't that just like him, Nan?" he demanded. "Many's the day—aye, and the night, too, for of late the nights have been bad here—we've thought of you, sir, and wished you were back in Port Agnew.

We knew what would happen to those scoundrels when
Mr. Donald got around to it." And he laughed the
asthmatic, contented chuckle of the aged as Nan related
briefly the story of Donald's recent activities.

Their conversation which followed was mostly of a
reminiscent character—recollections of boat-races in
the bight, fishing excursions off the coast, clambakes,
new boats, a dog which Donald had given Nan when he
left for prep school and which had since died of old
age. And all the while Nan Brent's child stood by Donald's knee, gazing up at him adoringly.

During a lull in the conversation, he created some
slight embarrassment by reiterating his belief that this
strange man must be his father, and appealed to his
mother for verification of his suspicions.

Poor child! His baby mind had but lately grasped
the fact that for him there was something missing in
the scheme of life, and, to silence his persistent ques-
tioning, Nan had told him that some day his father
would come to see them; whereupon, with the calm faith
of innocence, he had posted himself at the front gate,
to be in position to receive this beloved missing one when
the latter should appear. Donald skilfully diverted the
child's mind from this all-consuming topic by sliding
the boy down to his foot and permitting him to swing
gently there.

Presently Nan excused herself, for the purpose of
looking after the embers of Donald's recent raid. The
instant the door closed behind her, old Caleb Brent
looked across at his visitor.

"You've heard—of course, Mr. Donald?" he queried,
with a slight inclination of his head toward the door
through which his daughter had disappeared.

"Yes, Caleb. Misfortune comes in various guises."

"I would I could die," the pitiful old fellow whispered. "I will, soon, but, oh, what will my poor darling do then, Mr. Donald? After we first came here, I was that prosperous, sir, you wouldn't believe it. I gave Nan a good schooling, piano lessons, and fine dresses. We lived well, and yet we put by a thousand dollars in six years. But that's gone now, what with the expenses when the baby came, and my sickness that's prevented me from working. Thank God, sir, I have my three-quarter pay. It isn't much, but we're rent-free, and fuel costs us nothing, what with drift-wood and the waste from Darrow that comes down the river. Nan has a bit of a kitchen-garden and a few chickens—so we make out. But when I die, my navy-pay stops."

He paused, too profoundly moved by consideration of the destitution that would face Nan and her nameless boy to voice the situation in words. But he looked up at Donald McKaye, and the latter saw again that wistful look in his sea-blue eyes—the dumb pleading of a kind old lost dog. He thought of the thirty-eight-foot sloop old Caleb had built him—a thing of beauty and wondrously seaworthy; or the sense of obligation which had caused old Brent to make of the task a labor of love; of the long, lazy, happy days when, with Caleb and Nan for his crew, he had raced out of the bight twenty miles to sea and back again, for the sheer delight of driving his lee rail under until Nan cried out in apprehension.

Poor, sweet, sad Nan Brent! Donald had known her through so many years of gentleness and innocence —and she had come to this! He was consumed with pity for her. She had fallen, but—there were depths to which destitution and desperation might still drive her, just as there were heights to which she might climb again if some half-man would but give her a helping hand.

"Do you know the man, Caleb?" he demanded suddenly.

"No, I do not. I have never seen him. Nan wrote me when they were married, and told me his name, of course."

"Then there *was* a marriage, Caleb?"

"So Nan wrote me."

"Ah! Has Nan a marriage certificate?"

"I have never seen it. Seems their marriage wasn't legal. The name he gave wasn't his own; he was a bigamist."

"Then Nan knows his real name."

"Yes; when she learned that, she came home."

"But why didn't she prosecute him, Caleb? She owed that to herself and the child—to her good name and——"

"She had her reasons, lad."

"But you should have prosecuted the scoundrel, Caleb."

"I had no money for lawyers. I knew I was going to need it all for Nan and her child. And I thought her reasons sufficient, Donald. She said it would all come out right in the end. Maybe it will."

"Do you mean she knowingly accepted the inevitable disgrace when she might have—have—" He wanted to add, "proved herself virtuous," but, somehow, the words would not come. They didn't appear to him to be quite fair to Nan.

The old man nodded.

"Of course we haven't told this to anybody else," he hastened to add. " 'Twould have been useless. They'd have thought it a lie."

"Yes, Caleb—a particularly clumsy and stupid lie."

Caleb Brent looked up suddenly and searched, with an alert and wistful glance, the face of the young laird of Tyee.

"But you do not think so, do you?" he pleaded.

"Certainly not, Caleb. If Nan told you that, then she told you the truth."

"Thank you, lad."

"Poor old Caleb," Donald soliloquized, "you find it hard to believe it yourself, don't you? And it does sound fishy!"

"I don't believe it's Nan's fault," Donald found himself saying next. "She was always a good girl, and I can't look at her now and conceive her as anything but virtuous and womanly. I'll always be a good friend of hers, Caleb. I'll stand back of her and see that she gets a square deal—she and her son. When you're gone, she can leave Port Agnew for some city where she isn't known, and as 'Mrs. Brent' she can engage in some self-supporting business. It always struck me that Nan had a voice."

"She has, Mr. Donald. They had grand opera in Seattle, and I sent her up there to hear it and having a singing teacher hear her sing 'Alice, Where Art Thou.' He said she'd be earning a thousand dollars a night in five years, Mr. Donald, if somebody in New York could train her. That was the time," he concluded, "that she met *him!* He was rich and, I suppose, full of fine graces; he promised her a career if she'd marry him, and so he dazzled the child—she was only eighteen—and

she went to San Francisco with him. She says there
was some sort of marriage, but he gave her no such
gift as I gave her mother—a marriage certificate. She
wrote me she was happy, and asked me to forgive her
the lack of confidence in not advising with me—and of
course I forgave her, Mr. Donald. But in three months
he left her, and one night the door yonder opened and
Nan come in and put her arms round my neck and held
me tight, with never a tear—so I knew she'd cried her
fill long since and was in trouble." He paused several
seconds, then added, "Her mother was an admiral's
daughter—and she married me!" He appeared to suggest this latter as a complete explanation of woman's
frailty.

"The world is small, but it is sufficiently large to hide
a girl from the Sawdust Pile of Port Agnew. Of course,
Nan cannot leave you now, but when you leave her,
Caleb, I'll finance her for her career. Please do not
worry about it."

"I'm like Nan, sir," he murmured. "I'm beyond tears,
or I'd weep, Mr. Donald. God will reward you, sir. I
can't begin to thank you."

"I'm glad of that. By the way, who is towing the
garbage-barge to sea nowadays?"

"I don't know, sir. Mr. Daney hired somebody else
and his boat when I had to quit because of my sciatica."

"Hereafter, we'll use your boat, Caleb, and engage a
man to operate it. The rental will be ten dollars per
trip, two trips a week, eighty dollars a month. Cheap
enough; so don't think it's charity. Here's the first
month's rental in advance. I'm going to run along
now, Caleb, but I'll look in from time to time, and if
you should need me in the interim, send for me."

He kissed little Don Brent, who set up a prodigious shriek at the prospect of desertion and brought his mother fluttering into the room. He watched her soothe the youngster and then asked:

"Nan, where do you keep the arnica now? I cut my knuckles on that yellow rascal."

She raised a sadly smiling face to his.

"Where would the arnica be—if we had any, Donald?" she demanded.

"Where it used to be, I suppose. Up on that shelf, inside the basement of that funny old half-portion grandfather's clock and just out of reach of the pendulum."

"You do remember, don't you? But it's all gone so many years ago, Donald. We haven't had a boy around to visit us since you left Port Agnew, you know. I'll put some tincture of iodine on your knuckles, however."

"Do, please, Nan."

A little later, he said:

"Do you remember, Nan, the day I stuck my finger into the cage of old Mrs. Biddle's South American parrot to coddle the brute and he all but chewed it off?"

She nodded.

"And you came straight here to have it attended to, instead of going to a doctor."

"You wept when you saw my mangled digit. Remember, Nan? Strange how that scene persists in my memory! You were so sweetly sympathetic I was quite ashamed of myself."

"That's because you always were the sweetest boy in the world and I was only the garbage-man's daughter," she whispered. "There's a ridiculous song about the garbage-man's daughter. I heard it once, in vaudeville—in San Francisco."

"If I come over some evening soon, will you sing for me, Nan?"

"I never sing any more, Don."

"Nobody but you can ever sing 'Carry Me Back to Old Virginy' for me."

"Then I shall sing it, Don."

"Thank you, Nan."

She completed the anointing of his battle-scarred knuckles with iodine, and, for a moment, she held his hand, examining critically an old ragged white scar on the index-finger of his right hand. And quite suddenly, to his profound amazement, she bent her head and swiftly implanted upon that old scar a kiss so light, so humble, so benignant, so pregnant of adoration and gratitude that he stood before her confused and inquiring.

"Such a strong, useful big hand!" she whispered. "It has been raised in defense of the sanctity of my home —and until you came there was 'none so poor to do me reverence.' "

He looked at her with sudden, new interest. Her action had almost startled him. As their eyes held each other, he was aware, with a force that was almost a shock, that Nan Brent was a most unusual woman. She was beautiful; yet her physical beauty formed the least part of her attractiveness, perfect as that beauty was. Instinctively, Donald visualized her as a woman with brains, character, nobility of soul; there was that in her eyes, in the honesty and understanding with which they looked into his, that compelled him, in that instant, to accept without reservation and for all time the lame and halting explanation of her predicament he had recently heard from her father's lips. He longed to tell her so. Instead, he flushed boyishly and said, quite impersonally:

"Yes; you're beautiful as women go, but that's not the right word to express you. Physically, you might be very homely, but if you were still Nan Brent you would be sweet and compelling. You remind me of a Catholic chapel; there's always one little light within that never goes out, you know. So that makes you more than beautiful. Shall I say—glorious?"

She smiled at him with her wistful, sea-blue eyes—a smile tender, maternal, all-comprehending. She knew he was not seeking to flatter her, that the wiles, the artifices, the pretty speeches of the polished man of the world were quite beyond him.

"Still the same old primitive pal," she murmured softly; "still thinking straight, talking straight, acting straight, and—dare I say it, Donald?—seeing straight. I repeat, you always were the sweetest boy in the world —and there is still so much of the little boy about you." Her hand fluttered up and rested lightly on his arm. "I'll not forget this day, my dear friend."

It was characteristic of him that, having said that which was uppermost in his mind, he should remember his manners and thank her for dressing his knuckles. Then he extended his hand in farewell.

"When you come again, Donald," she pleaded, as he took her hand, "will you please bring me some books? They're all that can keep me sane—and I do not go to the public library any more. I have to run the gantlet of so many curious eyes."

"How long is it since you have been away from the Sawdust Pile?"

"Since before my baby came."

He was silent a minute, pondering this. Since old Caleb had become house-ridden, then, she had been without books. He nodded assent to her request.

"If I do not say very much, you will understand, nevertheless, how grateful I am," she continued. "To-day, the sun has shone. Whatever your thoughts may have been, Donald, you controlled your face and you were decent enough not to say, 'Poor Nan.'"

He had no answer to that. He was conscious only of standing helpless in the midst of a terrible tragedy. His heart ached with pity for her, and just for old sake's sake, for a tender sentiment for lost youth and lost happiness of the old comradely days when she had been Cinderella and he the prince, he wished that he might take her in a fraternal embrace and let her cry out on his breast the agony that gnawed at her heart like a worm in an apple. But it was against his code to indicate to her by word or action that she was less worthy than other women and hence to be pitied, for it seemed to him that her burden was already sufficient.

"Let me know if those people return to annoy you, Nan," was all he said. Then they shook hands very formally, and the young laird of Tyee returned to the mill-office to report to Andrew Daney that the Sawdust Pile had been cleaned out, but that, for the present at least, they would get along with the old drying-yard.

Somehow, the day came to an end, and he went home with tumult in his soul.

VII

AN unerring knowledge of men in general and of his own son in particular indicated to Hector McKaye, upon the instant that the latter appeared at the family dinner-table, that his son's first day in command had had a sobering effect upon that young man. He had gone forth that morning whistling, his eyes alert with interest and anticipation; and a feeling of profound contentment had come to The Laird as he watched Donald climb into his automobile and go briskly down the cliff highway to Port Agnew. Here was no unwilling exile, shackled by his father's dollars to a backwoods town and condemned to labor for the term of his natural life. Gladly, eagerly, it seemed to Hector McKaye, his son was assuming his heritage, casting aside, without one longing backward glance, a brighter, busier, and more delightful world.

Although his son's new arena of action was beautiful and The Laird loved it with a passionate love, he was sufficiently imaginative to realize that, in Port Agnew, Donald might not be as happy as had been his father. Old Hector was sufficiently unselfish to have harbored no resentment had this been so. It had been his one anxiety that Donald might take his place in the business as a matter of duty to himself rather than as a duty to his father, and because he had found his life-work and was approaching it with joy, for The Laird was philosopher enough to know that labor without joy is as dead-sea fruit. Indeed, before the first day of his retirement had passed, he had begun to suspect that joy without labor was apt to be something less than he had anticipated.

The Laird observed in his son's eyes, as the latter took his place at table, a look that had not been there when Donald left for the mill that morning. His usually pleasant, "Evening, folks!" was perfunctory to-night; he replied briefly to the remarks addressed to him by his mother and sisters; the old man noted not less than thrice a slight pause with the spoon half-way to his mouth, as if his son considered some problem more important than soup. Mrs. McKaye and the girls chattered on, oblivious of these slight evidences of mental perturbation, but as The Laird carved the roast (he delighted in carving and serving his family, and was old-fashioned enough to insist upon his right, to the distress of the girls, who preferred to have the roast carved in the kitchen and served by the Japanese butler), he kept a contemplative eye upon his son, and presently saw Donald heave a slight sigh.

"Here's a titbit you always liked, son!" he cried cheerfully, and deftly skewered from the leg of lamb the crisp and tender tail. "Confound you, Donald; I used to eat these fat, juicy little lamb's tails while you were at college, but I suppose, now, I'll have to surrender that prerogative along with the others." In an effort to be cheerful and distract his son's thoughts, he attempted this homely badinage.

"I'll give you another little tale in return, dad," Donald replied, endeavoring to meet his father's cheerful manner. "While we were away, a colony of riff-raff from Darrow jumped old Caleb Brent's Sawdust

Pile, and Daney was weak enough to let them get away with it. I'm somewhat surprised. Daney knew your wishes in the matter; if he had forgotten them, he might have remembered mine, and if he had forgotten both, it would have been the decent thing to have thrown them out on his own responsibility."

So that was what lay at the bottom of his son's perturbation! The Laird was relieved.

"Andrew's a good man, but he always needed a leader, Donald," he replied. "If he didn't lack initiative, he would have been his own man long ago. I hope you did not chide him for it, lad."

"No; I did not. He's old enough to be my father, and, besides, he's been in the Tyee Lumber Company longer than I. I did itch to give him a rawhiding, though."

"I saw smoke and excitement down at the Sawdust Pile this morning, Donald. I dare say you rectified Andrew's negligence."

"I did. The Sawdust Pile is as clean as a hound's tooth."

Jane looked up from her plate.

"I hope you sent that shameless Brent girl away, too," she announced, with the calm attitude of one whose own virtue is above reproach.

Donald glared at her.

"Of course I did not!" he retorted. "How thoroughly unkind and uncharitable of you, Jane, to hope I would be guilty of such a cruel and unmanly action!"

The Laird waved his carving-knife.

"Hear, hear!" he chuckled. "Spoken like a man, my son. Jane, my dear, if I were you, I wouldn't press this matter further. It's a delicate subject."

"I'm sure I do not see why Jane should not be free to express her opinion, Hector." Mrs. McKaye felt impelled to fly to the defense of her daughter. "You know as well as we do, Hector, that the Brent girl is quite outside the pale of respectable society."

"We shall never agree on what constitutes 'respectable society,' Nellie," The Laird answered whimsically. "There are a few in that Seattle set of yours I find it hard to include in that category."

"Oh, they're quite respectable, father," Donald protested.

"Indeed they are, Donald! Hector, you amaze me," Mrs. McKaye chided.

"They have too much money to be anything else," Donald added, and winked at his father.

"Tush, tush, lad!" the old man murmured. "We shall get nowhere with such arguments. The world has been at that line of conversation for two thousand years, and the issue's still in doubt. Nellie, will you have a piece of the well-done?"

"You and your father are never done joining forces against me," Mrs. McKaye protested, and in her voice was the well-known note that presaged tears should she be opposed further. The Laird, all too familiar with this truly feminine type of tyranny, indicated to his son, by a lightning wink, that he desired the conversation diverted into other channels, whereupon Donald favored his mother with a disarming smile.

"I'm going to make a real start to-morrow morning, mother," he announced brightly. "I'm going up in the woods and be a lumberjack for a month. Going to grow warts on my hands and chew tobacco and develop into a brawny roughneck."

"Is that quite necessary?" Elizabeth queried, with a slight elevation of her eyebrows. "I understood you were going to manage the business."

"I am—after I've learned it thoroughly, Lizzie."

"Don't call me 'Lizzie,'" she warned him irritably.

"Very well, Elizabeth."

"In simple justice to those people from Darrow that you evicted from the Sawdust Pile, Don, you should finish your work before you go. If they were not fit to inhabit the Sawdust Pile, then neither is Nan Brent. You've got to play fair." Jane had returned to the attack.

"Look here, Jane," her brother answered seriously: "I wish you'd forget Nan Brent. She's an old and very dear friend of mine, and I do not like to hear my friends slandered."

"Oh, indeed!" Jane considered this humorous, and indulged herself in a cynical laugh.

"Friend of his?" Elizabeth, who was regarded in her set as a wit, a reputation acquired by reason of the fact that she possessed a certain knack for adapting slang humorously (for there was no originality to her alleged wit), now bent her head and looked at her brother incredulously. "My word! That's a rich dish."

"Why, Donald dear," his mother cried reproachfully, "surely you are jesting!"

"Not at all. Nan Brent isn't a bad girl, even if she is the mother of a child born out of wedlock. She stays at home and minds her own business, and lets others mind theirs."

"Donald's going to be tragic. See if he isn't," Elizabeth declared. "Come now, old dear; if Nan Brent isn't a bad woman, just what is your idea of what constitutes badness in a woman? It would be interesting to know your point of view."

"Nan Brent was young, unsophisticated, poor, and trusting when she met this fellow, whoever he may be. He wooed her, and she loved him—or thought she did, which amounts to the same thing until one discovers the difference between thinking and feeling. At first, she thought she was married to him. Later, she discovered she was not—and then it was too late."

"It wouldn't have been too late with some—er—good people," The Laird remarked meaningly.

"In other words," Donald went on, "Nan Brent found herself out on the end of a limb, and then the world proceeded to saw off the limb. It is true that she is the mother of an illegitimate child, but if that child was not—at least in so far as its mother is concerned—conceived in sin, I say it isn't illegitimate, and that its mother is not a bad woman."

"Granted—if it's true; but how do you know it to be true?" Jane demanded. She had a feeling that she was about to get the better of her brother in this argument.

"I do not *know* it to be true, Jane."

"*Voilà!*"

"But—I believe it to be true, Jane."

"Why?"

"Because Nan told her father it was true, and old Caleb told me when I was at his house this morning. So I believe it. And I knew Nan Brent when she was a young girl, and she was sweet and lovely and virtuous. I talked with her this morning, and found no reason to change my previous estimate of her. I could only feel for her a profound pity."

" 'Pity is akin to love,' " Elizabeth quoted gaily. "Mother, keep an eye on your little son. He'll be going in for settlement-work in Port Agnew first thing we know."

"Hush, Elizabeth!" her mother cried sharply. She was highly scandalized at such levity. The Laird salted and peppered his food and said nothing. "Your attitude is very manly and sweet, dear," Mrs. McKaye continued, turning to her son, for her woman's intuition warned her that, if the discussion waxed warmer, The Laird would take a hand in it, and her side would go down to inglorious defeat, their arguments flattened by the weight of Scriptural quotations. She had a feeling that old Hector was preparing to remind them of Mary Magdalen and the scene in the temple. "I would much rather hear you speak a good word for that unfortunate girl than have you condemn her."

"A moment ago," her son reminded her, with some asperity, for he was sorely provoked, "you were demanding the right of free speech for Jane, in order that she might condemn her. Mother, I fear me you're not quite consistent."

"We will not discuss it further, dearie. It is not a matter of such importance that we should differ to the point of becoming acrimonious. Besides, it's a queer topic for dinner-table conversation."

"So say we all of us," Elizabeth struck in laconically. "Dad, will you please help me to some of the well-done?"

"Subjects," old Hector struck in, "which, twenty

years ago, only the family doctor was supposed to be
familiar with or permitted to discuss are now being
agitated in women's clubs, books, newspapers, and the
public schools. You can't smother sin or the facts of
life unless they occur separately. In the case of Nan
Brent they have developed coincidently; so we find it
hard to regard her as normal and human."

"Do you condone her offense, Hector?" Mrs. Mc-
Kaye demanded incredulously.

"I am a firm believer in the sacredness of marriage.
I cannot conceive of a civilization worth while without it," The Laird declared earnestly. "Nevertheless,
while I know naught of Nan Brent's case, except that
which is founded on hearsay evidence, I can condone
her offense because I can understand it. She might
have developed into a far worse girl than it appears
from Donald's account she is. At least, Nellie, she bore
her child and cherishes it, and, under the rules of society as we play it, that required a kind of courage
in which a great many girls are deficient. Give her
credit for that."

"Apparently she has been frank," Elizabeth answered
him coolly. "On the other hand, father McKaye, her
so-called courage may have been ignorance or apathy
or cowardice or indifference. It all depends on her
point of view."

"I disagree with mother that it is not a matter of
importance," Donald persisted. "It is a matter of
supreme importance to me that my mother and sisters
should not feel more charity toward an unfortunate
member of their sex; and I happen to know that it is
a matter of terrible importance to Nan Brent that in
Port Agnew people regard her as unclean and look at

her askance. And because that vacillating old Daney didn't have the courage to fly in the face of Port Agnew's rotten public opinion, he subjected Nan Brent and her helpless old father to the daily and nightly association of depraved people. If *he* should dare to say one word against——"

"Oh, it wasn't because Andrew was afraid of public opinion, lad," Hector McKaye interrupted him dryly. "Have you no power o' deduction? 'Twas his guid wife that stayed his hand, and well I know it."

"I dare say, dad," Donald laughed. "Yes; I suppose I'll have to forgive him."

"She'll be up to-morrow, my dear, to discuss the matter with you," The Laird continued, turning to his wife. "I know her well. Beware of expressing an opinion to her." And he bent upon all the women of his household a smoldering glance.

Apparently, by mutual consent, the subject was dropped forthwith. Donald's silence throughout the remainder of the meal was portentous, however, and Mrs. McKaye and her daughters were relieved when, the meal finished at last, they could retire with good grace and leave father and son to their cigars.

"Doesn't it beat hell?" Donald burst forth suddenly, apropos of nothing.

"It does, laddie."

"I wonder why?"

The Laird was in a philosophical mood. He weighed his answer carefully.

"Because people prefer to have their thoughts manufactured for them; because fanatics and hypocrites have twisted the heart out of the Christian religion in the grand scramble for priority in the 'Who's Holier than

Who' handicap; because people who earnestly believe
that God knows their inmost thoughts cannot refrain
from being human and trying to put one over on
Him." He smoked in silence for a minute, his calm
glance on the ceiling. "Now that you are what you
are, my son," he resumed reflectively, "you'll begin to
know men and women. They who never bothered to seek
your favor before will fight for it now—they do the
same thing with God Almighty, seeking to win his
favor by outdoing him in the condemnation of sin. A
woman's virtue, lad, is her main barricade against the
world; in the matter of that, women are a close corporation. Man, how they do stand together! Their
virtue's the shell that protects them, and when one of
them leaves her shell or loses it, the others assess her
out of the close corporation, for she's a minority stock-
holder."

"Mother and the girls are up to their eyebrows in
the work of an organization in Seattle designed to salvage female delinquents," Donald complained. "I can't
understand their attitude."

Old Hector hooted.

"They don't do the salvaging. Not a bit of it! That
unpleasant work is left to others, and the virtuous and
respectable merely pay for it. Ken ye not, boy, 'twas
ever the habit of people of means to patronize and coddle the lowly. If they couldn't do that, where would be
the fun of being rich? Look in the Seattle papers.
Who gets the advertising out of a charity ball if it
isn't the rich? They organize it and they put it over,
with the public paying for a look at them, and they
attending the ball on complimentary tickets, although
I will admit that when the bills are paid and the last

shred of social triumph has been torn from the affair,
the Bide-a-Wee Home for Unmarried Mothers can have
what's left—and be damned to them."

Donald laughed quietly.

"Scotty, you're developing into an iconoclast. If
your fellow plutocrats should hear you ranting in that
vein, they'd call you a socialist."

"Oh, I'm not saying there aren't a heap of excep-
tions. Many's the woman with a heart big enough to
mother the world, although, when all's said and done;
'tis the poor that are kind to the poor, the unfortunate
that can appreciate and forgive misfortune. I'm glad
you stood by old Brent and his girl," he added approv-
ingly.

"I intend to accord her the treatment which a gentleman always accords the finest lady in the land, dad."

"Or the lowest, my son. I've noticed that kind are
not altogether unpopular with our finest gentlemen.
Donald, I used to pray to God that I wouldn't raise a
fool. I feel that he's answered my prayers, but if you
should ever turn hypocrite, I'll start praying again."

VIII

DONALD left the following morning in the automobile for the logging-camps up-river, and because of his unfamiliarity with their present location, his father's chauffeur drove him up. He was to be gone all week, but planned to return Saturday afternoon to spend Sunday with his family.

As the car wound up the narrow river road, Donald found himself thinking of Nan Brent and her tragedy. Since his visit to the Sawdust Pile the day before, two pictures of her had persisted in his memory, every detail of both standing forth distinctly.

In the first, she was a shabby, barelegged girl of thirteen, standing in the cockpit of his sloop, holding the little vessel on its course while he and old Caleb took a reef in the mainsail. The wilderness of gold that was her uncared-for hair blew behind her like a sunny burgee; her sea-blue eyes were fixed on the mainsail, out of which she adroitly spilled the wind at the proper moment, in order that Donald and her father might haul the reef-points home and make them fast. In his mind's eye, he could see the pulse beating in her throat as they prepared to come about, for on such occasions she always became excited; he saw again the sweet curve of her lips and her uplifted chin; he heard again her shrill voice crying, "Ready, about!" and saw the spokes spin as she threw the helm over and crouched from the swinging boom, although it cleared her pretty head by at least three feet. He listened again to her elfin laugh as she let the sloop fall off sufficiently to take the lip of a comber over the starboard counter and force Donald and her father to seek shelter from the spray in the lee of the mainsail, from which sanctuary, with more laughter, she presently routed them by causing the spray to come in over the port counter.

The other picture was the pose in which he had seen her the morning previous at the Sawdust Pile, when, to hide her emotion, she had half turned from him and gazed so forlornly out across the Bight of Tyee. It had struck him then, with peculiar force, that Nan Brent never again would laugh that joyous elfin laugh of other days. He had seen the pulse beating in her creamy neck again—a neck fuller, rounder, glorious with the beauty of fully developed womanhood. And the riot of golden hair was subdued, with the exception of little wayward wisps that whipped her white temples. Her eyes, somewhat darker now, like the sea near the horizon after the sun has set but while the glory of the day still lingers, were bright with unshed tears. The sweet curves of her mouth were drawn in pain. The northwest trade-wind blowing across the bight had whipped her gingham dress round her, revealing the soft curves of a body, the beauty of which motherhood had intensified rather than diminished. Thus she had stood, the outcast of Port Agnew, and beside her the little badge of her shame, demanding the father he had never known and would never see.

The young laird of Tyee wondered what sort of man could have done this thing—this monumental wickedness. His great fists were clenched as there welled within him a black rage at the scoundrel who had so

wantonly wrecked that little home on the Sawdust Pile.
He wondered, with the arrogance of his years, assuming
unconsciously the right of special privilege, if Nan
would ever reveal to him the identity of the villain.
Perhaps, some day, in a burst of confidence, she might.
Even if she did tell him, what could he do? To induce
the recreant lover to marry her openly and legally
would, he knew, be the world's way of "righting the
wrong" and giving the baby a name, but the mischief
had been done too long, and could never be undone unless, indeed, a marriage certificate, with proper dating,
could be flaunted in the face of an iconoclastic and
brutal world. Even then, there would remain that
astute and highly virtuous few who would never cease
to impart in whispers the information that, no matter
what others might think, *they* had their doubts. He
was roused from his bitter cogitations by the chauffeur
speaking.

"This is Darrow, Mr. Donald. I don't believe you've
seen it, have you? Darrow put in his mill and town
while you were away."

Donald looked over the motley collection of shacks
as the automobile rolled down the single unpaved
street.

"Filthy hole," he muttered. "Hello! There's one
of my late friends from the Sawdust Pile."

A woman, standing in the open door of a shanty on
the outskirts of the town had made a wry face and
thrust out her tongue at him. He lifted his hat gravely,
whereat she screamed a curse upon him. An instant
later, an empty beer-bottle dropped with a crash in the
tonneau, and Donald, turning, beheld in the door of a

Darrow groggery one of the Greek fishermen he had dis-
possessed.

"Stop the car!" Donald commanded. "I think that
man wants to discuss a matter with me."

"Sorry, sir, but I don't think it's wise to obey you
just now," his father's chauffeur answered, and trod on
the accelerator. "They call that place the 'Bucket of
Blood,' and you'll need something more than your fists
if you expect to enter there and come out under your
own power."

"Very well. Some other time, perhaps."

"You don't appear to be popular in Darrow, Mr.
Donald."

"Those people left the Sawdust Pile yesterday—in a
hurry," Donald explained. "Naturally, they're still
resentful."

"They were making quite a little money down there,
I believe. Folks do say business was good, and when
you take money from that kind of cattle you make a
worth-while enemy. If I were you, sir, I'd watch my
step in dark alleys, and I'd carry a gun."

"When I have to carry a gun to protect myself from
vermin like that mulatto and those shifty little Greeks,
I'll be a few years older than I am now, Henry. However, I suppose I'd be foolish to neglect your warning
to mind my step."

He spent a busy week in the woods, and it was his
humor to spend it entirely felling trees. The tough,
experienced old choppers welcomed him with keen interest and played freeze-out each night in the bunk-houses
to see which one should draw him for a partner next
day; for the choppers worked in pairs, likewise the
cross-cut men. Their bucolic sense of humor impelled

the choppers to speed up when they found themselves paired with the new boss, for it would have been a feather in the cap of the man who could make him quit or send him home at nightfall "with his tail dragging," as the woods boss expressed it.

Donald sported a wondrous set of blisters at the close of that first day, but after supper he opened them, covered them with adhesive tape, and went back to work next morning as if nothing had happened. During those five days, he learned considerable of the art of dropping a tree exactly where he desired it, and bringing it to earth without breakage. He rode down to Port Agnew with the woods crew on the last log-train Saturday night, walked into the mill office, and cashed in his time-slip for five days' work as a chopper. He had earned two dollars a day and his board and lodging. His father, who had driven into town to meet him, came to the window and watched him humorously.

"So that's the way you elect to work it, eh?" he queried. "I told Daney to pay you my salary when I quit."

"I like to feel that I'm earning my stipend," Donald replied, "so it pleases me to draw the wages of the job I'm working at. When I'm thoroughly acquainted with all the jobs in the Tyee Lumber Company, or at least have a good working knowledge of them, I think I'll be a better boss."

The Laird took his son's big brown hands in his and looked at the palms.

"I rather think I like it so," he answered. "A man whose hands have never bled or whose back has never ached is a poor man to judge a labor dispute. 'Twould improve you if you were a married man and had to live on that for a week, less twenty-five cents for your hospital dues. The choppers pay a dollar a month toward the hospital, and that covers medical attendance for them and their families."

Donald laughed and flipped a quarter over to the cashier, then turned and handed ten dollars to a wiry little chopper standing in line.

"I was feeling so good this morning I bet Sandy my week's pay I could fell a tree quicker than he and with less breakage. He won in a walk," he explained to The Laird.

"Come with me," his father ordered, and led him into the office.

From the huge safe he selected a ledger, scanned the index, and opened it at a certain account headed, "Sandy Clough." To Sandy's credit each month, extending over a period of fifteen years, appeared a credit of thirty dollars.

"That's what it's costing me to have discovered Sandy," his father informed him; "but since I had served an apprenticeship as a chopper, the time required to discover Sandy was less than half an hour. I watched him one day when he didn't know who I was —so I figured him for a man and a half and raised him a dollar a day. He doesn't know it, however. If he did, he'd brag about it, and I'd have to pay as much to men half as good. When he's chopped for us twenty years, fire him and give him that. He's earned it. Thus endeth the first lesson, my son. Now come home to dinner."

After dinner, Donald returned to town to buy himself some working-clothes at the general store. His purchases completed, he sought the juvenile department.

"I want some kid's clothing," he announced. "To fit a child of three. Rompers, socks, shoes—the complete outfit. Charge them to my account and send them over to Nan Brent at the Sawdust Pile. I'll give you a note to enclose with them."

Notwithstanding the fact that she was an employe of the Tyee Lumber Company, the girl who waited on him stared at him frankly. He noticed this and bent upon her a calm glance that brought a guilty flush to her cheek. Quickly she averted her eyes, but, nevertheless she had a feeling that the young laird of Tyee was still appraising her, and, unable to withstand the fascination peculiar to such a situation, she looked at him again to verify her suspicions—and it was even so. In great confusion she turned to her stock, and Donald, satisfied that he had squelched her completely, went into the manager's office, wrote, and sealed the following note to Nan Brent:

Saturday night.

FRIEND NAN:

Here are some duds for the young fellow. You gave me the right to look after him, you know; at least, you didn't decline it. At any rate, I think you will not mind accepting them from me.

I sent to Seattle for some books I thought you might like. They have probably arrived by parcel-post. Sent you a box of candy, also, although I have forgotten the kind you used to prefer.

Been up in the logging-camp all week, chopping, and I ache all over. Expect to be hard and not quite so weary by next week-end, and will call over for Sunday dinner.

Sincerely,   DONALD McKAYE.

He spent Sunday at The Dreamerie, and at four o'clock Sunday afternoon boarded the up train and returned to the logging-camp. Mrs. Andrew Daney, seated in Sunday-afternoon peace upon her front veranda, looked up from the columns of the *Churchman* as the long string of logging-trucks wound round the base of the little knoll upon which the general manager's home stood; but even at a distance of two blocks, she recognized the young laird of Tyee in the cab with the engineer.

"Dear, dear!" this good soul murmured. "And such a nice young man, too! I should think he'd have more consideration for his family, if not for himself."

"Who's that?" Mr. Daney demanded, emerging from behind the Seattle *Post-Intelligencer*.

"Donald McKaye."

"What about him?" Mr. Daney demanded, with slight emphasis on the pronoun.

"Oh, nothing; only——"

"Only what?"

"People say he's unduly interested in Nan Brent."

"If he is, that's his business. Don't let what people say trouble you, Mrs. Daney."

"Well, can I help it if people will talk?"

"Yes—when they talk to you."

"How do you know they've been talking to me, Andrew?" she demanded foolishly.

"Because you know what they say." Andrew Daney rose from the wicker deck-chair in which he had been lounging and leveled his index-finger at the partner of his joys and sorrows. "You forget Donald McKaye and that Brent girl," he ordered. "It's none of your business. All Don has to say to me is, 'Mr. Daney, your job is vacant'—and, by Judas Priest, it'll be vacant. Remember that, my dear."

"Nonsense, dear. The Laird wouldn't permit it— after all these years."

"If it comes to a test of strength, I'll lose, and don't you forget it. Old sake's sake is all that saved me from a run-in with Donald before he had been in command fifteen minutes. I refer to that Sawdust Pile episode. You dissuaded me from doing my duty in that matter, Mary, and my laxity was not pleasing to Donald. I don't blame him a whit."

"Did he say anything?" she demanded, a trifle alarmed.

"No; but he looked it."

"How did he look, Andrew?"

"He looked," her husband replied, "like the Blue Bonnets coming over the border—that's what he looked like. Then he went down to the Sawdust Pile like a raging demon, cleaned it out in two twos, and put it to the torch. You be careful what you say to people, Mary. Get that boy started once, and he'll hark back to his paternal ancestors; and if The Laird has ever told you the history of that old claymore that hangs on the wall in The Dreamerie, you know that the favorite outdoor sports of the McKaye tribe were fighting and foot-racing—with the other fellow in front."

"The Laird is mild enough," she defended.

"Yes, he is. But when he was young, he could, and frequently did, whip twice his weight in bear-cats. Old as he is to-day, he's as sound as a man of forty; he wouldn't budge an inch for man or devil."

Mrs. Daney carefully folded the *Churchman*, laid it aside, and placed her spectacles with it.

"Andrew, I know it's terrible of me to breathe such a thing, but—did it ever occur to you that—perhaps —the father of Nan Brent's child might be——"

"Donald?" he exploded incredulously.

She nodded, and about her nod there was something of that calm self-confidence of an attorney who is winning his case and desires to impress that fact upon the jury.

"By God, woman," cried Daney, "you have the most infernal ideas——"

"Andrew! Remember it's the Sabbath!"

"It's a wonder my language doesn't shrivel this paper. Now then, where in hades do you get this crazy notion?" Daney was thoroughly angry. She gazed up at him in vague apprehension. Had she gone too, far? Suddenly he relaxed. "No; don't tell me," he growled. "I'll not be a gossip. God forgive me, I was about to befoul the very salt I eat. I'll not be disloyal."

"But, Andrew dear, don't you know I wouldn't dare breathe it to anyone but you?"

"I don't know how much you'd dare. At any rate, I'll excuse you from breathing it to me, for I'm not interested. I know it isn't true."

"Then, Andrew, it is your duty to tell me why you know it isn't true, in order that I may set at rest certain rumors——"

"You—mind—your—own—business, Mary!" he cried furiously, punctuating each word with a vigorous tap of his finger on the arm of her chair. "The Mc-Kayes meet their responsibilities as eagerly as they do their enemies. If that child were young Donald's, he'd have married the Brent girl, and if he had demurred about it, The Laird would have ordered him to."

"Thank you for that vote of confidence in the Mc-Kaye family, Andrew," said a quiet voice. "I think you have the situation sized up just right."

Andrew Daney whirled; his wife glanced up, startled, then half rose and settled back in her chair again, for her legs absolutely refused to support her. Standing at the foot of the three steps that led off the veranda was Hector McKaye!

"I drove Donald down from The Dreamerie to catch the up train, and thought I'd drop over and visit with you a bit," he explained. "I didn't intend to eavesdrop, and I didn't—very much; but since I couldn't help overhearing such a pertinent bit of conversation, I'll come up and we'll get to the bottom of it. Keep your seat, Mrs. Daney."

The advice was unnecessary. The poor soul could not have left it. The Laird perched himself on the veranda railing, handed the dumfounded Daney a cigar, and helped himself to one.

"Well, proceed," The Laird commanded. His words apparently were addressed to both, but his glance was fixed on Mrs. Daney—and now she understood full well her husband's description of the McKaye look.

"I had finished what I had to say, Mr. McKaye," Andrew Daney found courage to say.

"So I noted, Andrew, and right well and forcibly you said it. I'm grateful to you. I make no mistake, I think, if your statement wasn't in reply to some idle tale told your good wife and repeated by her to you—in confidence, of course, as between man and wife."

KINDRED OF THE DUST 77

"If you'll excuse me, Mr. McKaye, I—I'd rather not —discuss it!" Mary Daney cried breathlessly.

"I would I did not deem it a duty to discuss it myself, Mary. But you must realize that when the tongue of scandal touches my son, it becomes a personal matter with me, and I must look well for a weapon to combat it. You'll tell me now, Mary, what they've been saying about Donald and Caleb Brent's daughter."

"Andrew will tell you," she almost whispered, and made as if to go. But The Laird's fierce eyes deterred her; she quailed and sat down again.

"Andrew cannot tell me, because Andrew doesn't know," The Laird rebuked her kindly. "I heard him tell you not to tell him, that he wasn't a gossip, and wouldn't befoul the salt he ate by being disloyal, or words to that effect. Is it possible, Mary Daney, that you prefer me to think you are not inspired by similar sentiments? Don't cry, Mary—compose yourself."

"Idleness is the mother of mischief, and since the children have grown up and left home, Mary hasn't enough to keep her busy," Daney explained. "So, womanlike and without giving sober thought to the matter, she's been listening to the idle chattering of other idle women. Now then, my dear," he continued, turning to his wife, "that suspicion you just voiced didn't grow in your head. Somebody put it there—and God knows it found fertile soil. Out with it now, wife! Who've you been gossiping with?"

"I'll name no names," the unhappy woman sobbed; "but somebody told me that somebody else was down at the Sawdust Pile the day Donald burned those shacks, and after be burned them he spent an hour in the Brent cottage, and when he came out he had the

baby in his arms. When he left, the child made a great
to-do and called him, 'daddy.' "

The Laird smiled.

"Well, Mary, what would you expect the boy to
do? Beat the child? To my knowledge, he's been
robbing the candy department of my general store for
years, and the tots of Port Agnew have been the bene-
ficiaries of his vandalism. He was born with a love of
children. And would you convict him on the prattle of
an innocent child in arms?"

"Certainly not, Mr. McKaye. I understand. Well
then, on Saturday night he sent over a complete outfit
of clothing for the child, with a note in the bundle——"

"Hm-m-m."

"And then somebody remembered that the child's
name is Donald."

"How old is that child, Mrs. Daney?"

She considered.

"As I recall it, he'll be three years old in October."

"Since you're a married woman, Mrs. Daney," The
Laird began, with old-fashioned deprecation for the
blunt language he was about to employ, "you'll admit
that the child wasn't found behind one of old Brent's
cabbages. This is the year 1916."

But Mrs. Daney anticipated him.

"They've figured it out," she interrupted, "and Donald was home from college for the holidays in 1912."

"So he was," The Laird replied complacently. "I'd
forgotten. So that alibi goes by the board. What else
now? Does the child resemble my son?"

"Nobody knows. Nan Brent doesn't receive visitors,
and she hasn't been up-town since the child was born."

"Is that all, Mary?"

"All I have heard so far."

Old Hector was tempted to tell her that, in his opinion, she had heard altogether too much, but his regard for her husband caused him to refrain.

"It's little enough, and yet it's a great deal," he answered. "You'll be kind enough, Mary, not to carry word of this idle gossip to The Dreamerie. I should regret that very much."

She flushed with the knowledge that, although he forgave her, still he distrusted her and considered a warning necessary. However, she nodded vigorous acceptance of his desire, and immediately he changed the topic. While, for him, the quiet pleasure he had anticipated in the visit had not materialized and he longed to leave at once, for Daney's sake he remained for tea. When he departed, Mrs. Daney ran to her room and found surcease from her distress in tears, while her husband sat out on the veranda smoking one of The Laird's fine cigars, his embarrassment considerably alleviated by the knowledge that his imprudent wife had received a lesson that should last for the remainder of her life.

About eight o'clock, his wife called him to the telephone. The Laird was on the wire.

"In the matter of the indiscreet young lady in the store, Andrew," he ordered, "do not dismiss her or reprimand her. The least said in such cases is soonest mended."

"Very well, sir."

"Good-night, Andrew."

"Good-night, sir."

"Poor man!" Daney sighed, as he hung up. "He's

thought of nothing else since he heard about it; it's a canker in his heart. I wish I dared indicate to Donald the fact that he's being talked about—and watched—by the idle and curious, in order that he may bear himself accordingly. He'd probably misunderstand my motives, however."

IX

DURING the week, Mary Daney refrained from broaching the subject of that uncomfortable Sunday afternoon, wherefore her husband realized she was thinking considerably about it and, as a result, was not altogether happy. Had he suspected, however, the trend her thoughts were taking, he would have been greatly perturbed. Momentous thoughts rarely racked Mrs. Daney's placid and somewhat bovine brain, but once she became possessed with the notion that Nan Brent was the only human being possessed of undoubted power to create or suppress a scandal which some queer feminine intuition warned her impended, the more firmly did she become convinced that it was her Christian duty to call upon Nan Brent and strive to present the situation in a common-sense light to that erring young woman.

Having at length attained to this resolution, a subtle peace settled over Mrs. Daney, the result, doubtless, of a consciousness of virtue regained, since she was about to right a wrong to which she had so thoughtlessly been a party. Her decision had almost been reached when her husband, coming home for luncheon at noon on Saturday, voiced the apprehension which had harassed him during the week.

"Donald will be home from the woods to-night," he announced, in troubled tones. "I do hope he'll not permit that big heart of his to lead him into further

kindnesses that will be misunderstood by certain people
in case they hear of them. I have never known a man
so proud and fond of a son as The Laird is of Donald."

"Nonsense!" his wife replied complacently. "The
Laird has forgotten all about it."

"Perhaps. Nevertheless, he will watch his son, and
if, by any chance, the boy should visit the Sawdust
Pile——"

"Then it will be time enough to worry about him,
Andrew. In the meantime, it's none of our business,
dear. Eat your luncheon and don't think about it."

He relapsed into moody silence. When he had departed for the mill office, however, his wife's decision
had been reached. Within the hour she was on her way
to the Sawdust Pile, but as she approached Caleb
Brent's garden gate, she observed, with a feeling of
gratification, that, after all, it was not going to be
necessary for her to be seen entering the house or leaving it. Far up the strand she saw a woman and a little
child sauntering.

Nan Brent looked up at the sound of footsteps
crunching the shingle, identified Mrs. Daney at a glance,
and turned her head instantly, at the same time walking
slowly away at right angles, in order to obviate a meeting. To her surprise, Mrs. Daney also changed her
course, and Nan, observing this out of the corner of
her eye, dropped her apronful of driftwood and turned
to face her visitor.

"Good afternoon, Miss Brent. May I speak to you
for a few minutes?"

"Certainly, Mrs. Daney."

Mrs. Daney nodded condescendingly and sat down on the white sand.

"Be seated, Miss Brent, if you please."

"Well, perhaps if we sit down, we will be less readily recognized at a distance." Nan replied smilingly, and was instantly convinced that she had read her visitor's mind aright, for Mrs. Daney flushed slightly. "Suppose," the girl suggested gently, "that you preface what you have to say by calling me 'Nan.' You knew me well enough to call me that in an earlier and happier day, Mrs. Daney."

"Thank you, Nan. I shall accept your invitation and dispense with formality." She hesitated for a beginning, and Nan, observing her slight embarrassment, was gracious enough to aid her by saying:

"I dare say your visit has something to do with the unenviable social position in which I find myself in Port Agnew, Mrs. Daney, for I cannot imagine any other possible interest in me to account for it. So you may be quite frank. I'm sure nothing save a profound sense of duty brought you here, and I am prepared to listen." This was a degree of graciousness the lady had not anticipated, and it put her at her ease immediately.

"I've called to talk to you about Donald McKaye," she began abruptly.

"At the solicitation of whom?"

"Nobody." Mrs. Daney sighed. "It was just an idea of mine."

"Ah—I think I prefer it that way. Proceed, Mrs. Daney."

"Young Mr. McKaye is unduly interested in you,

Nan—at least, that is the impression of a number of people in Port Agnew."

"I object to the use of the adverb 'unduly' in connection with Mr. Donald's interest in my father and me. But no matter. Since Port Agnew has no interest in me, pray why, Mrs. Daney, should I have the slightest interest in the impressions of these people you refer to and whose volunteer representative you appear to be?"

"There! I knew you would be offended!" Mrs. Daney cried, with a deprecatory shrug. "I'm sure I find this a most difficult matter to discuss, and I assure you, I do not desire to appear offensive."

"Well, you are; but I can stand it, and whether I resent it or not cannot be a matter of much import to you or the others. And I'll try not to be disagreeable. Just why did you come to see me, Mrs. Daney?"

"I might as well speak plainly, Miss Brent. Donald McKaye's action in ridding the Sawdust Pile of your neighbors has occasioned comment. It appears that this was his first official act after assuming his father's place in the business. Then he visited you and your father for an hour, and your child, whom it appears you have named Donald, called him 'daddy.' Then, last Saturday night, Mr. McKaye sent over some clothing for the boy——"

"Whereupon the amateur detectives took up the trail," Nan interrupted bitterly. "And you heard of it immediately."

"His father heard of it also," Mrs. Daney continued. "It worries him."

"It should not. He should have more faith in his son, Mrs. Daney."

"He is a father, my dear, very proud of his son, very devoted to him, and fearfully ambitious for Donald's future."

"And you fear that I may detract from the radiance of that future? Is that it?"

"In plain English," the worthy lady replied brutally, "it is."

"I see your point of view very readily, Mrs. Daney. Your apprehensions are ridiculous—almost pathetic. Don McKaye's great sympathy is alone responsible for his hardihood in noticing me, and he is so much too big for Port Agnew that it is no wonder his motives are misunderstood. However, I am sorry his father is worried. We have a very great respect for The Laird; indeed, we owe him a debt of gratitude, and there is nothing my father or I would not do to preserve his peace of mind."

"The talk will die out, of course, unless something should occur to revive it, Miss Brent—I mean, Nan. But it would be just like Donald McKaye to start a revival of this gossip. He doesn't care a farthing for what people think or say, and he is too young to realize that one *must* pay *some* attention to public opinion. You realize that, of course."

"I ought to, Mrs. Daney. I think I have had some experience of public opinion," Nan replied sadly.

"Then, should Donald McKaye's impulsive sympathy lead him to—er——"

"You mean that I am to discourage him in the event——"

"Precisely, Miss Brent. For his father's sake."

"Not to mention your husband's position. Precisely, Mrs. Daney."

Mary Daney's heart fluttered.

"I have trusted to your honor, Nan—although I didn't say so in the beginning—not to mention my visit or this interview to a living soul."

"My 'honor!'" Nan's low, bitter laugh raked the Daney nerves like a rasp. "I think, Mrs. Daney, that I may be depended upon to follow my own inclinations in this matter. I suspect you have been doing some talking yourself and may have gone too far, with the result that you are hastening now, by every means in your power, to undo whatever harm, real or fancied, has grown out of your lack of charity."

"Nan, I beg of you——"

"Don't! You have no right to beg anything of me. I am not unintelligent and neither am I degraded. I think I possess a far keener conception of my duty than do you or those whom you have elected to represent; hence I regard this visit as an unwarranted impertinence. One word from me to Donald Mc-Kaye——"

Terror smote the Samaritan. She clasped her hands; her lips were pale and trembling.

"Oh, my dear, my dear," she pleaded, "you wouldn't breathe a word to him, would you? Promise me you'll say nothing. How could I face my husband if—if——" She began to weep.

"I shall promise nothing," Nan replied sternly.

"But I only came for his father's sake, you cruel girl!"

"Perhaps his father's case is safer in my hands than in yours, Mrs. Daney, and safest of all in those of his son."

The outcast of Port Agnew rose, filled her apron

with the driftwood she had gathered, and called to her child. As the little fellow approached, Mrs. Daney so far forgot her perturbation as to look at him keenly and decide, eventually, that he bore not the faintest resemblance to Donald McKaye.

"I'm sure, Nan, you will not be heartless enough to tell Donald McKaye of my visit to you," she pleaded, as the girl started down the beach.

"You have all the assurance of respectability, dear Mrs. Daney," Nan answered carelessly.

"You shall not leave me until you promise to be silent!" Mary Daney cried hysterically, and rose to follow her.

"I think you had better go, Mrs. Daney. I am quite familiar with the figure of The Laird since his retirement; he walks round the bight with his dogs every afternoon for exercise, and, if I am not greatly mistaken, that is he coming down the beach."

Mrs. Daney cast a terrified glance in the direction indicated. A few hundred yards up the beach she recognized The Laird, striding briskly along, swinging his stick, and with his two English setters romping beside him. With a final despairing "Please Nan; please do not be cruel!" she fled, Nan Brent smiling mischievously after her stout retreating form.

"I have condemned you to the horrors of uncertainty," the girl soliloquized. "How very, very stupid you are, Mrs. Daney, to warn me to protect him! As if I wouldn't lay down my life to uphold his honor! Nevertheless, you dear old bungling busybody, you are absolutely right, although I suspect no altruistic reason carried you forth on this uncomfortable errand."

Nan had heretofore, out of the bitterness of her

life, formed the opinion that brickbats were for the lowly, such as she, and bouquets solely for the great, such as Donald McKaye. Now, for the first time, she realized that human society is organized in three strata —high, mediocre, and low, and that when a mediocrity has climbed to the seats of the mighty, his fellows strive to drag him back, down to their own ignoble level—or lower. To Nan, child of poverty, sorrow, and solitude, the world had always appeared more or less incomprehensible, but this afternoon, as she retraced her slow steps to the Sawdust Pile, the old dull pain of existence had become more complicated and acute with the knowledge that the first ray of sunlight that had entered her life in three years was about to be withdrawn; and at the thought, tears, which seemed to well from her heart rather than from her eyes, coursed down her cheeks and a sob broke through her clenched lips.

Her progress homeward, what with the heavy bundle of driftwood, in her apron impeding her stride, coupled with the necessity for frequent pauses to permit her child to catch up with her, was necessarily slow—so slow, in fact, that presently she heard quick footsteps behind her and, turning, beheld Hector McKaye. He smiled, lifted his hat, and greeted her pleasantly.

"Good-afternoon, Miss Nan. That is a heavy burden of driftwood you carry, my dear. Here—let me relieve you of it. I've retired, you know, and the necessity for finding something to do— Bless my soul, the girl's crying!" He paused, hat in hand, and gazed at her with frank concern. She met his look bravely.

"Thank you, Mr. McKaye. Please do not bother about it."

"Oh, but I shall bother," he answered. "Remove your apron, girl, and I'll tie the wood up in it and carry it home for you."

Despite her distress, she smiled.

"You're such an old-fashioned gentleman," she replied. "So very much like your son—I mean, your son is so very much like you."

"That's better. I think I enjoy the compliment more when you put it that way," he answered. "Do not stand there holding the wood, my girl. Drop it."

She obeyed and employed her right hand, thus freed, in wiping the telltale tears from her sweet face.

"I have been lax in neighborly solicitude," The Laird continued. "I must send you over a supply of wood from the box factory. We have more waste than we can use in the furnaces. Is this your little man, Nan? Sturdy little chap, isn't he? Come here, bub, and let me heft you."

He swung the child from the sands, and while pretending to consider carefully the infant's weight, he searched the cherubic countenance with a swift, appraising glance.

"Healthy little rascal," he continued, and swung the child high in the air two or three times, smiling paternally as the latter screamed with delight. "How do you like that, eh?" he demanded, as he set the boy down on the sand again.

"Dood!" the child replied, and gazed up at The Laird yearningly. "Are you my daddy?"

But The Laird elected to disregard the pathetic query and busied himself gathering up the bundle of driftwood, nor did he permit his glance to rest upon Nan Brent's flushed and troubled face. Tucking the bundle under one arm and taking Nan's child on the other, he whistled to his dogs and set out for the Sawdust Pile, leaving the girl to follow behind him. He preceded her through the gate, tossed the driftwood on a small pile in the yard, and turned to hand her the apron.

"You are not altogether happy, poor girl!" he said kindly. "I'm very sorry. I want the people in my town to be happy."

"I shall grow accustomed to it, Mr. McKaye," Nan answered. "To-day, I am merely a little more depressed than usual. Thank you so much for carrying the wood. You are more than kind."

His calm, inscrutable gray glance roved over her. noting her beauty and her sweetness, and the soul of him was troubled.

"Is it something you could confide in an old man?" he queried gently. "You are much neglected, and I—I understand the thoughts that must come to you sometimes. Perhaps you would be happier elsewhere than in Port Agnew."

"Perhaps," she replied dully.

"If you could procure work—some profession to keep your mind off your troubles—I have some property in Tacoma—suburban lots with cottages on them." The Laird grew confused and embarrassed because of the thought that was in the back of his mind, and was expressing himself jerkily and in disconnected sentences. "I do not mean—I do not offer charity, for I take it you have had enough insults—well, you and your father could occupy one of those cottages at whatever you think you could afford to pay, and I would be happy to advance you any funds you might need until you—

could—that is, of course, you must get on your feet again, and you must have help—" He waved his hand. "All this oppresses me."

The remembrance of Mrs. Daney's interview with her prompted the girl to flash back at him.

" 'Oppresses,' Mr. McKaye? Since when?"

He gazed upon her in frank admiration for her audacity and perspicacity.

"Yes," he admitted slowly; "I dare say I deserve that. Yet, mingled with that ulterior motive you have so unerringly .discerned, there is a genuine, if belated, desire to be decently human. I think you realize that also."

"I should be stupid and ungrateful did I not, Mr. McKaye. I am sorry I spoke just now as I did, but I could not bear——"

"To permit me to lay the flattering unction to my soul that I had gotten away with something, eh?" he laughed, much more at his ease, now that he realized how frank and yet how tactful she could be.

"It wasn't quite worthy of you—not because I might resent it, for I am nobody, but because you should have more faith in yourself and be above the possibility of disturbance at the hands—or rather, the tongues—of people who speak in whispers." She came close to him suddenly and laid her hand lightly on his forearm, for she was speaking with profound earnestness. "I am your debtor, Mr. McKaye, for that speech you found it so hard to make just now, and for past kindnesses from you and your son. I cannot accept your offer. I would like to, did my pride permit, and were it not for the fact that such happiness as is left to my father can only be found by the Bight of Tyee. So, while he

lives I shall not desert him. As for your apprehensions"
—she smiled tolerantly and whimsically—"though flattering to me, they are quite unnecessary, and I beg
you to rid your mind of them. I am—that which I am;
yet I am more than I appear to be to some and I shall
not wantonly or wilfully hurt you—or yours."

The Laird of Tyee took in both of his the slim hand
that rested so lightly on his sleeve—that dainty left
hand with the long, delicate fingers and no wedding-
ring.

"My dear child," he murmured, "I feel more than I
dare express. Good-by and may God bless you and be
good to you, for I fear the world will not." He bowed
with old-fashioned courtesy over her hand and departed; yet such was his knowledge of life that now his
soul was more deeply troubled than it had been since
his unintentional eavesdropping on his manager's gar-
rulous wife.

"What a woman!" he reflected. "Brains, imagination, dignity, womanly pride, courage, beauty and—
yes; I agree with Donald. Neither maid, wife, nor
widow is she—yet she is not, never has been, and never
will be a woman without virtue. Ah, Donald, my son,
she's a bonny lass! For all her fall, she's not a common woman and my son is not a common man—I
wonder—Oh, 'tis lies, lies, lies, and she's heard them
and knows they're lies. Ah, my son, my son, with the
hot blood of youth in you—you've a man's head and
heart and a will of your own— Aye, she's sweet—
that she is— I wonder!"

X

A T the front of Caleb Brent's little house there was
a bench upon which the old man was wont to sit
on sunny days—usually in the morning, before the
brisk, cool nor'west trade-wind commenced to blow.
Following Hector McKaye's departure, Nan sought
this bench until she had sufficiently mastered her emotions to conceal from her father evidence of a distress
more pronounced than usual; as she sat there, she
revolved the situation in her mind, scanning every
aspect of it, weighing carefully every possibility.

In common with the majority of human kind, Nan
considered herself entitled to life, liberty, and the pur-
suit of happiness, and now, at a period when, in the
ordinary course of events, all three of these necessary
concomitants of successful existence (for, to her, life
meant something more than mere living) should have
been hers in bounteous measure, despite the handicap
under which she had been born, she faced a future so
barren that sometimes the distant boom of the breakers
on Tyee Head called to her to desert her hopeless fight
and in the blue depths out yonder find haven from the
tempests of her soul.

In an elder day, when the Sawdust Pile had been
Port Agnew's garbage-dump, folks who clipped their
rose bushes and thinned out their marigold plants had
been accustomed to seeing these slips take root again
and bloom on the Sawdust Pile for a brief period after

their ash-cans had been emptied there; and, though she
did not know it, Nan Brent bore pitiful resemblance to
these outcast flowers. Here, on the reclaimed Sawdust
Pile, she had bloomed from girlhood into lovely womanhood—a sweet forget-me-not in the Garden of Life,
she had been transplanted into Eden until Fate, the
grim gardener, had cast her out, to take root again
on the Sawdust Pile and ultimately to wither and die.

It is terrible for the great of soul, the ambitious, the
imaginative, when circumstances condemn them to life
amid dull, uninteresting, drab, and sometimes sordid
surroundings. Born to love and be loved, Nan Brent's
soul beat against her environment even as a wild bird,
captured and loosed in a room, beats against the win-
dow-pane. From the moment she had felt within her
the vague stirrings of womanhood, she had been wont
to gaze upon the blue-back hills to the east, to the
horizon out west, wondering what mysteries lay beyond,
and yearning to encounter them. Perhaps it was the
sea-faring instinct, the *Wanderlust* of her forebears;
perhaps it was a keener appreciation of the mediocrity
of Port Agnew than others in the little town possessed,
a realization that she had more to give to life than life
had to give to her. Perhaps it had been merely the
restlessness that is the twin of a rare heritage—the
music of the spheres—for with such had Nan been
born. It is hard to harken for the reedy music of Pan
and hear only the whine of a sawmill or the boom of
the surf.

Of her mother, Nan had seen but little. Her recollections of her mother were few and vague; of her
mother's people, she knew nothing save the fact that
they dwelt in a world quite free of Brents, and that

her mother had committed a distinctly social *faux pas* in marrying Caleb Brent she guessed long before Caleb Brent, in his brave simplicity, had imparted that fact to her. An admiral's daughter, descendant of an old and wealthy Revolutionary family, the males of which had deemed any calling other than the honorable profession of arms as beneath the blood and traditions of the family, Nan's mother had been the pet of Portsmouth until, inexplicably, Caleb Brent, a chief petty officer on her father's flag-ship, upon whom the hero's medal had just been bestowed, had found favor in her eyes. The ways of love, as all the philosophers of the ages are agreed, are beyond definition or understanding; even in his own case, Caleb Brent was not equal to the task of understanding how their love had grown, burgeoned into an engagement, and ripened into marriage. He only knew that, from a meek and well-disciplined petty officer, he had suddenly developed the courage of a Sir Galahad, and, while under the influence of a strange spell, had respectfully defied the admiral, who had foolishly assumed that, even if his daughter would not obey him, his junior in the service would. Then had come the baby girl, Nan, the divorce—pressed by the mother's family—and the mother's death.

If his wife had discerned in him the nobility that was apparent to his daughter— Poor old hero! But Nan always checked her meditations at this point. They didn't seem quite fair to her mother.

Seated on the bench this afternoon, Nan reviewed her life from her sixth year, the year in which her father had claimed her. Until her eighteenth year, she had not been unhappy, for, following their arrival in Port

Agnew, her father had prospered to a degree which permitted his daughter the enjoyment of the ordinary opportunities of ordinary people. If she had not known extravagance in the matter of dress, neither had she known penury; when her feminine instinct impelled her to brighten and beautify the little home on the Sawdust Pile from time to time, she had found that possible. She had been graduated with honors from the local high school, and, being a book-lover of catholic taste and wide range, she was, perhaps, more solidly educated than the majority of girls who have had opportunities for so-called higher education. With the broad democracy of sawmill towns, she had not, in the days gone by, been excluded from the social life of the town, such as it was, and she had had her beaus, such as they were. Sometimes she wondered how the choir in the Presbyterian church had progressed since she, once the mezzo-soprano soloist, had resigned to sing lullabys to a nameless child, if Andrew Daney still walked on the tips of his shoes when he passed the collection-plate, and if the mortgage on the church had ever been paid.

She rose wearily and entered the little house. Old Caleb sat at the dining-room table playing solitaire. He looked up as she entered, swept the cards into a heap and extended his old arm to encircle her waist as she sat on the broad arm of his chair. She drew his gray head down on her breast.

"Dadkins," she said presently, "Donald McKaye isn't coming to dinner to-morrow after all."

"Oh, that's too bad, Nan! Has he written you? What's happened?"

"No; he hasn't written me, and nothing's happened. I have decided to send him word not to come."

"Aren't you feeling well, my dear?"

"It isn't that, popsy-wops. He's the new laird of Tyee now, and he must be careful of the company he keeps."

Old Caleb growled in his throat.

"Much he cares what people think."

"I know it. And much I care what people think, for I've grown accustomed to their thoughts. But I do care what his father thinks, for, of course, he has plans for Donald's future, and if Donald, out of the kindness of his heart, should become a frequent visitor here, The Laird would hear of it sooner or later— sooner, perhaps, for it would never occur to Donald to conceal it—and then the poor laird would be worried. And we don't owe The Laird that, father Brent!"

"No; we do not." The old face was troubled.

"I met Mrs. Daney on the beach, and it was she who gave me the intimation that The Laird had heard some cruel gossip that was disturbing him."

"I'm sorry. Well, use your own judgment, daughter."

"I'm sure Donald will understand," she assured him. "And he will not think the less of us for doing it."

She got up and went to the peculiar and wholly impractical little desk which Mrs. McKaye had picked up in Italy and which Donald, calm in the knowledge that his mother would never use it or miss it, had given her to help furnish the house when first they had come to the Sawdust Pile. On a leaf torn from a tablet, she wrote:

THE SAWDUST PILE, Saturday Afternoon.
DEAR DONALD:

I had planned to reserve my thanks for the books and the candy until you called for dinner to-morrow. Now,

I have decided that it will be better for you not to come
to dinner to-morrow, although this decision has not been
made without father and me being sensible of a keen feeling of disappointment. We had planned to sacrifice an
old hen that has outlived her margin of profit, hoping that,
with the admixture of a pinch of saleratus, she would
prove tender enough to tempt the appetite of a lumberjack, but, upon sober second thought, it seems the part
of wisdom to let her live.

We honor and respect you, Donald. You are so very
dear to us that we wish to cherish always your good opinion of us; we want everybody in Port Agnew to think of
you as we do. People will misunderstand and misconstrue
your loyalty to the old friends of your boyhood if you
dare admit your friendship. Indeed, some have already
done so. I thank you for the books and the candy, but
with all my heart I am grateful to you for a gift infinitely
more precious but which is too valuable for me to accept.
I shall have to treasure it at a distance. Sometimes, at
colors, you might wave to
Your old friend,
NAN BRENT.

Her letter completed, she sealed it in a plain white
envelop, after which she changed into her best dress
and shoes and departed up-town.

Straight to the mill office of the Tyee Lumber Company she went, her appearance outside the railing in
the general office being the signal for many a curious
and speculative glance from the girls and young men
at work therein. One of the former, with whom Nan
had attended high school, came over to the railing and,
without extending a greeting, either of word or smile,
asked, in businesslike tones,

"Whom do you wish to see?"

In direct contrast with this cool salutation, Nan inclined her head graciously and smilingly said:

"Why, how do you do, Hetty? I wonder if I might be permitted a minute of Mr. Daney's time."

"I'll see," Hetty replied, secretly furious in the knowledge that she had been serenely rebuked, and immediately disappeared in the general manager's office. A moment later, she emerged. "Mr. Daney will see you, Miss Brent," she announced. "First door to your right. Go right in."

"Thank you very much, Hetty."

Andrew Daney, seated at a desk, stood up as she entered.

"How do you do, Nan?" he greeted her, with masculine cordiality, and set out a chair. "Please be seated and tell me what I can do to oblige you."

A swift scrutiny of the private office convinced her that they were alone; so she advanced to the desk and laid upon it the letter she had addressed to Donald McKaye.

"I would be grateful, Mr. Daney, if you would see that Mr. Donald McKaye receives this letter when he comes in from the woods to-night," she replied. Daney was frankly amazed.

"Bless my soul," he blurted, "why do you entrust me with it? Would it not have been far simpler to have mailed it?"

"Not at all, Mr. Daney. In the first place, the necessity for writing it only developed an hour ago, and in order to be quite certain Mr. McKaye would receive it this evening, I would have had to place a special-delivery stamp upon it. I did not have a special-delivery stamp; so, in order to get one, I would have had to go to the post-office and buy it. And the instant I did that, the girl on duty at the stamp-window would have gone to the mail-chute to get the letter and read the address. So I concluded it would be far more simple and safe to entrust my letter to you. More-over," she added, "I save ten cents."

"I am very greatly obliged to you, Nan," Daney answered soberly. "You did exactly right," Had she conferred upon him a distinct personal favor, his ex-pression of obligation could not have been more sincere. He took a large envelop of the Tyee Lumber Company, wrote Donald's name upon it, enclosed Nan's letter in this large envelop, and sealed it with a mighty blow of his fist. "Now then," he declared, "what people do not know will not trouble them. After you go, I'll place this envelop in Don's mail-box in the outer office. I think we understand each other," he added shrewdly.

"I think we do, Mr. Daney."

"Splendid fellow, young Donald! Thundering fine boy!"

"I agree with you, Mr. Daney. If Donald has a fault, it is his excessive democracy and loyalty to his friends. Thank you so much, Mr. Daney. Good-afternoon."

"Not at all—not at all! All this is quite confidential, of course, otherwise you would not be here." He bowed her to the door, opened it for her, and bowed again as she passed him. When she had gone, he summoned the young lady whom Nan had addressed as "Hetty."

"Miss Fairchaild," he said, " 'phone the local sales-

office and tell them to deliver a load of fire-wood to the
Brent house at the Sawdust Pile."

Two minutes later, the entire office force knew that
Nan Brent had called to order a load of fire-wood, and
once more the world sagged into the doldrums.

XI

AT six o'clock Donald came in from the logging-camp. Daney made it his business to be in the entry of the outer office when his superior took his mail from his box, and, watching narrowly, thought he observed a frown on the young laird's face as he read Nan Brent's letter. Immediately he took refuge in his private office, to which he was followed almost immediately by Donald.

"That's your handwriting, Mr. Daney," he said, thrusting the large envelop under Daney's nose. "Another letter in a smaller envelop was enclosed by you in this large one. You knew, of course, who wrote it."

"Miss Brent brought it personally."

Donald started slightly. He was amazed.

"I take it," he continued, after a slight pause, "that it was entirely your idea to conceal from the office force the fact that Miss Brent had written me this letter."

"It was, Don."

"I am at a loss to know why you took such a precaution." Donald's eyes met Daney's in frank suspicion; the latter thought that he detected some slight anger in the younger man's bearing.

"I can enlighten you, Don. Miss Brent was at some pains to conceal the fact that she had written you a letter; she brought it to me to be handed to you, rather than run the risk of discovery by dropping it in

the post-office for special delivery. Some of the girls
in our office went to school with Nan Brent and might
recognize her handwriting if they saw the envelop. I
saw Hetty Fairchaild looking over your letters rather
interestedly the other day, when she was sorting the
mail and putting it in the boxes."

"The entire procedure appears to me to be peculiar
and wholly unnecessary. However, I'm obliged to you,
Mr. Daney, for acceding so thoroughly to Nan's apparent wishes." He frowned as he tore the envelop into
shreds and dropped them in Daney's waste-basket. "I'm
afraid some young women around this plant are going
to lose their jobs unless they learn to restrain their
curiosity and their tongues," he added.

"I thought I was still general manager," Daney
reminded him gently. "Hiring and firing have always
been my peculiar prerogatives."

"Forgive me, Mr. Daney. They shall continue to
be." The young Laird grinned at the rebuke; Daney
smiled back at him, and the somewhat charged atmosphere cleared instantly.

"By the way, Donald, your father is in town. He's
going up to Seattle to-night on the seven-ten train.
Your mother and the girls left earlier in the week. He's
dining at the hotel and wishes you to join him there.
He figured that, by the time you could reach The
Dreamerie, shave, bathe, and dress, it would be too
late to have dinner with him there and still allow him
time to catch his train."

"How does idleness sit on my parent, Mr. Daney?"

"Not very well, I fear. He shoots and fishes and
takes long walks with the dogs; he was out twice in

your sloop this week. I think he and your mother and the girls plan a trip to Honolulu shortly."

"Good!" Donald yawned and stretched his big body. "I've lost eight pounds on this chopping-job," he declared, "and I thought I hadn't an ounce of fat on me. Zounds, I'm sore! But I'm to have an easy job next week. I'm to patrol the skid-roads with a grease-can. That woods boss is certainly running me ragged."

"Well, your innings will come later," Daney smiled.

At the mill office, Donald washed, and then strolled over to the hotel to meet his father. Old Hector grinned as Donald, in woolen shirt, mackinaw, corduroy trousers, and half-boots came into the little lobby, for in his son he saw a replica of himself thirty years agone."

"Hello, dad!" Donald greeted him.

"Hello, yourself!"

The father, in great good humor, joined his son, and they proceeded to dine, chaffing each other good-naturedly the while, and occasionally exchanging pleasantries with their neighbors at adjoining tables. The Laird was in excellent spirits, a condition which his interview that afternoon with Nan Brent had tended to bring about; during the period that had elapsed between his subsequent doubts and his meeting with his son, he had finally decided that the entire matter was a mare's nest and had dismissed it from his mind.

After dinner, they walked down to the railroad station together, Donald carrying his father's bag. While The Laird was at the ticket-window purchasing his transportation, his son walked over to a baggage-truck to rest the bag upon it. As the bag landed with a thud, a man who had been seated on the truck with

his back toward Donald glanced over his shoulder in
a leisurely way, and, in that glance, the latter recognized one of the Greeks he had evicted from the Sawdust
Pile—the same man who had thrown a beer-bottle at
him the day he motored through Darrow.

"What are you doing in Port Agnew?" Donald demanded.

To his query, the fellow replied profanely that this
was none of his interrogator's affair.

"Well, it is some of my affair," the new boss of Tyee
replied. "I have a crow to pluck with you, anyhow,
and I'm going to pluck it now." He grasped the Greek
by his collar and jerked him backward until the man
lay flat on his back across the baggage-truck; then,
with his horny left hand, Donald slapped the sullen face
vigorously, jerked the fellow to his feet, faced him in
the direction of Darrow, and, with a vigorous kick,
started him on his way. "That's for throwing beer-
bottles!" he called after the man. "And hereafter you
keep out of Port Agnew. Your kind are not welcome
here."

The Greek departed into the night cursing, while
The Laird, still at the ticket-window, glanced inter-
estedly from his son to the Greek and then back to
Donald.

"What's the idea, son?" he demanded.

"A recent dweller on the Sawdust Pile," his son replied easily. "He declared war on me, so, naturally, he
comes into my territory at his own risk. That scum
from Darrow must keep out of our town, dad, and force
is the only argument they can understand. Daney
gave them a free hand and spoiled them, but I'm going
to teach them who's boss around here now. Besides,

I owe that fellow a poke. He insulted Nan Brent. There would have been a bill for repairs on the scoundrel if I had caught him the day I drove his gang off the Sawdust Pile."

"Well, I approve of your sentiments, Donald, but, nevertheless, it's a poor practise for a gentleman to fight with a mucker, although," he added whimsically, "when I was your age I always enjoyed a go with such fellows. That man you just roughed is George Chirakes, and he's a bad one. Knifed three of his countrymen in a drunken riot in Darrow last fall, but got out of it on a plea of self-defense. Keep your eye on the brute. He may try to play even, although there's no real courage in his kind. They're born bushwhackers." The Laird glanced at his watch and saw that it still lacked eight minutes of train-time. "Wait for me a minute," he told his son. "I want to telephone Daney on a little matter I overlooked this afternoon."

He entered the telephone-booth in the station and called up Andrew Daney.

"McKaye speaking," he announced. "I've just discovered Donald has an enemy—that Greek, Chirakes, from Darrow. Did Dirty Dan come in from the woods to-night?"

"I believe he did. He usually comes in at week-ends."

"Look him up immediately, and tell him to keep an eye on Donald, and not to let him out of his sight until the boy boards the logging-train to-morrow night to go back to the woods. Same thing next week-end, and when Donald completes his tour of duty in the woods, transfer Dan from the logging-camp and give him a job in the mill, so he can watch over the boy when he's abroad nights. He is not, of course, to let my son know he is under surveillance."

"I will attend to the matter immediately," Daney promised, and The Laird, much relieved, hung up and rejoined his son.

"Take care of yourself—and watch that Greek, boy," he cautioned, as he swung aboard the train.

Donald stood looking after the train until the tail-lights had disappeared round a curve.

XII

DANEY readily discovered in a pool-hall the man he sought. "Dirty Dan" O'Leary was a chopper in the McKaye employ, and had earned his sobriquet, not because he was less cleanly than the average lumber-jack but because he was what his kind described as a "dirty" fighter. That is to say, when his belligerent disposition led him into battle, which it frequently did, Mr. O'Leary's instinct was to win, quickly and decisively, and without consideration of the niceties of combat, for a primitive person was Dirty Dan. Fast as a panther, he was as equally proficient in the use of all his extremities, and, if hard pressed, would use his teeth. He was a stringy, big-boned man of six feet, and much too tall for his weight, wherefore belligerent strangers were sometimes led to the erroneous conclusion that Mr. O'Leary would not be hard to upset. In short, he was a wild, bad Irishman who had gotten immovably fixed in his head an idea that old Hector McKaye was a "gr-rand gintleman," and a gr-rand gintleman was one of the three things that Dirty Dan would fight for, the other two being his personal safety and the love of battle.

Daney drew Dirty Dan out of the pool-hall and explained the situation to him. The knowledge that The Laird had, in his extremity, placed reliance on him moved Dirty Dan to the highest pitch of enthusiasm and loyalty. He pursed his lips, winked one of his piggy 'eyes craftily, and, without wasting time in words of assurance, set forth in search of the man he was to follow and protect. Presently he saw Donald entering the butcher shop; so he stationed himself across the street and watched the young laird of Tyee purchase a fowl and walk out with it under his arm. Keeping his man dimly in view through the gloom, Dirty Dan, from the opposite side of the street, followed on velvet feet to the outskirts of the town, where Donald turned and took a path through some vacant lots, arriving at last at the Sawdust Pile. Dirty Dan heard him open and close the gate to Caleb Brent's garden.

"Oh, ho, the young divil!" Dirty Dan murmured, and immediately left the path, padding softly out into the grass in order that, when the door of Caleb Brent's house should be opened, the light from within might not shine forth and betray him. After traversing a dozen steps, he lay down in the grass and set himself patiently to await the reappearance of his quarry.

In response to several clearly audible knocks, the front door failed to open, and Dirty Dan heard Don walk round the house to the back door.

"The young divil!" he reiterated to himself. "Faith, whin the cat's away the mice'll play, an' divil a worrd o' lie in that! Begorra, I'm thinkin' the ould gintleman'd be scandalized could he know where his darlin' bhoy is this minute—here, wait a minute Daniel, ye gossoon. Maybe, 'tis for this I've been sint to watch the lad an' not for to protect him. If it is, faith 'tis a job I'm not wishful for, shpyin' on me own boss." He pondered the matter. Then: "Well, sorra wan o' me knows. What if the young fella do be in love wit' her an' his father have wind of it! Eh? What thin,

Daniel? A scandal, that's what, an', be the toe-nails o' Moses, nayther The Laird nor his son can afford that. I'll take note o' what happens, but, be the same token, 'tis not to Misther Daney I'll make me report, but to the ould man himself. Sh—what's that?"

His ear being close to the ground, Dirty Dan had caught the sound of slow, cautious footsteps advancing along the little path. He flattened himself in the grass and listened, the while he hoped fervently that those who walked the path (for he knew now there were more than one) would not leave it as he had done and at the same point. Should they inadvertently tread upon him, Dirty Dan felt that the honor of the McKaye family and the maintenance of the secret of his present employment would demand instant and furious battle— on suspicion.

The unknown pedestrians paused in the path.

"Ah done tol' you-all Ah'm right," Dirty Dan heard one of them say.

"Ha!" thought Dirty Dan. "A dirrty black naygur! I can tell be the v'ice of him."

One of his companions grunted, and another said, in accents which the astute Mr. O'Leary correctly judged to be those of a foreigner of some sort:

"All right. W'en he's come out, we jumpa right here. Wha's matter, eh?"

"Suits me," the negro replied. "Let's set down, an' fo' de Lawd's sake, keep quite 'twell he come."

Dirty Dan heard them move off to the other side of the path and sit down in the grass.

"So 'tis that big buck yeller naygur from Darrow an' two o' the Greeks," he mused. "An' God knows I never did like fightin' in the dark. They'll knife me as sure as pussy is a cat."

Decidedly, the prospect did not appeal to Dirty Dan. However, he had his orders to protect The Laird's son; he had his own peculiar notions of honor, and in his wild Irish heart there was not one drop of craven blood. So presently, with the stealth of an animal, he crawled soundlessly away until he judged it would be safe for him to stand up and walk, which he did with infinite caution.

He reached the gate, passed like a wraith through it, and round to the side of Caleb Brent's home, in momentary dread of discovery by a dog. He breathed a sigh of relief when, the outcry failing to materialize, he decided the Brents were too poor to maintain a dog; whereupon he filled his pipe, lighted it, leaned up against the house, and, for the space of an hour, stood entranced, for from Caleb Brent's poor shanty there floated the voice of an angel, singing to the notes of a piano.

"Glory be!" murmured the amazed Daniel. "Sure, if that's what the young fella hears whin he calls, divil a bit do I blame him. Oh, the shweet v'ice of her—an' singin' 'The Low-backed Car'!"

Despite the wicked work ahead of him, Dirty Dan was glad of the ill fortune which had sent him hither. He had in full measure the Gael's love of music, and when, at length, the singing ceased and reluctantly he made up his mind that the concert was over, he was thrilled to a point of exaltation.

"Begorra, I didn't expect to be piped into battle," he reflected humorously—and sought the Brent wood-pile, in which he poked until his hard hands closed over a hard, sound, round piece of wood about three feet long. He tested it across his knee, swung it over his head, and decided it would do.

"Now thin, for the surprise party," he reflected grimly, and walked boldly to the gate, which he opened and closed with sufficient vigor to advertise his coming, even if his calked boots on the hard path had not already heralded his advance. However, Dirty Dan desired to make certain; so he pursed his lips and whistled softly the opening bars of "The Low-backed Car" in the hope that the lilting notes would still further serve to inculcate in the lurking enemy the impression that he was a lover returning well content from his tryst. As he sauntered along, he held his bludgeon in readiness while his keen eyes searched—and presently he made out the crouching figures.

"The naygur first—to hold me, whilst the Greeks slip a dirk in me," he decided shrewdly.

He heard the scuttering rush start, and, with the shock of combat, his carefully prearranged plan of battle quite fled his mercurial mind. He met the charge with a joyous screech, forgot that he had a club, and kicked viciously out with his right foot. His heavy logger's boots connected with something soft and yielding, which instinct told Mr. O'Leary was an abdomen; instinct, coupled with experience, informed him further that no man could assimilate that mighty kick in the abdomen and yet remain perpendicular, whereupon Dirty Dan leaped high in the air and came down with both terrible calked boots on something which gave slightly under him and moaned. On the instant, he received a light blow in the breast and knew he had been stabbed.

He remembered his club now; as he backed away swiftly, he swung it, and, from the impact, concluded he had struck a neck or shoulder. That was the luck of night-fighting; so, with a bitter curse, Dirty Dan swung again, in the pious hope of connecting with a skull; he scored a clean miss and was, by the tremendous force of his swing, turned completely round. Before he could recover his balance, a hand grasped his ankle and he came down heavily on his face; instantly, his assailant's knees were pressed into his back. With a mighty heave he sought to free himself, at the same time flinging both long legs upward, after the fashion of one who strives to kick himself in the small of the back; whereupon a knife drove deep into his instep, and he realized he had not acted a split second too soon to save himself from a murderous thrust in the kidneys —a Greek's favorite blow.

In battle, Dirty Dan's advantage lay always in his amazing speed and the terrible fury of his attack during the first five minutes. Even as he threw up his feet, he drew back, an elbow and crashed it into his enemy's ribs; like a flash, his arm straightened, and his sinewy hand closed over the wrist of an arm that struggled in vain to strike downward. Holding the wrist securely, Dirty Dan heaved upward, got his left elbow under his body, and rested a few moments; another mighty heave, and he tossed off the Greek, and, whirling with the speed of a pin-wheel, was on top of his man. He had momentarily released his hold on the Greek's wrist, however, and he had to fight for another hold now—in the dark. Presently he captured it, twisted the arm in the terrible hammer-lock, and broke it; then, while the Greek lay writhing in agony, Mr.

O'Leary leaped to his feet and commenced to play with his awful boots a devil's tatoo on that portion of his enemy's superstructure so frequently alluded to in pugilistic circles as "the slats." After five or six kicks, however, he paused, due to a difficulty in breathing; so he struck a match and surveyed the stricken field.

The big mulatto and two Greeks lay unconscious before him; in the flickering light of the match, two blood-stained dirks gleamed in the grass, so, with a minute attention to detail, Dirty Dan possessed himself of these weapons, picked up his club, and, reasoning shrewdly that Donald McKaye's enemies had had enough combat for a few weeks at least, the dauntless fellow dragged the fallen clear of the path, in order that his youthful master might not stumble over them on his way home, and then disappeared into the night. Half and hour later, smeared with dust and blood, he crawled up the steps of the Tyee Lumber Company's hospital on his hands and knees and rapped feebly on the front door. The night nurse came out and looked him over.

"I'm Dirty Dan O'Leary," he wheezed; "I've been fightin' agin."

The nurse called the doctor and two orderlies, and they carried him into the operating-room.

"I'm not the man I used to be," Dirty Dan whispered, "but glory be, ye should see the other fellers." He opened his hand, and two blood-stained clasp-knives rolled out; he winked knowingly, and indulged in humorous reminiscences of the combat while he was being examined.

"You're cut to strings and ribbons, Dan," the doctor informed him, "and they've stuck you in the left lung.

You've lost a lot of blood. We may pull you through, but I doubt it."

"Very well," the demon replied composedly.

"Telephone Judge Alton to come and get his dying statement," the doctor ordered the nurse, but Dirty Dan raised a deprecating hand.

" 'Twas a private, personal matther," he declared. " 'Twas settled satisfacthory. I'll not die, an' I'll talk to no man but Misther Daney. Sew me up an' plug me lung, an' be quick about it, Docthor."

When Andrew Daney came, summoned by telephone, Dirty Dan ordered all others from the room, and Daney saw that the door was closed tightly after them. Then he bent over Dirty Dan.

"Where's Donald?" he demanded.

"That's neither here nor there, sir," Mr. O'Leary replied evasively. "He's safe, an' never knew they were afther him. T'ree o' thim, sir, the naygur and two Greeks. I kidded thim into thinkin' I was Misther McKaye; 'tis all over now, an' ye can find out what two Greeks it was by those knives I took for evidence. I cannot identify thim, but go up to Darrow in the mornin' an' look for a spreckled mulatter, wan Greek wit' a broken right arm, an' another wit' a broken neck, but until I die, do nothin'. If I get well, tell them to quit Darrow for good agin' the day I come out o' the hospital. Good-night to you, sir, an' thank ye for callin'."

From the hospital, Andrew Daney, avoiding the lighted main street, hastened to the Sawdust Pile. A light still burned in Caleb Brent's cottage; so Daney stood aloof in the vacant lot and waited. About ten o'clock, the front door opened, and, framed in the light

of the doorway, the general manager saw Donald Mc-
Kaye, and beside him Nan Brent.

"Until to-morrow at five, Donald, since you will persist in being obstinate," he heard Nan say, as they
reached the gate and paused there. "Good-night, dear."

Andrew Daney waited no longer, but turned and
fled into the darkness.

XIII

HAVING done that which her conscience dictated, Nan Brent returned to her home a prey to many conflicting emotions, chief of which were a quiet sense of exaltation in the belief that she had played fair by both old Hector and his son, and a sense of depression in the knowledge that she would not see Donald McKaye again. As a boy, she had liked him tremendously; as a man, she knew she liked him even better.

She was quite certain she had never met a man who was quite fit to breathe the same air with Donald McKaye; already she had magnified his virtues until, to her, he was rapidly assuming the aspect of an arch-angel—a feeling which bordered perilously on ado-ration.

But deep down in her woman's heart she was afraid, fearing for her own weakness. The past had brought her sufficient anguish—she dared not risk a future filled with unsatisfied yearning that comes of a great love suppressed or denied.

She felt better about it as she walked homeward; it seemed that she had regained, in a measure, some peace of mind, and as she prepared dinner for her father and her child, she was almost cheerful. A warm glow of self-complacency enveloped her. Later, when old Caleb and the boy had retired and she sat before the little wood fire alone with her thoughts, this feeling of self-conscious rectitude slowly left her, and int its place crept a sense of desolation inspired by one thought that obtruded upon her insistently, no matter how desperately she drove her mind to consider other things. She was not to see him again—no, never any more. Those fearless, fiery gray eyes that were all abeam with tenderness and complete understanding that day he left her at the gate; those features that no one would ever term handsome, yet withal so rugged, so strong, so pregnant of character, so peculiarly winning when lighted by the infrequent smile—she was never to gaze upon them again. It did not seem quite fair that, for all that the world had denied her, it should withhold from her this inconsequent delight. This was carrying misfortune too far; it was terrible — unbearable almost——

A wave of self-pity, the most acute misery of a tortured soul, surged over her; she laid her fair head on her arms outspread upon the table, and gave herself up to wild sobbing. In her desolation, she called aloud, piteously, for that mother she had hardly known, as if she would fain summon that understanding spirit and in her arms seek the comfort that none other in this world could give her. So thoroughly did she abandon herself to this first—and final—paroxysm of despair that she failed to hear a tentative rap upon the front door and, shortly, the tread of rough-shod feet on the board walk round the house. Her first intimation that some one had arrived to comfort her came in the shape of a hard hand that thrust itself gently under her chin and lifted her face from her arms.

Through the mist of her tears she saw only the vague outlines of a man clad in heavy woolen shirt and mackinaw, such as her father frequently wore.

"Oh, father, father!" she cried softly, and laid her head on his breast, while her arms went round his neck. "I'm so terribly unhappy! I can't bear it—I can't! Just—because he chose to be—kind to us—those gossips—as if anybody could help being fond of him——"

She was held tight in his arms.

"Not your father, Nan." Donald murmured in a low voice.

She drew away from him with a sharp little cry of amazement and chagrin, but his great arms closed round her and drew her close again.

"Poor dear," he told her, "you were calling for your mother. You wanted a breast to weep upon, didn't you? Well, mine is here for you."

"Oh, sweetheart, you mustn't!" she cried passionately, her lips unconsciously framing the unspoken cry of her heart as she strove to escape from him.

"Ah, but I shall!" he answered. "You've called me 'sweetheart,' and that gives me the right." And he kissed her hot cheek and laughed the light, contented little laugh of the conqueror, nor could all her frantic pleadings and struggling prevail upon him to let her go. In the end, she did the obvious, the human thing. She clasped him tightly round the neck, and, forgetting everything in the consuming wonder of the fact that this man loved her with a profound and holy love, she weakly gave herself up to his caresses, satisfying her heart-hunger for a few blessed, wonderful moments before hardening herself to the terrible task of impressing upon him the hopelessness of it all and sending him upon his way. By degrees, she cried herself dry-eyed and leaned against him, striving to collect her dazed thoughts. And then he spoke.

"I know what you're going to say, dear. From a wordly point of view, you are quite right. Seemingly, without volition on our part, we have evolved a distressing, an impossible situation——"

"Oh, I'm so glad that you understand!" she gasped.

"And yet," he continued soberly, "love such as ours is not a light thing to be passed lightly by. To me, Nan Brent, you are sacred; to you, I yearn to be all things that—the—other man was not. I didn't realize until I entered unannounced and found you so desolate that I loved you. For two weeks you have been constantly in my thoughts, and I know now that, after all, you were my boyhood sweetheart."

"I know you were mine," she agreed brokenly. "But that's just a little tender memory now, even if we said nothing about it then. We are children no longer, Donald dear; we must be strong and not surrender to our selfish love."

"I do not regard it as selfish," he retorted soberly. "It seems most perfectly natural and inevitable. Why, Nan, I didn't even pay you the preliminary compliment of telling you I loved you or asking you if you reciprocated my affection. It appeared to me I didn't have to; that it was a sort of mutual understanding —for here we are. It seems it just was to be—like the law of gravitation."

She smiled up at him, despite her mental pain.

"I'm not so certain, dear," she answered, "that I'm not wicked enough to rejoice. It will make our renunciation all the easier—for me. I have known great sorrow, but to-night, for a little while, I have surrendered myself to great happiness, and nothing—nothing—can ever rob me of the last shred of that. Yo are my man, Donald. The knowledge that you love me is going to draw much of the sting out of existence. I know I cannot possess you, but I can resign myself to that and not be embittered."

"Well," he answered dully, "I can give you up— because I have to; but I shall never be resigned about it, and I fear I may be embittered. Is there no hope, Nan?"

"A faint one—some day, perhaps, if I outlive another."

"I'll wait for that day, Nan. Meanwhile, I shall ask no questions. I love you enough to accept your love on faith, for, by God, you're a good woman!"

Her eyes shown with a wonderful radiance as she drew his face down to hers and kissed him on the lips.

"It's sweet of you to say that; I could love you for that alone, were there nothing else, Donald. But tell me, dear, did you receive my letter?"

"Yes—and ignored it. That's why I'm here."

"That was a risk you should not have taken."

He looked thoughtfully at the multicolored flame of the driftwood fire.

"Well, you see, Nan, it didn't occur to me that I was taking a risk; a confession of love was the last thing I would have thought would happen."

"Then why did you disregard that letter that cost me such an effort to write?"

"Well," he replied slowly, "I guess it's because I'm the captain of my soul—or try to be, at any rate. I didn't think it quite fair that you should be shunned; it occurred to me that I wouldn't be playing a manly part to permit the idle mewing of the Port Agnew tabbies to frighten me away. I didn't intend to fall in

love with you— Oh, drat my reasons! I'm here because I'm here. And in the matter of that old hen—"
He paused and favored her with a quizzical smile.

"Yes?"

"I brought a substitute hen with me—all ready for the pot, and if I can't come to dinner to-morrow, I'm going to face a very lonely Sunday."

"You ridiculous boy! Of course you may come, although it must be the final visit. You realize that we owe it to ourselves not to make our burden heavier than it's going to be."

He nodded.

" 'Eat, drink and be merry, for to-morrow we may be dead,' " he quoted. "Let's sit down and talk it over. I haven't sat in front of a driftwood fire since I was a boy. Queer how the salt in the wood colors the flames, isn't it?"

It occurred to her for a fleeting moment that they two were driftwood, and that the salt of their tears would color their lives as the years consumed them. But she banished from her mind all thought of everything save the present. With a contented little sigh she seated herself beside him; her hand stole into his and, soothed and sustained by the comforting touch, each of the other, gradually the first terror of their predicament faded; ere long, Donald reminded her of her promise, and she stole to the old square piano and sang for him while, without, Dirty Dan O'Leary crouched in the darkness and thrilled at the rippling melody.

At ten o'clock, when Donald left the Sawdust Pile, he and Nan had arrived at a firm determination to

follow separate paths, nor seek to level the barrier
that circumstance had raised between them.

"Some day—perhaps," he whispered, as he held her
to his heart in the dark at the garden gate. "While
I live, I shall love you. Good-by, old sweetheart!"

XIV

TRUE to his promise, Daniel P. O'Leary declined to die that night.

"Confound your belligerent soul!" the doctor growled at dawn. "I believe you're too mean to die."

"We'll make it a finish fight," whispered Daniel.

"I'll go you," the doctor answered, and sent for digitalis and salt solution.

There was one other soul in Port Agnew who did not sleep that night, either. Andrew Daney's soul, shaken by what was to him a cosmic cataclysm, caused that good man to rise at five o'clock and go down to the hospital for another look at Dirty Dan. To his anxious queries the doctor shook a dubious head, but the indomitable O'Leary smiled wanly.

"Go on wit' ye!" he wheezed faintly. "I'll win be a hair-line decision."

At seven o'clock, when the telegraph-station opened, Andrew Daney was waiting at the door. He entered and sent a telegram to The Laird.

Return immediately.

In the late afternoon, Hector McKaye returned to Port Agnew and at once sought Daney, who related to him exactly what had occurred. The shadow of profound worry settled over The Laird's face.

"Dan refuses to disclose anything regarding Donald's movements," Daney continued, "where he followed the boy or where the fight took place. I only know that Donald was not present; Dan, fortunately, overheard the plot, inculcated, by some means, the idea in those scoundrels' heads that he was Donald, and took the fight off the boy's hands. He claimed he fought a winning fight, and he is right. The mulatto died in Darrow this morning. One of the Greeks has a smashed shoulder, and the other a broken arm and four broken ribs. How they ever got home to Darrow is a mystery."

"The third Greek must have waited near the river-mouth with a boat, Andrew. Have you any idea where Donald spent the evening?"

"Yes, sir; but he's free, white, and twenty-one, and he's my superior. I prefer not to discuss his movements."

"Andrew, I command you to."

"I refuse to be commanded, sir."

"That's all I wanted to know. He visited the Brents, and you know it." He saw by the flush on Daney's old face that he had hit the mark. "Well, I'm obliged to you, Andrew. You've done your full duty; so we'll not discuss the matter further. The situation will develop in time, and, meanwhile, I'll not spy on my boy. I wonder if that Darrow gang will talk."

"I imagine not, sir—that is, if Dirty Dan keeps his own counsel. They will fear prosecution if Dan dies; so they will be silent awaiting the outcome of his injuries. If he lives, they will still remain silent, awaiting his next move. Dan will probably admit having been jumped in the dark by three unknown men and that he defended himself vigorously; he can fail to identify the Greeks, and the Greeks cannot do less than fail to identify Dirty Dan, who can plead self-defense if the coroner's jury delves too deeply into the mulatto's death. I imagine they will not. At any rate, it's up to Dan whether Donald figures in the case or not, and Dan will die before he'll betray the confidence."

"That's comforting," The Laird replied. "Will you be good enough to drive me home to The Dreamerie, Andrew?"

At The Dreamerie, old Hector discovered that his son had left the house early in the afternoon, saying he would not be home for dinner. So The Laird sat him down and smoked and gazed out across the Bight of Tyee until sunset, when, a vague curiosity possessing him, he looked down to the Sawdust Pile and observed that the flag still flew from the cupola. The night shadows gathered, but still the flag did not come down; and presently round The Laird's grim mouth a little prescient smile appeared, with something of pain in it.

"Dining out at Brent's," he soliloquized, "and they're so taken up with each other they've forgotten the flag. I do not remember that the Brent girl ever forgot it before. She loves him."

XV

FOLLOWING his parting with Nan Brent on Saturday night, Donald McKaye went directly to the mill office, in front of which his car was parked, entered the car, and drove home to The Dreamerie, quite oblivious of the fact that he was not the only man in Port Agnew who had spent an interesting and exciting evening. So thoroughly mixed were his emotions that he was not quite certain whether he was profoundly happy or incurably wretched. When he gave way to rejoicing in his new-found love, straightway he was assailed by a realization of the barriers to his happiness—a truly masculine recognition of the terrible bar sinister to Nan's perfect wifehood induced a veritable shriveling of his soul, a mental agony all the more intense because it was the first unhappiness he had ever experienced.

His distress was born of the knowledge that between the Sawdust Pile and The Dreamerie there stretched a gulf as wide and deep as the Bight of Tyee. He was bred of that puritanical stock which demands that the mate for a male of its blood must be of original purity, regardless of the attitude of leniency on the part of that male for lapses from virtue in one of his own sex. This creed, Donald had accepted as naturally, as inevitably as he had accepted belief in the communion of saints and the resurrection of the dead. His father's daughter-in-law, like Cæsar's wife, would

have to be above suspicion; while Donald believed Nan
Brent to be virtuous, or, at least, an unconscious, unwilling, and unpremeditating sinner, non-virtuous by
circumstance instead of by her own deliberate act, he
was too hard-headed not to realize that never, by the
grace of God, would she be above suspicion. Too well
he realized that his parents and his sisters, for whom he
entertained all the affection of a good son and brother,
would, unhampered by sex-appeal and controlled wholly
by tradition, fail utterly to take the same charitable
view, even though he was honest enough with himself
to realize that perhaps his own belief in the matter
was largely the result of the wish being father to the
thought.

Curiously enough, he dismissed, quite casually, consideration of the opinions his mother and sisters, their
friends and his, the men and women of Port Agnew
might entertain on the subject. His apprehensions
centered almost entirely upon his father. His affection for his father he had always taken for granted.
It was not an emotion to exclaim over. Now that he
realized, for the first time, his potential power to hurt
his father, to bow that gray head in grief and shame
and humiliation, he was vouchsafed a clearer, all-comprehending vision of that father's love, of his goodness,
his manliness, his honor, his gentleness, and his fierce,
high pride; to Donald simultaneously came the knowledge of his own exalted love for the old man. He knew
him as no other human being knew him or ever would
know him; whence he knew old Hector's code—that a
clean man may not mate with an unclean woman without
losing caste.

He and Nan had discussed the situation but briefly,

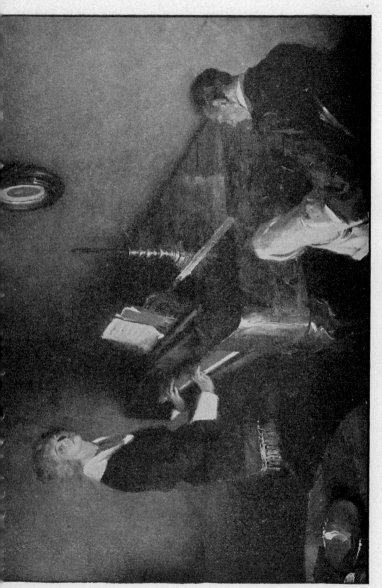

SHE STOLE TO THE OLD SQUARE PIANO AND SANG FOR HIM.

for they were young, and the glory of that first perfect hour could not be marred by a minute consideration of misery in prospect. To-night, they had been content to forget the world and be happy with each other, apparently with the mutual understanding that they occupied an untenable position, one that soon must be evacuated.

Yes; he was the young laird of Tyee, the heir to a principality, and it would be too great a strain on mere human beings to expect his little world to approve of its highest mating with its lowest. Prate as we may of democracy, we must admit, if we are to be honest with ourselves, that this sad old world is a snobocracy. The very fact that man is prone to regard himself as superior to his brother is the leaven in the load of civilization; without that quality, whether we elect to classify it as self-conceit or self-esteem, man would be without ambition and our civilization barren of achievement. The instinct for the upward climb—the desire to reach the heights—is too insistent to be disregarded. If all men are born equal, as the framers of our Constitution so solemnly declared, that is because the brains of all infants, of whatsoever degree, are at birth incapable of thought. The democracy of any people, therefore, must be predicated upon their kindness and charity—human characteristics which blossom or wither according to the intensity of the battle for existence. In our day and generation, therefore, democracy is too high-priced for promiscuous dissemination; wherefore, as in an elder day, we turn from the teaching of the Man of Galilee and cling to tradition.

Tradition was the stone in the road to Donald Mc-

Kaye's happiness, and his strength was not equal to the task of rolling it away.

Despair enveloped him. Every fiber of his being, every tender, gallant instinct drew him toward this wonder-girl that the world had thrust aside as unworthy. His warm, sympathetic heart ached for her; he knew she needed him as women like her must ever need the kind of man he wanted to be, the kind he had always striven to be. Had he been egotist enough to set a value upon himself, he would have told himself she was worthy of him; yet a damnable set of damnable man-made circumstances over which he had no control hedged them about and kept them apart. It was terrible, so he reflected, to know that, even if Nan should live the life of a saint from the hour of her child's birth until the hour of her death, a half-century hence, yet would she fail to atone for her single lapse while there still lived one who knew—and remembered. He, Donald McKaye, might live down a natural son, but Nan Brent could not. The contemplation of this social phenomenon struck him with peculiar force, for he had not hitherto considered the amazing inequalities of a double standard of morals.

For the first time in his life, he could understand the abject deference that must be shown to public opinion. He, who considered himself, and not without reason, a gentleman, must defer to the inchoate, unreasoning, unrelenting, and barbaric point of view of men and women who hadn't sense enough to pound sand in a rat-hole or breeding enough to display a reasonable amount of skill in the manipulation of a knife and fork. Public opinion! Bah! Deference to a fetish, a shibboleth, to the ancient, unwritten law that one must not

KINDRED OF THE DUST   131

do that which hypocrites condemn and cowards fear to
do, unless, indeed, one can "get away with it."

Ah, yes! The eleventh commandment: "Thou shalt
not be discovered." It had smashed Nan Brent, who
had violated it, desolated her, ruined her—she who had
but followed the instinct that God Almighty had given
her at birth—the instinct of sex, the natural yearning of a trustful, loving heart for love, motherhood,
and masculine protection from a brutal world. More.
Not satisfied with smashing her, public opinion insisted
that she should remain in a perennial state of smash.
It was abominable!

Nan had told him she had never been married, and
a sense of delicacy had indicated to him that this was
a subject upon which he must not appear to be curious. To question her for the details would have been
repugnant to his nicely balanced sense of the fitness of
things. Nevertheless, he reflected, if her love had been
illicit, was it more illicit than that of the woman who
enters into a loveless marriage, induced to such action
by a sordid consideration of worldly goods and gear?
Was her sin in bearing a child out of wedlock more
terrible than that of the married woman who shud-
ders at the responsibilities of motherhood, or evades
the travail of love's fulfilment by snuffing out little
lives in embryo? He thought not. He recalled an
evening in New York when he had watched a policeman following a drab of the streets who sought to evade
him and ply her sorry trade in the vicinity of Herald
Square; he remembered how that same policeman had
abandoned the chase to touch his cap respectfully and
open her limousine door for the heroine (God save the
mark!) of a scandalous divorce.

"Damn it!" he murmured. "It's a rotten, cruel world, and I don't understand it. I'm all mixed up." And he went to bed, where, his bodily weariness overcoming his mental depression, he slept.

He was man enough to scorn public opinion, but human enough to fear it.

XVI

THE heir of the Tyee mills and forests was not of a religious turn of mind for all his strict training in Christian doctrine, although perhaps it would be more to the point to state that he was inclined to be unorthodox. Nevertheless, out of respect to the faith of his fathers, he rose that Sunday morning and decided to go to church. Not that he anticipated any spiritual benefit would accrue to him by virtue of his pilgrimage down to Port Agnew; in his heart of hearts he regarded the pastor as an old woman, a man afraid of the world, and without any knowledge of it, so to speak. But old Hector was a pillar of the church; his family had always accompanied him thither on Sundays, and a sense of duty indicated to Donald that, as the future head of the clan, he should not alter its customs.

By a strange coincidence, the Reverend Mr. Tingley chose as the text for his sermon the eighth chapter of the Gospel according to St. John from the first to the eleventh verses, inclusive. Donald, instantly alert, straightened in the pew, and prepared to listen with interest to the Reverend Mr. Tingley's opinion of the wisdom of Jesus Christ in so casually disposing of the case of the woman taken in adultery.

"Dearly beloved," the pastor began, carefully placing an index-finger between the leaves of his Bible to mark the passage he had just read, "the title of my sermon this Sunday shall be: 'The First Stone. Let him who is without sin cast it.' "

"Banal, hypocritical ass!" Donald soliloquized. "She was the mezzo-soprano soloist in your choir four years, and you haven't tried to help her since she came back to the Sawdust Pile."

It was a good sermon, as sermons go. In fact, the Reverend Mr. Tingley, warming to his theme, quite outdid himself on the subject of charity as practised by his Redeemer, and, as a result, was the recipient of numberless congratulatory handshakes later at the church door. Donald agreed that it was an unusually good sermon—in theory; but since he knew it would collapse in practise, he avoided Mr. Tingley after service.

On the steps of the church he was accosted by Andrew Daney and the latter's wife, who greeted him effusively. Unfortunately for Mrs. Daney, Nan, in one of those bursts of confidence that must ever exist between lovers, had informed Donald the night previous of the motherly soul's interest in his affairs; wherefore he returned Mrs. Daney's warm greeting with such chilly courtesy that she was at no loss to guess the reason for it and was instantly plunged into a slough of terror and despair. She retained sufficient wit, however, to draw her husband away, thus preventing him from walking with Donald.

"I want to tell him about Dirty Dan," Daney protested, in a low voice. "As the boss, he ought to be told promptly of any injury to an employe."

"Never mind Dirty Dan," she retorted. "He'll hear of it soon enough. Let us congratulate Mr. Tingley on his sermon."

Donald, having turned his back on them almost rudely, strode down the street to his car and motored back to The Dreamerie. He spent the remainder of the morning force-breaking a setter puppy to retrieve; at one o'clock, he ate a cold luncheon, and immediately thereafter drove down to Port Agnew and brazenly parked his car in front of Caleb Brent's gate.

He entered without the formality of knocking, and Nan met him in the tiny entrance-hall.

"I couldn't wait until dinner-time," he explained. "Nobody home at The Dreamerie—" He took her face in his calloused hands, drew her to him. "You're sweet in that calico gown," he informed her, waiving a preliminary word of greeting. "I love you," he added softly, and kissed her. She clung to him.

"You should not have come here in broad daylight," she protested. "Oh, you big, foolish, impulsive dear! Don't you realize I want to protect you from the tongue of scandal? If you persist in forgetting who you are, does it follow that I should pursue a similar course?"

He ignored her argument.

"I'll help you get dinner, old blue-eyes," he suggested. "Let me shuck some corn or shell some peas or string some beans—any job where I can sit and look at you and talk to you."

"It will please me if you'll visit a little while with father Caleb," she suggested. "He's out on the sunporch. He's far from well this morning. Do cheer him up, Donald dear."

Old Caleb hailed him with a pleasure that was almost childish. During the two weeks that had elapsed since Donald had seen him last, he had failed markedly.

"Well, how does the old sailor feel this morning?" Donald queried casually, seating himself opposite the old man.

"Poorly, Mr. Donald; poorly." He turned, satisfied himself that Nan was busy in the kitchen, and then leaned toward his visitor. "I've got my sailing-orders," he whispered confidentially. The man who had won a Congressional medal of honor, without clearly knowing why or how, had not changed with the years. He advanced this statement as a simple exposition of fact.

"Think so, Caleb?" Donald answered soberly.

"I know it."

"If you have no desire to live, Caleb, of course nature will yield to your desires. Remember that and buck up. You may have your sailing-orders, but you can keep the bar breaking indefinitely to prevent you from crossing out."

"I've done that for a year past. I do not wish to die and leave her, for my three-quarter pay stops then. But I suffer from angina pectoris. It's the worry, Mr. Donald," he added.

"Worry as to the future of Nan and the child?"

"Aye, lad."

"Well, Caleb, your worries are unnecessary. I feel it my duty to tell you that I love Nan; she loves me, and we have told each other so. She shall not suffer when you are gone. She has indicated to me that, some day, this—this mess may be cleared up; and when that happens, I shall marry Nan."

"So Nan told me this morning. I was wondering if you'd speak to me about it, and I'm glad you have done so—promptly. You—you—honor us, Mr. Donald; you do, indeed. You're the one man in the world I can trust her with, whether as good friend or husband—only, her husband you'll never be."

"I see breakers ahead," Donald admitted. He had no desire to dissemble with this straightforward old father.

"We're poor folk and plain, but—please God!—we're decent and we know our place, Mr. Donald. If your big heart tells you to dishonor yourself in the eyes of your world and your people—mark you, lad, I do not admit that an alliance with my girl could ever dishonor you in your own eyes—Nan will not be weak enough to permit it."

"I have argued all that out with myself," Donald confessed miserably, "without having arrived at a conclusion. I have made up my mind to wait patiently and see what the future may bring forth."

"It may be a long wait."

"It will be worth while. And when you have sailed, I'll finance her to leave Port Agnew and develop her glorious voice."

"You haven't the right, Mr. Donald. My girl has some pride."

"I'll gamble a sizable sum on her artistic future. The matter will be arranged on a business basis. I shall lend her the money, and she shall pay me back with interest."

"Nan has a woman's pride. The obligation would remain always, even though the money should be repaid."

"I think we'll manage to adjust that," Donald countered confidently.

"Ah, well," the old fellow answered; "we've always been your debtors. And it's a debt that grows."

He loaded his pipe and was silent, for, after the fashion of the aged, he dared assume that his youthful auditor would understand just how the Brents regarded him.

"Well, my heart's lighter for our talk, lad," he declared presently. "If you don't mind, I'll have a little nap."

Donald, grateful for the dismissal, returned to the kitchen, where Nan was preparing the vegetables. Her child at once clamored for recognition, and, almost before he knew it, Donald had the tyke in his lap and was saying,

"Once upon a time there was a king and he had three sons——"

"He isn't interested in kings and princes, dear," Nan interrupted. "Tell him the story of the bad little rabbit."

"But I don't know it, Nan."

"Then you'll fail as a daddy to my boy. I'm surprised. If Don were your own flesh and blood, you would know intuitively that there is always a bad little rabbit and a good little rabbit. They dwell in a hollow tree with mother Rabbit and father Rabbit."

"Thanks for the hint. I shall not fail in this job of dadding. Well then, bub, once upon a time there was a certain Mr. Johnny Rabbit who married a very beautiful lady rabbit whose name was Miss Molly Cottontail. After they were married and had gone to keep house under a lumber-pile, Mr. Hezekiah Coon came along and offered to rent them some beautifully furnished apartments in the burned-out stump of a hemlock tree. The rent was to be one nice ear of sweet corn every month——"

The tale continued, with eager queries from the interested listener—queries which merely stimulated the young laird of Tyee to wilder and more whimsical flights of fancy, to the unfolding of adventures more and more thrilling and unbelievable until, at last, the recital began to take on the character of an Arabian Nights' tale that threatened to involve the entire animal kingdom, and only ceased when, with a wealth of mournful detail, Donald described the tragic death and funeral of the gallant young Johnny Rabbit, his fatherless audience suddenly burst into tears and howled lugubriously; whereupon Donald was hard put to it to bring Johnny Rabbit back to life mysteriously but satisfactorily, and send him scampering home to the hollow hemlock tree, there to dwell happily ever after.

His tale completed, Donald happened to glance toward Nan. She was regarding him with shining eyes.

"Donald," she declared, "it's a tremendous pity you haven't a boy of your own. You're just naturally intended for fatherhood."

He grinned.

"My father has been hinting rather broadly that a grandson would be the very last thing on earth to make him angry. He desires to see the name and the breed and the business in a fair way of perpetuation before he passes on."

"That is the way of all flesh, Donald."

"I wish it were not his way. My inability to comply with his desires isn't going to render dad or me any happier."

"Dear old boy, what a frightful predicament you're in!" she murmured sympathetically. "I wish I could be quite certain you aren't really in love with me, Donald."

"Life would be far rosier for all concerned if I were quite certain I was mistaking an old and exalted friendship for true love. But I'm not. You're the one woman in the world for me, and if I cannot have you, I'll have none other— Hello! Weeping has made this young fellow heavy-lidded, or else my fiction has bored him, for he's nodding."

"It's time for his afternoon nap, Donald." She removed the sleepy tot from his arms and carried him away to his crib. When she returned, she resumed her task of preparing dinner.

"Nan," Donald queried suddenly, "have I the right to ask you the name of the man who fathered that child?"

"Yes," she answered soberly; "you have. I wish, however, that you would not ask me. I should have to decline to answer you."

"Well, then, I'll not ask. Nevertheless, it would interest me mightily to know why you protect him."

"I am not at all desirous of protecting him, Donald. I am merely striving to protect his legal wife. His marriage to me was bigamous; he undertook the task of leading a dual married life, and, when I discovered it, I left him."

"But are you certain he married you?"

"We went through a marriage ceremony which, at the time, I regarded as quite genuine. Of course, since it wasn't legal, it leaves me in the status of an unmarried woman."

"So I understood from your father. Where did this ceremony take place?"

"In San Francisco." She came over, sat down beside him, and took one of his hard, big hands in both of hers. "I'm going to tell you as much as I dare," she informed him soberly. "You have a right to know, and you're too nice to ask questions. So I'll not leave you to the agonies of doubt and curiosity. You see, honey dear, father Brent wanted me to have vocal and piano lessons, and to do that I had to go to Seattle once a week, and the railroad-fare, in addition to the cost of the lessons, was prohibitive until your father was good enough to secure me a position in the railroad-agent's office in Port Agnew. Of course, after I became an employe of the railroad company, I could travel on a pass, so I used to go up to Seattle every Saturday, leaving here on the morning train. Your father arranged matters in some way so that I worked but five days a week."

"Naturally. Dad's a pretty heavy shipper over the line."

"I would receive my lessons late Saturday afternoons, stay overnight with a friend of mine, and return to Port Agnew on Sunday. *He* used to board the train at—well, the name of the station doesn't matter—every Saturday, and one day we got acquainted, quite by accident as it were. Our train ran through an open switch and collided with the rear end of a freight; there was considerable excitement, and everybody spoke to everybody else, and after that it didn't appear that we were strangers. The next Saturday, when he boarded the train, he sat down in the same seat with me and asked permission to introduce himself. He was very nice, and his manners were beautiful; he didn't act in the least like a man who desired to 'make a mash.' Finally, one day, he asked me to have dinner with him in Seattle, and I accepted. I think that was because I'd never been in a fashionable restaurant in all my life. After dinner, he escorted me to the studio, and on Sunday morning we took the same train home again. He was such good company and such a jolly, worldly fellow—so thoughtful and deferential! Can't you realize, Donald, how he must have appealed to a little country goose like me?

"Well, finally, daddy Brent learned that Signor Moretti, a tenor who had retired from grand opera, had opened a studio in San Francisco. We both wanted Moretti to pass on my voice, but we couldn't afford the expense of a journey to San Francisco for two, so daddy sent me alone. I wrote—that man about our plans, and told him the name of the steamer I was sailing on. Your father gave me a passage on one of his steam-schooners, and when we got to the dock in San Francisco——"

"*He* was there, eh? Came down by train and beat the steamer in." Donald nodded his comprehension. "What did Moretti say about your voice?"

"The usual thing. My Seattle teacher had almost ruined my voice, he declared, but, for all that, he was very enthusiastic and promised me a career within five years if I would place myself unreservedly in his hands. Of course, we couldn't afford such an expensive career, and the realization that I had to forego even the special inducements Signor Moretti was generous

enough to make me quite broke my heart. When I told
him about it—we were engaged by that time—he suggested that we get married immediately, in order that
I might reside with him in San Francisco and study
under Moretti. So we motored out into the country
one day and were married at San José. He asked
me to keep our marriage secret on account of some
clause in his father's will, but I insisted upon my right
to tell daddy Brent. Poor old dear! My marriage
was such a shock to him; but he agreed with me that
it was all for the best——"

"Well, I was quite happy for three months. My
husband's business interests necessitated very frequent
trips North——"

"What business was he in, Nan?"

"That is immaterial," she evaded him. "Presently,
Signor Moretti contracted a severe cold and closed
his studio for a month. My husband—I suppose I
must call him that to identify him when I refer to him
—had just gone North on one of his frequent trips,
and since he always kept me generously supplied with
money, I decided suddenly to take advantage of
Moretti's absence to run up to Port Agnew and visit
my father.

"In Seattle, as I alighted from the train, I saw my
husband in the station with another woman. I recognized her. She was a friend of mine—a very dear,
kind, thoughtful friend of several years' standing—
the only woman friend I had in the world. I loved
her dearly; you will understand when I tell you that
she had frequently gone out of her way to be kind
to me. It struck me as strange that he had never admitted knowing her, although frequently he had heard

me speak of her. While I stood pondering the situation, he took her in his arms and kissed her good-by and boarded the train without seeing me. I slipped out of the station without having been seen by either of them; but while I was waiting for a taxicab, my friend came out of the station, saw me, and rushed up to greet me. It developed, in the course of our conversation following the usual commonplaces of greeting, that she had been down to the station to see her husband off on the train for San Francisco."

Donald whistled softly.

"How did you manage to get away with it, Nan?" he demanded incredulously.

"All my life I have been used to doing without things," she replied simply. "I suppose that helped a little. The shock was not so abrupt that I lost my presence of mind; you see, I had had a few minutes to adjust myself after seeing him kiss her in the station—and just then the taxicab came up and I escaped. Then I came home to the Sawdust Pile. I wrote him, of course, and sent the letter by registered mail, in order to make certain he would receive it. He did, but he did not answer. There was no reason why he should, for he was quite safe. I had assured him there was no necessity for worry on my account."

"Of all the crazy, fool things for you to do!" Donald cried sharply. "Why under the canopy did you deem it necessary to sacrifice yourself for him? Surely you did not love him——"

"I'm afraid I never loved him," she interrupted. "I—I thought I did, although, if he hadn't been away so frequently after our marriage, I would have learned to love him dearly, I think."

"Just human nature," Donald suggested. "Something akin to what trapshooters and golfers call a mental hazard."

"Of course he married me under an assumed name, Donald."

"Did you ever see a marriage certificate?"

"Oh, yes; I had to sign it in the presence of the minister."

Donald was relieved.

"Then, you great goose of a girl, you can clear your record any time you desire. The minister forwarded the marriage certificate to the state capital, and it is registered there with the State Board of Health. After registration, it was returned to the minister whose signature appeared on the certificate as the officiating clergyman. The minister undoubtedly returned the certificate to your husband."

"I never saw it again."

"What if you did not? You can procure a certified copy from the record in the county-clerk's office or from the records of the State Board of Health. Marriage records, old dear, are fairly well protected in our day and generation."

"I wrote to the State Board of Health at Sacramento. There is no record of my marriage there."

"That's strange. Why didn't you write the county clerk of the county in which the license was issued?"

She smiled at him.

"I did. I had to, you know. My honor was at stake. The license was issued in Santa Clara County."

"Well, it will be a simple matter to comb the list of ministers until we find the one that tied the knot.

A certified copy of the marriage license, with a sworn affidavit by the officiating clergyman——"

"The officiating clergyman is dead. A private detective agency in San Francisco discovered that for us."

"But couldn't you cover your tracks, Nan? Under the circumstances, a lie—any kind of deceit to save your good name—would have been pardonable."

"I couldn't help being smirched. Remember, my father was the only person in Port Agnew who knew I had been married; he heeded my request and kept the secret. Suddenly I returned home with a tale of marriage in anticipation of my ability to prove it. In that I failed. Presently my baby was born. People wondered who my husband was, and where he kept himself; some of the extremely curious had the hardihood to come here and question me. Was my husband dead? Of course not. Had I fibbed and told them he was, they would have asked when and where and the nature of the disease that carried him off. Was I divorced? Again I was confronted with the necessity for telling the truth, because a lie could be proved. Then the minister, to quiet certain rumors that had reached him—he wanted me to sing in the choir again, and there was an uproar when he suggested it—wrote to the California State Board of Health. When he received a reply to his letter, he visited me to talk it over, but I wasn't confiding in Mr. Tingley that day. He said I might hope for salvation if I confessed my wickedness and besought forgiveness from God. He offered to pray for me and with me. He meant well—poor, silly dear!—but he was so terribly incredulous that presently I told him

I didn't blame him a bit and suggested that I be permitted to paddle my own canoe, as it were. Thanked him for calling, but told him he needn't call again. He departed in great distress."

"I hold no brief for the Reverend Tingley, Nan; but I'll be shot if your story will hold water in a world that's fairly well acquainted with the frailty of human-kind. Of course I believe you—and, for some fool reason, I'm not ashamed of my own intelligence in so believing. I have accepted you on faith. What sets my reason tottering on its throne is the fact that you insist upon protecting this scoundrel."

"I insist upon protecting his wife. I love her. She has been kind to me. She's the only friend of my own sex that I have ever known. She's tubercular, and will not live many years. She has two children—and she adores her scamp of a husband. If I cannot convict that man of bigamy, would it not be foolish of me to cry? And why should I inflict upon her, who has shown me kindness and love, a brimming measure of humiliation and sorrow and disgrace? I can bear my burden a year or two longer, I think; then, when she is gone, I can consider my vindication." She patted his hand to emphasize her unity of purpose. "That's the way I've figured it all out—the whole, crazy-quilt pattern, and if you have a better scheme, and one that isn't founded on human selfishness, I'm here to listen to it."

A long silence fell between them.

"Well, dear heart?" she demanded finally.

"I wasn't thinking of *that*," he replied slowly. "I was just trying to estimate how much more I love you this minute than I did five minutes ago."

He drew her golden head down on his shoulder and held her to him a long time without speaking. It was Nan who broke the spell by saying:

"When the time comes for my vindication, I shall ask you to attend to it for me, dear. You're my man—and I think it's a man's task."

His great fingers opened and closed in a clutching movement. He nodded.

XVII

WHEN Donald returned to The Dreamerie about eleven o'clock, he was agreeably surprised to nd his father in the living-room.

"Hello, dad!" he greeted The Laird cheerfully. Glad to see you. When did you get back?"

"Came down on the morning train, Donald."

They were shaking hands now. The Laird mo-oned him to a chair, and asked abruptly.

"Where have you been all day, son?"

"Well, I represented the clan at church this morn-g, and, after luncheon here, I went down to visit the rents at the Sawdust Pile. Stayed for dinner. Old aleb's in rather bad shape mentally and physically, d I tried to cheer him up. Nan sang for me— ite like old times."

"I saw Nan Brent on the beach the other day. ite a remarkable young woman. Attractive, I should y," the old man answered craftily.

"It's a pity, dad. She's every inch a woman. Hard a girl with brains and character to find herself such a sorry tangle."

The Laird's heavy heart was somewhat lightened the frankness and lack of suspicion with which his a had met his blunt query as to where he had been ending his time. For the space of a minute, he ap-ared to be devoting his thoughts to a consideration Donald's last remark; presently he sighed, faced son, and took the plunge.

149

"Have you heard anything about a fight down near the Sawdust Pile last night, my son?" he demanded.

His son's eyes opened with interest and astonishment.

"No; I did not, dad. And I was there until nearly ten o'clock."

"Yes; I was aware of that, and of your visit there to-day and this evening. Thank God, you're frank with me! That yellow scoundrel and two Greeks followed you there to do for you. After you roughed the Greek at the railroad station, it occurred to me that you had an enemy and might hold him cheaply, so, just before I boarded the train, I telephoned Daney to tell Dirty Dan to shadow you and guard you. So well did he follow orders that he lies in the company hospital now at the point of death. As near as I can make out the affair, Dirty Dan inculcated in those bushwhackers the idea that he was the man they were after; he went to meet them and took the fight off your hands."

"Good old Dirty Dan! I'll wager a stiff sum he did a thorough job." The young laird of Tyee rose and ruffled his father's gray head affectionately. "Thoughful, canny old fox!" he continued. "I swear I'm all puffed up with conceit when I consider the kind of father I selected for myself."

"Those scoundrels would have killed you," old Hector reminded him, with just a trace of emotion in his voice. "And if they'd done that, sonny, your old father'd never held up his head again. There are two things I could not stand up under—your death and"—he sighed, as if what he was about to say hurt him cruelly—"the wrong kind of a daughter-in-law."

"We will not fence with each other," his son answered soberly. "There has never been a lack of confidence between us, and I shall not withhold anything
from you. You are referring to Nan, are you not?"

"I am, my son."

"Well?"

"I am not a cat, and it hurts me to be an old dog,
but—I saw Nan Brent recently, and we had a bit of
talk together. She's a bonny lass, Donald, and I'm
thinking 'twould be better for your peace of mind—
and the peace of mind of all of us—if you saw less
of her."

"You think, then, father, that I'm playing with
fire."

"You're sitting on an open barrel of gunpowder with
a lighted torch in your hand."

Donald returned to his chair and faced his father.

"Let us suppose," he suggested, "that the present
unhappy situation in which Nan finds herself did not
exist. Would you still prefer that I limit my visits
to, say, Christmas and Easter?"

The Laird scratched the back of his head in perplexity.

"I'm inclined to think I wouldn't," he replied. "I'd
consider your best interests always. If you married
a fine girl from Chicago or New York, she might not
be content to dwell with you in Port Agnew."

"Then Nan's poverty—the lowliness of her social
position, even in Port Agnew, would not constitute a
serious bar?"

"I was as poor as Job's turkey once myself—and
your mother's people were poorer. But we came of
good blood."

"Well, Nan's mother was a gentlewoman; her grandfather was an admiral; her great-grandfather a commodore, her great-great-granduncle a Revolutionary colonel, and her grandmother an F. F. V. Old Caleb's ancestors always followed the sea. His father and his grandfather were sturdy old Yankee shipmasters. He holds the Congressional medal of honor for conspicuous gallantry in action over and above the call of duty. The Brent blood may not be good enough for some, but it's a kind that's good enough for me!"

"All that is quite beside the question, Donald. The fact remains that Nan Brent loves you."

"May I inquire on what grounds you base that statement, dad?"

"On Saturday night, when you held her in your arms at parting, she kissed you." Donald was startled, and his features gave indubitable indication of the fact. His father's cool gray eyes were bent upon him kindly but unflinchingly. "Of course," he continued, in even tones, "you would not have accepted that caress were you not head over heels in love with the girl. You are not low enough to seek her favor for another reason."

"Yes; I love her," Donald maintained manfully. "I have loved her for years—since I was a boy of sixteen —only, I didn't realize it until my return to Port Agnew. I can't very well help loving Nan, can I, dad?"

To his amazement, his father smiled at him sympathetically.

"No; I do not see how you could very well help yourself, son," he replied. "She's an extraordinary young woman. After my brief and accidental interview with her recently, I made up my mind that there would be something radically wrong with you if you didn't fall in love with her."

His son grinned back at him.

"Proceed, old lumberjack!" he begged. "Your candor is soothing to my bruised spirit."

"No; you cannot help loving her, I suppose. Since you admit being in love with her, the fact admits of no argument. It has happened, and I do not condemn you for it. Both of you have merely demonstrated in the natural, human way that you are natural human beings. And I'm grateful to Nan for loving you. I think I should have resented her not doing so, for it would demonstrate her total lack of taste and appreciation of my son. She informed me, in so many words, that she wouldn't marry you."

"Nan has the capacity, somewhat rare in a woman, of keeping her own counsel. That is news to me, dad. However, if you had waited about two minutes, I would have informed you that I do not intend to marry Nan—" He paused for an infinitesimal space and added, "yet."

The Laird elevated his eyebrows.

" 'Yet?' " he repeated.

Donald flushed a little as he reiterated his statement with an emphatic nod.

"Why that reservation, my son?"

"Because, some day, Nan may be in position to prove herself that which I know her to be—a virtuous woman—and when that time comes, I'll marry her in spite of hell and high water."

Old Hector sighed. He was quite familiar with the fact that, while the records of the county clerk of Santa Clara County, California, indicated that a marriage license had been issued on a certain date to a certain man and one Nan Brent, of Port Agnew, Washington, there was no official record of a marriage between the two. The Reverend Mr. Tingley's wife had sorrowfully imparted that information to Mrs. McKaye, who had, in turn, informed old Hector, who had received the news with casual interest, little dreaming that he would ever have cause to remember it in later years. And The Laird was an old man, worldly-wise and of mature judgment. His soul wore the scars of human perfidy, and, because he could understand the weakness of the flesh, he had little confidence in its strength. Consequently, he dismissed now, with a wave of his hand, consideration of the possibility that Nan Brent would ever make a fitting mate for his son.

"It's nice of you to believe that, Donald. I would not destroy your faith in human nature, for human nature will destroy your faith in time, as it has destroyed mine. I'm afraid I'm a sort of doubting Thomas. I must see in order to believe; I must thrust my finger into the wound. I wonder if you realize that, even if this poor girl should, at some future time, be enabled to demonstrate her innocence of illicit love, she has been hopelessly smeared and will never, never, be quite able to clean herself."

"It matters not if *I* know she's a good woman. That is all sufficient. To hell with what the world thinks! I'm going to take my happiness where I find it."

"It may be a long wait, my son."

"I will be patient, sir."

"And, in the meantime, I shall be a doddering old man, without a grandson to sweeten the afternoon of my life, without a hope for seeing perpetuated all those things that I have considered worth while because I created them. Ah, Donald, lad, I'm afraid you're going to be cruel to your old father!"

"I have suffered with the thought that I might appear to be, dad. I have considered every phase of the situation; I was certain of the attitude you would take, and I feel no resentment because you have taken it. Neither Nan nor I had contemplated the condition which confronts us. It happened—like that," and Donald snapped his fingers. "Now the knowledge of what we mean to each other makes the obstacles all the more heart-breaking. I have tried to wish, for your sake, that I hadn't spoken—that I had controlled myself, but, for some unfathomable reason, I cannot seem to work up a very healthy contrition. And I think, dad, this is going to cause me more suffering than it will you."

A faint smile flitted across old Hector's stern face. Youth! Youth! It always thinks it knows!

"This affair is beyond consideration by the McKayes, Donald. It is utterly impossible! You must cease calling on the girl."

"Why, father?"

"To give you my real reason would lead to endless argument in which you would oppose me with more or less sophistry that would be difficult to combat. In the end, we might lose our tempers. Let us say, therefore, that you must cease calling on the lass because I desire it."

"I'll never admit that I'm ashamed of her, for I am not!" his son burst forth passionately.

"But people are watching you now—talking about you. Man, do ye not ken you're your father's son?"

A faint note of passion had crept into The Laird's tones; under the stress of it, his faint Scotch brogue increased perceptibly. He had tried gentle argument, and he knew he had failed; in his desperation, he decided to invoke his authority as the head of his clan. "I forbid you!" he cried firmly, and slapped the huge leather arm of his chair. "I charge you, by the blood that's in you, not to bring disgrace upon my house!"

A slight mistiness which Donald, with swelling heart, had noted in his father's eyes a few moments before was now gone. They flashed like naked claymores in the glance that Andrew Daney once had so aptly described to his wife.

For the space of ten seconds, father and son looked into each other's soul and therein each read the other's answer. There could be no surrender.

"You have bred a man, sir, not a mollycoddle," said the young laird quietly. "I think we understand each other." He rose, drew the old man out of his chair, and threw a great arm across the latter's shoulders. "Good-night, sir," he murmured humbly, and squeezed the old shoulders a little.

The Laird bowed his head but did not answer. He dared not trust himself to do so. Thus Donald left him, standing in the middle of the room, with bowed head a trifle to one side, as if old Hector listened for advice from some unseen presence. The Laird of Tyee had thought he had long since plumbed the heights and depths of the joys and sorrows of fatherhood. The tears came presently.

A streak of moonlight filtered into the room as the moon sank in the sea and augmented the silver in a head

that rested on two clasped hands, while Hector Mc-
Kaye, kneeling beside his chair, prayed to his stern
Presbyterian God once more to save his son from the
folly of his love.

XVIII

IT had been Donald McKaye's intention to go up to the logging-camp on the first log-train leaving for the woods at seven o'clock on Monday morning, but the news of Dirty Dan's plight caused him to change his plans. Strangely enough, his interview with his father, instead of causing him the keenest mental distress, had been productive of a peculiar sense of peace. The frank, sympathetic, and temperate manner in which the old laird had discussed his affair had conduced to produce this feeling. He passed a restful night, as his father observed when the pair met at the breakfast-table.

"Well, how do you feel this morning, son?" the old man queried kindly.

"Considerably better than I did before our talk last night, sir," Donald answered.

"I haven't slept," old Hector continued calmly, "although I expect to have a little nap during the day. Just about daylight a comforting thought stole over me."

"I'm glad to hear it, dad."

"I've decided to repose faith in Nan, having none at all in you. If she truly loves you, she'll die before she'll hurt you."

"Perhaps it may be a comfort to you to know that she has so expressed herself to me."

"Bless her poor heart for that! However, she told me practically the same thing."

He scooped his eggs into the egg-cup and salted and peppered them before he spoke again. Then:

"We'll not discuss this matter further. All I ask is that you'll confine your visits to the Sawdust Pile to the dark of the moon; I trust to your natural desire to promote my peace of mind to see to it that no word of your—affair reaches your mother and sisters. They'll not handle you with the tact you've had from me."

"I can well believe that, sir. Thank you. I shall exercise the utmost deference to your desires consistent with an unfaltering adherence to my own code."

There it was again—more respectful defiance! Had he not, during the long, distressing hours of the night, wisely decided to leave his son's case in the hands of God and Nan Brent, The Laird would have flown into a passion at that. He compromised by saying nothing, and the meal was finished in silence.

After breakfast, Donald went down to the hospital to visit Dirty Dan. O'Leary was still alive, but very close to death; he had lost so much blood that he was in a state of coma.

"He's only alive because he's a fighter, Mr. McKaye," the doctor informed Donald. "If I can induce some good healthy man to consent to a transfusion of blood, I think it would buck Dan up considerably."

"I'm your man," Donald informed him. It had occurred to him that Dirty Dan had given his blood for the House of McKaye; therefore, the least he could do was to make a partial payment on the debt.

The doctor, knowing nothing of the reason for Dirty Dan's predicament, was properly amazed.

"You—the boss—desire to do this?" he replied.

"We can get one of this wild rascal's comrades——"

"That wild rascal is my comrade, doctor. I'm more or less fond of Dan." He had removed his coat and was already rolling up his sleeve. "I'm half Gael," he continued smilingly, "and, you know, we must not adulterate Dirty Dan's blood any more than is absolutely necessary. Consider the complications that might ensue if you gave Dan an infusion of blood from a healthy Italian. The very first fight he engaged in after leaving this hospital, he'd use a knife instead of nature's weapons. Get busy!"

But the doctor would take no liberties with the life-blood of the heir of Tyee until he had telephoned to The Laird.

"My son is the captain of his own soul," old Hector answered promptly. "You just see that you do your job well; don't hurt the boy or weaken him too greatly."

An hour after the operation, father and son sat beside Dirty Dan's bed. Presently, the ivory-tinted eye-lids flickered slightly, whereat old Hector winked sagely at his son. Then Dirty Dan's whiskered upper lip twisted humorously, and he whispered audibly:

"Ye young divil! Oh-ho, ye young vagabond! Faith, if The Laird knew what ye're up to this night, he'd—break yer—back—in two halves!"

Hector McKaye glanced apprehensively about, but the nurse had left the room. He bent over Dirty Dan.

"Shut up!" he commanded. "Don't tell everything you know!"

O'Leary promptly opened his eyes and gazed upon The Laird in profound puzzlement.

"Wild horrses couldn't dhrag it out o' me," he protested. "Ask me no questions an' I'll tell ye no lies."

He subsided into unconsciousness again. The doctor entered and felt of his pulse.

"On the up-grade," he announced. "He'll do."

"Dan will obey the voice of authority, even in his delirium," The Laird whispered to his son, when they found themselves alone with the patient once more. "I'll stay here until he wakes up rational, and silence him if, in the mean time, he babbles. Run along home, lad."

At noon, Dirty Dan awoke with the light of reason and belligerency in his eyes, whereupon The Laird questioned him, and developed a stubborn reticence which comforted the former to such a degree that he decided to follow his son home to The Dreamerie.

XIX

A WEEK elapsed before Hector McKaye would permit his son to return to his duties. By that time, the slight wound in the latter's arm where the vein had been opened had practically healed. Dirty Dan continued to improve, passed the danger-mark, and began the upward climb to his old vigor and pugnacity. Port Agnew, stirred to discussion over the affray, forgot it within three days, and on the following Monday morning Donald returned to the woods. The Laird of Tyee carried his worries to the Lord in prayer, and Nan Brent frequently forgot her plight and sang with something of the joy of other days.

A month passed. During that month, Donald had visited the Sawdust Pile once and had written Nan thrice. Also, Mrs. Andrew Daney, hard beset because of her second experience with the "Blue Bonnet" glance of a McKaye, had decided to remove herself from the occasions of gossip and be in a position to claim an alibi in the event of developments. So she abandoned Daney to the mercies of a Japanese cook and departed for Whatcom to visit a married daughter. From Whatcom, she wrote her husband that she was enjoying her visit so much she hadn't the slightest idea when she would return, and, for good and sufficient reasons, Daney did not urge her to change her mind.

Presently, Mrs. McKaye and her daughters returned to Port Agnew. His wife's letters to The Laird had

162

failed to elicit any satisfactory reason for his continued stay at home, and inasmuch as all three ladies
were deferring the trip to Honolulu on his account,
they had come to a mutual agreement to get to close
quarters and force a decision.

Mrs. McKaye had been inside The Dreamerie somewhat less than five minutes before her instinct as a
woman, coupled with her knowledge as a wife, informed
her that her spouse was troubled in his soul. Always
tactless, she charged him with it, and when he denied
it, she was certain of it. So she pressed him further,
and was informed that he had a business deal on; when
she interrogated him as to the nature of it (something she had not done in years), he looked at her
and smoked contemplatively. Immediately she changed
the subject of conversation, but made a mental resolve to keep her eyes and her ears open.

The Fates decreed that she should not have long to
wait. Donald came home from the logging-camp the
following Saturday night, and the family, having finished dinner, were seated in the living-room. The Laird
was smoking and staring moodily out to sea, Donald
was reading, Jane was at the piano softly playing ragtime, and Mrs. McKaye and Elizabeth were knitting
socks for suffering Armenians when the telephone-bell
rang. Jane immediately left the piano and went out
into the entrance-hall to answer it, the servants having
gone down to Port Agnew to a motion-picture show.
A moment later, she returned to the living-room, leaving the door to the entrance-hall open.

"You're wanted on the telephone, Don!" she cried
gaily. "Such a sweet voice, too!"

Mrs. McKaye and Elizabeth looked up from their

knitting. They were not accustomed to having Donald
called to the telephone by young ladies. Donald laid
his magazine aside and strode to the telephone; The
Laird faced about in his chair, and a harried look
crept into his eyes.

"Close the door to the entrance-hall, Jane," he commanded.

"Oh, dear me, no!" his spoiled daughter protested.
"It would be too great a strain on our feminine curiosity not to eavesdrop on Don's little romance."

"Close it!" The Laird repeated. He was too late.
Through the open door, Donald's voice reached them:

"Oh, you poor girl! I'm so sorry, Nan dear. I'll be
over immediately." His voice dropped several octaves,
but the words came to the listeners none the less distinctly. "Be brave, sweetheart."

Mrs. McKaye glanced at her husband in time to see
him avert his face; she noted how he clutched the arm
of his chair.

To quote a homely phrase, the cat was out of the
bag at last. Donald's face wore a troubled expression
as he reentered the living-room. His mother spoke
first.

"Donald! *My* son!" she murmured tragically.

"Hum-m-!" The Laird grunted. The storm had
broken at last, and, following the trend of human nature, he was conscious of sudden relief.

Jane was the first to recover her customary aplomb.

"Don dear," she cooed throatily, "are we mistaken
in our assumption that the person with whom you have
just talked is Nan Brent?"

"Your penetration does you credit, Jane. It was."

"And did our ears deceive us or did we really hear you call her 'dear' and 'sweetheart'?"

"It is quite possible," Donald answered. He crossed the room and paused beside his father. "Caleb Brent blinked out a few minutes ago, dad. It was quite sudden. Heart-trouble. Nan's all alone down there, and of course she needs help. I'm going. I'll leave to you the job of explaining the situation to mother and the girls. Good-night, pop; I think you understand."

Mrs. McKaye was too stunned, too horrified, to find refuge in tears.

"How dare that woman ring you up?" she demanded haughtily. "The hussy!"

"Why, mother dear, she has to have help," her son suggested reproachfully.

"But why from you, of all men? I forbid you to go!" his mother quavered. "You must have more respect for us. Why, what will people say?"

"To hell with what people say! They'll say it, anyhow," roared old Hector. Away down in his proud old heart he felt a few cheers rising for his son's manly action, albeit the necessity for that action was wringing his soul. " 'Tis no time for idle spierin'. Away with you, lad! Comfort the puir lass. 'Tis no harm to play a man's part. Hear me," he growled; "I'll nae have my soncy lad abused."

"Dad's gone back to the Hielands. 'Nough said." Elizabeth had recovered her customary jolly poise. Wise enough, through long experience, to realize that when her father failed to throttle that vocal heritage from his forebears, war impended, she gathered up her knitting and fled to her room.

Jane ran to her mother's side, drew the good lady's

head down on her shoulder, and faced her brother. "Shame! Shame!" she cried sharply. "You ungrateful boy! How could you hurt dear mother so!"

This being the cue for her mother to burst into violent weeping, forthwith the poor soul followed up the cue. Donald, sore beset, longed to take her in his arms and kiss away her tears, but something warned him that such action would merely serve to accentuate the domestic tempest, so, with a despairing glance at old Hector, he left the room.

"Pretty kettle o' fish you've left me to bring to a boil!" the old man cried after him. "O Lord! O Lord! Grant me the wisdom of Solomon, the patience of Job, and the cunning of Judas Iscariot! God help my mildewed soul!"

XX

THE instant the front door closed behind her son, Mrs. McKaye recovered her composure. Had the reason been more trifling, she would have wept longer, but, in view of its gravity, her common sense (she possessed some, when it pleased her to use it) bade her be up and doing. Also, she was smitten with re- morse. She told herself she was partly to blame for this scourge that had come upon the family; she had neglected her son and his indulgent father. She, who knew so well the peculiar twists of her husband's mental and moral make-up, should not be surprised if he cast a tolerant eye upon his son's philanderings; seemingly the boy had always been able to twist his father round his finger, so to speak. She sat up, dabbed her eyes, kissed Jane lovingly as who should say, "Well, thank God, here is one child I can rely upon," and turned upon the culprit. Her opening sentence was at once a summons and an invitation.

"Well, Hector?"

"It happened while you were away—while we were both away, Nellie. I was gone less than forty-eight hours—and he had compromised himself."

"You don't mean—really compromised himself!" Jane cried sharply, thus bringing upon her The Laird's attention. He appeared to transfix her with his index- finger.

"To bed with you, young lady!" he ordered. "Your mother and I will discuss this matter without any of your pert suggestions or exclamations. I'm far from pleased with you, Jane. I told you to shut that door, and you disobeyed me. For that, you shall suffer due penance. Six months in Port Agnew, my dear, to teach you obedience and humility. Go!"

Jane departed, sniffling, and this stern evidence of The Laird's temper was not lost upon his wife. She decided to be tactful, which, in her case, meant proceeding slowly, speaking carefully, and listening well. Old Hector heaved himself out of his great chair, came and sat down on the divan with his wife, and put his arm round her.

"Dear old Nellie!" he whispered, and kissed her.

For the moment, they were lovers of thirty-odd years agone; their children forgotten, they were sufficient unto themselves.

"I know just how you feel, Nellie. I have done my best to spare you—I have not connived or condoned. And I'll say this for our son: He's been open and aboveboard with her and with me. He's young, and in a moment of that passion that comes to young men—aye, and young women, too, for you and I have known it— he told her what was in his heart, even while his head warned him to keep quiet. It seems to me sometimes that 'tis something that was to be."

"Oh, Hector, it mustn't be! It cannot be!"

"I'm hoping it will not be, Nellie. I'll do my best to stop it."

"But, Hector, why did you support him a moment ago?"

He flapped a hand to indicate a knowledge of his own incomprehensible conduct.

"She'd called for him, Nellie. Poor bairn, her heart went out to the one she knew would help her, and, by God, Nellie, I felt for her! You're a woman, Nellie. Think—if one of your own daughters was wishful for a kind word and a helping hand from an honorable gentleman and some fool father forbade it. Nellie wife, my heart and my head are sore tangled, sore tangled——"

His voice broke. He was shaken with emotion. He had stood much and he had stood it alone; while it had never occurred to him to think so, he had been facing life pretty much alone for a decade. It would have eased his surcharged spirit could he have shed a few manly tears, if his wife had taken his leonine old head on her shoulder and lavished upon him the caresses his hungry heart yearned for. Unfortunately, she was that type of wife whose first and only thought is for her children. She was aware only that he was in a softened mood, so she said,

"Don't you think you've been a little hard on poor Jane, Hector dear?"

"No, I do not. She's cruel, selfish, and uncharitable."

"But you'll forgive her this once, won't you, dear?"

He considered.

"Well, if she doesn't heckle Donald—" he began, but she stopped further proviso with a grateful kiss, and immediately followed Jane up-stairs to break the good news to her. She and Jane then joined Elizabeth in the latter's room, and the trio immediately held what their graceless relative would have termed "a lodge of sorrow." Upon motion of Jane, seconded by Elizabeth, it was unanimously resolved that the honor of the family must be upheld. At all cost. They laid out a plan of campaign.

XXI

UPON his arrival in Port Agnew, Donald called upon one Sam Carew. In his youth, Mr. Carew had served his time as an undertaker's assistant, but in Port Agnew his shingle proclaimed him to his world as a "mortician." Owing to the low death-rate in that salubrious section, however, Mr. Carew added to his labors those of a carpenter, and when outside jobs of carpentering were scarce, he manufactured a few plain and fancy coffins.

Donald routed Sam Carew out of bed with the news of Caleb Brent's death and ordered him down to the Sawdust Pile in his capacity of mortician; then he hastened there himself in advance of Mr. Carew. Nan was in the tiny living-room, her head pillowed on the table, when Donald entered, and when she had sobbed herself dry-eyed in his arms, they went in to look at old Caleb. He had passed peacefully away an hour after retiring for the night; Nan had straightened his limbs and folded the gnarled hands over the still heart; in the great democracy of death, his sad old face had settled into peaceful lines such as had been present in the days when Nan was a child and she and her father had been happy building a home on the Sawdust Pile. As Donald looked at him and reflected on the tremendous epics of a career that the world regarded as commonplace, when he recalled the sloop old Caleb had built for him with so much pride and pleas-

ure, the long-forgotten fishing trips and races in the
bight, the wondrous tales the old sailor had poured
into his boyish ears, together with the affection and
profound respect, as for a superior being, which the
old man had always held for him, the young laird of
Tyee mingled a tear or two with those of the orphaned
Nan.

"I've told Sam Carew to come for him," he informed
Nan, when they had returned to the living-room. "I
shall attend to all of the funeral arrangements. Funeral the day after to-morrow, say in the morning.
Are there any relatives to notify?"

"None that would be interested, Donald."

"Do you wish a religious service?"

"Certainly not by the Reverend Tingley."

"Then I'll get somebody else. Anything else?
Money, clothes?"

She glanced at him with all the sweetness and tenderness of her great love lambent in her wistful sea-
blue eyes.

"What a poor thing is pride in the face of circumstances," she replied drearily. "I haven't sufficient
strength of character to send you away. I ought to,
for your own sake, but since you're the only one that
cares, I suppose you'll have to pay the price. You
might lend me a hundred dollars, dear. Perhaps some
day I'll repay it."

He laid the money in her hand and retained the hand
in his; thus they sat gazing into the blue flames of the
driftwood fire—she hopelessly, he with masculine helplessness. Neither spoke, for each was busy with personal problems.

The arrival of Mr. Carew interrupted their sad

thoughts. When he had departed with the harvest of his grim profession, the thought that had been uppermost in Donald's mind found expression.

"It's going to be mighty hard on you living here alone."

"It's going to be hard on me wherever I live—alone," she replied resignedly.

"Wish I could get some woman to come and live with you until we can adjust your affairs, Nan. Tingley's wife's a good sort. Perhaps——"

She shook her head.

"I prefer my own company—when I cannot have yours."

A wave of bitterness, of humiliation swept over him in the knowledge that he could not ask one of his own sisters to help her. Truly he dwelt in an unlovely world.

He glanced at Nan again, and suddenly there came over him a great yearning to share her lot, even at the price of sharing her shame. He was not ashamed of her, and she knew it; yet both were fearful of revealing that fact to their fellow mortals. The conviction stole over Donald McKaye that he was not being true to himself, that he was not a man of honor in the fullest sense or a gentleman in the broadest meaning of the word. And that, to the heir of a principality, was a dangerous thought.

He then took tender leave of the girl and walked all the way home. His father had not retired when he reached The Dreamerie, and the sight of that stern yet kindly and wholly understandable person moved him to sit down beside The Laird on the divan and take the old man's hand in his childishly.

"Dad, I'm in hell's own hole!" he blurted. "I'm so unhappy!"

"Yes, son; I know you are. And it breaks me all up to think that, for the first time in my life, I can't help you. All the money in the world will not buy the medicine that'll cure you."

"I have to go through that, too, I suppose," his son complained, and jerked his head toward the stairs, where, as a matter of fact, his sister Jane crouched at the time, striving to eavesdrop. "I had a notion, as I walked home, that I'd refuse to permit them to discuss my business with me."

"This particular business of yours is, unfortunately, something which they believe to be their business, also. God help me, I agree with them!"

"Well, they had better be mighty careful how they speak of Nan Brent," Donald returned darkly. "This is something I have to fight out alone. By the way, are you going to old Caleb's funeral, dad?"

"Certainly. I have always attended the funerals of my neighbors, and I liked and respected Caleb Brent. Always reminded me of a lost dog. But he had a man's pride. I'll say that for him."

"Thank you, father. Ten o'clock, the day after to-morrow, from the little chapel. There isn't going to be a preacher present, so I'd be obliged if you'd offer a prayer and read the burial service. That old man and I were pals, and I want a real human being to preside at his obsequies."

The Laird whistled softly. He was on the point of asking to be excused, but reflected that Donald was bound to attend the funeral and that his father's presence would tend to detract from the personal side of the unprecedented spectacle and render it more of a matter of family condescension in so far as Port Agnew was concerned.

"Very well, lad," he replied; "I'm forced to deny you so much 'twould be small of me not to grant you a wee favor now and then. I'll do my best. And you might send a nurse from the company hospital to stay with Nan for a week or two."

"Good old file!" his son murmured gratefully, and, bidding his father good-night, climbed the stairs to his room. Hearing his footsteps ascending, Jane emerged from the rear of the landing; simultaneously, his mother and Elizabeth appeared at the door of the latter's room. He had the feeling of a captured missionary running the gantlet of a forest of spears *en route* to a grill over a bed of coals.

"Donald dear," Elizabeth called throatily, "come here."

"Donald dear is going to bed," he retorted savagely. "'Sufficient unto the day is the evil thereof.' Good-night!"

"But you *must* discuss this matter with us!" Jane clamored. "How can you expect us to rest until we have your word of honor that you——"

The Laird had appeared at the foot of the stairs, having followed his son in anticipation of an interview which he had forbidden.

"Six months, Janey," he called up; "and there'll be no appeal from that decision. Nellie! Elizabeth! Poor Jane will be lonesome in Port Agnew, and I'm not wishful to be too hard on her. You'll keep her company."

There was a sound of closing doors, and silence settled over The Dreamerie, that little white home that The Laird of Tyee had built and dedicated to peace and love. For he was the master here.

DONALD BOWED HIS HEAD. "I CAN'T GIVE HER UP, FATHER."

XXII

CALEB BRENT'S funeral was the apotheosis of simplicity. Perhaps a score of the old sailor's friends and neighbors attended, and there were, perhaps, half a dozen women—motherly old souls who had known Nan intimately in the days when she associated with their daughters and who felt in the presence of death a curious unbending of a curious and indefinable hostility. Sam Carew, arrayed in the conventional habiliments of his profession, stood against the wall and closed his eyes piously when Hector McKaye, standing beside old Caleb, spoke briefly and kindly of the departed and with a rough eloquence that stirred none present—not even Nan, who, up to that moment, entirely ignorant of The Laird's intention, could only gaze at him, amazed and incredulous—more than it stirred The Laird himself. The sonorous and beautiful lines of the burial service took on an added beauty and dignity as he read them, for The Laird believed! And when he had finished reading the service, he looked up, and his kind gaze lay gently on Nan Brent as he said:

"My friends, we will say a wee bit prayer for Caleb wi' all the earnestness of our hearts. O Lorrd, now that yon sailor has towed out on his last long cruise, we pray thee to gie him a guid pilot—aye, an archangel, for he was ever an honest man and brave—to guide him to thy mansion. Forgie him his trespasses and

in thy great mercy grant comfort to this poor bairn
he leaves behind. And thine shall be the honor and
the glory, forever and ever. Amen!"

None present, except Donald, realized the earnestness of that prayer, for, as always under the stress of
deep emotion, The Laird had grown Scotchy. Mrs.
Tingley, a kindly little soul who had felt it her Christian duty to be present, moved over to the little organ,
and Nan, conspicuous in a four-year-old tailored suit
and a black sailor-hat, rose calmly from her seat
and stood beside the minister's wife. For a moment, her
glance strayed over the little audience. Then she sang—
not a hymn, but just a little song her father had
always liked—the haunting, dignified melody that has
been set to Stevenson's "Requiem."

> Under the wide and starry sky,
> Dig the grave and let me lie.
> Glad did I live and gladly die,
>   And I laid me down with a will.
>
> This be the verse you grave for me:
> *Here he lies where he longed to be.*
> *Home is the sailor, home from sea,*
>   *And the hunter, home from the hill.*

The Laird, watching her narrowly, realized the effort it was costing her; yet her glorious voice did not
break or quiver once. "You wonderful, wonderful
woman!" he thought, moved to a high pitch of admiration for her independence and her flagrant flaunting
of tradition. "What a wife for my boy—what a
mother for my grandson—if you hadn't spoiled it all!"

She rode to the cemetery in The Laird's car with

The Laird, Donald, and Mrs. Tingley. Leaning on
Donald's arm, she watched them hide old Caleb beneath the flowers from the gardens of The Dreamerie;
then The Laird read the service at the grave and they
returned to the Sawdust Pile, where Nan's child (he
had been left at home in charge of a nurse from the
Tyee Lumber Company's hospital) experienced more
or less difficulty deciding whether Donald or The Laird
was his father.

The Laird now considered his duty to Caleb Brent
accomplished. He remained at the Sawdust Pile a
period barely sufficient for Nan to express her sense of
obligation.

"In a month, my dear girl," he whispered, as he
took her hand, "you'll have had time to adjust yourself and decide on the future. Then we'll have a little
talk."

She smiled bravely up at him through misty eyes
and shook her head. She read his thoughts far better
than he knew.

Father and son repaired to the private office at the
mill, and The Laird seated himself in his old swivel
chair.

"Now then, lad," he demanded, "have I been a good
sport?"

"You have, indeed, father! I'm grateful to you."

"You needn't be. I wouldn't have missed that funeral for considerable. That girl can sing like an angel,
and, man, the courage of her! 'Twas sweet of her,
singing to old Caleb like that, but I much mistake if
she won't be talked about for it. 'Twill be said she's
heartless." He handed his son a cigar and snipped
the end off one for himself. "We'll be needing the

Sawdust Pile now for a drying-yard," he announced complacently.

"You mean——"

"I mean, my son, that you're dreaming of the impossible, and that it's time for you to wake up. I want no row about it. I can't bear to hear your mother and sisters carrying on longer. I'll never get over thinking what a pity it is that girl is damaged goods. She must not be wife to son of mine."

The young laird of Tyee bowed his head.

"I can't give her up, father," he murmured. "By God, I can't!"

"There can be no happiness without honor, and you'll not be the first to make our name a jest in the mouths of Port Agnew. You will write her and tell her of my decision; if you do not wish to, then I shall do it for you. Trust her to understand and not hold it against you. And it is my wish that you should not see her again. She must be cared for, but when that time comes, I shall attend to it; you know me well enough to realize I'll do that well." He laid his hand tenderly on the young man's shoulder. "This is your first love, my son. Time and hard work will help you forget—and I'll wait for my grandson."

"And if I should not agree to this—what?"

"Obey me for a month—and then ask me that question if you will. I'm—I'm a bit unprepared for an answer on such short notice."

Donald bowed his head.

"Very well, sir. I'll think it over for a month—on one condition."

"Thank you, my son," said The Laird of Tyee. "And what is the condition?"

"Let mother and the girls go to Seattle or Honolulu or Shanghai or some other seaport—anywhere,
provided they're not at The Dreamerie when I return
to Port Agnew. I'm going to spend that damnable
month in the woods, week-ends and all, and wrestle
with this problem."

Old Hector smiled a small smile.

"I'm an old ass," he declared. "Have it your own
way, only—by the gods, I ought to teach them sense.
I've spoiled them, and I ought to unspoil them. They
drive me crazy, much as I love them."

The Laird went home that afternoon lighter of heart
than he had been for a month. He told himself that
his firm stand with Donald had rather staggered that
young man, and that a month of reflection, far from
the disturbing influence of Nan Brent's magnetic presence, would induce Donald to adopt a sensible course.

XXIII

SINCE that night when Mr. Daney, standing aloof in the dark vacant lot close to the Sawdust Pile, had seen Donald McKaye, in the light cast through the open door of Caleb Brent's cottage, take Nan Brent in his arms and kiss her, since he had heard Nan Brent's voice apply to the young laird of Port Agnew a term so endearing as to constitute a verbal caress, his practical and unromantic soul had been in a turmoil of apprehension.

It seemed to him that in old Hector he noted signs of deep mental perturbation. Also, he told himself, he detected more shades than lights in Donald's usually pleasant features; so, knowing full well that which he knew and which neither The Laird nor Donald suspected him of knowing, to wit: that a declaration of love had been made between Nan Brent and the heir to the Tyee millions, Mr. Daney came to the conclusion, one evening about a week after old Caleb's funeral, that something had to be done—and done quickly—to avert the scandal which impended. To his way of reasoning, however, it appeared that nothing along this line was possible of accomplishment while Nan Brent remained in Port Agnew; so Mr. Daney brought to play all of his considerable intelligence upon the problem of inducing her to leave.

Now, to render Port Agnew untenable for Nan, thus forcing her to retreat, was a task which Mr.

Daney dismissed not only as unworthy of him but
also as impossible. As a director of the Bank of Port
Agnew, he had little difficulty in ascertaining that
Caleb Brent's savings-account had been exhausted;
also, he realized that the chartering of Caleb's motor-
boat, Brutus, to tow the municipal garbage-barge
to sea and return, had merely been Donald's excuse to
be kind to the Brents without hurting their gentle
pride. To cancel the charter of the Brutus now would
force Nan to leave Port Agnew in order to support
herself, for Daney could see to it that no one in Port
Agnew employed her, even had anyone in Port Agnew
dared run such risk. Also, the Tyee Lumber Company might bluff her out of possession of the Sawdust
Pile. However, Donald would have to be reckoned with
in either case, and Mr. Daney was not anxious to
have the weight of his young master's anger fall on
his guilty head. He saw, therefore, that some indi-
rect means must be employed.

Now, Mr. Daney wisely held, in contradiction to
any number of people not quite so hard-headed as
he, that absence does *not* tend to make the heart grow
fonder—particularly if sufficient hard work and worry
can be supplied to prevent either party to the separa-
tion thinking too long or too intensely of the ab-
sentee. Within a decent period following Nan's hoped-
for departure from Port Agnew, Mr. Daney planned
to impress upon The Laird the desirability of a trip
to the Orient, while he, Daney, upon the orders of a
nerve-specialist, took a long sea voyage. Immediately the entire burden of seeing that the Tyee Lumber
Company functioned smoothly and profitably would
fall upon Donald's young and somewhat inexperienced

shoulders. In the meantime, what with The Laird's money and the employment of a third party or parties, it would be no trick at all to induce Nan Brent to move so far from Port Agnew that Donald could not, in justice to his business interests, desert those interests in order to pay his court to her.

"Dog my cats!" Mr. Daney murmured, at the end of a long period of perplexity. "I have to force the girl out of Port Agnew, and I can never do so while that motor-boat continues to pay her eighty dollars a month. She cannot exist on eighty dollars a month elsewhere, but she can manage very nicely on it here. And yet, even with that confounded charter canceled, we're stuck with the girl. She cannot leave Port Agnew without sufficient funds to carry her through for a while, and she'd die before she'd accept the gift of a penny from anybody in Port Agnew, particularly the McKayes. Even a loan from The Laird would be construed as a roundabout way of buying her off."

Mr. Daney pondered his problem until he was almost tempted to butt his poor head against the office wall, goat-fashion, in an attempt to stimulate some new ideas worth while. Nevertheless, one night he wakened from a sound sleep and found himself sitting up in bed, the possessor of a plan so flawless that, in sheer amazement, he announced aloud that he would be—jiggered. Some cunning little emissary of the devil must have crept in through his ear while he slept and planted the brilliant idea in Mr. Daney's brain.

Eventually, Mr. Daney lay down again. But he could not go to sleep; so he turned on the electric bedside-lamp and looked at his watch. It was midnight

—and at midnight no living creature, save possibly an adventurous or amorous cat, moved in Port Agnew; so Mr. Daney dressed, crept down-stairs on velvet feet, in order not to disturb the hired girl, and stepped forth into the night. Ten minutes later, he was down at the municipal garbage-barge, moored to the bulkhead of piles along the bank of the Skookum.

He ventured to strike a match. The gunwale of the barge was slightly below the level of the bulkhead; so Mr. Daney realized that the tide had turned and was at the ebb—otherwise, the gunwale would have been on a level with the bulkheads. He stepped down on the barge, made his way aft to the Brutus, moored astern, and boarded the little vessel. He struck another match and looked into the cabin to make certain that no member of the barge-crew slept there. Finding no one, he went into the engine-room and opened the sea-cock. Then he lifted up a floor-board, looked into the bilge, saw that the water therein was rising, and murmured,

"Bully—by heck!"

He clambered hastily back aboard the barge, cast off the mooring-lines of the Brutus, and with a boat-book gave her a shove which carried her out into the middle of the river. She went bobbing away gently on the ebb-tide, bound for the deep water out in the Bight of Tyee where, when she settled, she would be hidden forever and not be a menace to navigation. Mr. Daney watched her until she disappeared in the dim starlight before returning to his home and so, like Mr. Pepys, to bed, where he had the first real sleep in weeks. He realized this in the morning and marveled at it, for he had always regarded himself as a man of tender conscience and absolutely incapable of committing a maritime crime. Nevertheless, he whistled and wore a red carnation in his lapel as he departed for the mill office.

XXIV

FOLLOWING the interview with his father, subsequent to Caleb Brent's funeral, Donald McKaye
realized full well that his love-affair, hitherto indefinite as to outcome, had crystallized into a definite
issue. For him, there could be no evasion or equivo-
cation; he had to choose, promptly and for all time,
between his family and Nan Brent—between respectability, honor, wealth, and approbation on one hand,
and pity, contempt, censure, and poverty on the other.
Confronting this *impasse*, he was too racked with tor-
ment to face his people that night and run the gantlet
of his mother's sad, reproachful glances, his father's
silence, so eloquent of mental distress, and the studied
scorn, amazement, and contempt in the very attitudes
of his selfish and convention-bound sisters. So he
ate his dinner at the hotel in Port Agnew, and after
dinner his bruised heart took command of his feet
and marched him to the Sawdust Pile.

The nurse he had sent down from the Tyee Lumber Company's hospital to keep Nan company until
after the funeral had returned to the hospital, and
Nan, with her boy asleep in her lap, was seated in
a low rocker before the driftwood fire when Donald
entered, unannounced save for his old-time triple tap
at the door. At first glance, it was evident to him
that the brave reserve which Nan had maintained at
the funeral had given way to abundant tears when

187

she found herself alone at home, screened from the gaze of the curious.

He knelt and took both outcasts in his great strong arms, and for a long time held them in a silence more eloquent than words.

"Well, my dear," she said presently, "aren't you going to tell me all about it?"

That was the woman of it. She knew.

"I'm terribly unhappy," he replied. "Dad and I had a definite show-down after the funeral. His order—not request—is that I shall not call here again."

"Your father is thinking with his head; so he thinks clearly. You, poor dear, are thinking with your heart controlling your head. Of course you'll obey your father. You cannot consider doing anything else."

"I'm not going to give you up," he asserted doggedly.

"Yes; you are going to give me up, dear heart," she replied evenly. "Because I'm going to give you up, and you're much too fine to make it hard for me to do that."

"I'll not risk your contempt for my weakness. It *would* be a weakness—a contemptible trick—if I should desert you now."

"Your family has a greater claim on you, Donald. You were born to a certain destiny—to be a leader of men, to develop your little world, and make of it a happier place for men and women to dwell in. So, dear love, you're just going to buck up and be spunky and take up your big life-task and perform it like the gentleman you are."

"But what is to become of you?" he demanded, in desperation.

"I do not know. It is a problem I am not going to consider very seriously for at least a month. Of course I shall leave Port Agnew, but before I do, I shall have to make some clothes for baby and myself."

"I told my father I would give him a definite answer regarding you in a month, Nan. I'm going up in the woods and battle this thing out by myself."

"Please go home and give him a definite answer to-night. You have not the right to make him suffer so," she pleaded.

"I'm not prepared to-night to abandon you, Nan. I must have some time to get inured to the prospect."

"Did you come over to-night to tell me good-by before going back to the woods, Donald?"

He nodded, and deliberately she kissed him with great tenderness.

"Then—good-by, sweetheart," she whispered. "In our case, the least said is soonest mended. And please do not write to me. Keep me out of your thoughts for a month, and perhaps I'll stay out."

"No hope," he answered, with a lugubrious smile. "However, I'll be as good as I can. And I'll not write. But—when I return from that month of exile, do not be surprised if I appear to claim you for good or for evil, for better or for worse."

She kissed him again—hurriedly—and pressed him gently from her, as if his persistence gave her cause for apprehension.

"Dear old booby!" she murmured. "Run along home now, won't you, please?"

So he went, wondering why he had come, and the following morning, still wrapped in a mental fog, he departed for the logging-camp, but not until his sister

Jane had had her long-deferred inning. While he was in the garage at The Dreamerie, warming up his car, Jane appeared and begged him to have some respect for the family, even though, apparently, he had none for himself. Concluding a long and bitter tirade, she referred to Nan as "that abandoned girl."

Poor Jane! Hardly had she uttered the words before her father appeared in the door of the garage.

"One year, Janey," he announced composedly. "And I'd be pleased to see the photograph o' the human being that'll make me revoke that sentence. I'm fair weary having my work spoiled by women's tongues."

"I'll give you my photograph, old pepper-pot," Donald suggested. "I have great influence with you, have I not?"

The Laird looked up at him with a fond grin.

"Well?" he parried.

"You will remit the sentence to one washing of the mouth with soap and water to cleanse it of those horrid words you just listened to."

"That's not a bad idea," the stern old man answered. "Janey, you may have your choice, since Donald has interceded for you."

But Jane maintained a freezing silence and swept out of the garage with a mien that proclaimed her belief that her brother and father were too vulgar and plebeian for her.

"I'm having the deil's own time managing my family," old Hector complained, "but I'll have obedience and kindness and justice in my household, or know the reason why. Aye—and a bit of charity," he added grimly. He stood beside the automobile and held up his hand up for his son's. "And you'll be gone a month, lad?" he queried.

Donald nodded.

"Too painful—this coming home week-ends," he explained. "And Nan has requested that I see no more of her. You have a stanch ally in her, dad. She's for you all the way."

Relief showed in his father's troubled face.

"I'm glad to know that," he replied. "You're the one that's bringing me worry and breaking down her good resolutions and common sense." He leaned a little closer, first having satisfied himself, by a quick, backward glance, that none of the women of the family was eavesdropping, and whispered: "I'm trying to figure out a nice way to be kind to her and give her a good start in life without insulting her. If you should have a clear thought on the subject, I'd like your advice, son. 'Twould hurt me to have her think I was trying to buy her off."

"As I view the situation, all three of us have to figure our own angles for ourselves. However, if a happy thought should dawn on me, I'll write you. Think it over a few weeks, and then do whatever seems best."

So they parted.

XXV

A FEW days subsequent to Andrew Daney's secret scuttling of the motor-boat Brutus, Nan Brent was amazed to receive a visit from him.

"Good-morning, Nan," he saluted her. "I have bad news for you."

"What, pray?" she managed to articulate. She wondered if Donald had been injured up in the woods.

"Your motor-boat's gone."

This was, indeed, bad news. Trouble showed in Nan's face.

"Gone where?" she faltered.

"Nobody knows. It disappeared from the garbage-barge, alongside of which it was moored. I've had men searching for it two days, but we've given it up as lost. Was the Brutus, by any chance, insured against theft?"

"Certainly not."

"Well, the Tyee Lumber Company used reasonable care to conserve your property, and while there's a question whether the company's responsible for the loss of the boat if it's been stolen, even while under charter to us, nevertheless, you will be reimbursed for the value of the boat. Your father had it up for sale last year. Do you recall the price he was asking?"

"He was asking considerably less than he really believed the Brutus to be worth," Nan replied honestly. "He would have sold for fifteen hundred dollars, but

192

the Brutus was worth at least twenty-five hundred.
Values shrink, you know, when one requires ready cash.
And I do not agree with you that no responsibility
attaches to the Tyee Lumber Company, although, under
the circumstances, it appears there is no necessity for
argument."

"We'll pay twenty-five hundred rather than descend
to argument," Daney replied crisply, "although personally I am of the opinion that two thousand would
be ample." He coughed a propitiatory cough and
looked round the Sawdust Pile appraisingly. "May I
inquire, my girl," he asked presently, "what are your
plans for the future?"

"Certainly, Mr. Daney. I have none."

"It would be a favor to the Tyee Lumber Company
if you had, and that they contemplated removal to
some other house. The Laird had planned originally
to use the Sawdust Pile for a drying-yard"—he smiled
faintly—"but abandoned the idea rather than interfere
with your father's comfort. Of course, The Laird
hasn't any more title to the Sawdust Pile than you
have—not as much, in fact, for I do believe you could
make a squatter's right stick in any court. Just at
present, however, we have greater need of the Sawdust
Pile than ever. We're getting out quite a lot of airplane spruce for the British government, and since
there's no doubt we'll be into the war ourselves one of
these days, we'll have to furnish additional spruce for
our own government. Spruce has to be air-dried, you
know, to obtain the best results, and—well, we really
need the Sawdust Pile. What will you take to abandon
it and leave us in undisputed possession?"

"Nothing, Mr. Daney."

"Nothing?"

"Precisely—nothing. We have always occupied it on The Laird's sufferance, so I do not think, Mr. Daney," she explained, with a faint smile, "that I shall turn pirate and ingrate now. If you will be good enough to bring me over twenty-five hundred dollars in cash to-day, I will give you a clearance for the loss of the Brutus and abandon the Sawdust Pile to you within the next three or four days."

His plan had worked so successfully that Daney was, for the moment, rendered incapable of speech.

"Will you be leaving Port Agnew?" he sputtered presently. "Or can I arrange to let you have a small house at a modest rental——"

She dissipated this verbal camouflage with a disdainful motion of her upflung hand.

"Thank you. I shall leave Port Agnew—forever. The loss of the Brutus makes my escape possible," she added ironically.

"May I suggest that you give no intimation of your intention to surrender this property?" he suggested eagerly. "If word of your plan to abandon got abroad, it might create an opportunity for some person to jump the Sawdust Pile and defy us to dispossess him."

Mr. Daney sought, by this subterfuge, to simulate an interest in the physical possession of the Sawdust Pile which he was far from feeling. He congratulated himself, however, that, all in all, he had carried off his mission wonderfully well, and departed with a promise to bring over the money himself that very afternoon. Indeed, so delighted was he that it was with difficulty that he restrained himself from unburdening to The Laird, when the latter dropped in at the mill office that afternoon, the news that before the week should be out Nan Brent would be but a memory in Port Agnew. Later, he wondered how far from Port Agnew she would settle for a new start in life and whether she would leave a forwarding address. He resolved to ask her, and he did, when he reappeared at the Sawdust Pile that afternoon with the money to reimburse Nan for the loss of the Brutus.

"I haven't decided where I shall go, Mr. Daney," Nan informed him truthfully, "except that I shall betake myself some distance from the Pacific Coast—some place where the opportunities for meeting people who know me are nebulous, to say the least. And I shall leave no forwarding address. When I leave Port Agnew"—she looked Mr. Daney squarely in the eyes as she said this—"I shall see to it that no man, woman, or child in Port Agnew—not even Don McKaye or The Laird, who have been most kind to me—shall know where I have gone."

"I'm sorry matters have so shaped themselves in your life, poor girl, that you're feeling bitter," Mr. Daney replied, with genuine sympathy, notwithstanding the fact that he would have been distressed and puzzled had her bitterness been less genuine. In the realization that it *was* genuine, he had a wild impulse to leap in the air and crack his ankles together for very joy. "Will I be seeing you again, Nan, before you leave?"

"Not unless the spirit moves you, Mr. Daney," she answered dryly. She had no dislike for Andrew Daney, but, since he was the husband of Mrs. Daney and under that person's dominion, she distrusted him.

"Well then, I'll bid you good-by now, Nan," he announced. "I hope your lot will fall in pleasanter places than Port Agnew. Good-by, my dear girl, and good luck to you—always."

"Good-by, Mr. Daney," she replied. "Thank you for bringing the money over."

XXVI

BY an apparent inconsistency in the natural order of human affairs, it seems that women are called upon far oftener than men to make the hardest sacrifices; also, the call finds them far more willing, if the sacrifice is demanded of them by love. Until Andrew Daney had appeared at the Sawdust Pile with the suddenness of a genie (and a singularly benevolent genie at that), Nan had spent many days wondering what fate the future held in store for her. With all the ardor of a prisoner, she had yearned to leave her jail, although she realized that freedom for her meant economic ruin. On the Sawdust Pile, she could exist on the income from the charter of the Brutus, for she had no rent to pay and no fuel to buy; her proximity to the sea, her little garden and a few chickens still further solved her economic problems. Away from the Sawdust Pile, however, life meant parting with her baby. She would have to place him in some sort of public institution if she would be free to earn a living for them both, and she was not aware that she possessed any adaptability for any particular labor which would enable her to earn one hundred dollars a month, the minimum sum upon which she could, by the strictest economy, manage to exist and support her child. Too well she realized the difficulty which an inexperienced woman has in securing employment in an office or store at a wage which, by the wildest stretch of the imagination, may be termed lucrative,

and, lacking funds wherewith to tide her over until
she should acquire experience, or even until she should
be fortunate enough to secure any kind of work, inevitable starvation faced her. Her sole asset was her
voice; she had a vague hope that if she could ever
acquire sufficient money to go to New York and buy
herself just sufficient clothing to look well dressed and
financially independent, she might induce some vaudeville impresario to permit her to spend fifteen minutes
twice or four times daily, singing old-fashioned songs
to the proletariat at something better than a living
wage. She had an idea for a turn to be entitled, "Songs
of the 'Sixties."

The arrival of Andrew Daney with twenty-five hundred dollars might have been likened to an eleventh-
hour reprieve for a condemned murderer. Twenty-five
hundred dollars! Why, she and Don could live two
years on that! She was free—at last! The knowledge
exalted her—in the reaction from a week of contem-
plating a drab, barren future, she gave no thought
to the extreme unlikelihood of anyone's daring to steal
a forty-foot motor-boat on a coast where harbors are
so few and far between as they are on the Pacific. Had
old Caleb been alive, he would have informed her that
such action was analogous to the theft of a hot stove,
and that no business man possessed of a grain of common sense would have hastened to reimburse her for
the loss after an inconsequential search of only two
days. Had she been more worldly wise, she would have
known that business men do not part with twenty-five
hundred dollars that readily—otherwise, they would not
be business men and would not be possessed of twenty-
five hundred dollars. Nan only realized that, in handing

her a roll of bank-notes with a rubber band round
them, Andrew Daney had figuratively given her the key
to her prison, against the bars of which her soul had
beaten for three long years.

Now, it is doubtful whether any woman ever loved a
man without feeling fully assured that she, more than
any other person, was better equipped to decide exactly
what was best for that man. Her woman's intuition
told Nan that Donald McKaye was not to be depended
upon to conserve the honor of the McKaye family by
refraining from considering an alliance with her. Also,
knowing full well the passionate yearnings of her own
heart and the weakness of her economic position, she
shrank from submitting herself to the task of repelling
his advances. Where he was concerned, she feared
her own weakness—she, who had endured the brutality
of the world, could not endure that the world's brutality
should be visited upon him because of his love for her.
Strong of will, self-reliant, a born fighter, and as stiff-
necked as his father, his yearning to possess her, coupled
with his instinct for fair play, might and probably
would lead him to tell the world to go hang, that he
would think for himself and take his happiness where he
found it. By all means, this must be prevented. Nan
felt that she could not permit him to risk making a
sorry mess of a life of promise.

Consumed with such thoughts as these, it was obvious
that Nan should pursue but one course—that is, leave
Port Agnew unannounced and endeavor to hide herself where Donald McKaye would never find her. In
this high resolve, once taken, she did not falter; she
even declined to risk rousing the suspicions of the townspeople by appearing at the general store to purchase

badly needed articles of clothing for herself and her
child. She resolved to leave Port Agnew in the best
clothes she had, merely pausing a few days in her flight
—at Vancouver, perhaps—to shop, and then continuing
on to New York.

On the morning of her departure, the butcher's boy,
calling for an order, agreed, for fifty cents, to transport
her one small trunk on his cart to the station. The
little white house which she and her father had built
with so much pride and delight, she left furnished as
it was and in perfect order. As she stood at the front
door and looked back for the last time, the ticking of
the clock in the tiny dining-and-living room answered
her mute, "Good-by, little house; good-by," and,
though her heart was full enough, she kept back the
tears until she saw the flag flying bravely at the cupola.

"Oh, my love, my love!" she sobbed. "I mustn't
leave it flying there, flaunting my desertion in your
dear eyes."

Blinded by her tears, she groped her way back to
the house, hauled down the flag, furled it, and laid it
away in a bureau drawer. And this time, when she
left the house, she did not look back.

At the station, she purchased a ticket for Seattle
and checked her trunk at the baggage-room counter.
As she turned from the counter and started for the
waiting-room, she caught the interested eyes of old
Hector McKaye bent upon her. He lifted his hat and
walked over to her.

"I happened to be looking down at the Sawdust Pile
when you hauled your flag down this morning," he
explained, in a low voice. "So I knew you were going

away. That's why I'm here." To this extraordinary speech, the girl merely replied with an inquiring look. "I wonder if you will permit me to be as kind to you as I can," he continued. "I know it sounds a bit blunt and vulgar to offer you money, but when one needs money——"

"I have sufficient for my present needs," she replied. "Mr. Daney has paid me for the loss of my motor-boat, you know. You are very kind; but I think I shall have no need to impose further on your generosity. I think the twenty-five hundred dollars will last me nicely until I have made a new start in life."

"Ah!" The Laird breathed softly. "Twenty-five hundred dollars. Yes, yes! So he did; so he did! And are you leaving Port Agnew indefinitely, Nan?"

"Forever," she replied. "We have robbed you of the ground for a drying-yard for nearly ten years, but this morning the Sawdust Pile is yours."

"Bless my soul!" The Laird ejaculated. "Why, we are not at all in distress for more drying-space."

"Mr. Daney intimated that you were. He asked me how much I would take to abandon my squatter's right, but I declined to charge you a single cent." She smiled up at him a ghost of her sweet, old-time whimsical smile. "It was the first opportunity I had to be magnanimous to the McKaye family, and I hastened to take advantage of it. I merely turned the key in the lock and departed."

"Daney has been a trifle too zealous for the Tyee interests, I fear," he replied gently. "And where do you plan to live?"

"That," she retorted, still smilingly, "is a secret. It may interest you, Mr. McKaye, to know that I am not even leaving a forwarding address for my mail. You see, I never receive any letters of an important nature."

He was silent a moment, digesting this. Then,

"And does my son share a confidence which I am denied?"

"He does not, Mr. McKaye. This is my second opportunity to do the decent thing toward the McKaye family—so I am doing it. I plan to make rather a thorough job of it, too. You—you'll be very kind and patient with him, will you not? He's going to feel rather badly, you know, but, then, I never encouraged him. It's all his fault, I think—I tried to play fair— and it was so hard." Her voice sunk to a mere whisper. "I've always loved Donald, Mr. McKaye. Most people do; so I have not regarded it as sinful on my part."

"You are abandoning him of your own free will——"

"Certainly. I have to. Surely you must realize that?"

"Yes, I do. I have felt that he would never abandon you." He opened and closed his big hands nervously, and was plainly a trifle distrait. "So—so this is your idea of playing the game, is it?" he demanded presently. She nodded. "Well," he replied helplessly, "I would to God I dared be as good a sport as you are, Nan Brent! Hear me, now, lass. Think of the thing in life you want to do and the place where you want to do it——"

She interrupted him.

"No, no, Mr. McKaye; there can be no talk of money between us. I cannot and will not take your son—for his sake, and for my own sake I cannot and will not accept of your kindness. Somehow, some place, I'm going to paddle my own canoe."

"Guid lass; guid lass," he whispered huskily. "Remember, then, if your canoe upsets and spills you, a wire to me will right you, and no questions asked. Good-by, my dear, and good luck to you!"

He pressed her hand, lifted his hat, and walked briskly away in the direction of The Tyee Lumber Company's office, quite oblivious of the fact that his interview with Nan Brent had been observed by a person to whom the gods had given at birth a more than average propensity of intrigue, romance, and general cussedness—Mr. Daniel J. O'Leary, of whom more anon.

From the station, Hector McKaye hurried over to the mill office and entered Andrew Daney's room.

"Andrew," he began, "you've been doing things. What became of old Caleb Brent's motor-boat?"

"I opened the seacock, cast it off, and let it drift out into the bight on the ebb-tide one night recently."

"Why?"

"In order that I might have a logical and reasonable excuse to furnish Nan Brent with sufficient funds to leave this town and make a new start elsewhere. I have charged the twenty-five hundred to your personal account on the company books."

"You also indulged in some extraordinary statements regarding our pressing need for the Sawdust Pile as a drying-yard."

"We can use it, sir," Daney replied. "I felt justified in indicating to the girl that her room was desired to her company. Your son," he added deliberately, "was treading on soft ground, and I took the license of an old friend and, I hope, a faithful servant, to rid him of temptation."

"I shall never be done with feeling grateful to you,

Andrew. The girl is leaving on the train that's just pulling out, and—the incident is closed. My son is young. He will get over it. Thank you, Andrew, dear friend, until you're better paid—as you will be some day soon."

"I'll have need of your friendship if Donald ever discovers my part in this deal. He'll fire me out o' hand."

"If he does, I'll hire you back."

"Hell will pop when he finds the bird has flown, sir."

"Let it pop! That kind of popping is music in my ears. Hark, Andrew lad! There's the train whistling for Darrow's Crossing. From there on the trail is lost—lost—*lost*, I tell you! O Lord, God of Hosts, I thank Thee for Thy great mercy!"

And, quite suddenly, old Hector sat down and began to weep.

XXVII

NAN BRENT'S departure from the Sawdust Pile
was known to so few in Port Agnew that it was
fully ten days before the news became general; even
then it excited no more than momentary comment, and
a week later when Donald McKaye returned to town,
somewhat sooner than he had anticipated, Port Agnew
had almost forgotten that Nan Brent had ever lived
and loved and sinned in its virtuous midst. Even the
small gossip about her and the young laird had subsided, condemned by all, including the most thoughtless,
as a gross injustice to their favorite son, and consequently dismissed as the unworthy tattling of unworthy,
suspicious old women. Life in the busy little sawmill
town had again sagged into the doldrums.

For several days, a feeling of lassitude had been
stealing over Donald. At first he thought it was mental
depression, but when, later, he developed nausea, lack
of appetite, and pains in his head, back, and extremities,
it occurred to him that he wasn't feeling well physically
and that The Dreamerie was to be preferred to his
rough pine shanty in the woods, even though in the
latter he had sanctuary from the female members of
his family.

He came in unexpectedly on the last log-train on
Saturday night; tired, with throbbing head and trembling legs, he crawled off the caboose at the log dump
and made his way weakly up to the mill office. It was

deserted when he got there at half-past six, but in his mail-box he found something which he had promised himself would be there, despite certain well-remembered assurances to the contrary. It was a letter from Nan. He tore the envelop eagerly and read:

Donald dear, I love you. That is why I am leaving you. We shall not meet again, I think. If we should, it will doubtless be years hence, and by that time we shall both have resigned ourselves to this present very necessary sacrifice. Good-by, poor dear.

Always your sweetheart,

NAN.

He read and reread the letter several times. It was undated. Presently, with an effort, he recovered the envelop from the waste-basket and examined the postmark. The letter had been mailed from Seattle, but the post-date was blurred.

With the letter clutched in his hand, he bent forward and pillowed his hot face in his arms, outspread upon his father's old desk. He wanted to weep—to sob aloud in a childish effort to unburden his heart, scourged now with the first real sorrow of his existence. His throat contracted; something in his breast appeared to have congealed, yet for upward of an hour he neither moved nor gave forth a sound. At last, under the inspiration of a great hope that came apparently without any mental effort or any desire for hope, so thoroughly crushed was he, the black, touseled head came slowly up. His face, usually ruddy beneath the dark, suntanned skin but now white and haggard, showed a fleeting little smile, as if he grinned at his own weakness and lack of faith; he rose unsteadily and clumped out of the office-building.

Gone! Nan gone—like that! No, no! He would not believe it. She might have intended to go—she might have wanted to go—she might even have started to go—but she had turned back! She loved him; she was his. During those long days and nights up in the woods, he had fought the issue with himself and made up his mind that Nan Brent was the one woman in the world for him, that there could never, by God's grace, be any other, and that he would have her, come what might and be the price what it would. Rather than the fortune for which his father had toiled and sacrificed, Donald preferred Nan's love; rather than a life of ease and freedom from worry, he looked forward with a fierce joy to laboring with his hands for a pittance, provided he might have the privilege of sharing it with her. And The Dreamerie, the house his father had built with such great, passionate human hopes and tender yearnings, the young laird of Port Agnew could abandon without a pang for that little white house on the Sawdust Pile. Round steak and potatoes, fried by the woman destined to him for his perfect mate, would taste better to him than the choicest viands served by light stepping servitors in his father's house.

What, after all, was there worth while in the world for him if he was to be robbed of his youth and his love? For him, the bare husks of life held no allurement; he was one of that virile, human type that rejects the doctrine of sacrifice, denial, and self-repression in this life for the greater glory of God and man's promise of a reward in another life, of which we wot but little and that little not scientifically authenticated. He

wanted the great, all-compelling, omnipotent Present,
with its gifts that he could clutch in his fierce hands or
draw to his hungry heart. To hell with the future. He
reflected that misers permit their thoughts to dwell
upon it and die rich and despised, leaving to the apostles
of the Present the enjoyment of the fruits of a foolish
sacrifice.

"She came back. I know she did," he mumbled, as he
groped his way through the dark of the drying-yard.
"I'm sick. I must see her and tell her to wait until I'm
well. The damned dirty world can do what it jolly
well pleases to me, but I'll protect her from it. I will
—by God!"

He emerged into the open fields beyond which lay
the Sawdust Pile, snuggled down on the beach. The
Brent cottage was visible in the dim starlight, and he
observed that there was no light in the window; nevertheless, his high faith did not falter. He pressed on,
although each step was the product of an effort, mental
and physical. His legs were heavy and dragged, as if
he wore upon, his logger's boots the thick, leaden soles
of a deep-sea diver.

At the gate, he leaned and rested for a few minutes,
then entered the deserted yard and rapped at the front
door; but his summons bringing no response, he staggered round to the back door and repeated it. He
waited half a minute and then banged furiously with
his fist upon the door-panel. Still receiving no response,
he seized the knob and shook the door until the little
house appeared to rattle from cellar to cupola.

"Nan! Nan! Where are you?" he called. "It is I—
Donald. Answer me, Nan. I know you haven't gone
away. You wouldn't! Please answer me, Nan!"

But the only sound he heard was the labored pumping of his own heart and the swish of the wavelets against the timbered buttress of the Sawdust Pile. The conviction slowly came to his torpid brain that he was seeking admittance to a deserted house, and he leaned against the door and fought for control of himself. Presently, like a stricken animal, he went slowly and uncertainly away in the direction whence he had come.

Andrew Daney had put out the cat and wound the clock and was about to ascend to his chamber (now, alas, reoccupied by Mrs. Daney, upon whom the news of Nan's departure had descended like a gentle rainfall over a hitherto arid district) when he heard slow footsteps on his front veranda. Upon going to the door and peering out, he was amazed to see Donald McKaye standing just outside.

"Well, bless my soul!" Daney declared. "So it's you Donald. Come in, lad; come in."

Donald shook his head.

"No, I've only come to stay a minute, Mr. Daney. Thank you, sir. I—I notice you're running a light track from the drying-yard down to the Sawdust Pile. Stumbled over it in the dark a few minutes ago, and I—" He essayed a ghastly smile, for he desired to remove the sting from the gentle rebuke he purposed giving the general manger—"couldn't seem to remember having ordered that track—or—suggesting that it be laid."

"Quite so, Donald; quite so," Daney answered. "I did it on my own initiative. Nan Brent has abandoned the Sawdust Pile—moved away from Port Agnew, you know; so I decided to extend the drying-yard, and squat on the Sawdust Pile before some undesirable took possession."

"Hm-m-m! I see. Well, suppose Nan takes a notion to return to Port Agnew, Mr. Daney. She'll find our drying-yard something of a nuisance, will she not?"

"Oh, but she's not coming back," Daney assured him, with all the confidence of one free from the slightest doubt on the subject.

"She might. I could see rather dimly into the kitchen and it appears Miss Brent left her little home furnished."

"Yes, she did, Donald. I believe she just turned the key in the lock and went away."

"Know where she went, Mr. Daney?"

"No. She didn't even leave a forwarding address for her mail."

The young laird of Tyee lurched up to Mr. Daney and laid a heavy hand on the older man's shoulder.

"How do you know that?" he demanded, and there was a growl in his voice. "Has Mrs. Daney been asking the postmaster?"

Mr. Daney saw that, for some inexplicable reason, he was in for a bad five minutes or more. His youthful superior's face was white and beaded with perspiration. Daney had a suspicion that Donald had had a drink or two.

"There has been no gossip, Donald," he answered crisply. "Get that notion out of your head. I would protect you from gossip, for I think I know my duty to the McKayes. I learned that lesson a long time ago," he added, with spirit.

"You haven't answered my question, Mr. Daney," Donald persisted.

"I shall. I know, because she told me herself." Mr. Daney had not intended that Donald should ever discover that he had had an interview with Nan Brent, but his veracity had, for the moment, appeared to him to be questioned by his superior, and he was too truthful, too thoroughly honest to attempt now to protect his reputation for truth-telling by uttering a small fib, albeit he squirmed inwardly at the terrible necessity for such integrity.

"Ah! Then Nan called upon you again?"

Mr. Daney sighed.

"No, I called upon her."

"With reference to what?"

"To settle with her for the loss of the Brutus."

"When did you lose the Brutus."

Mr. Daney pulled at his ear, gazed at the porch light, rubbed his Adam's apple, and gave the exact date.

"What happened to the Brutus?"

"She just disappeared, Donald. She was tied up alongside the barge——"

The heavy hand on Mr. Daney's shoulder tightened a little. Donald was merely holding fast to the general manager in order to stay on his feet, but Mr. Daney credited him with being the victim of rising anger.

"When did Nan leave Port Agnew, Mr. Daney?"

"Let me see, Donald." Mr. Daney tugged at his beard. "Why, she left two weeks ago yesterday. Yes; she left on the nineteenth."

"When did you settle with her for the loss of the Brutus?"

"On the sixteenth," Daney answered glibly.

"How much?"

"Twenty-five hundred dollars. It was more than the

Brutus was worth, but I disliked to appear niggardly
in the matter, Donald. I knew you and your father
would approve whatever sum I settled for—and the
loss of the little boat provided a nice opportunity for
generosity without hurting the girl's pride."

"Yes—thank you, Mr. Daney. That was kind and
thoughtful of you." Donald spoke the words slowly
as if he searched his brain carefully for each word and
then had to coax his tongue into speaking it. "You
settled, then, two days after the boat disappeared
Fast work. Nobody up here would steal the boat
Too much distance between ports—run short of gaso
line, you know, on her limited tank capacity—and if
anybody had purchased cased gasoline around here
to load on deck, you'd know of it. Hard to conceal o
disguise a forty-foot boat, too." His fingers closed like
steel nippers over Mr. Daney's shoulder. "Where di
you hide the boat, Mr. Daney? Answer me. I'll no
be trifled with."

"I scuttled her—if you must have the truth."

"I knew you wouldn't lie to me. On whose orders
Mr. Daney? My father's?"

"No, sir; it was my own idea." Daney's face wa
white with mental and physical distress and red wit
confusion, by turns. His shoulder was numb.

"Why?"

"I figured that if the girl had some money to mak
a new start elsewhere, she'd leave Port Agnew, whic
would be best for all concerned."

"Why, Andrew Daney, you old hero! Cost you some
thing to confess that, didn't it? Well—I guessed yo
or my father had induced her to go, so I conclude
to start the investigation with you." He passed hi

and over his white dripping brow before resuming hat he had to say. "The Tyee Lumber Company isn't quipped to carry on its pay-roll Mr. Donald McKaye nd the man who interferes in his personal affair, even hough actuated by a kindly interest. You rip up that rack you're laying and leave Nan's home alone. Then ou clean up your desk and hand me your resignation. m sick—and your damned interference hurts. Sorry; ut you must go. Understand? Nan's coming back— nderstand? Coming back—devilish hot night—for iis time of year, isn't it? Man, I'm burning up."

It came to Mr. Daney that the young laird was acting a a most peculiar manner. Also, he was talking that ay. Consequently, and what with the distress of being ismissed from the McKaye service in such cavalier ashion, the general manager decided to twist out from nder that terrible grasp on his shoulder.

Instantly, Donald released from this support, swayed id clutched gropingly for Mr. Daney's person.

"Dizzy," he panted. "Head's on strike. Mr. Daney, here the devil are you? Don't run away from me. ou damned old muddler, if I get my hands on you I'll ick you apart—yes, I will—to see—what makes you). You did it. Yes, you did—even if you're too upidly honest—to lie about it. Glad of that, though, .r. Daney. Hate liars and interfering duffers. Ah— ie cold-blooded calculation of it—took advantage of :r poverty. She's gone—nobody knows— May God imn your soul to the deepest hell— Where are you? ll kill you—no, no; forgive me, sir— Yes, you've een faithful, and you're an old employe— I wish you very pleasant good-evening, sir."

He stepped gingerly down the three wide stairs,

pitched forward, and measured his length in a bed of
pansies. Mr. Daney came down, struck a match, and
looked at his white face. Donald was apparently unconscious; so Mr. Daney knelt, placed his inquisitive
nose close to the partly open lips, and sniffed. Then he
swore his chiefest oath.

"Hell's bells and panther-tracks! He isn't drunk.
He's sick."

Fifteen minutes later, the young Laird of Port Agnew
reposed in the best room of his own hospital, and Andrew Daney was risking his life motoring at top speed
up the cliff road to The Dreamerie with bad news for
old Hector. Mrs. McKaye and the girls had retired,
but The Laird was reading in the living-room when
Daney entered unannounced.

Old Hector looked up at his general manager from
under his white, shaggy brow.

"Ye, Andrew," he saluted the latter gently, "I see by
your face it's not welcome news you bring. Out with
it, man."

So Andrew came "out with it," omitting no detail,
and at the conclusion of his recital, the old man wagged
his head to emphasize his comprehension.

"My son is not a dull man by any means," he said
presently. "He knows what he knows—a man sure of
himself always—and oh, Andrew man, because of the
brain of him and the sweet soul of him, it breaks my
heart to give pain to him. And what does the doctor
say?"

"From a cursory examination he suspects typhoid
fever."

"Ah, that's bad, bad, Andrew."

"The boy has the strength of a Hercules, sir. He'll beat through, never fear."

"Well, he'll not die to-night, at any rate," old Hector answered, "and I can do no good puttering round the hospital to-night. Neither would I alarm his mother and the girls. Send for the best medical brains in the country, Andrew, and don't quibble at the cost. Pay them what they ask. 'Twill be cheap enough if they save him. Good-night, Andrew, and thank you kindly." He stood up and laid his hand affectionately upon the shoulder of his faithful servant and walked with him thus to the door. "My good Andrew," he murmured, and propelled the general manager gently outside, "there's no need to worry over the dismissal. When the lad's well, he'll rescind his order, so, in the meantime, do not leave us."

"But—if he shouldn't rescind it?" Daney pleaded anxiously. Although he was comfortably fixed with this world's goods and had long since ceased to work for monetary reward, the Tyee Lumber Company was, nevertheless, part of his life, and to be dismissed from its service was akin to having some very necessary part of him amputated.

"Tush, man; tush! Don't be building a mare's nest," old Hector answered and closed the door upon him. For The Laird was losing control of himself and he could not bear that any human eye should gaze upon his weakness.

XXVIII

THE morning following Donald's admittance to the hospital, the company doctor confirmed his original diagnosis that the patient was suffering from an attack of typhoid fever. The disease had evidently been two weeks incubating, for the woods boss reported that his superior had complained of being "under the weather" for ten days before yielding to the former's repeated advice to go down to Port Agnew and have the doctor look him over. As a result of Donald's stubborn refusal to acknowledge his illness, the disease had reached a fair stage of development by the time he received medical attention.

He was not delirious when The Laird and Mrs. McKaye reached the hospital that morning, however, they were permitted to see him for but a few minutes only.

"Has he a fighting chance?" old Hector demanded bluntly of the doctor. It seemed to him that his son's face already wore the look of one doomed to dissolution at an early date.

"Yes, he has, Mr. McKaye," the doctor replied gravely; "provided he'll fight. You will understand that in typhoid fever the mortality rate is rather high —as high as thirty per cent. However, in the case of Donald, who is a husky athlete, I should place the odds at about ten to one that he'll survive an attack of even more than moderate severity. That is," he added, "under the most favorable conditions."

"Well, what's wrong with the conditions in this case?" The Laird demanded crisply. "You can have anything you want—if you're shy on material to work with, and I've sent for the best physician in the state to come here and consult with you."

"The hospital conditions are perfect, Mr. McKaye. What I mean is this: It is a well recognized principle of medical practice that a patient combating a disease of extreme severity and high mortality is sustained quite as much by his courage and a passionate desire to get well—in a word, by his morale—as he is by his capacity for physical resistance. Your son is, I think, slightly depressed mentally. That is the sole reason I see to warrant apprehension."

"Oh—so that's all, eh?" The Laird was relieved. "Then don't worry about him. He'll put up a battle— never fear. Why, he never quit in all his life. However, in case he might need a bit of encouragement from his old daddy from time to time, you'll have a room made ready for me. I'll stay here till he's out of danger."

That was a terrible week on old Hector. The nurse, discovering that his presence appeared to excite her patient, forbade him the room; so he spent his days and part of his nights prowling up and down the corridor, with occasional visits to the mill office and The Dreamerie, there to draw such comfort from Daney and his family as he might. While his temperature remained below a hundred and four, Donald would lie in a semi-comatose condition, but the instant the thermometer crept beyond that point he would commence to mutter incoherently. Suddenly, he would announce, so

loudly The Laird could hear every word, that he contemplated the complete and immediate destruction of
Andrew Daney and would demand that the culprit be
brought before him. Sometimes he assumed that Daney
was present, and the not unusual phenomenon atten-
dant upon delirium occurred. When in good health
Donald never swore; neither would he tolerate rough
language in his presence from an employe; nevertheless, in his delirium he managed, at least once daily, to
heap upon the unfortunate Daney a generous helping
of invective of a quality that would have made a mule-
skinner blush. Sometimes Mr. Daney was unfortunate
enough to drop in at the hospital in time to hear this
stream of anathema sounding through the corridor;
upon such occasions he would go into The Laird's room
and he and old Hector would eye each other grimly but
say never a word.

Having demolished Mr. Daney with a verbal broad-
side, Donald would appear to consider his enemy dead
and direct his remarks to Nan Brent. He would reproach her tenderly for leaving Port Agnew without
informing him of her intention; he assured her he loved
her, and that unless she returned life would not be
worth living. Sometimes he would call upon old dead
Caleb to reason with her in his behalf. About
that time he would be emerging from a Brand bath
and, with the decline of his temperature, his mutterings
and complaints gradually grew incoherent again and
he would sleep.

Thus two weeks passed. Donald showed no sign of
the improvement which should ordinarily be looked for
in the third week, and it was apparent to the doctors
and nurses who attended him that the young Laird was

not making a fight to get well—that his tremendous physical resistance was gradually being undermined. His day-nurse it was who had the courage, womanlike, to bring the matter to an issue.

"He's madly in love with that Nan girl he's always raving about," she declared. "From all I can gather from his disconnected sentences, she has left Port Agnew forever, and he doesn't know where she is. Now, I've seen men—little, weak men—recover from a worse attack of typhoid than this big fellow has, and he ought to be on the up-grade now, if ever—yet he's headed down-hill. About next week he's going to start to coast, unless Nan Brent shows up to take him by the hand and lead him back up-hill. I believe she could do it— if she would."

"I believe she could, also," the doctor agreed. "Perhaps you've noticed that, although his family have listened to him rave about her, they have never given the slightest indication that they know what he is raving about. The girl's tabu, apparently."

"The Laird appears to be a human being. Have you spoken to him about this—Nan girl?"

"I tried to—once. He looked at me—and I didn't try any more. The fact is," the doctor added, lowering his voice, "I have a notion that old Hector, through Daney, gave the girl money to leave the country."

"If he knew what an important personage she is at this minute, he'd give her more money to come back— if only just long enough to save his son. Have you spoken to Mr. Daney?"

"No; but I think I had better. He has a great deal of influence with The Laird, and since I have no doubt they were in this conspiracy together, Daney may ven-

ture to discuss with the old man the advisability of
bringing the girl back to Port Agnew."

"If she doesn't appear on the scene within ten
days——"

"I agree with you. Guess I'll look up Mr. Daney."

He did. Daney was at his desk in the mill office
when the doctor entered and, without the least circum-
locution, apprised him of the desperate state to which
Donald was reduced.

"I tell you, Mr. Daney," he declared, and pounded
Daney's desk to emphasize his statement, "everything
that medical science can do for that boy has been
done, but he's slipping out from under us. Our last
hope lies in Nan Brent. If she can be induced to come
to his bedside, hold his hand, and call him pet names
when he's rational, he'll buck up and win out. There
are no dangerous physical complications to combat
now. They are entirely mental."

While the physician was speaking, Andrew Daney's
face had gradually been taking on the general color-
tones of a ripe old Edam cheese. His chin slowly sagged
on his breast; his lips parted in horror and amazement until, finally, his mouth hung open slackly, foolishly; presently, two enormous tears gathered in the
corners of his eyes and cascaded slowly across his cheeks
into his whiskers. He gripped the arms of his chair.

"O God, forgive me!" he moaned. "The Laird doesn't
know where she is, and neither do I. I induced her to
go away, and she's lost somewhere in the world. To
find her now would be like searching a haystack for a
needle."

"But you might telegraph a space-ad to every leading newspaper in the country. The Laird can afford

to spend a million to find her—if she can be found in a hurry. Why, even a telegram from her would help to buck him up."

But Andrew Daney could only sway in his chair and quiver with his profound distress.

"The scandal!" he kept murmuring, "the damned scandal! I'll have to go to Seattle to send the telegrams. The local office would leak. And even if we found her and induced her to come back to save him, she'd—she'd have to go away again—and if she wouldn't—if he wouldn't permit her—why, don't you see how impossible a situation has developed? Man, can Donald McKaye wed Nan Brent of the Sawdust Pile?"

"My interest in the case is neither sentimental nor ethical. It is entirely professional. It appears to me that in trying to save this young fellow from the girl, you've signed his death warrant; now it is up to you to save him from himself, and you're worrying because it may be necessary later to save the girl from him or him from the girl. Well, I've stated the facts to you, and I tried to state them to The Laird. Do as you think best. If the boy dies, of course, I'll swear that he was doomed, anyhow, due to perforation of the intestines."

"Yes, yes!" Daney gasped. "Let The Laird off as lightly as you can."

"Oh, I'll lie cheerfully. By the way, who is this girl? I haven't been in Port Agnew long enough to have acquired all the gossip. Is she impossible?"

"She's had a child born out of wedlock."

"Oh, then she's not a wanton?"

"I'm quite sure she is not."

"Well, I'll be damned! So that's all that's wrong with her, eh?" Like the majority of his profession, this physician looked up such a *contretemps* with a kindly and indulgent eye. In all probability, most of us would if we but knew as many of the secrets of men as do our doctors and lawyers.

Long after the doctor had left him alone with his terrible problem, Mr. Daney continued to sit in his chair, legs and arms asprawl, chin on breast. From time to time, he cried audibly:

"O Lord! O my God! What have I done? What shall I do? How shall I do it? O Lord!"

He was quite too incoherent for organized prayer; nevertheless his agonized cry to Omnipotence was, indeed, a supplication to which the Lord must have inclined favorably, for, in the midst of his desolation and bewilderment, the door opened and Dirty Dan O'Leary presented himself.

XXIX

THANKS to the constitution of a Nubian lion, Dirty Dan's wounds and contusions had healed very rapidly and after he got out of hospital, he spent ten days in recuperating his sadly depleted strength. His days he spent in the sunny lee of a lumber pile in the drying-yard, where, in defiance of the published ordinance, he smoked plug tobacco and perused the *Gaelic American*.

Now, Mr. O'Leary, as has been stated earlier in this chronicle, was bad black Irish. Since the advent of Oliver Cromwell into Ireland, the males of every generation of the particular tribe of O'Leary to which Dirty Dan belonged had actively or passively supported the battles of Ould Ireland against the hereditary enemy across the Channel, and Dirty Dan had suckled this holy hatred at his mother's breast; wherefore he regarded it in the light of his Christian duty to keep that hate alive by subscribing to the *Gaelic American* and believing all he read therein anent the woes of the Emerald Isle. Mr. O'Leary was also a member of an Irish-American revolutionary society, and was therefore aware that presently his kind of Irish were to rise, cast off their shackles (and, with the help o' God and the German kaiser) proclaim the Irish Republic.

For several months past, Daniel's dreams had dwelt mostly with bayonet-practice. Ordinary bayonets, however, were not for him. He dreamed his trusty steel

223

was as long as a cross-cut saw, and nightly he skewered
British soldiers on it after the fashion of kidneys and
bacon *en brochette*. For two months he had been saving his money toward a passage home to Ireland and
the purchase of a rifle and two thousand rounds of
ammunition—soft-nose bullets preferred—with the
pious intention of starting with "th' bhoys" at the very
beginning and going through with them to the bloody
and triumphant finish.

Unfortunately for Dirty Dan, his battle in defense
of Donald McKaye had delayed his sortie to the fields
of martyrdom. On the morning that Nan Brent left
Port Agnew, however, fortune had again smiled upon
The O'Leary. Meeting Judge Moore, who occupied two
local offices—justice of the peace and coroner—upon
the street, that functionary had informed Dan that the
public generally, and he and the town marshal in particular, traced an analogy between the death of the
mulatto in Darrow and Mr. O'Leary's recent sojourn
in the Tyee Lumber Company's hospital, and thereupon, verbally subpoenaed him to appear before a coroner's jury the following day at ten o'clock A. M., then
and there to tell what he knew about said homicide.

Dirty Dan received this summons with outward nonchalance but tremendous secret apprehensions, and immediately fled for advice to no less a person than Andrew Daney.

However, the Fates ordained that Andrew Daney
should be spared the trouble of advising Dirty Dan, for,
as the latter came shuffling down the hall toward Daney's office door, The Laird emerged from his old office
and accosted his henchman.

"Well, Dan!" he greeted the convalescent, "how do you find yourself these days?"

"Poorly, sir, poorly," Dirty Dan declared. " 'Twas only yisterd'y I had to take the other side av the shtreet to av'id a swamper from Darrow, sir."

The Laird smiled.

"Well, Dan, I think it's about time I did something to make you feel better. I owe you considerable for that night's work, so here's a thousand dollars for you, my boy. Go down to southern California or Florida for a month or two, and when you're back in your old form, report for duty. I have an idea Mr. Donald intends to make you foreman of the loading-sheds and the drying-yard when you're ready for duty."

"God bless ye, me lord, an' may the heavens be your bed!" murmured the astounded lumberjack, as The Laird produced his wallet and counted into Dan's grimy, quivering paw ten crisp hundred-dollar bills. "Oh, t'ank you, sor; t'ank you a t'ousand times, sor. An' ye'll promise me, won't ye, to sind for me firrst-off if ye should be wantin' some blackguard kilt?"

"I assure you, Dan, you are my sole official killer," laughed The Laird, and shook the O'Leary's hand with great heartiness. "Better take my advice about a good rest, Dan."

"Sor, I'll be afther havin' the vacation o' me life."

"Good-by, then, and good luck to you, Dan!"

"Good-by, an' God bless ye, sor!"

Five minutes later, Daniel J. O'Leary was in the general store fitting on what he termed a "Sunday suit." Also, he bought himself two white shirts of the "b'iled" variety, a red necktie, a brown Derby hat, and a pair of shoes, all too narrow to accommodate comfort-

ably his care-free toes. Next, he repaired to the bar-
ber-ship, where he had a hair-cut and a shave. His
ragged red mustache, ordinarily of the soup-strainer
pattern, he had trimmed, waxed, and turned up at each
end; the barber put much pomade on his hair and
combed it in a Mazeppa, with the result that when
Daniel J. O'Leary appeared at the railroad station the
following morning, and purchased a ticket for New
York City, Hector McKaye, loitering in front of the
station on the lookout for Nan Brent, looked at and
through Mr. O'Leary without recognizing him from
Adam's off ox.

It is, perhaps, superfluous to remark that Dirty Dan
was about to embark upon an enterprise designed to
make his dreams come true. He was headed for Ireland
and close grips with the hated redcoats as fast as train
and steamer could bear him.

Now, Mr. O'Leary had never seen Nan Brent, although he had heard her discussed in one or two bunk-
houses about the time her child had been born. Also,
he was a lumberjack, and since lumberjacks never speak
to the "main push" unless first spoken to, he did not
regard it as all necessary to bring himself to Hector
McKaye's notice when his alert intelligence informed
him that The Laird had failed to recognize him in his
going-away habiliments. Further, he could see with
half an eye that The Laird was waiting for somebody,
and when that somebody appeared on the scene, the imp
of suspicion in Dirty Dan's character whispered: "Begorra, is the father up to some shenanigans like the
son? Who's this girrl? I dunno. A young widder,
belike, seein' she has a youngster wit' her."

He saw Nan and The Laird enter into earnest con-

versation, and his curiosity mastering him, he ventured
to inquire of a roustabout who was loading baggage on
a truck who the young lady might be. Upon receiving
the desired information, he, with difficulty repressed
a whistle of amazement and understanding; instantly
his active imagination was at work.

The girl was leaving Port Agnew. That was evident.
Also, The Laird must have known of this, for he had
reached the station before the girl and waited for her.
Therefore, he must have had something to do with inducing her to depart. Mr. O'Leary concluded that it
was quite within the realm of possibility that The Laird
had made it well worth her while to refrain from wrecking the honor of his house, and he watched narrowly
to observe whether or not money passed between them.

One thing puzzled Dirty Dan extremely. That was
the perfectly frank, friendly manner in which his employer and this outcast woman greeted each other, the
earnestness with which they conversed, and the effect of
the woman's low-spoken words upon the color of Hector
McKaye's face. When The Laird took his leave, the
lumberjack noted the increased respect—the emotion,
even—with which he parted from her. The lumberjack heard him say, "Good-by, my dear, and good luck
to you wherever you go"; so it was obvious Nan Brent
was not coming back to Port Agnew. Knowing what
he knew, Mr. O'Leary decided that, upon the whole,
here was good riddance to the McKaye family of rub-
bish that might prove embarrassing if permitted to remain dumped on the Sawdust Pile.

"Poor gurrl," he reflected as he followed Nan aboard
the train. "She have a sweet face, that she have, God

forgive her! An be th' Rock av Cashel, she have a v'ice like an angel from heaven."

He sat down in a seat behind her and across the aisle, and all the way to Seattle he stared at the back of her neck or the beautiful rounded profile of her cheek. From time to time, he wondered how much Hector McKaye had paid her to disappear out of his son's life, and how that son would feel, and what he would say to his father when he discovered his light o' love had flown the cage.

The following morning Mr. O'Leary boarded a tourist-sleeper on the Canadian Pacific, and, to his profound amazement, discovered that Nan Brent and her child occupied a section in the same car.

"Begorra, she couldn't have shtuck the ould man very deep at that, or 'tis in a standard shleeper an' not a tourist she'd be riding," he reflected. "What the divil's up here at all, at all, I dunno."

Dirty Dan saw her enter a taxicab at the Grand Central Station in New York.

"I wonder if the young Caddyheck himself'll meet her here," Mr. O'Leary reflected, alive with sudden suspicion, and springing into the taxicab that drew in at the stand the instant the taxi bearing Nan and her child pulled out, he directed the driver to follow the car ahead, and in due course found himself before the entrance to a hotel in lower Broadway—one of that fast disappearing number of fifth-class hotels which were first-class thirty years ago.

Dirty Dan hovered in the offing until Nan had registered and gone up to her room. Immediately he registered also, and, while doing so, observed that Nan had signed her real name and given her address as Port

Agnew, Washington. With unexpected nicety, Dirty Dan decided not to embarrass her by registering from Port Agnew also, so he gave his address as Seattle.

For two days, he forgot the woes of Ireland and sat round the stuffy lobby, awaiting Nan Brent's next move. When he saw her at the cashier's window paying out, he concealed himself behind a newspaper, and watched her covertly as the clerk gave instructions to the head porter regarding the disposition of her baggage. The instant she left the hotel, accompanied by her child, Dirty Dan approached the porter and said with an insinuating smile:

"I'd give a dollar to know the address the young lady wit' the baby bhoy give you f'r the delivery av her trunk."

The porter reached for the dollar and handed Dirty Dan a shipping tag containing the address. Mr. O'Leary laboriously wrote the address in a filthy little memorandum-book, and that afternoon made a point of looking up Nan's new habitation. He discovered it to be an old brownstone front in lower Madison Avenue, and a blue-and-gold sign over the area fence indicated to Mr. O'Leary that, from an abode of ancient New York aristocracy, the place had degenerated into a respectable boarding-house.

" 'Tis true," Dirty Dan murmured. "She's given the young fella the go-by. Hurro! An' I'm bettin' I'm the only lad in the wide, wide wurrld that knows where she's gone. Faith, but wouldn't Misther Donald pay handsomely for the information in me little book."

Having, as he judged, followed the mystery to its logical conclusion, Mr. O'Leary was sensible of a sudden waning of his abnormal curiosity in Nan Brent's affairs. He acknowledged to himself that he had spent time and money on a matter that was absolutely none of his business, but excused himself upon the ground that if he hadn't investigated the matter thoroughly, his failure to do so might annoy him in the future. If, for no other reason than the desirability of being on the inside track of this little romance of a rich man's son, his action was to be commended. People have no business disappearing without leaving a trace or saying good-by to those that love them. Dirty Dan hadn't the least idea of selling his information to Donald Mc-Kaye, but something in his peculiar mental make-up caused him to cherish a secret for its own sake; he had a true Irishman's passion for being "in the know," and now that he was in it, he was tremendously satisfied with himself and dismissed the entire matter from his mind. Old Ireland and her woes were again paramount, so Mr. O'Leary presented himself before the proper authorities and applied for a passport to visit Ireland.

Now, while Daniel J. did not know it, one of the first questions the applicant for a passport is required to answer is his reason for desiring to make the journey, and during the Great War, as everybody of mature years will recall, civilians were not permitted to subject themselves to the dangers of a ruthless submarine war without good and sufficient reason. Mr. O'Leary had a reason—to his way of thinking, the noblest reason in all the world; consequently he was proud of it and not at all inclined to conceal it.

"I'm goin' over there," he declared, with profane emphasis, "to kill all the damned English I can before they kill me."

His interlocutor gravely wrote this reply down in

Mr. O'Leary's exact language and proceeded to the other questions. When the application was completed, Dirty Dan certified to the correctness of it, and was then smilingly informed that he had better go back where he came from, because his application for a passport was denied. Consumed with fury, the patriot thereupon aired his opinion of the Government of the United States, with particular reference to its representative then present, and in the pious hope of drowning his sorrows, went forth and proceeded to get drunk.

When drunk, Mr. O'Leary always insisted, in the early stages of his delirium, on singing Hibernian ballads descriptive of the unflinching courage, pure patriotism and heroic sacrifices of the late Owen Roe O'Neill and O'Donnell Abu. Later in the evening he would howl like a timber-wolf and throw glasses, and toward morning he always fought it out on the floor with some enemy. Of course, in the sawmill towns of the great Northwest, where folks knew Mr. O'Leary and others of his ilk, it was the custom to dodge the glasses and continue to discuss the price of logs. Toward Dirty Dan, however, New York turned a singularly cold shoulder. The instant he threw a glass, the barkeeper tapped him with a "billy"; then a policeman took him in tow, and the following morning, Dirty Dan, sick, sore, and repentant was explaining to a police judge that he was from Port Agnew, Washington, and really hadn't meant any harm. He was, therefore, fined five dollars and ordered to depart forthwith for Port Agnew, Washington, which he did, arriving there absolutely penniless and as hungry as a cougar in midwinter. He fled over to the mill kitchen, tossed about five dollars worth of ham and eggs and hot biscuit into his empty being, and began to take stock of life. Naturally, the first thing he recalled in mind was The Laird's remark that Donald planned to make him foreman of the loading-sheds and drying-yards; so he wasted no time in presenting himself before Donald's office door. To his repeated knocking there was no reply, so he sought Mr. Daney.

"Hello, Dan! You back?" Daney greeted him. "Glad to see you. Looking for Mr. Donald?"

"Yes, sor; thank you, sor."

"Mr. Donald is ill in the company's hospital. We're afraid, Dan, that he isn't going to pull through."

"Glory be!" Mr. O'Leary gasped, horrified on two counts. First, because he revered his young boss, and, second, because the latter's death might nullify his opportunity to become foreman of the loading-sheds and drying-yard. "Sure, what's happened to the poor bhoy?"

Before Daney could answer, a terrible suspicion shot through the agile and imaginative O'Leary brain. In common with several million of his countrymen, he always voiced the first thought that popped into his head; so he lowered that member, likewise his voice, peered cunningly into Andrew Daney's haggard face, and whispered:

"Don't tell me he tried to commit suicide, what wit' his poor broken heart an' all!"

It was Andrew Daney's turn to peer suspiciously at Dirty Dan. For a few seconds, they faced each other like a pair of belligerent game-cocks. Then said Daney:

"How do you know his heart was broken?"

Dirty Dan didn't know. The thought hadn't even

occurred to him until ten seconds before; yet, from
the solemnity of Daney's face and manner, he knew
instantly that once more his feet were about to tread the
trails of romance, and the knowledge imbued him with
a deep sense of importance.

He winked knowingly.

"Beggin' yer pardon, Misther Daney an' not m'anin'
the least offinse in life, but—I know a lot about that
young man—yis, an' the young leddy, too—that divil a
sowl on earth knows or is goin' to find out." He tried a
shot in the dark. "That was a clever bit o' wurrk
gettin' her out o' Port Agnew——"

Andrew Daney's hands closed about Dirty Dan's collar, and he was jerked violently into the latter's office,
while Daney closed and locked the door behind them.
The general manager was white and trembling.

"You damned, cunning mick, you!" he cried, in a
low voice. "I believe you're right. You do know a lot
about this affair——"

"Well, if I do, I haven't talked about it," Dirty Dan
reminded him with asperity.

"You knew the girl had left Port Agnew and why,
do you not?" Daney demanded.

"Of course I do. She left to plaze The Laird an' get
rid o' the young fella. Whether Th' Laird paid her to
go or not, I don't know, but I'll say this: 'If he gave
her anythin' at all, 'twas damned little.'"

"He didn't give her a red cent," Daney protested.

"I believe you, sor," Mr. O'Leary assured him, as
solemn as a Supreme Court justice. "I judged so be
the way she traveled an' the hotel she shtopped at."

Daney made another dive at the returned prodigal,
but Mr. O'Leary evaded him.

"Where did she travel, and what hotel did she put up at?" the general manager demanded.

"She traveled to the same places an' put up at the same hotels that I did," Dirty Dan replied evasively, for his natural love for intrigue bade him hoard his secret to the last.

Daney sat down and said very quietly: "Dan, do you know where Nan Brent may be found?"

"Where she *may* be found? Faith, I can tell you where she can be found—but I'll not."

"Why not?"

"Because 'tis her secret, an' why should I share it wit' you, m'anin' no disrespect, sor, at that?"

"Your sentiments do you honor, Dan—a heap more honor than I ever thought you possessed. If Mr. Donald's life should happen to be the price of your silence, however, you'd tell me, wouldn't you?"

"I would. The young gintlemin's blood runs in my veins, sor."

"Thank you, Dan. Give me her address."

"Number one eighty-five Madison Avenue, Noo Yorrk City," Dirty Dan replied promptly. "More I do not know. Am I on the pay-roll agin?"

"You bet! I'll pick out a good job for you as soon as I find time to think about it."

"Could I have a dollar or two in advance—" the wanderer began, as Daney hastened toward the door.

"Certainly." The door slammed, and Dirty Dan could hear the general manager shouting in the general office. "Dirty Dan is back. Give him some money."

Mr. O'Leary sighed contentedly.

"Oh-ho, 'tis the great life we live," he murmured, and

hastened outside to present himself at the cashier's window, while Andrew Daney continued on to the Tyee Lumber Company's hospital, tiptoed down the corridor to the room where the young Laird of Port Agnew lay dying, and rapped lightly on the door. A nurse came out and closed the door after her.

"Well?" Daney demanded.

"No change. His temperature fell two degrees during the night and he slept a little, but the fever is up again this morning, and he's raving again. Any news at your end?"

"Yes. I have the girl's address. She's in New York. Is his father inside?"

"Yes."

"Ask him to step into the reception room for a few minutes, please."

The Laird appeared promptly in response to this message, and the two men walked slowly down the hall to the reception-room. Daney closed the door and resolutely faced The Laird.

"The doctors and the nurses tell me things, sir, they're afraid to tell you," he began. "Ordinarily, the boy should be able to fight this thing through successfully, for he has a splendid body and a lot of resistance, but the fact of the matter is, he isn't trying. He doesn't want to get well."

The Laird's face went white.

"They believe this?" he cried sharply.

"They do. His subconscious mind clings to the memory of his loss. He keeps calling for her in his delirium, doesn't he? Now that he is assured she has dropped out of his life forever, he doesn't give a snap

whether school keeps or not—and the doctors cannot
cure him. If the girl were here—well, she might. Her
very presence would bring about a strong mental and
physical reaction—" He paused a moment. Then, "I
know where she can be found."

The Laird raised his haggard face and though his
stern gray eyes were dull with agony, yet Daney saw
in them the light of an unfaltering resolution.

"I have left my son's honor and his life in the hands
of God Almighty. I have made my bed and I'll lie in
it," he panted.

"But if the boy should die——"

"Rather that than—than——"

"But you're not going to take a chance on his pulling through, in the face of the advice of the doctors that
only the girl's presence can stimulate him to a desire
to live. I tell you, Hector McKaye, man, he's dying
because he is not interested in living."

"God's will be done, Andrew. If I asked her to come
back and save my lad, I'd have to surrender him to
her, and I would be derelict in my duty as a father if
I permitted that. Better that he should pass out now
than know the horror of a living death through all the
years to come. God knows best. It is up to Him. Let
there be no talk of this thing again, Andrew." Abruptly he quitted the room and returned to his vigil by
the side of the son who was at once the light and the
shadow of his existence.

The nurse came stealthily to the reception-room
entrance and looked in inquiringly. Daney shook his
head, so she came into the room and pointed at him a
singularly commanding index-finger.

"If that old man is permitted to have his stubborn way, Donald McKaye will die," she declared.

"So will old Hector. He'll be dead of a broken heart within the year."

"He's sacrificing his son to his Scotch pride. Now, his mother is far more bitter against the girl than The Laird is; in her distress she accuses the Brent girl of destroying her son. Nevertheless, Mrs. McKaye's pride and resentment are not so intense that she will sacrifice her son to them."

"Then give her this address," Daney suggested weakly, and handed it over. "I'm caught between the upper and nether millstone, and I don't care what happens to me. Damn the women, say I. Damn them! Damn them! They're the ones that do all the talking, set up a cruel moral code, and make a broad-minded, generous man follow it."

"Thanks for the compliment," the nurse retorted blithely. "If I had time, I'd discuss the matter with you to your disadvantage, but, fortunately, I have other fish to fry. My job is to keep Donald McKaye alive for the next five or six days until Nan Brent can get here. She'll come. I know she will. She'd lie down in the street and die for him. I know it. I spent two days with her when her father was dead, and let me tell you something, Mr. Daney: 'She's too good for them. There! I feel better now.' "

"What a remarkable woman!" Mr. Daney reflected, as he walked back to the mill office. "What a truly remarkable woman!" Then he remembered the complications that were about to ensue, and to the wonderment of several citizens of Port Agnew, he paused in front of the postoffice, threw both arms aloft in an agitated flourish, and cried audibly:

"Hell's bells and panther-tracks! I'd give a ripe peach to be in hell or some other seaport. O Lordy, Lordy, Lordy! And all the calves got loose!"

XXX

AS a wife, it is probable that Nellie McKaye had not been an altogether unqualified success. She lacked tact, understanding and sympathy where her husband was concerned; she was one of that numerous type of wife who loses a great deal of interest in her husband after their first child is born. The Laird's wife was normally intelligent, peacefully inclined, extremely good-looking both as to face and figure, despite her years, and always abnormally concerned over what the most inconsequential people in the world might think of her and hers. She had a passion for being socially "correct." Flights of imagination were rarely hers; on the few occasions when they were, her thoughts had to do with an advantageous marriage for Jane and Elizabeth, who, it must be confessed, had not had very good luck holding on to the few eligible young bachelors who had seemed, for a brief period, to regard them with serious intent. The poor soul was worried about the girls, as well she might be, since the strides of time were rapidly bearing both into the sere-and-yellow-leaf period of life. For her son, she had earnest, passionate mother love, but since, like all mothers, she was obsessed with the delusion that every girl in the world, eligible and ineligible, was busy angling for her darling, she had left his matrimonial future largely to his father. Frequently her conscience smote her for her neglect of old Hector, but she smoothed it by promising herself to devote more time to him, more study to his masculine needs for wifely devotion, as soon as Elizabeth and Jane should be settled.

Her son's acute illness and the possibility that he might not survive it had brought her closer to The Laird than these twain had been in twenty years; the blow that had all but crushed him had not even staggered her, for she told herself that, during this crisis she must keep her feet and her head. A wave of pity for her husband and a tinge of shame for her years of neglect of him revived more than a modicum of the old honeymoon tenderness, and, to her mild amazement, she discovered that she was still, in old Hector's eyes, young and beautiful; her breast, her lips, still had power to soothe and comfort.

In those trying days she was The Laird's greatest asset. With maternal stubbornness, she resolutely refused to entertain the thought that her son might die. She could understand the possibility of some other woman's son dying, but not hers! she, who knew him so well (or thought she did, which amounts to the same thing), met with gentle tolerance and contempt the portentous nods and anxious glances of doctors and trained nurses. 'Fraid-cats—every last one of them! She told old Hector so and, to a considerable extent, succeeded in making him believe it.

After The Laird's interview with Andrew Daney he came home that night to The Dreamerie, and, to please Nellie, he pretended to partake of some dinner. Also, during the course of the meal he suddenly decided to relate to his wife and daughters as much as he knew of the course of the affair between Donald and Nan Brent; he repeated his conversation with Nan on the

two occasions he had spoken with her, and gave them
to understand that his efforts to induce Donald to "be
sensible" had not been successful. Finally, his distress
making him more communicative, he related the cunning
stratagem by which Daney had made it possible for
Donald to be separated from the source of temptation.

Elizabeth was the first to comment on his extraordinary revelations when he appeared to have finished his
recital.

"The girl has a great deal more character than I
supposed," she opined in her soft, throaty contralto.

"She played the game in an absolutely ripping manner!" Jane declared enthusiastically. "I had no idea
she was possessed of so much force. Really, I should
love to be kind to her, if that were at all possible
now."

The Laird smiled but without animus.

"You had ample opportunity once, Janey," he reminded her. "But then, of course, unlike Donald and
myself, you had no opportunity for realizing what a
fine, wholesome lass she is." He lowered his gaze and
rolled a bread-crumb nervously between thumb and
forefinger. "They tell me at the hospital, Nellie," he
began again presently, "that her absence is killing our
boy—that he'll die if she doesn't come back. They've
been whispering to Daney, and this afternoon he mentioned the matter to me." Three pairs of eyes bent
upon him; gazes of mingled curiosity and distress.
"Have you heard aught of such talk from the doctors
and nurses," he continued, addressing them collectively.

"I have," said Mrs. McKaye meekly, and the two girls
nodded. "I think it's all poppycock," Jane added.

"It isn't all poppycock, my dear," old Hector re-

buked her. He rolled another bread-crumb. "Andrew
has her address," he resumed after a long silence.
"She's in New York. He asked me to wire her to come
immediately, or else permit him to wire her in my
name. I refused. I told Daney that our boy's case was
in the hands of God Almighty."

"Oh, Hector!" Mrs. McKaye had spoken. There
was gentle reproach and protest in her voice, but she
camouflaged it immediately by adding: "You poor
dear, to be called upon to make such a decision."

"His decision was absolutely right," Elizabeth declared. "I'd almost prefer to see my brother decently
dead than the laughing-stock of the town, married to a
woman that no respectable person would dare receive in
her home."

Old Hector looked up in time to see Jane nod approval of her sister's sentiments, and Mrs. McKaye,
by her silence, appeared also to agree with them. The
Laird reached forth and laid his great hand over
hers.

"Poor Nellie!" he murmured affectionately. "'Tis
hard to stand between our love and duty, is it not, lass?
By God, sweetheart, I had to do it. I couldn't stand
to see him wedded wie a lass that any man or woman
could throw mud at." His voice shook with the intensity of his emotion; his flashing glance swept the board
in pitiful defiance. "I have a right to protect my
honor and the honor of my house!" he cried sharply.
"Is not Jesus Christ the embodiment of honor? How
can He blame me if I trust in His power and discretion. I've prayed to Him—ach, man, how I've prayed
to Him— to keep my son from makin' a fule o' himself———"

"Now, there you go again, Hector, dear," his wife soothed. She rose from her place at the table, came round to him, put her arms around his great neck, and laid her cheek against his. "An open confession is good for the soul, they say, Hector. I'm glad you've taken us into your confidence, because it permits us to share with you an equal burden of this heart-breaking decision. But you mustn't feel badly, father. Haven't I told you our boy isn't going to die?"

"Do you really think so, Nellie?" he pleaded childishly, and for the hundredth time.

"Silly old Hector! I know so." And this time there was in her voice such a new note of confidence and in her eyes such a gleam of triumph that she actually did succeed in comforting him. "Ah, well, God's will be done," he said piously, and attacked his dinner again, while Mrs. McKaye slipped out of the room and upstairs on some pretext. Once in her bedroom, she seized the extension telephone and called up Andrew Daney.

"Andrew," she said softly but distinctly, "this is Nellie McKaye speaking. Hector and I have been discussing the advisability of sending for the Brent girl."

"I—I was goin' to take the matter up with you, Mrs. McKaye. I had a talk with your husband this afternoon, but he was a bit wild——"

"He isn't so wild now, Andrew. He's talked it over with the girls and me. It's a terrible alternative, Andrew, but it simply means our boy's life for the gratification of our own selfish family pride——"

"Exactly! Exactly! And though I understand just now you feel, Mrs. McKaye, after all, now, it's only a nine days' wonder, and you can't keep people from talk-

ing anyhow, unless you gag the brutes. The boy has
been raving, and some of the hospital attendants have
talked, and the gossip is all over town again. So why
not send for her? She doesn't have to marry him just
because her presence will revive his sinking morale——"

"Certainly not. My idea, exactly, Andrew. Well,
Andrew, suppose you telegraph her——"

"No, no, no! I'll telephone her. Remember, we have
a transcontinental telephone service nowadays. She
might not realize the vital necessity for speed; she might
question her right to come if I tried to cover the situation in a telegram. But, catch her on the 'phone, Mrs.
McKaye, and you can talk to her and convince her."

"Oh, that's perfectly splendid! Place the call for me
immediately, Andrew, please. And—Andrew, don't
mention to Hector what I've done. He wants to do it,
poor man, but he simply cannot bring himself to the
point of action."

"Don't I know it?" Daney's voice rose triumphant.
"The blessed old duffer!" he added. "I'll put in a call
for New York immediately. We ought to get it through
in an hour or two."

XXXI

IT was Mr. Daney's task to place the call for Nan Brent in New York City and while he did not relish the assignment, nevertheless he was far from shrinking from it. While the citizens of Port Agnew had been aware for more than two years that transcontinental telephoning was possible, they knew also that three minutes of conversation for twenty-five dollars tended to render silence more or less golden. As yet, therefore, no one in Port Agnew had essayed the great adventure; wherefore, Mr. Daney knew that when he did his conversation would be listened to eagerly by every telephone operator in the local office and a more or less garbled report of same circulated through the town before morning unless he took pains to prevent it. This he resolved to do, for the Tyee Lumber Company owned the local telephone company and it was quite generally understood in Port Agnew that Mr. Daney was high, low, and jack and the game, to use a sporting expression.

He stood by the telephone a moment after hanging up the receiver, and tugged at his beard reflectively.

"No," he murmured presently, "I haven't time to motor up-country forty or fifty miles and place the call in some town where we are not known. It just isn't going to be possible to smother this miserable affair; sooner or later the lid is going to fly off, so I might as well be game and let the tail go with the hide. Oh, damn it, damn it! If I didn't feel fully responsible for this dreadful state of affairs, I would most certainly stand from under!"

He turned from the 'phone and beheld Mrs. Daney, alert of countenance and fairly pop-eyed with excitement. She grasped her husband by the arm.

"You have a private line from the mill office to The Dreamerie," she reminded him. "Have the call run in on your office telephone, then call Mrs. McKaye, and switch her in. We can listen on the office extensions."

Upon his spouse Mr. Daney bent a look of profound contempt.

"When I consider the loyalty, the love, the forebearance, and Christian charity that have been necessary to restrain me from tearing asunder that which God, in a careless moment, joined together, Mary, I'm inclined to regard myself as four-fifths superman and the other fifth pure angel," he declared coldly. "This is something you're not in on, woman, and I hope the strain of your curiosity will make you sick for a week."

He seized his hat and fled, leaving his wife to shed bitter, scalding tears at his cruel words. Poor thing! She prided herself upon being the possessor of a superior brand of virtue and was always quick to take refuge in tears when any one decried that virtue; indeed, she never felt quite so virtuous as when she clothed herself, so to speak, in an atmosphere of patient resignation to insult and misunderstanding. People who delude themselves into the belief that they can camouflage their own nastiness and weaknesses from discovery by intelligent persons are the bane of existence, and in his better half poor Daney had a heavy cross to bear.

He left the house wishing he might dare to bawl aloud with anguish at the knowledge that he was yoked for life to a woman of whom he was secretly ashamed; he wished he might dare to get fearfully intoxicated and remain in that condition for a long time. In his youth, he had been shy and retiring, always envying the favor which the ladies appeared to extend to the daring devils of his acquaintance; consequently, his prenuptial existence had not been marked by any memorable amourous experiences, for where other young men sowed wild oats Mr. Daney planted a sweet forget-me-not. As a married man, he was a model of respectability— sacrosanct, almost. His idea of worldly happiness consisted in knowing that he was a solid, trustworthy business man, of undoubted years and discretion, whom no human being could blackmail. Now, as he fled from the odor of respectability he yearned to wallow in deviltry, to permit his soul, so long cramped in virtue, to expand in wickedness.

On his way down-town he met young Bert Darrow, son of the man after whom the adjacent lumber-town had been christened. Mr. Darrow had recently been indicted under the Mann law for a jolly little interstate romance. But yesterday, Mr. Daney had regarded Bert Darrow as a wastrel and had gone a block out of his way to avoid the scapegrace; to-night, however, Bert appealed to him as a man of courage, a devil of a fellow with spirit, a lover of life in its infinite moods and tenses, a lad with a fine contempt for public opinion and established morals. Morals? Bah, what were they! In France, Bert Darrow would have earned for himself a wink and a shrug, as though to say: "Ah, these young fellows! One must watch out for the rascals!" In the United States, he was a potential felon.

"Evening, Bert," Mr. Daney saluted him pleasantly, and paused long enough to shake the latter's hand. "I saw your ad in the Seattle *P. I.* this morning. You young dog! Hope you crawl out of that mess all right."

"*C'est la guerre,*" Bert murmured nonchalantly. "Thanks, awfully."

Mr. Daney felt better after that brief interview. He had clasped hands with sin and felt now like a human being.

He went directly to the local telephone office and placed his New York call with the chief operator, after which he sat in the manager's office and smoked until ten o'clock, when New York reported "Ready!"

"You young ladies," said Mr. Daney, addressing the two young women on duty, "may take a walk around the block. Port Agnew will not require any service for the next twenty minutes."

They assimilated his hint, and when he was alone with the chief operator Mr. Daney ordered her to switch the New York call on to Mrs. McKaye at The Dreamerie. Followed ten minutes of "Ready, Chicago." "All right, New York. Put your party on the line!"—a lot of persistent buzzing and sudden silence. Then: "Hello, Port Agnew."

Mr. Daney, listening on the extension in the office of the manager, recognized the voice instantly as Nan Brent's.

"Go on, Mrs. McKaye," he ordered. "That's the Brent girl calling Port Agnew."

"Hello, Miss Brent. This is Donald McKaye's mother speaking. Can you hear me distinctly?"

"Yes, Mrs. McKaye, quite distinctly."

"Donald is ill with typhoid fever. We are afraid he is not going to get well, Miss Brent. The doctors say that is because he does not want to live. Do you understand why this should be?"

"Yes; I think I understand perfectly."

"Will you come back to Port Agnew and help save him? We all think you can do it, Miss Brent. The doctors say you are the only one that can save him." There was a moment of hesitation. "His family desires this, then?" "Would I telephone across the continent if we did not?"

"I'll come, Mrs. McKaye—for his sake and yours. I suppose you understand why I left Port Agnew. If not, I will tell you. It was for his sake and that of his family."

"Thank you. I am aware of that, Miss Brent. Ah— of course you will be amply reimbursed for your time and trouble, Miss Brent. When he is well—when all danger of a relapse has passed—I think you realize, Miss Brent, all of the impossible aspects of this unfortunate affair which render it necessary to reduce matters strictly to a business basis."

"Quite, dear Mrs. McKaye. I shall return to Port Agnew—on business—starting to-morrow morning. If I arrive in time, I shall do my best to save your son, although to do so I shall probably have to promise not to leave him again. Of course, I realize that you do not expect me to keep that promise."

"Oh, I'm so sorry, my dear girl, that I cannot say 'No' to that. But then, since you realized, in the first place, how impossible——"

"Good-night. I must pack my trunk."

"Just a minute, my girl," Andrew Daney interrupted. "Daney speaking. When you get to Chicago, call up the C. M. St. P. station. I'll have a special train waiting there for you."

"Thank you, Mr. Daney. I'm sorry you cannot charter an airplane for me from New York to Chicago. Good-night, and tell Donald for me whatever you please."

"Send him a telegram," Daney pleaded. "Good-by." He turned to the chief operator and looked her squarely in the eyes. "The Laird likes discreet young women," he announced meaningly, "and rewards discretion. If you're not the highest paid chief operator in the state of Washington from this on, I'm a mighty poor guesser."

The girl smiled at him, and suddenly, for the first time in all his humdrum existence, Romance gripped Mr. Daney. He was riotously happy—and courageous! He thrust a finger under the girl's chin and tilted it in a most familiar manner, at the same time pinching it with his thumb.

"Young woman," he cautioned her, "don't you ever be prim and smug! And don't you ever marry any man until you're perfectly wild to do it; then, were he the devil himself, follow your own natural impulses." He let go her chin and shook his forefinger between her eyes. "I'd rather be happy than virtuous," the amazing man continued. "The calm placidity that comes of a love of virtue and the possession of it makes me sick! Such people are dull and stupid. They play hide-and-seek with themselves, I tell you. Suspicious little souls peering out of windows and shocked to death at everything they see or hear—condemn everything they do not understand. Damn it, girl, give me the virtue that's had to fight like the devil to stay on its feet—the kind that's been scratched and has had the corners knocked off in contact with the world and still believes that God made man to his own image and likeness. I tell you, the Lord knew what he was about when he invented the devil. If he hadn't, we'd all be so nasty-nice nobody could trust the other fellow further'n you can throw a bear up-hill by the tail. I tell you, young woman, sin is a great institution. Why, just think of all the fun we have in life—we good people—forgiving our neighbor his trespasses as he does not forgive us for trespassing against him."

And with this remarkable statement, Mr. Daney betook himself to his home. Mrs. Daney, a trifle red and watery about the eyes and nose, sat up in bed and demanded to be informed what had kept him down-town so late.

"Would you sleep any better if you knew?" he demanded.

She said she would not.

"Then, woman, resign yourself to the soft embrace of Bacchus, the god of sleep," he replied, mixed metaphorically. "As for me, my dear, I'm all talked out!"

XXXII

DONALD, trembling on the brink of Beyond, not
from his disease but from the exhaustion incident
to it, was conscious when his father entered the room
and sat down beside his bed.

"Well, lad," he greeted the boy with an assumption
of heartiness he was far from feeling, "and have you no
good news for your old father this morning. Tell me
you're feeling better, lad."

"Read the telegram," Donald whispered, and old
Hector, seeing a telegram lying on the bed, picked it up.
It was dated from New York that morning, and the
Laird read:

Due Port Agnew Friday morning. Remember the last
line in the fairy-tale. Love and kisses from your
SWEETHEART.

"God bless my soul!" The Laird almost shouted.
"Who the devil is 'Sweetheart'?"

"Only—have one—Scotty. Sorry—for you—but do
you—happen to know—last line—fairy-tale? Tell you.
'And so—they—were married—and lived—happy—
ever—after.'"

Fell a long silence. Then, from The Laird:

"And you're going to wait for—her, my son?"

"Certainly. Foolish die—now. I'll try—to wait.
Try hard."

He was still trying when Nan Brent stepped off the special train at Port Agnew on Friday morning. She was heavily veiled, and because of the distinctly metropolitan cut of her garments, none recognized her. With her child trotting at her side, she walked swiftly to the company hospital, and the nurse, who had been watching for her, met her at the door. The girl raised a white, haggard face, and her sad blue eyes asked the question. The nurse nodded, led her down the hall, pointed to the door of Donald's room, and then picked up Nan's child and carried him off to the hospital kitchen for a cookie.

The outcast of Port Agnew entered. Hector Mc-Kaye sat by the bed, gazing upon his son, who lay with closed eyes, so still and white and emaciated that a sudden fear rose in Nan's mind. Had she arrived too late?

The Laird turned and gazed at her an instant with dull eyes, then sprang to meet her.

"Well, lass," he demanded, and there was a belligerent and resentful note in his voice, "is this playing the game?" She nodded, her blurred eyes fixed upon his son, and old Hector's face softened with a tenderness almost paternal. "Then," he whispered, "you didn't mean that—about the last line of the fairy-tale?"

Her head moved in negation, but she did not look at him. She had eyes only for the wreck of the man she loved.

"I heard you needed me—to save him, Mr. McKaye. So I'm here—to save him, if I can—for you—nothing more."

He bowed to her, deeply, humbly, as if she were in truth the grandest lady in the land, then left the room hurriedly. Nan approached the bed and leaned over Donald, gazing at him for several minutes, for he was not as yet aware of her presence. Suddenly she commenced to sing softly the song he loved: "Carry Me Back to Old Virginny," and her hand stole into his. The little grin that crept over his bearded face was ghastly; after the first bar, she bent and laid her cool cheek against his.

"Well, old shipmate," she murmured in his ear, "I'm back."

" 'God's in—his heaven,' " he whispered. " 'All's right—with the—world.' "

XXXIII

FROM the company hospital, The Laird went straight to his general manager's office. Entering, he strode to Daney's desk and transfixed that harassed individual with an accusing finger.

"Andrew, this is your work, is it not?"

Mr. Daney's heart skipped a beat, but he remembered this was Friday morning. So he decided not to be foolish and spar for time by asking The Laird what work he referred to. Also, having read somewhere that, in battle, the offensive frequently wins—the defensive never—he glared defiantly at The Laird and growled.

"Well, what are you going to do about it?" His demeanor appeared to say: "This is my work, and I'm proud of it."

To Daney's profound amazement, The Laird smiled benignantly and thrust out his hand, which Mr. Daney shook gingerly, as one might a can of nitroglycerin.

"I thank you more than you will ever realize, Andrew, for taking this matter out of my hands. I left the decision up to the Almighty and evidently he inspired you to disobey me and save the day—without compromising me."

"Pooh! That's the easiest thing I do." Mr. Daney's courage had returned with a rush. "For heaven's sake, don't talk about it, sir. I placed a call for the girl on the telephone—at your expense. Yes, sir; I talked with her clear across the continent, and before

255

she even started from New York, it was understood that she is to jilt Donald the minute the doctors pronounce him strong enough to stand jilting."

"She told me, practically, the same thing. Oh, Andrew, Andrew, my boy, this is bully work! Bully! Bully!"

Mr. Daney replied to this encomium with a deprecatory shrug and hoped The Laird would never ask *him who had made the bargain.* Thus far, he flattered himself, he had not strayed from the straight and narrow path of strict veracity, and he hoped he would not have to. To obviate this, he decided to get rid of The Laird immediately; so he affected embarrassment; fussed with the pile of mail on his desk, and growled:

"All right, boss. If you're satisfied, I am. I haven't been able to sleep very well since I started mixing in your family affairs, and without sleep a man cannot hold up his job. I've got a lot of work to do, and I cannot have any idle, interfering fellows stampeding round my office; so I suggest that you run up to The Dreamerie to break the good news to your poor wife and the girls, and let me get something done."

"All right, Andrew; I'll go in a minute. Er—ah— you're certain, Andrew, the girl understands quite thoroughly that I haven't had a thing to do with bringing her back to Port Agnew?" The Laird smote the desk resolutely; he desired to be absolutely certain of his ground.

Mr. Daney looked up with a slight frown.

"I'll answer your question with another. Have you seen and talked with Nan Brent this morning?"

"Yes. I did—the minute she entered Donald's room."

"And you demanded a show-down then and there?"

Parenthetically it may be stated that Mr. Daney's intimate knowledge of The Laird's character prompted this question. He was certain of an affirmative reply.

"I did."

"And her answer was satisfactory?"

"Absolutely!"

"So I judged from the fact that you shook hands with me upon entering my office. I had expected nothing more nor less than instant dismissal . . . Well, since you desire the girl's testimony confirmed, I repeat that she came out here on the distinct understanding that Donald's family had not receded from its original position. This is a business trip, pure and simple, in so far as the McKaye family is concerned, although I grant you there is a heap of sentiment on Nan's part —at least sufficient to persuade her to do anything for the boy's sake. She places his welfare above her own."

The Laird nodded.

"The girl is capable of doing the most unexpected things, Andrew. I really think she'll play the game. When she told me what her intentions were, I believe she stated the absolute truth."

"Well, let us hope she doesn't change them, sir. Remember, she has no more intention of marrying him this morning than she had when she fled from Port Agnew. I was certain of that when listening to her on the telephone the other night. However, sir, I want to go on record, here and now, as disclaiming responsibility for anything that may occur hereafter. I am not the seventh son of a seventh son, and neither was I born with a caul. Hence, I do not pretend to foretell future events with any degree of exactitude. I simply guarantee you, sir, that the girl realizes that you have had nothing whatsoever, directly or indirectly, to do with the request for her return. Also, I give you my word of honor that I have not made her a single promise—directly or indirectly."

"Well, I am relieved. I dreaded the thought that I might be compromised—indirectly, for, as you well know, Andrew, I have a repugnance to asking favors from anybody to whom I am not prepared to grant them. My son is my chief happiness. Now, if I were to ask her to save my happiness, while at the same time reserving the right to deny the girl hers—well, thank God, I'm saved that embarrassment! Thanks to you, you fox!" he added.

"Bless my wicked heart! I'm glad you've gone and that I'm out of it so easy," the general manager soliloquized, as the door closed behind The Laird.

He reached for the telephone and called Mrs. McKaye at The Dreamerie.

"Your husband is on his way home, Mrs. McKaye," he advised her. "The girl is here, The Laird has met her and talked with her and is quite happy over the situation. However, I want to warn you that you will avoid unpleasantness by keeping from him the fact that you asked the Brent girl to come back to Port Agnew. He thinks I did that, and I have not seen fit, for reasons of my own, to deny it."

"Why, I asked you not to tell him, Andrew," she replied, surprised that he should forget it.

"I know. But you had planned to tell him yourself if, after the girl had arrived, you discovered he was secretly pleased that she had come."

"Yes; that is true. However, since you say Hector

is quite pleased with the situation, why should I not tell him, Andrew?"

"I have a suspicion the news will trouble him. He is quite willing to accept of the girl's services, as it were, but not at the behest of any member of his family. Better hear what he has to say on the subject before you commit yourself, Mrs. McKaye."

"Oh, I think I can be depended upon to manage Hector," she replied confidently, and hung up, for already through the window she could see The Laird's car taking the grade up Tyee Head. He arrived a few minutes later and entered smilingly, rubbing his hands as indicative of his entire satisfaction with the universe as constituted that morning.

"My dears, I have wonderful news for you!" he announced.

Elizabeth, warned by her mother of the impending announcement, and already in the latter's confidence regarding the long-distance conversation with Nan Brent, interrupted him. She was a born actress.

"Oh, do tell us quickly, daddy dear," she gushed, and flew to throw her arms round his neck. Over his shoulder she winked at Jane and her mother and grimaced knowingly.

"Donald's going to pull through. The doctors feel certain he'll take in the slack on his life-line, now that the Brent girl has suddenly turned up. In fact, the lad has been holding his own since he received a telegram from her some days back. I didn't tell you about that, my dears, not being desirous of worrying you; and since it was no doings of mine, I saw it could not be helped, and we'd have to make the best of it."

"Oh, daddy! How could you? That's perfectly

dreadful news!" the artful Elizabeth cried, while her
mother raised her eyes resignedly upward and clasped
her hands so tightly that they trembled. The Laird
thought his wife sought comfort from above; had he
known that she had just delivered a sincere vote of
thanks, he would not have hugged her to his heart, as
he forthwith proceeded to do.

"Now, now, Nellie, my dear," he soothed her, "it's all
for the best. Don't cross your bridges before you come
to them. Wait till I tell you everything. That fox,
Daney, had the common sense to call the girl on the
telephone and explain the situation; he induced her to
come out here and tease that soft-hearted moonstruck
son of ours back to life. And when Donald's strong
enough to stand alone—by Jupiter, that's exactly how
he's going to stand!—We're not the slightest bit compromised, my dears. The McKaye family is absolutely
in the clear. The girl has done this solely for Donald's sake."

"Hector McKaye," Jane declared, "you've really got
to do something very handsome for Andrew Daney."

"Yes, indeed," Elizabeth cooed.

"Dear, capable, faithful Andrew!" Mrs. McKaye
sighed.

"Ah, he's a canny lad, is Andrew," old Hector declared happily. "He took smart care not to compromise me, for well he knows my code. When I re-
jected his suggestion that I send for the lass, Andrew
knew why without asking foolish questions. Well, he
realized that if I should ask her to come and save my
son, I would not be unfair enough to tell her later that
she was not a fit wife for that son. As a matter o'
manly principle, I would have had to withdraw my

opposition, and Donald could wed her if he liked and with my blessing, for all the bitter cost. I did not build The Dreamerie with the thought that Donald would bring a wife like this Brent lass home to live in it, but —God be thanked!—the puir bairn loves him too well to ruin him——"

He broke off, wiping his eyes, moist now with the pressure of his emotions, and while he was wiping them, Mrs. McKaye and her daughters exchanged frightened glances. Elizabeth's penchant for ill-timed humor disappeared; she stood, alert and awed, biting her lip. Jane's eyebrows went up in quick warning to her mother, who paled and flushed alternately. The latter understood now why Andrew Daney had taken the precaution to warn her against the danger of conjugal confidences in the matter of Nan Brent; devoutly she wished she had had the common sense to have left those delicate negotiations entirely in the hands of dear, capable, faithful Andrew, for, delicate as they had been, she realized now, when it was too late, that in all probability Mr. Daney, although a mere man, would have concluded them without compromising the McKaye family. Surely he would have had the good taste to assure Nan that he was acting entirely upon his own initiative.

On the instant, Mrs. McKaye hated the unfortunate general manager. She told herself that, had he been possessed of the brains of a chipmunk, he would have pointed out to her the danger of her course; that he had not done so was proof that the craven had feared to compromise himself. He had made a cat's-paw of her, that's what he had done! He had taken advantage of a momentary lack of caution—the result of her impetuous mother love. Ah, what a blockhead the man was, not to have warned her of the diplomatic dangers she was risking! At that moment, placid Nellie Mc-Kaye could have shrieked with fury; it would have been a relief to her if she could have stuck her hatpin in that monumental chucklehead, Daney. Like so many of her sex, the good lady's code of sportsmanship was a curious one, to say the least. It had not been prudence but an instinctive desire to protect her son that had moved her to be careful when begging Nan to return to Port Agnew, to indicate that this request predicated no retirement from the resolute stand which the family had taken against the latter's alliance with Donald. In a hazy, indefinite way, she had realized the importance of nullifying any tendency on her part to compromise herself or her family by the mere act of telephoning to Nan, and with the unintentional brutality of a not very intelligent, tactless woman she had taken this means of protection.

Curiously enough, it had not occurred to her until this moment that she had done something shameful and cruel and stupid and unwomanly. She shriveled mentally in the contemplation of it. Not until her husband had so unexpectedly revealed to her a hitherto hidden facet of his character—his masculine code of an eye for an eye and a tooth for a tooth—did she realize how dreadfully she had blundered. She realized now that, without having given the slightest thought to the commission of an act unworthy of her womanhood, she had acted because, to her, the end appeared to justify the means; never given to self-analysis, she had merely followed the imperative call of her mother love to the point where nothing mattered save results.

She looked up tearfully at The Laird. For thirty-odd years she had lived with this strange soul; yet she had not known until now how fierce was his desire for independence, how dear to him was his passion for self-respect. Even now, she found it difficult to understand why, even if he had been able to subdue his pride to the point of asking Nan Brent to preserve life in that which was dearer to him than his own life, his passion for always giving value received should preclude bargaining with the girl. It was plain to her, therefore, that her husband could never love their son as his mother loved him, else, in a matter of life or death, he would not have paused to consider the effect on himself of any action that might safeguard his son's existence. She knew what he had thought when Daney first proposed the matter to him. That sort of thing wasn't "playing the game." Poor, troubled soul! She did not know that he was capable of playing any game to the finish, even though every point scored against him should burn like a branding-iron.

The Laird, noting her great distress, held her fondly in his arms and soothed her; manlike, he assumed that she wept because her heart was overflowing with joy. For half an hour he chatted with her; then, with a light step and a cheerful "Good-by, Nellie, wife," he entered his automobile and drove back to town.

His departure was the signal for Jane and Elizabeth to rally to their mother's side and inaugurate a plan of defense.

"Well, mother dear," Elizabeth opined calmly, "it appears that you've spilled the beans."

"What a funny old popsy-wops it is, to be sure!" Jane chirped. "It's fine to be such a grand old sport, but so dreadfully inconvenient! Beth, can you imagine what father McKaye would say if he only knew?"

"I wouldn't mind the things he'd say. The things he'd do would be apt to linger longest in our memories."

"Oh, my dears, what shall I do?" poor Mrs. McKaye quavered.

"Stand pat, should necessity ever arise, and put the buck up to Mr. Daney," the slangy Elizabeth suggested promptly. "He has warned you not to confess to father, hasn't he? Now, why did he do this? Answer: Because he realized that if dad should learn that you telephoned this odious creature from the Sawdust Pile, the head of our clan would consider himself compromised—bound by the action of a member of his clan, as it were. Then we'll have a wedding and after the wedding we'll all be thrown out of The Dreamerie to make room for Master Don and his consort. So, it appears to me, since Mr. Daney has warned you not to tell, mother dear, that he cannot afford to tell on you himself—no, not even to save his own skin."

"You do not understand, Elizabeth," Mrs. McKaye sobbed. "It isn't because that stupid Andrew cares a snap of his finger for us; it's because he's devoted to Hector and doesn't want him worried or made unhappy."

And in this observation, it is more than probable that the lady spoke more truly than she realized.

"Oh, well, if that's the case, it's all as clear as mud!" Jane cried triumphantly. "If the worst should ever come to the worst, Mr. Daney will lie like a gentleman and—why, he has already done so, silly! Of course he has, and it's rather gallant of him to do it, I think."

"He's an imbecile, and why Hector has employed him all these years—why he trusts him so implicitly, I'm sure I am at a loss to comprehend." Mrs. McKaye complained waspishly.

"Dear, capable, faithful Andrew!" Elizabeth mimicked her mother's speech earlier in the day. "Cheer up, ma! Cherries are ripe." She snapped her fingers, swayed her lithe body, and undulated gracefully to the piano, where she brought both hands down on the keys with a crash, and played ragtime with feverish fury for five minutes. Then, her impish nature asserting itself, she literally smashed out the opening bars of the Wedding March from Lohengrin, and shouted with glee when her mother, a finger in each ear, fled from the room.

XXXIV

MR. DANEY worked through a stack of mail with his stenographer, dismissed her, and, in the privacy of his sanctum, lighted his pipe and proceeded to mend his fences. In the discretion of the chief operator at the telephone exchange, he had great confidence; in that of Mrs. McKaye, none at all. He believed that the risk of having the secret leak out through Nan herself was a negligible one, and, of course (provided he did not talk in his sleep) the reason for Nan's return was absolutely safe with him. Indeed, the very fact that The Laird had demanded and received an explanation from the girl would indicate to Nan that Mrs. McKaye had acted on her own initiative; hence, Nan would, in all probability, refrain from disclosing this fact to The Laird in any future conversations.

Reasoning further, Daney concluded there would be no future conversations. The Laird, following his usual custom of refraining from discussing a subject already settled to his satisfaction, could be depended upon to avoid a discussion of any kind with Nan Brent in future, for such discussions would not be to his interest, and he was singularly adept in guarding that interest.

His cogitations were interrupted by a telephone-call from Mrs. McKaye. The good soul's first gust of resentment having passed, she desired to thank him for his timely warning and to assure him that, on the subject of that transcontinental telephone-conversation she and her daughters could be depended upon to remain as silent as the Sphinx.

This information relieved Mr. Daney greatly. "After all," he confided to the cuspidor, "it is up to the girl whether we fish or cut bait. But then, what man in his senses can trust a woman to stay put. Females are always making high dives into shoal water, and those tactless McKaye women are going to smear everything up yet. You wait and see."

The longer Mr. Daney considered this situation, the more convinced did he become that mischief was brewing. Did not periods of seraphic calm always precede a tornado? In the impending social explosion, a few hard missiles would most certainly come his way, and in a sudden agony of apprehension and shame because he had told The Laird a half-truth, he sprang to his feet, resolved to seek old Hector, inform him that Mrs. McKaye had compromised the family, and thus enable him to meet the issue like a gentleman. But this decision was succeeded by the reflection that perhaps this action would merely serve to precipitate a situation that might not be evolved in the ordinary course of affairs. Furthermore, he could not afford to betray Mrs. McKaye on the mere suspicion that, sooner or later, she would betray herself, for this would savor of too much anxiety to save his own skin at her expense. "I'm a singularly unhappy old duffer," he groaned and kicked his inoffending waste-basket across the office. "The females! The mischief-making, bungling, thoughtless, crazy females! There are millions of wonderful, angelic women in this terrible world, but what I want to know is: Where the Sam Hill do they hide themselves?"

XXXV

NAN did not remain at the hospital more than fifteen minutes. She was ill at ease there; it was no
comfort to her to gaze upon the pallid, wasted face of
the man she loved when she realized that, by her presence here, she was constituting herself a party to a
heart-breaking swindle, and must deny herself the joy
of gazing upon that same beloved countenance when,
later, it should be glowing with health and youth and
high hopes. He was too weak to speak more than a
few words to her. The faintest imaginable pressure of
his hand answered the pressure of hers. It appeared to
be a tremendous effort for him to open his eyes and look
up at her. When, however, he had satisfied his swim-
ming senses that she was really there in the flesh, he
murmured:

"You'll not—run away—again? Promise?"

"I promise, dear. The next time I leave Port Agnew,
I'll say good-by."

"You must not—leave—again. Promise?"

She knew his life might be the reward of a kindly
lie; so she told it, bravely and without hesitation. Was
she not there for that purpose?

"Good—news! If I get—well, will you—marry me,
Nan?" She choked up then; nevertheless, she nodded.

"More good—news! Wait for me—Sawdust Pile—
sweetheart."

She interpreted this as a dismissal, and gratefully

made her exit. From the hospital office she telephoned orders to the butcher, the baker, the grocer, and the milk-
man, forcibly separated little Don from the nurse, and
walked down through Port Agnew to the Sawdust Pile.

The old-fashioned garden welcomed her with its fra-
grance; her cat, which she had been unable to give away
and had not the heart to destroy at the time of her
departure, came to the little white gate to meet her and
rubbed against her, purring contentedly—apparently
none the worse for a month of vagabondage and richer
by a litter of kittens that blinked at Nan from under
the kitchen stoop. From across the Bight of Tyee, the
morning breeze brought her the grateful odor of the
sea, while the white sea-gulls, prinking themselves on
the pile-butts at the outer edge of the Sawdust Pile,
raised raucous cries at her approach and hopped
toward her in anticipation of the scraps she had been
wont to toss them. She resurrected the key from its
hiding-place under the eaves, and her hot tears fell so
fast that it was with difficulty she could insert it in
the door. Poor derelict on the sea of life, she had
gone out with the ebb and had been swept back on the
flood, to bob around for a little while in the cross-cur-
rents of human destinies before going out again with
the ebb.

The air in the little house was hot and fetid; so she
threw open the doors and windows. Dust had accumulated everywhere and, with a certain detachment,
she noted, even in her distress, that she had gone away
without closing the great square piano. She ran her
fingers over the dusty keys and brought forth a few
sonorous chords; then she observed that the little, ancient, half-portion grandfather's clock had died of in-

anition; so she made a mental note to listen for the twelve-o'clock whistle on the Tyee mill and set the clock by it. The spigot over the kitchen sink was leaking a little, and it occurred to her, in the same curious detached way, that it needed a new gasket.

She sighed. Once more, in this silent little house so fraught with happy memories, the old burden of existence was bearing upon her—the feeling that she was in jail. For a month she had been free—free to walk the streets, to look in shop windows, to seek a livelihood and talk to other human beings without that terrible feeling that, no matter how pleasant they might appear to be, their eyes were secretly appraising her —that they were *thinking*. And now to be forced to abandon that freedom——

"Oh, well! It can't last forever," she soliloquized, and, blinking away her tears, she proceeded to change into a house dress and put her little home in order. Presently, the local expressman arrived with her baggage and was followed by sundry youths bearing sundry provisions; at twelve-thirty, when she and young Don sat down to the luncheon she had prepared, her flight to New York and return appeared singularly unreal, like the memory of a dream.

She visited the hospital next day, choosing an hour when Port Agnew was at its evening meal and too preoccupied with that important detail to note her coming and going. She returned to her home under cover of darkness.

At the hospital, she had received a favorable report of the patient's progress. His physicians were distinctly encouraged. Nan looked in on her lover for a minute, and then hurried away on the plea that her

baby was locked in at the Sawdust Pile, in the absence
of some one to care for him; she had the usual maternal presentiment that he was playing with matches.

As she was going out she met The Laird and Mrs.
McKaye coming in. Old Hector lifted his hat and said
quite heartily:

"How do you do, my dear girl. The news this evening is most encouraging—thanks to you, I'm told—so
we are permitted to see Donald for five minutes. Nellie,
my dear, you remember little Nan Brent, do you not?"

Mrs. McKaye's handsome mouth contracted in a
small, automatic smile that did not extend to her eyes.
She acknowledged Nan's "Good-evening, Mrs. Mc-
Kaye," with a brief nod, and again favored the girl
with another property smile, between the coming and
going of which her teeth flashed with the swiftness of
the opening and closing of a camera shutter.

"We are *so* grateful to you, Miss Brent," she murmured. And then, womanlike, her alert brown eyes,
starting their appraisal at Nan's shoes, roved swiftly
and calmly upward, noting every item of her dress,
every soft seductive curve of her healthy young body.
Her glance came to a rest on the girl's face, and for
the space of several seconds they looked at each other
frankly while old Hector was saying:

"Aye, grateful indeed, Nan. We shall never be out
of your debt. There are times when a kindness and a
sacrifice are all the more welcome because unexpected,
and we had no right to expect this of you. God bless
you, my dear, and remember—I am always your friend."

"Yes, indeed," his wife murmured, in a voice that,
lacking his enthusiasm, conveyed to Nan the informa-

tion that The Laird spoke for himself. She tugged gently at her husband's arm; again the automatic smile; with a cool: "Good-night, Miss Brent. Thank you again—*so* much," she propelled The Laird toward the hospital entrance. He obeyed promptly, glad to escape a situation that was painful to him, for he had realized that which his wife did not credit him with having suf· ficiently acute perception to realize—to-wit, that his wife's camouflage was somewhat frayed and poorly manufactured. *She had not played the game with him.* It would have cost her nothing to have been as kindly and sincere as he had been toward this unfortunate girl; nevertheless, while he had sensed her deficiency, his wife had carried the affair off so well that he could not advance a sound argument to convince her of it. So he merely remarked dryly as the hospital door closed behind them:

"Nellie, I'm going to propound a conundrum for you. Why did your greeting of the Brent girl remind me of that Louis Quinze tapestry for which you paid sixty thousand francs the last time you were abroad?"

"I loathe conundrums, Hector," she replied coldly. "I do not care to guess the answer."

"The answer is: Not quite genuine," he retorted mild-ly, and said no more about it.

After that visit, Nan went no more to the hospital. She had met Donald's mother for the first time in four years and had been greeted as "Miss Brent," although in an elder day when, as a child, Donald had brought her to The Dreamerie to visit his mother and sisters, and later when she had sung in the local Presbyterian choir, Mrs. McKaye and her daughters had been wont to greet her as "Nan." The girl did not relish the prospect of facing again that camera-shutter smile and she shrank with the utmost distress from a chance meeting at the hospital with Elizabeth or Jane McKaye. As for The Laird, while she never felt ill at ease in his presence, still she preferred to meet him as infrequently as possible. As a result of this decision, she wrote Andrew Daney, and after explaining to him what she intended doing and why, asked him if he would not send some trustworthy person to her every evening with a report of Donald's progress.

Accordingly, Dirty Dan O'Leary, hat in hand and greatly embarrassed, presented himself at the Sawdust Pile the following evening under cover of darkness, and handed her a note from Daney. Donald's condition was continuing to improve. For his services, Mr. O'Leary was duly thanked and given a bouquet from Nan's old-fashioned garden for presentation to the invalid. Tucked away in the heart of it was a tiny envelop that enclosed a message of love and cheer.

Dirty Dan was thrilled to think that he had been selected as the intermediary in this secret romance. Clasping the bouquet in his grimy left hand, he bowed low and placed his equally grimy right in the region of his umbilicus.

"Me hearrt's wit' ye, agra," he declared. "Sure 'tis to the divil an' back agin I'd be the proud man to go, if 'twould be a favor to ye, Miss Brint."

"I know you would, Dan," she agreed, tactfully setting the wild rascal at his ease when addressing him by his Christian name. "I know what you did for Mr. Donald that night. I think you're very, very wonderful. I haven't had an opportunity heretofore to tell you how grateful I am to you for saving him."

Here was a mystery! Mr. O'Leary in his Sunday clothes bound for Ireland resembled Dirty Dan O'Leary in the raiment of a lumberjack, his wild hair no longer controlled by judicious applications of pomade and his mustache now—alas—returned to its original state of neglect, as a butterfly resembles a caterpillar. Without pausing to consider this, Dirty Dan, taking the license of a more or less privileged character, queried impudently:

"An' are ye glad they sint for ye to come back?"

She decided that Mr. O'Leary was inclined to be familiar; so she merely looked at him and her cool glance chilled him.

"Becuz if ye are," he continued, embarrassed, "ye have me to thank for it. 'Tis meself that knows a thing or two wit'out bein' told. Have ye not been surprised that they knew so well where to find ye whin they wanted ye?"

She stared at him in frank amazement.

"Yes, I have been tremendously interested in learning the secret of their marvelous perspicacity."

"I supplied Misther Daney wit' your address, allanah."

"How did you know it? Did The Laird——"

"He did not. I did it all be mesel'. Ah, 'tis the romantic divil I am, Miss Brint. Sure I got a notion ye were runnin' away an' says I to meself, says I: 'I don't like this idjee at all, at all. These mysterious disappearances are always leadin' to throuble.' Sure, what if somebody should die an' lave ye a fortun'? What good would it be to ye if nobody could find ye? An' in back o' that agin," he assured her cunningly, "I realized what a popular laddy buck I'd be wit'

Misther Donald if I knew what he didn't know but was wishful o' knowin'?"

"But how did you procure my address in New York?" she demanded.

"Now, I'm a wise man, but if I towld ye that, ye'd be as wise as I am. An' since 'twould break me heart to think anybody in Port Agnew could be as wise as me-sel', ye'll have to excuse me from blatherin' all I know."

"Oh, but you must tell me, Dan. There are reasons why I should know, and you wouldn't refuse to set my mind at ease, would you?"

Dirty Dan grinned and played his ace.

"If ye'll sing 'The Low-backed Car' an' 'She Moved Through the Fair' I'll tell ye," he promised. "Sure I listened to ye the night o' the battle, an' so close to death was I, sure I t'ought 'twas an angel from glory singin'. Troth, I did."

She sat down, laughing, at the antiquated piano, and sang him the songs he loved; then, because she owed him a great debt she sang for him "Kathleen Mavourneen," "Pretty Molly Brannigan," "The Harp That Once Thro' Tara's Halls," and "Killarney." Dan stood just outside the kitchen door, not presuming to enter, and when the last song was finished, he had tears in his piggy little eyes; so he fled with the posies, nor tarried to thank her and wish her a pleasant good-night. Neither did he keep his promise by telling her how he came to know her New York address.

"Let me hear anny blackguard mintion that one's name wit' a lack o' respect," Mr. O'Leary breathed, as he crossed the vacant lots, "an' I'll break the back o' him in two halves! Whirro-o-o! Sure I'd make a mummy out o' him!"

XXXVI

A MONTH passed, and to the Sawdust Pile one evening, instead of Dirty Dan, there came another messenger. It was Mr. Daney. To Nan's invitation to enter and be seated, he gave ready acceptance; once seated, however, he showed indubitable evidence of uneasiness, and that he was the bearer of news of more than ordinary interest was apparent by the nervous manner in which he twirled his hat and scattered over her clean floor a quantity of sawdust which had accumulated under the rim during his peregrinations round the mill that day.

"Well, Nan, he went home to The Dreamerie this afternoon," the general manager began presently. "Got up and dressed himself unaided, and insisted on walking out to the car without assistance. He's back on a solid diet now, and the way he's filling up the chinks in his superstructure is a sight to marvel at. I expect he'll be back on the job within a month."

"That is wonderful news, Mr. Daney."

"Of course," Daney continued, "his hair is falling out, and he'll soon be as bald as a Chihuahua dog. But—it'll grow in again. Yes, indeed. It'll grow in."

"Oh dear! I do hope it will grow out," she bantered, in an effort to put him at his ease. "What a pity if his illness should leave poor Don with a head like a thistle—with all the fuzzy-wuzzy inside."

He laughed.

"I'm glad to find you in such good spirits, Nan, because I've called to talk business. And, for some reason or other, I do not relish my job."

"Then, suppose I dismiss you from this particular job, Mr. Daney. Suppose I decline to discuss business."

"Oh, but business is something that has to be discussed sooner or later," he asured her, on the authority of one whose life had been dedicated to that exacting duty. "I suppose you've kept track of your expenses since you left New York. That, of course, will include the outlay for your living-expenses while here, and in order to make doubly certain that we are on the safe side, I am instructed to double this total to cover the additional expenses of your return to New York. And if you will set a value upon your lost time from the day you left New York until your return, both days inclusive, I will include that in the check also."

"Suppose I should charge you one thousand dollars a day for my lost time," she suggested curiously.

"I should pay it without the slightest quibble. The Laird would be delighted to get off so cheaply. He feels himself obligated to you for returning to Port Agnew——"

"Did The Laird send you here to adjust these financial details with me, Mr. Daney?"

"He did not. The matter is entirely in my hands. Certainly, in all justice, you should be reimbursed for the expenses of a journey voluntarily incurred for the McKaye benefit."

"Did he say so?"

"No. But I know him so well that I have little difficulty in anticipating his desires. I am acting under

Mrs. McKaye's promise to you over the telephone to reimburse you."

"I am glad to know that, Mr. Daney. I have a very high regard for Donald's father, and I should not care to convict him of an attempt to settle with me on a cash basis for declining to marry his son. I wish you would inform The Laird, Mr. Daney, that what I did was done because it pleased me to do it for his sake and Donald's. They have been at some pains, throughout the years, to be kind to the Brents, but, unfortunately for the Brents, opportunities for reciprocity have always been lacking until the night Mrs. McKaye telephoned me in New York. I cannot afford the gratification of very many desires—even very simple ones, Mr. Daney—but this happens to be one of the rare occasions when I can. To quote Sir Anthony Gloster, 'Thank God I can pay for my fancies!' The Laird doesn't owe me a dollar, and I beg you, Mr. Daney, not to distress me by offering it."

"But, my dear girl, it has cost you at least five hundred dollars——"

"What a marvelous sunset we had this evening, Mr. Daney. Did you observe it? My father always maintained that those curious clouds predicated sou'west squalls."

"I didn't come here, girl, to talk about sunsets. You're foolish if you do not accept——"

The outcast of Port Agnew turned upon Mr. Daney a pair of sea-blue eyes that flashed dangerously.

"I think I have paid my debt to the McKayes," she declared, and in her calm voice there was a sibilant little note of passion. "Indeed, I have a slight credit-balance due me, and though Mrs. McKaye and her daugh-

ters cannot bring themselves to the point of acknowl-
edging this indebtedness, I must insist upon collecting
it. In view of the justice of my claim, however, I cannot stultify my womanhood by permitting the Mc-
Kaye women to think they can dismiss the obligation by
writing a check. I am not an abandoned woman, Mr.
Daney. I have sensibilities and, strange to relate, I,
too, have pride—more than the McKayes I think sometimes. It is possible to insult me, to hurt me, and cause
me to suffer cruelty, and I tell you, Mr. Daney, I would
rather lie down and die by the roadside than accept one
penny of McKaye money."

Mr. Daney stared at her, visibly distressed.

"Why, what's happened?" he blurted.

She ignored him.

"I repeat that The Laird owes me nothing—not even
his thanks. I met him one night with Mrs. McKaye on
the hospital steps, and he tendered me his meed of
gratitude like the splendid gentleman he is."

"Oh, I see!" A great light had suddenly dawned on
Mr. Daney. "The Laird led trumps, but Nellie Mc-
Kaye revoked and played a little deuce?"

"Well, Mr. Daney, it seemed to me she fumbled the
ball, to employ a sporting metaphor. She bowed to me
—like this—and smiled at me—like that!" Her cool,
patronizing nod and the sudden contraction and relaxa-
tion of Nan's facial muscles brought a wry smile to old
Daney's stolid countenance. "Even if I felt that I
could afford to or was forced to accept reimbursement
for my expenses and lost time," Nan resumed, "her action precluded it. Can't you realize that, Mr. Daney?
And Jane and Elizabeth went her one—no, two—better. I'm going to tell you about it. I went up-town the

other day to send a telegram, and in the telegraph-office I met Donald's sisters. I knew they would not care to have me speak to them in public, so, when the telegrapher wasn't looking at me and intuition told me that Eliazbeth and Jane were, I glanced up and favored them with a very small but very polite smile of recognition."

"And then," quoted Mr. Daney, reaching into his ragbag of a mind and bringing up a remnant of Shakespeare, " 'there came a frost—a killing frost!' "

"Two hundred and forty-five degrees below zero, and not even a stick of kindling in the wood-box," she assured him humorously. "They looked at me, through me, over me, beyond me——"

"And never batted an eye?"

"Not even the flicker of an eyelash."

His canine loyalty bade Mr. Daney defend The Laird's ewe lambs.

"Well, maybe they didn't recognize you," he protested. "A good deal of water has run under a number of bridges since the McKaye girls saw you last."

"In that event, Mr. Daney, I charge that their manners would have been extremely bad. I know town dogs that smile at me when I smile at them. However, much as I would like to assure you that they didn't know me, I must insist, Mr. Daney, that they did."

"Well, now, how do you know, Nan?"

"A little devil took possession of me, Mr. Daney, and inspired me to smoke them out. I walked up and held out my hand to Jane. 'How do you do, Jane,' I said. 'I'm Nan Brent. Have you forgotten me?' "

Mr. Daney raised both arms toward the ceiling.

" 'Oh, God! cried the woodcock,—and away he flew!' What did the chit say?"

"She said, 'Why, not at all,' and turned her back on me. I then proffered Elizabeth a similar greeting and said, 'Surely, Elizabeth, *you* haven't forgotten me!' Elizabeth is really funny. She replied: 'So sorry! I've always been absent-minded!' She looked at me steadily with such a cool mirth in her eyes—she has nice eyes, too—and I must have had mirth in mine, also, because I remember that at precisely that minute I thought up a perfectly wonderful joke on Elizabeth and Jane and their mother. Of course, the poor Laird will not see the point of the joke, but then he's the innocent bystander, and innocent bystanders are always getting hurt."

"Ah, do not hurt him!" Daney pleaded anxiously. "He's a good, kind, manly gentleman. Spare him! Spare him, my dear!"

"Oh, I wouldn't hurt him, Mr. Daney, if I did not know I had the power to heal his hurts."

Suddenly she commenced to laugh, albeit there was in her laugh a quality which almost caused Mr. Daney to imagine that he had hackles on his back and that they were rising. He much preferred the note of anger of a few minutes previous; with a rush all of his old apprehensions returned, and he rasped out at her irritably:

"Well, well! What's this joke, anyhow? Tell me and perhaps I may laugh, too."

"Oh, no, Mr. Daney, you'd never laugh at this one. You'd weep."

"Try me."

"Very well. You will recall, Mr. Daney, that when Mrs. McKaye rang me up in New York, she was careful, even while asking me to return, to let me know my place?"

"Yes, yes. I was listening on the line. I heard her, and I thought she was a bit raw. But no matter. Proceed."

"Well, since she asked me to return to Port Agnew, I'm wondering who is going to ask me to go away again?"

"I'll be shot if I will! Ha! Ha! Ha!" And Mr. Daney threw back his head and laughed the most enjoyable laugh he had known since the night an itinerant hypnotist, entertaining the citizens of Port Agnew, had requested any adventurous gentleman in the audience who thought he couldn't be hypnotized, to walk up and prove it. Dirty Dan O'Leary had volunteered, had been mesmerized after a struggle, and, upon being told that he was Dick Whittington's cat, had proceeded to cut some feline capers that would have tickled the sensibilities of a totem-pole. Mr. Daney's honest cachinnations now were so infectious that Nan commenced to laugh with him—heartily, but no longer with that strident little note of resentment, and cumulatively, as Mr. Daney's mirth mounted until the honest fellow's tears cascaded across his ruddy cheeks.

"Egad, Nan," he declared presently, "but you have a rare sense of humor! Yes, do it. Do it! Make 'em all come down—right here to the Sawdust Pile! Make 'em remember you—all three of 'em—make 'em say please! Yes, sir! 'Please Nan, forgive me for forgetting. Please Nan, forgive me for smiling like the head of an old fiddle. Please, Nan, get out of Port Agnew so we can sleep nights. Please, Nan, be careful not to say "Good-by." Please, Nan, knock out a couple of your front teeth and wear a black wig and a sunbonnet, so nobody'll recognize you when you leave, follow you, and learn your address.'" He paused to wipe his eyes. "Why, dog my cats, girl, you've got 'em where the hair is short; so make 'em toe the scratch!"

"Well, of course," Nan reminded him, "they are not likely to toe the scratch unless they receive a hint that toeing scratches is going to be fashionable in our best Port Agnew circles this winter."

Mr. Daney arched his wild eyebrows, pursed his lips, popped his eyes, and looked at Nan over the rims of his spectacles.

"Very well, my dear girl, I'll be the goat. A lesson in humility will not be wasted on certain parties. But suppose they object? Suppose they buck and pitch and sidestep and bawl and carry on? What then?"

"Why," Nan replied innocently, regarding him in friendly fashion with those wistful blue eyes, "you might hint that I'm liable to go to The Laird and tell him I regard him as a very poor sport, indeed, to expect me to give up his son, in view of the fact that his son's mother sent for me to save that son's life. Do you know, dear Mr. Daney, I suspect that if The Laird knew his wife had compromised him so, he would be a singularly wild Scot!"

"Onward, Christian soldier, marching as to war!" cried Mr. Daney, and, seizing his hat from the table, he fled into the night.

XXXVII

UPON reaching his home, Mr. Daney telephoned to Mrs. McKaye.

"It is important," he informed her, "that you, Miss Jane and Miss Elizabeth come down to my office tomorrow for a conference. I would come up to The Dreamerie to see you, but Donald is home now, and his father will be with him; so I would prefer to see you down-town. I have some news of interest for you."

The hint of news of interest was sufficient to secure from Mrs. McKaye a promise to call at his office with the girls at ten o'clock the following morning.

"What is this interesting news, Andrew?" Mrs. Daney asked, with well-simulated disinterestedness. She was knitting for the French War-Relief Committee a pair of those prodigious socks with which well-meaning souls all over these United States have inspired many a poor little devil of a *poilu* with the thought that the French must be regarded by us as a Brobdingnagian race.

"We're arranging a big blowout, unknown to The Laird and Donald, to celebrate the boy's return to health. I'm planning to shut down the mill and the logging-camps for three days," he replied glibly. Of late he was finding it much easier to lie to her than to tell the truth, and he had observed with satisfaction that Mrs. Daney's bovine brain assimilated either with equal avidity.

"How perfectly lovely!" she cooed, and dropped a stitch which later would be heard from on the march, in the shape of a blister on a Gallic heel. "You're so thoughtful and kind, Andrew! Sometimes I wonder if the McKayes really appreciate your worth."

"Well, we'll see," he answered enigmatically and went off to bed.

It was with a feeling of alert interest that he awaited in his office, the following morning, the arrival of the ladies from The Dreamerie. They arrived half an hour late, very well content with themselves and the world in general, and filling Mr. Daney's office with the perfume of their presence. They appeared to be in such good fettle, indeed, that Mr. Daney took a secret savage delight in dissipating their nonchalance.

"Well, ladies," he began, "I decided yesterday that it was getting along toward the season of the year when my thoughts stray as usual toward the Sawdust Pile as a drying-yard. So I went down to see if Nan Brent had abandoned it again—and sure enough, she hadn't." He paused exasperatingly, after the fashion of an orator who realizes that he has awakened in his audience an alert and respectful interest. "Fine kettle of fish brewing down there," he resumed darkly, and paused again, glanced at the ceiling critically as if searching for leaks, smacked his lips and murmured confidentially a single word: "Snag!"

" 'Snag!' "   In chorus.

"Snag! In some unaccountable manner, it appears that you three ladies have aroused in Nan Brent a spirit of antagonism——"

"Nonsense!"

"The idea!"

"Fiddlesticks!"

"I state the condition as I found it. I happen to know that the girl possesses sufficient means to permit her to live at the Sawdust Pile for a year at least."

"But isn't she going away?" Mrs. McKaye's voice rose sharply. "Is she going to break her bargain?"

"Oh, I think not, Mrs. McKaye. She merely complained to me that somebody begged her to come back to Port Agnew; so she's waiting for somebody to come down to the Sawdust Pile and beg her to go away again. She's inclined to be capricious about it, too. One person isn't enough. She wants three people to call, and she insists that they be—ah—ladies!"

"Good gracious, Andrew, you don't mean it?"

"I am delivering a message, Mrs. McKaye."

"She must be spoofing you," Jane declared.

"Well, she laughed a good deal about it, Miss Jane, and confided to me that a bit of lurking devil in your sister's eyes the day you both met her in the telegraph office gave her the inspiration for this joke. She believes that she who laughs last laughs best."

Mrs. McKaye was consumed with virtuous indignation.

"The shameless hussy! Does she imagine for a moment that I will submit to blackmail, that my daughters or myself could afford to be seen calling upon her at the Sawdust Pile?"

"She wants to force us to recognize her, mother." Jane, recalling that day in the telegraph-office, sat staring at Daney with flashing eyes. She was biting the finger of her glove.

"Nothing doing," Elizabeth drawled smilingly

Mr. Daney nodded his comprehension.

"In that event, ladies," he countered, with malignant joy in his suppressed soul, "I am requested to remind you that The Laird will be informed by Miss Brent that she considers him a very short sport, indeed, if he insists upon regarding her as unworthy of his son, in view of the fact that his son's mother considered her a person of such importance that she used the transcontinental telephone in order to induce——"

"Yes, yes; I know what you're going to say. Do you really think she would go as far as that, Andrew?" Mrs. McKaye was very pale.

"Beware the anger of a woman scorned," he quoted.

"In the event that she should, Mr. Daney, we should have no other alternative but to deny it." Elizabeth was speaking. She still wore her impish glacial smile. "As a usual thing, we are opposed to fibbing on the high moral ground that it is not a lady's pastime, but in view of the perfectly appalling results that would follow our failure to fib in this particular case, I'm afraid we'll have to join hands, Mr. Daney, and prove Nan Brent a liar. Naturally, we count on your help. As a result of his conversation with you, father believes you did the telephoning."

"I told him half the truth, but no lie. I have never lied to him, Miss Elizabeth, and I never shall. When Hector McKaye asks me for the truth, he'll get it." In Mr. Daney's voice there was a growl that spoke of slow, quiet fury at the realization that this cool young woman should presume to dictate to him.

"I think you'll change your mind, Mr. Daney. You'll not refuse the hurdle when you come to it. As for this wanton Brent girl, tell her that we will think her proposition over and that she may look for a call from us.

We do not care how long she looks, do we mother?"
And she laughed her gay, impish laugh. "In the meantime, Mr. Daney, we will do our best to spare ourselves
and you the ignominy of that fib. The doctors will
order Donald away for a complete rest for six months,
and dad will go with him. When they're gone that
Brent house on the Sawdust Pile is going to catch fire
—accidently, mysteriously. The man who scuttled the
Brent's motor-boat surely will not scruple at such a
simple matter as burning the Brent shanty. Come,
mother. Jane, for goodness' sake, do buck up! Good-
by, dear Mr. Daney."

He stared at her admiringly. In Elizabeth, he discerned, for the first time, more than a modicum of her
father's resolute personality; he saw clearly that she
dominated her mother and Jane and, like The Laird,
would carry her objective, once she decided upon it, regardless of consequences.

"Good-morning, ladies. I shall repeat your message
—verbatim, Miss Elizabeth," he assured the departing
trio.

And that night he did so.

"They neglected to inform you how much time they
would require to think it over, did they not?" Nan interrogated mildly. "And they didn't tell you approxi-
mately when I should look for their visit?"

"No," he admitted.

"Oh, I knew they wouldn't submit," Nan flung back
at him. "They despise me—impersonally, at first and
before it seemed that I might dim the family pride;
personally, when it was apparent that I could dim it if
I desired. Well, I'm tired of being looked at and
sneered at, and I haven't money enough left to face New

York again. I had dreamed of the kind of living I might earn, and when the opportunity to earn it was already in my grasp, I abandoned it to come back to Port Agnew. I had intended to play fair with them, although I had to lie to Donald to do that, but—they hurt something inside of me—something deep that hadn't been hurt before—and—and now——"

"Now *what!*" Mr. Daney cried in anguished tones.

"If Donald McKaye comes down to the Sawdust Pile and asks me to marry him, I'm going to do it. I have a right to happiness; I'm—I'm tired—sacrificing—Nobody cares—no appreciation—Nan of the Sawdust Pile will be—mistress of The Dreamerie—and when they —enter house of mine—they shall be—humbler than I. They shall——"

As Mr. Daney fled from the house, he looked back through the little hall and saw Nan Brent seated at her tiny living-room table, her golden head pillowed in her arms outspread upon the table, her body shaken with great, passionate sobs. Mr. Daney's heart was constricted. He hadn't felt like that since the Aurora Stock Company had played "East Lynne" in the Port Agnew Opera House.

XXXVIII

AT the Sawdust Pile the monotony of Nan Brent's life remained unbroken; she was marking time, waiting for something to turn up. Since the last visit of the McKaye ambassador she had not altered her determination to exist independent of financial aid from the McKaye women or their father,—for according to her code, the acceptance of remuneration for what she had done would be debasing. Nan had made this decision even while realizing that in waiving Mr. Daney's proffer of reimbursement she was rendering impossible a return to New York with her child. The expenses of their journey and the maintenance of their brief residence there; the outlay for clothing for both and the purchase of an additional wardrobe necessitated when, with unbelievable good luck she had succeeded in securing twenty weeks time over a high-class vaudeville circuit for her "Songs of the 'Sixties," had, together with the cost of transportation back to Port Agnew, so depleted her resources that, with the few hundred dollars remaining, her courage was not equal to the problem which unemployment in New York would present; for with the receipt of Mrs. McKaye's message, Nan had written the booking agent explaining that she had been called West on a matter which could not be evaded and expressed a hope that at a later date the "time" might be open to her. Following her return to the Sawdust Pile she had received a brief communication stating that there would be no opening for her until the following year. The abandonment of her contract and the subsequent loss of commissions to the agent had seriously peeved that person.

The receipt of this news, while a severe disappointment, had not caused her to flinch, for she had, in a measure, anticipated it and with the calmness of desperation already commenced giving thought to the problem of her future existence. In the end she had comforted herself with the thought that good cooks were exceedingly scarce—so scarce, in fact, that even a cook with impedimenta in the shape of a small son might be reasonably certain of prompt and well-paid employment. Picturing herself as a kitchen mechanic brought a wry smile to her sweet face, but—it was honorable employment and she preferred it to being a waitress or an underfed and underpaid saleswoman in a department store. For she could cook wonderfully well and she knew it; she believed she could dignify a kitchen and she preferred it to cadging from the McKayes the means to enable her to withstand the economic siege incident to procuring a livelihood more dignified and remunerative.

Thus she had planned up to the day of her unexpected meeting with Jane and Elizabeth McKaye in the Port Agnew telegraph office. On that day, something had happened—something that had constituted a distinct event in Nan Brent's existence and with which the well-bred insolence of the McKaye girls had nothing to do. Indirectly old Caleb Brent had been responsible, for by the mere act of dying, his three-quarter pay as a retired sailor had automatically terminated, and Nan had written the Navy Department notifying it accordingly.

Now, the death of a retired member of the Army or Navy, no matter what his grade may be, constitutes news for the service journals, and the fact that old Caleb had been a medal of honor man appeared, to the editor of one of these journals, to entitle the dead sailor to three hundred words of posthumous publicity. Subsequently, these three hundred words came under the eye of a retired admiral of the United States Navy, who thereby became aware that he had an orphaned grand-daughter residing in Port Agnew, Washington.

As a man grows old he grows kindlier; those things which, at middle age, appear so necessary to an unruffled existence, frequently undergo such a metamorphosis, due to the corroding effects of time, that at eighty one has either forgotten them or regards them as something to be secretly ashamed of. Thus it was with Nan's grandfather. His pride and dignity were as austere as ever, but his withered heart yearned for the love and companionship of one of his own blood; now that Caleb Brent was dead, the ancient martinet forgot the offense which this simple sailor had committed against the pride of a long line of distinguished gentlemen, members of the honorable profession of arms. He thought it over for a month, and then wrote the only child of his dead daughter, asking her to come to him, hinting broadly that his days in the land were nearly numbered and that, in the matter of worldly goods he was not exactly a pauper.

Having posted this letter the old admiral waited patiently for an answer, and when this answer was not

forthcoming within the time he had set, he had tele-
graphed the postmaster of Port Agnew, requesting information as to her address. This telegram the postmaster had promptly sent over to Nan and it was for
the purpose of replying to it that she had gone to the
telegraph office on the day when Fate decreed that
Jane and Elizabeth McKaye should also be there.

After her return to the Sawdust Pile that day Nan's
thoughts frequently adverted to the Biblical line: "The
Lord giveth and the Lord taketh away." Certainly,
in her case, He appeared to be working at cross pur-
poses. At a time when she had resigned herself to
domestic labor in order to avoid starvation, her aris-
tocratic, arrogant, prideful grandfather had seen fit
to forgive her dead father and offer her shelter from the
buffets of the world; yet, even while striving, apparently to be kind, she knew that the reason underlying his
invitation was plain, old-fashioned heart-hunger, a tender conscience and a generous admixture of human selfishness. She smiled bitterly at his blunt hint of a
monetary reward following his demise; it occurred to
her that the stubborn old admiral was striving to buy
that which he might have had for a different asking.

She read the admiral's letter for the twentieth time
—and from the thick white page her glance went to her
child. Would he be welcome in that stern old sea dog's
home? Would his great-grandfather forget the bar sinister of little Don's birth and would her own misfortune be viewed by him with the tenderness and perfect
understanding accorded her by old Caleb? She did not
think so; and with the remembrance of her dead father,
the flames of revolt leaped in her heart. He had been

loyal to her and she would be loyal to him. No, no! She was not yet prepared to come fawning to the feet of that fierce old man who had robbed her father of his happiness. What right had he to expect forgiveness, *sans* the asking, *sans* an acknowledgment of his heartlessness?

With a bitter smile she wrote him a long letter, relating in detail the incident of her marriage, the birth of her child, her standing in Port Agnew society and her belief that all of this rendered acceptance of his invitation impossible, if she were to act with deference to his point of view and still remain loyal to the memory of her dead father. For these reasons she declined, thanked him for his kindness and remained his very sincerely. When she had posted this letter she felt better, and immediately took up the case of the Mc-Kayes.

Until that moment she had not considered seriously the possibility of a marriage with the young Laird of Port Agnew as a means of humiliating these women who had humiliated her. The thought had occurred to her in the telegraph office and at the moment had held for her a certain delightful fascination; prior to that meeting her resolution not to permit Donald McKaye to share her uncertain fortunes had been as adamant. But long and bitter reflection upon the problem thrust upon her by her grandfather had imbued her with a clearer, deeper realization of the futility of striving to please everybody in this curious world, of the cruelty of those who seek to adjust to their point of view that of another fully capable of adjusting his own; of the appalling lack of appreciation with which her piteous sacrifice would meet from the very persons who shrank from the ignominy incident to non-sacrifice on the part of her whom they held in open contempt!

Donald McKaye was not unintelligent. He was a man, grown, with all a man's passions, with all the caution to be expected in one of his class. If he still loved her sufficiently, following a period of mature deliberation and fierce opposition from his people, to offer her honorable marriage, would she not be a fool to cast away such a priceless gift? How few men know love so strong, so tender, so unselfish, that they do not shrink from sharing with the object of their love, the odium which society has always set upon the woman taken in adultery.

In rejecting his proffered sacrifice, she had told herself that she acted thus in order to preserve his happiness, although at the expense of her own. By so doing Nan realized that she had taken a lofty, a noble stand; nevertheless, who was she that she should presume to decide just wherein lay the preservation of his happiness? In her grandfather's letter before her she had ample evidence of the miscarriage of such pompous assumptions.

There is a latent force in the weakest of women, an amazing capacity for rebellion in the meekest and a regret for lost virtue even in the most abandoned. Nan was neither weak, meek, nor abandoned; wherefore, to be accorded toleration, polite contumely and resentment where profound gratitude and admiration were her due, had aroused in her a smouldering resentment which had burned like a handful of oil-soaked waste tossed into a corner. At first a mild heat; then a dull red glow of spontaneous combustion progresses —and presently flame and smoke.

It is probable that mere man, who never has been able to comprehend the intensity of feeling of which a woman is capable, is not equal to the problem of realizing the effect of solitude, misunderstanding and despair upon the mind of a woman of more than ordinary sensibilities and imagination. The seed of doubt, planted in such soil, burgeons rapidly, and when, upon the very day that Mr. Daney had made his last call at the Sawdust Pile, Nan, spurred to her decision by developments of which none but she was aware, had blazed forth in open rebellion and given the Tyee Lumber Company's general manager the fright of his prosaic existence.

XXXIX

AFTER leaving the Sawdust Pile, Mr. Daney walked
twice around the Bight of Tyee before arriving
at a definite decision as to his future conduct in this
intrigue, participation in which had been thrust upon
him by his own loyalty to his employer and the idiocy
of three hare-brained women. Time and again as he
paced the lonely strand, Mr. Daney made audible reference to the bells of the nether regions and the presence of panther tracks! This was his most terrible
oath and was never employed except under exceptional
circumstances.

At length Mr. Daney arrived at a decision. He
would have nothing further to do with this horrible
love affair. In the rôle of Dan Cupid's murderer he
was apparently a Tumble Tom; for three months he had
felt as if he trod thin ice—and now he had fallen
through! "I'll carry no more of their messages," he
declared aloud. "I'll tell them so and wash my hands
of the entire matter. If there is to be any asking
of favors from that girl the McKaye women can do
it."

It was after midnight when he returned to his home
and his wife was sitting up to receive an explanation of
his nocturnal prowlings. However, the look of desperation with which he met her accusing glance frightened
her into silence, albeit she had a quiet little crying
spell next morning when she discovered on the floor of

Mr. Daney's room quite a quantity of sand which had worked into his shoes during his agitated spring around Tyee Beach. She was quite certain he had indulged in a moonlight stroll on the seashore with a younger and prettier woman, so she resolved to follow him when next he fared forth and catch the traitor red-handed.

To her surprise, Mr. Daney went out no more o' nights. He had kept his word given to himself, and on the morning succeeding his extraordinary interview with Nan he had again summoned the ladies of the McKaye family to his office for a conference. However, the capable Elizabeth was the only one of the trio to present herself, for this young woman—and not without reason—regarded herself as Mr. Daney's mental superior; she was confident of her ability to retain his loyalty should he display a tendency to betray them.

"Well, dear Mr. Daney," she murmured in her melted-butter voice, "what new bugaboo have you developed for us?"

"You do not have to bother calling upon the Brent girl, Miss Elizabeth. She says now that if Donald asks her to marry him she'll accept. She has an idea she'll be mistress of The Dreamerie."

Elizabeth arched her eyebrows. "What else?" she queried amiably.

"That's all—from Nan Brent. I have a small defi to make on my own account, however, Miss Elizabeth. From this minute on I wash my hands of the private affairs of the McKaye family. My job is managing your father's financial affairs. Believe me, the next move in this comedy-drama is a wedding—if Donald asks her in all seriousness to marry him—that is, if he insists on it. He may insist and then again he may not, but if he should, I shall not attempt to stop him. He's free, white and twenty-one; he's my boss and I hope I know my place. Personally, I'm willing to wager considerable that he'll marry her, but whether he does or not—I'm through."

Elizabeth McKaye sighed. "That means we must work fast, Mr. Daney. Donald will be feeling strong enough within two weeks to call on her; he may even motor down to the Sawdust Pile within ten days. Mother has already broached the subject of taking him away to southern California or Florida for a long rest; Dad has seconded the motion with great enthusiasm—and that stubborn Donald has told them frankly that he isn't going away for a rest."

"Gosh!" Mr. Daney gasped. "That makes it a little binding, eh?"

She met his clear glance thoughtfully and said: "If her house should burn down—accidentally—to-day or to-night, when she and her baby aren't in it, she'll have to leave Port Agnew. There isn't a house in town where she could find shelter, and you could see to it that all the rooms in the hotel are taken."

"You forget, my dear," he replied with a small smile. "I have no further interest in this affair and moreover, I'm not turning firebug—not this year."

"You refuse to help us?"

"Absolutely. What is to be will be, and I, for one, have decided not to poke my finger into the cogs of destiny."

"Well—thanks awfully for what you've already done, Mr. Daney." Again she smiled her bright, impish smile. "Good-morning."

"Good-morning, Miss Elizabeth."

As she left the office, Mr. Daney noted her débutante slouch and gritted his teeth. "Wonder if they'll call on Nan now, or make a combined attack on the boy and try bluff and threats and tears," he soliloquized.

As a matter of fact they tried the latter. The storm broke after luncheon one day when Donald declared he felt strong enough to go down to Port Agnew, and, in the presence of the entire family, ordered the butler to tell his father's chauffeur to bring the closed car around to the door. Immediately, the astute Elizabeth precipitated matters by asking her brother sharply if his projected visit to Port Agnew predicated also a visit to the Sawdust Pile.

"Why, yes, Elizabeth," he answered calmly.

The Laird scowled at her, but she ignored the scowl; so old Hector flashed a warning glance to Jane and her mother—a glance that said quite plainly: "Let there be no upbraiding of my son."

"Do you think it is quite—ah, delicate of you, Donald, to call upon any young lady at her apartments in the absence of a proper chaperon, even if the lady herself appears to have singularly free and easy views on the propriety of receiving you thus?"

He saw that she was bound to force the issue and was rather relieved than otherwise. With a mental promise to himself to keep his temper at all hazards he replied: "Well, Elizabeth, I'll admit the situation is a trifle awkward, but what cannot be cured must be endured. You see, I want to have a talk with Nan Brent and I cannot do so unless I call upon her at the Sawdust Pile. It is impossible for us to meet on neutral ground, I fear. However, if you will write her a nice friendly little note and invite her up here to visit me, the question of a chaperon will be solved and I will postpone my visit until she gets here."

"Don't be a fool," she retorted bitterly.

"As for Nan's free and easy views on the subjects, who in Port Agnew, may I ask, expects her to act differently? Why, therefore, since she is fully convinced that I possess a few of the outward appearances of a gentleman, should she fear to receive me in her home? To conform to the social standards of those who decry her virtue? Elizabeth, you expect too much, I fear."

"Hear, hear," cried The Laird. He realized that Elizabeth was not to be denied, so he thought best to assume a jocular attitude during the discussion.

"Father," his eldest daughter reminded him. "It is your duty to forbid Donald doing anything which is certain to bring his family into disrepute and make it the target for the tongue of scandal."

"Oh, leave him alone, you pestiferous woman," old Hector cried sharply. "Had it not been for the girl he would not be living this minute, so the least he can do is to express his compliments to her. Also, since this disagreeable topic has again been aired, let me remind you that the lass isn't going to marry Donald. She came out here, Donald," he continued, turning to his son, "with the distinct understanding that her job was to humor you back to health, and for that you owe her your thanks and I'm willing you should call on her and express them. Don't flattter yourself that she'll marry you, my boy. I've had a talk with her—since you must know it, sooner or later—and she promised me she wouldn't."

The young Laird's face paled a little but he maintained his composure. "I greatly fear you misunderstood her, father," he replied gently. "She promised me she'd marry me. You see," he added looking the old man resolutely in the face, "I think she's virtuous, so I'm going to marry her."

His father smiled sadly. "Poor lad. God knows I'm sorry for you, but—well, go see her and let's have the issue settled once for all. For God's sake, lad, grant me peace of mind. End it to-day, one way or the other."

"Ah, yes, you're brave," Elizabeth flung at her father. "You're so certain that girl will keep her promise, aren't you? Well, I happen to have been informed, on very good authority, that she intends to betray you. She had made the statement that she'll marry Donald if he asks her—again."

"The girl doesn't impress me as one who would lie, Elizabeth. Who told you this?"

"Andrew Daney."

"Bear with me a moment, son, till I call Andrew on the telephone," the Laird requested, and went into the telephone booth under the stairs in the reception hall. When he emerged a few minutes later his face was pale and haggard.

"Well? What did I tell you?" Elizabeth's voice was triumphant.

Her father ignored her. Placing himself squarely before his son, he bent forward slightly and thrust his aggressive face close to Donald's. "I command you to respect the honor of my house," he cried furiously. "For the last time, Donald McKaye, ha' done wie this woman, or—" and his great arm was outflung in a sweeping gesture that denoted all too forcibly the terrible sentence he shrank from speaking.

"Are you offering me an alternative?" Donald's voice was low and very calm, but his brown eyes were blazing with suppressed rage. "The Dreamerie or—" and he swung and pointed to the Brent cottage far below them on the Sawdust Pile.

"Aye," his father cried in a hard cracked voice. "Aye!"

Donald looked over at his mother with the helplessness of a child who has fallen and hurt himself. "And you, mother? What do you say to this?"

She thought she would faint. "You—you must obey your father," she quavered. Until her son should marry Nan Brent she could not force herself to the belief that he could possibly commit such an incredible offense.

"The opinions of you and Jane," Donald continued, turning to each sister in turn, "do not interest me particularly, but while the polls are open you might as well vote. If I marry Nan Brent are you each prepared to forget that I am your brother?"

Elizabeth nodded calmly. She had gone too far now to develop weakness when an assumption of invincible strength might yet win the day.

"I couldn't receive such a peculiar sister-in-law," Jane murmured, evidently close to tears. "Surely, you would not expect us to take such a woman to our hearts, Donald dear?"

"I did not build The Dreamerie for yon lass," The Laird burst forth passionately.

His son stood with bowed head. "Have you, mother, or you, my sisters, been down to the Sawdust Pile

to thank Nan for inspiring me—no matter how—with
a desire to live? I think you realize that until she
came I was too unhappy—too disgusted with life—to
care whether I got well or not? Have you absolved
yourselves of an obligation which must be perfectly
evident to perfect ladies?"

"We have not." Elizabeth's calm voice answered
him. "What the girl did was entirely of her own volition. She did it for your sake, and since it is apparent that she plans to collect the reward of her disinterested effort we have considered that a formal expression of thanks would be superfluous."

"I see. I see. Well, perhaps you're right. I shall
not quarrel with your point of view. And you're all
quite certain you will never recede from your attitude
of hostility toward Nan—under no circumstances, to
recognize her as my wife and extend to her the hospi-
tality of The Dreamerie?"

He challenged his father with a look and the old man
slowly nodded an affirmative. His mother thought Donald was about to yield to their opposition and nodded
likewise. "I have already answered that question,"
Jane murmured tragically, and Elizabeth again reminded him that it was not necessary for him to make
a fool of himself.

"Well, I'm glad this affair has been ironed out—at
last," Donald assured them. "I had cherished the hope
that when you knew Nan better—" He choked up for
a moment, then laid his hands on his father's shoulders.
"Well, sir," he gulped, "I'm going down to the Sawdust Pile and thank Nan for saving my life. Not," he
added bitterly, "that I anticipate enjoying that life to

the fullest for some years to come. If I did not believe that time will solve the problem——"

The Laird's heart leaped. "Tush, tush, boy. Run along and don't do anything foolish." He slapped Donald heartily across the back while the decisive sweep of that same hand an instant later informed the women of his household that it would be unnecessary to discuss this painful matter further.

"I understand just how you feel, dad. I hold no resentment," Donald assured him, and dragged The Laird close to him in a filial embrace. He crossed the room and kissed his mother, who clung to him a moment, tearfully; seeing him so submissive, Jane and Elizabeth each came up and claimed the right to embrace him with sisterly affection.

The butler entered to announce that the car was waiting at the front door. Old Hector helped his son into a great coat and Mrs. McKaye wound a reefer around his neck and tucked the ends inside the coat. Then The Laird helped him into the car; as it rolled slowly down the cliff road, Old Hector snorted with relief.

"By Judas," he declared, "I never dreamed the boy would accept such an ultimatum."

"Well, the way to find out is to try," Elizabeth suggested. "Sorry to have been forced to disregard that optical S. O. S. of yours, Dad, but I realized that we had to strike now or never."

"Whew-w-w!" The Laird whistled again.

WITH the license of long familiarity, Donald knocked at the front door of the Brent cottage to anounce his arrival; then, without awaiting permission to enter, he opened the door and met Nan in the tiny hall hurrying to admit him.

"You—Donald!" she reproved him. "What are you doing here? You shouldn't be out."

"That's why I came in," he retorted drily and kissed her. "And I'm here because I couldn't stand The Dreamerie another instant. I wanted my mother and sisters to call on you and thank you for having been so nice to me during my illness, but the idea wasn't received very enthusiastically. So, for the sheer sake of doing the decent thing I've called myself. It might please you," he added, "to know that my father thought I should."

"He is always tactful and kind," she agreed.

She led him to her father's old easy chair in the living room.

"As Dirty Dan O'Leary once remarked in my presence," he began, "it is a long lane that hasn't got a saloon at the end of it. I will first light a cigarette, if I may, and make myself comfortable, before putting you on the witness stand and subjecting you to a severe cross-examination. Seat yourself on that little hassock before me and in such a position that I can look squarely into your face and note flush of guilt when you fib to me."

She obeyed, with some slight inward trepidation, and sat looking up at him demurely.

"Nan," he began, "did anybody ever suggest to you that the sporty thing for you to do would be to run away and hide where I could never find you?"

She shook her head.

"Did anybody ever suggest to you that the sporty thing for you to do would be to return to Port Agnew from your involuntary exile and inspire me with some enthusiasm for life?"

His keen perception did not fail to interpret the slight flush of embarrassment that suffused Nan's face. "I object to that question, your honor," she replied with cleverly simulated gaiety, "on the ground that to do so would necessitate the violation of a confidence."

"The objection is sustained by the court. Did my father or Andrew Daney, acting for him, ever offer you any sum of money as a bribe for disappearing out of my life?"

"No. Your father offered to be very, very kind to me the morning I was leaving. We met at the railroad station and his offer was made *after* I informed him that I was leaving Port Agnew forever—and why. So I know he made the offer just because he wanted to be kind—because he is kind."

"Neither he nor Daney communicated with you in anyway following your departure from Port Agnew?"

"They did not."

"Before leaving New York or immediately after your return to Port Agnew, did you enter into verbal agreement with any member of my family or their representative to nurse me back to health and then jilt me?"

"I did not. The morning I appeared at the hospital

your father, remembering my statement to him the morning I fled from Port Agnew, suspected that I had had a change of heart. He said to me: 'So this is your idea of playing the game, is it?' I assured him then that I had not returned to Port Agnew with the intention of marrying you, but merely to stiffen your morale, as it were. He seemed quite satisfied with my explanation, which I gave him in absolute good faith."

"Did he ever question you as to how you ascertained I was ill?"

"No. While I cannot explain my impression, I gathered at the time that he knew."

"He credited Andrew Daney with that philanthropic job, Nan. He does not know that my mother communicated with you."

"Neither do you, Donald. I have not told you she did."

"I am not such a stupid fellow as to believe you would ever tell me anything that might hurt me, Nan. One does not relish the information that one's mother has not exhibited the sort of delicacy one expects of one's mother," he added bluntly.

"It is not nice of you to say that, Donald. How do you know that Mr. Daney did not send for me?"

He smiled tolerantly. "Before Daney would dare do that he would consult with my father, and if my father had consented to it he would never have left to Daney the task of requesting such a tremendous favor of you for his account. If Daney ever consulted my father as to the advisability of such a course, my father refused to consider it."

"What makes you think so, old smarty?"

"Well, I know my father's code. He had no hesitancy

in permitting you to know that you were not welcome
as a prospective daughter-in-law, although he was not
so rude as to tell you why. He left that to your imagination. Now, for my father to ask a favor of anybody is very unusual. He has a motto that a favor
accepted is a debt incurred, and he dislikes those perennial debts. My father is a trader, my dear. If he had,
directly or indirectly, been responsible for your return
to Port Agnew for the purpose of saving his son's life,
he would not be—well, he just wouldn't do it," he
explained with some embarrassment. "He couldn't do
it. He would say to you, 'My son is dying because
he finds life uninteresting without you. If you return,
your presence will stimulate in him a renewed interest
in life and he will, in all probability, survive. If you
are good enough to save my son from death you are
good enough to share his life, and although this wedding is about going to kill me, nevertheless we will
pull it off and make believe we like it.' "

"Nonsense," she retorted.

"Knowing how my father would act under such circumstances, I was dumfounded when he informed me
this afternoon that you had agreed to perform under
false pretenses. He was quite certain you would proceed to jilt me, now that I am strong enough to stand
it. He said you had promised him you would."

"I did not promise him. I merely told him truth-
fully what my firm intention was at the time he
demanded to be informed as to the nature of my intentions. I reserved my woman's right to change my
mind."

"Oh!"

"Had I made your father a definite promise I would

have kept it. If I were a party to such a contract with your father, Donald dear, all of your pleading to induce me to break it would be in vain."

"A contract without a consideration is void in law," he reminded her. "Dad just figured he could bank on your love for me. He did you the honor to think it was so strong and wonderful that death would be a delirious delight to you in preference to spoiling my career by marrying me—well—Elizabeth disillusioned him!"

Nan's eyebrows lifted perceptibly.

"She informed my father in my presence," Donald continued, "that you had had a change of heart; that you were now resolved to accept me should I again ask you to marry me. It appears you had told Andrew Daney this—in cold blood as it were. So Dad went to the telephone and verified this report by Daney; then we had a grand show-down and I was definitely given my choice of habitation—The Dreamerie or the Sawdust Pile. Father, Mother, Elizabeth and Jane jointly and severally assured me that they would never receive you, so Nan, dear, it appears that I will have to pay rather a heavy price for the privilege of marrying you——"

"I have never told you I would marry you," she cried sharply.

"Yes, you did. That day in the hospital."

"That was a very necessary fib and you should not hold it against me. It was a promise absolutely not made in good faith."

"But did you tell Daney that you would accept me if I should ask you again to marry me?"

She was visibly agitated but answered him truth-fully. "Yes, I did."

"You said it in anger?"

"Yes." Very softly.

"Daney had come to you with an offer of monetary reward for your invaluable services to the McKaye family, had he not? And since what you did was not done for profit, you were properly infuriated and couldn't resist giving Daney the scare of his life? That was the way of it, was it not?"

Nan nodded and some tears that trembled on h long lashes were flicked off by the vigor of the nod; some of them fell on the big gaunt hands that held hers.

"I suppose you haven't sufficient money with which to return to New York?" he continued.

Again she nodded an affirmative.

"Just what are your plans, dear?"

"I suppose I'll have to go somewhere and try to procure a position as a cook lady."

"An admirable decision," he declared enthusiasti-cally. "I'll give you a job cooking for me, provided you'll agree to marry me and permit me to live in your house. I'm a man without a home and you've just *got* to take me in, Nan. I have no other place to lay my weary head."

She looked at him and through the blur of her tears she saw him smiling down at her, calmly, benignantly and with that little touch of whimsicality that was always in evidence and which even his heavy heart could not now subdue.

"You've—you've—chosen the Sawdust Pile?" she cried incredulously.

"How else would a man of spirit choose, old ship-mate?"

"But you're not marrying me to save me from poverty, Donald? You must be certain you aren't mistaking for love the sympathy which rises so naturally in that big heart of yours. If it's only a great pity— if it's only the protective instinct——"

"Hush! It's all of that and then some. I'm a man grown beyond the puppy-love stage, my dear—and the McKayes are not an impulsive race. We count the costs carefully and take careful note of the potential profits. And while I could grant my people the right to make hash of my happiness I must, for some inexplicable reason, deny them the privilege of doing it with yours. I think I can make you happy, Nan; not so happy, perhaps, that the shadow of your sorrow will not fall across your life occasionally, but so much happier than you are at present that the experiment seems worth trying, even at the expense of sacrificing the wordly pride of my people."

"Are you entertaining a strong hope that after you marry me, dear, your people will forgive you, make the best of what they consider a bad bargain and acknowledge me after a fashion? Do you think they will let bygones be bygones and take me to their hearts— for your sake?"

"I entertain no such silly illusion. Under no circumstances will they ever acknowledge you after a fashion, for the very sufficient reason that the opportunity to be martyrs will never be accorded my mother and sisters by yours truly, Donald McKaye, late Laird apparent of Port Agnew. Bless your sweet soul, Nan I have some pride, you know. I wouldn't permit them to tolerate you. I prefer open warfare every time."

"Have you broken with your people, dear?"

"Yes, but they do not know it yet. I didn't have the heart to raise a scene, so I merely gave the old pater a hug, kissed mother and the girls and came away. I'm not going back."

"You will—if I refuse to marry you?"

"I do not anticipate such a refusal. However, it does not enter into the matter at all in so far as my decision to quit The Dreamerie is concerned. I'm through! Listen, Nan. I could win my father to you —win him wholeheartedly and without reservation— if I should inform him that my mother asked you to come back to Port Agnew. My mother and the girls have not told him of this and I suspect they have encouraged his assumption that Andrew Daney took matters in his own hands. Father has not cared to inquire into the matter, anyhow, because he is secretly grateful to Daney (as he thinks) for disobeying him. Mother and the girls are forcing Daney to protect them; they are using his loyalty to the family as a club to keep him in line. With that club they forced him to come to you with a proposition that must have been repugnant to him, if for no other reason than that he knew my father would not countenance it. When you told him you would marry me if I should ask you again, to whom did Daney report? To Elizabeth, of course—the brains of the opposition. That proves to me that my father had nothing to do with it —why the story is as easily understood from deduction as if I had heard the details from their lips. But I cannot use my mother's peace of mind as a club to beat dad into line; I cannot tell him something that will almost make him hate mother and my sisters; I would not force him to do that which he does not desire to do because it is the kindly, sensible and humane course. So I shall sit tight and say nothing— and by the way, I love you more than ever for keeping this affair from me. So few women are true blue sports, I'm afraid."

"You must be very, very angry and hurt, Donald?"

"I am. So angry and hurt that I desire to be happy within the shortest possible period of elapsed time. Now, old girl, look right into my eyes, because I'm going to propose to you for the last time. My worldly assets consist of about a hundred dollars in cash and a six dollar wedding ring which I bought as I came through Port Agnew. With these wordly goods and all the love and honor and respect a man can possibly have for a woman, I desire to endow you. Answer me quickly. Yes or no?"

"Yes," she whispered.

"You chatterbox! When?"

"At your pleasure."

"That's trading talk. We'll be married this afternoon." He stretched out his long arms for her and as she slid off the low hassock and knelt beside his chair, he gathered her hungrily to him and held her there for a long time before he spoke again. When he did it was to say, with an air of wonder that was almost childlike:

"I never knew it was possible for a man to be so utterly wretched and so tremendously happy and all within the same hour. I love you so much it hurts." He released her and glanced at his watch. "It is now

two o'clock, Nan. If we leave here by three we can
reach the county seat by five o'clock, procure a license
and be married by six. By half past seven we will
have finished our wedding supper and by about ten
o'clock we shall be back at the Sawdust Pile. Put a
clean pair of rompers on the young fellow and let's
go! From this day forward we live, like the Sinn
Fein "For ourselves alone."

While Nan was preparing for that hurried ceremony,
Donald strolled about the little yard, looking over the
neglected garden and marking for future attention
various matters such as a broken hinge on the gate,
some palings off the fence and the crying necessity
for paint on the little white house, for he was striving
mightily to shut out all thought of his past life and
concentrate on matters that had to do with the future.
Presently he wandered out on the bulkhead. The great
white gulls which spent their leisure hours gravely con-
templating the Bight of Tyee from the decaying piling,
rose lazily at his approach and with hoarse cries of
resentment flapped out to sea; his dull glance followed
them and rested on a familiar sight.

Through the Bight of Tyee his father's barkentine
Kohala was coming home from Honolulu, ramping in
before a twenty mile breeze with every shred of canvas
drawing. She was heeled over to starboard a little
and there was a pretty little bone in her teeth; the
colors streamed from her mizzen rigging while from her
foretruck the house-flag flew. Idly Donald watched her
until she was abreast and below The Dreamerie and
her house-flag dipped in salute to the master watching
from the cliff; instantly the young Laird of Tyee saw
a woolly puff of smoke break from the terrace below

the house and several seconds later the dull boom of the signal gun. His heart was constricted. "Ah, never for me!" he murmured, "never for me—until he tells them to look toward the Sawdust Pile for the master!"

He strode out to the gate where his father's chauffeur waited with the limousine. "Take the car home," he ordered, "and as you pass through town stop in at the Central Garage and tell them to send a closed car over to me here."

The chauffeur looked at him with surprise but obeyed at once. By the time the hired car had arrived Nan and her child were ready, and just before locking the house Nan, realizing that they would not return to the Sawdust Pile until long after nightfall, hauled in the flag that floated over the little cupola; and for the second time, old Hector, watching up on the cliff, viewed this infallible portent of an event out of the ordinary. His hand trembled as he held his marine glasses to his blurred eyes and focussed on The Sawdust Pile, in time to see his son enter the limousine with Nan Brent and her child—and even at that distance he could see that the car in which they were departing from the Sawdust Pile was not the one in which Donald had left The Dreamerie. From that fact alone The Laird deduced that his son had made his choice; and because Donald was his father's son, imbued with the same fierce high pride and love of independence, he declined to be under obligation to his people even for the service of an automobile upon his wedding day.

The Laird stood watching the car until it was out

of sight; then he sighed very deeply, entered the house and rang for the butler.

"Tell Mrs. McKaye and the young ladies that I would thank them to come here at once," he ordered calmly.

They came precipitately, vaguely apprehensive. "My dears," he said in an unnaturally subdued voice, "Donald has just left the Sawdust Pile with the Brent lass to be married. He has made his bed and it is my wish that he shall lie in it."

"Oh, Hector!" Mrs. McKaye had spoken quaveringly. "Oh, Hector, dear, do not be hard on him!"

He raised his great arm as if to silence further argument. "He has brought disgrace upon my house. He is no longer son of mine and we are discussing him for the last time. Hear me, now. There will be no further mention of Donald in my presence and I forbid you, Nellie, you, Elizabeth and you, Jane, to have aught to do wie him, directly or indirectly."

Mrs. McKaye sat down abruptly and commenced to weep and wail her woe aloud, while Jane sought vainly to comfort her. Elizabeth bore the news with extreme fortitude; with unexpected tact she took her father by the arm and steered him outside and along the terrace walk where the agonized sobs and moans of her mother could not be heard—for what Elizabeth feared in that first great moment of remorse was a torrent of self-accusation from her mother. If, as her father had stated, Donald was en route to be married, then the mischief was done and no good could come out of a confession to The Laird of the manner in which the family honor had been compromised, not by Donald, but by his mother, aided and abetted by his sisters! The Laird, now quite dumb with distress, walked in silence with his eldest daughter, vaguely conscious of the comfort of her company and sympathy in his hour of trial.

When Elizabeth could catch Jane's attention through the window she cautiously placed her finger on her lip and frowned a warning. Jane nodded her comprehension and promptly bore her mother off to bed where she gave the poor soul some salutary advice and left her to the meager comfort of solitude and smelling salts.

Just before he retired that night, The Laird saw a light shine suddenly forth from the Sawdust Pile. So he knew his son had selected a home for his bride, and rage and bitterness mingled with his grief and mangled pride to such an extent that he called upon God to take him out of a world that had crumbled about his hoary head. He shook his fist at the little light that blinked so far below him and Mrs. McKaye, who had crept down stairs with a half-formed notion of confessing to The Laird in the hope of mitigating her son's offense—of, mother-like, taking upon her shoulders an equal burden of the blame—caught a glimpse of old Hector's face, and her courage failed her. Thoroughly frightened she returned noiselessly to her room and wept, dry-eyed, for the fountain of her tears had long since been exhausted.

Meanwhile, down at the Sawdust Pile, Nan was putting her drowsy son to bed; in the little living-room her husband had lighted the drift-wood fire and had drawn the old divan up to the blue flames. He was sitting with his elbows on his knees and his chin in his hands, outlining plans for their future, when Nan, having put her child to bed, came and sat down beside him. He glanced at her with troubled eyes and grinned a trifle foolishly.

"Happy?" he queried.

She nodded. "In a limited fashion only, dear heart. I'm thinking how wonderfully courageous you have been to marry me and how tremendously grateful I shall always be for your love and faith." She captured his right hand and fondled it for a moment in both of hers, smiling a little thoughtfully the while as if at some dear little secret. "Port Agnew will think I married you for money," she resumed presently; "your mother and sisters will think I married you to spite them and your father will think I married you because you insisted and because I was storm-tossed and had to find a haven from the world. But the real reason is that I love you and know that some day I am going to see more happiness in your eyes than I can see to-night."

Again, in that impulsive way she had, she bent and kissed his hand. "Dear King Cophetua," she murmured, "your beggar maid will never be done with adoring you." She looked up at him with a sweet and lovely wistfulness shining in her sea-blue eyes. "And the sweetest thing about it, you angelic simpleton," she added, "is that you will never, never, never know why."

THE first hint of the tremendous events impending came to Mr. Daney through the medium of no less an informant than his wife. Upon returning from the mill office on the evening of Donald McKaye's marriage, Mr. Daney was met at his front door by Mrs. Daney who cried triumphantly:

"Well, what did I tell you about Donald McKaye?"

Mr. Daney twitched inwardly, but answered composedly. "Not one-tenth of one per cent. of what I have discovered without your valuable assistance my dear."

She wrinkled the end of her nose disdainfully. "He's gone motoring with Nan Brent in a hired car, and they took the baby with them. They passed through town about half past two this afternoon and they haven't returned yet."

"How do you know all this?" he demanded coolly.

"I saw them as they passed by on the road below; I recognized that rent limousine of the Central Garage with Ben Nicholson driving it, and a few moments ago I telephoned the Central Garage and asked for Ben. He hasn't returned yet—and it's been dark for half an hour."

"Hum-m-m! What do you suspect, my dear?"

"The worst," she replied dramatically.

"What a wonderful fall day this has been," he remarked blandly as he hung up his hat. She turned

320

upon him a glance of fury; he met it with one so calm and impersonal that the good lady quite lost control of herself. "Why do you withhold your confidence from me?" she cried sharply.

"Because you wouldn't respect it, my dear; also, because I'm paid to keep the McKaye secrets and you're not."

"Is he going to marry her, Andrew? Answer me," she demanded.

"Unfortunately for you, Mrs. Daney, the young gentleman hasn't taken me into his confidence. Neither has the young lady. Of course I entertain an opinion on the subject, but since I am not given to discussing the intimate personal affairs of other people, you'll excuse my reticence on this subject, I'm sure. I repeat that this has been a wonderful fall day."

She burst into tears of futile rage and went to her room. Mr. Daney partook of his dinner in solitary state and immediately after dinner strolled down town and loitered around the entrance to the Central Garage until he saw Ben Nicholson drive in about ten o'clock.

"Hello, Ben," he hailed the driver as Ben descended from his seat. "I hear you've been pulling off a wedding."

Ben Nicholson lowered his voice and spoke out the corner of his mouth. "What do you know about the young Laird, eh, Mr. Daney? Say I could 'a' cried to see him throwin' himself away on that Jane."

Mr. Daney shrugged. "Oh, well, boys will be boys," he declared. "The bigger they are the harder they fall. Of course, Ben, you understand I'm not in position to say anything, one way or the other," he added parenthetically, and Ben Nicholson nodded comprehension. Thereupon Mr. Daney sauntered over to the cigar stand in the hotel, loaded his cigar case and went down to his office, where he sat until midnight, smoking and thinking. The sole result of his cogitations, however, he summed up in a remark he directed at the cuspidor just before he went home:

"Well, there's blood on the moon and hell will pop in the morning."

For the small part he had played in bringing Nan Brent back to Port Agnew, the general manager fully expected to be dismissed from the McKaye service within thirty seconds after old Hector should reach the mill office; hence with the heroism born of twelve hours of preparation he was at his desk at eight o'clock next morning. At nine o'clock The Laird came in and Mr. Daney saw by his face instantly that old Hector knew. The general manager rose at his desk and bowed with great dignity.

"Moritori salutamus, sir," he announced gravely.

"What the devil are you talking about, Daney?" The Laird demanded irritably.

"That's what the gladiators used to say to the Roman populace. It means, I believe, 'We who are about to die, salute you.' Here is my resignation, Mr. McKaye."

"Don't be an ass, Andrew," The Laird commanded and threw the proffered resignation into the waste basket. "Why should you resign?"

"To spare the trouble of discharging me, sir."

"What for?"

"Bringing the Brent girl back to Port Agnew. If I hadn't gotten her address from Dirty Dan I would never have suggested to——"

"Enough. We will not discuss what might have been, Andrew. The boy has married her, and since the blow has fallen nothing that preceded it is of the slightest importance. What I have called to say to you is this: Donald McKaye is no longer connected with the Tyee Lumber Company."

"Oh, come, come, sir," Daney pleaded. "The mischief is done. You'll have to forgive the boy and make the best of a bad business. What can't be cured must be endured, you know."

"Not necessarily. And you might spare me your platitude, Andrew," The Laird replied savagely. "I'm done with the lad forever, for son of mine he is no longer. Andrew, do you remember the time he bought that red cedar stumpage up on the Wiskah and unloaded it on me at a profit of two hundred thousand dollars?"

Mr. Daney nodded. "And you, in turn, sold it at a profit of fifty thousand," he reminded the irate old man.

"Donald did not retain that profit he made at my expense. 'Twas just a joke with him. He put the money into bonds and sent them to you with instructions to place them in my vault for my account." Mr. Daney nodded and The Laird resumed. "Take those bonds to the Sawdust Pile, together with a check for all the interest collected on the coupons since they came into my possession, and tell him from me that I'll take it kindly of him to leave Port Agnew and make a start for himself elsewhere as quickly as he can. He owes it to his family not to affront it by his presence in Port Agnew, giving ground for gossip and scandal and piling needless sorrow upon us. And

when the Sawdust Pile is again vacant you will remove the Brent house and put in the drying yard
you've planned this many a year."

"Very well, sir. It's not a task to my liking, but—"
His pause was eloquent.

"Have my old desk put in order for me. I'm back
in the harness and back to stay, and at that I'm not
so certain it isn't the best thing for me, under the
present circumstances. I dare say," he added, with a
sudden change of tone, "the news is all over Port
Agnew this morning."

Mr. Daney nodded.

"You will procure Donald's resignation as President
and have him endorse the stock I gave him in order to
qualify as a director of the company. We'll hold a
directors' meeting this afternoon and I'll step back
into the presidency."

"Very well, sir."

"You will cause a notice to be prepared for my signature, to be spread on the bulletin board in each
department, to the effect that Donald McKaye is no
longer connected in any way with the Tyee Lumber
Company."

"Damn it, man," Daney roared wrathfully, "have
you no pride? Why wash your dirty linen in public?"

"You are forgetting yourself, my good Andrew. If
you do not wish to obey my orders I shall have little
difficulty inducing your assistant to carry out my
wishes, I'm thinking." The Laird's voice was calm
enough; apparently he had himself under perfect control, but—the Blue-Bonnets-coming-over-the-Border
look was in his fierce gray eyes; under his bushy iron-
gray brows they burned like campfires in twin caverns

at night. His arms, bowed belligerently, hung tense at his side, his great hands opened and closed, a little to the fore; he licked his lips and in the brief silence that followed ere Mr. Daney got up and started fumbling with the combination to the great vault in the corner, old Hector's breath came in short snorts. He turned and, still in the same attitude, watched Daney while the latter twirled and fumbled and twirled. Poor man! He knew The Laird's baleful glance was boring into his back and for the life of him he could not remember the combination he had used for thirty years.

Suddenly he abandoned all pretense and turned savagely on The Laird.

"Get out of my office," he yelled. "I work for you, Hector McKaye, but I give you value received and in this office I'm king and be damned to you." His voice rose to a shrill, childish treble that presaged tears of rage. "You'll be sorry for this, you hard-hearted man. Please God I'll live to see the day your dirty Scotch pride will be humbled and you'll go to that wonderful boy and his wife and plead for forgiveness. Why, you poor, pitiful, pusillanimous old pachyderm, if the boy has dishonored you he has honored himself. He's a gallant young gentleman, that's what he is. He has more guts than a bear. He's *married* the girl, damn you—and that's more than you would have done at his age. Ah, don't talk to me! We were young together and I know the game you played forty years ago with the girl at the Rat Portage—yes, you—you with your youth and your hot passions—turning your big proud back on your peculiar personal god to wallow in sin and enjoy it."

"But I—I was a single man then," The Laird sputtered, almost inarticulate with fury and astonishment.

"He was a single man yesterday but he's a married man to-day. And she loves him. She adores him. You can see it in her eyes when his name is mentioned. And she had no *reason* to behave herself, had she? She has behaved herself for three long years, but did she win anybody's approbation for doing it? I'm telling you a masterful man like him might have had her without the wedding ring, for love's sake, if he'd cared to play a waiting game and stack the cards on her. After all, she's human."

Suddenly he commenced to weep with fury, the tears cascading into his whiskers making him look singularly ridiculous in comparison with the expression on his face, which was anything but grievous. "Marriage! Marriage!" he croaked. "I know what it is. I married a fat-head—and so did my wife. We've never known romance; never had anything but a quiet, well-ordered existence. I've dwelt in repression; never got out of life a single one of those thrills that comes of doing something daring and original and nasty. Never had an adventure; never had a woman look at me like I was a god; married at twenty and never knew the Grand Passion." He threw up his arms. "Oh-h-h, God-d-d! If I could only be young again I'd be a devil! Praise be, I know one man with guts enough to tell 'em all to go to hell."

With a peculiar little moving cry he started for the door.

"Andrew," The Laird cried anxiously. "Where are you going?"

"None of your infernal business," the rebel shrilled, "but if you must know, I'm going down to the Saw-

'dust Pile to kiss the bride and shake a man's hand and wish him well. After I've done that I'll deliver your message. Mark me, he'll never take those bonds."

"Of course he will, you old fool. They belong to him."

"But he refused to make a profit at the expense of his own father. He gave them to you and he's not an Indian giver."

"Andrew, I have never known you to act in such a peculiar manner. Are you crazy? Of course he'll take them. He'll have to take them in order to get out of Port Agnew. I doubt if he has a dollar in the world."

Mr. Daney beat his chest gorilla fashion. "He doesn't need a dollar. Boy and man, I've loved that— ahem! son of yours. Why, he always *did* have guts. Keep your filthy money. The boy's credit is good with me. I'm no pauper, even I if do work for you. I work for fun. Understand. Or do you, Hector Mc-Kaye?"

"If you dare to loan my son as much as a thin dime I'll fire you out of hand."

Mr. Daney jeered. "How?" he demanded very distinctly, and yet with a queer, unusual blending of the sentence with a single word, as if the very force of his breath had telescoped every syllable, "would you like to stand off in that corner there and take a long runnin' jump at yourself, proud father?"

"Out of this office! You're fired."

Mr. Daney dashed the tears from his whiskers and blew his nose. Then he pulled himself together with dignity and bowed so low he lost his center of gravity and teetered a little on his toes before recovering his balance. "Fired is GOOD," he declared. "Where do you get that stuff, eh? My dear old Furiosity, ain't my resignation in the wastebasket? Good-by, good luck and may the good Lord give you the sense God gives geese. I'm a better man than you are, Gunga Din."

The door banged open. Then it banged shut and The Laird was alone. The incident was closed. The impossible had come to pass. For the strain had been too great, and at nine o'clock on a working day morning, steady, reliable, dependable, automatic Andrew Daney having imbibed Dutch courage in lieu of Nature's own brand, was, for the first time in his life, jingled to an extent comparable to that of a boiled owl.

Mr. Daney's assistant thrust his head in the door, to disturb The Laird's cogitations. "The knee-bolters went out at the shingle mill this morning, sir," he announced. "They want a six and a half hour day and a fifty per cent. increase in wages, with a whole holiday on Saturday. There's a big Russian red down there exhorting them."

"Send Dirty Dan to me. Quick!"

A telephonic summons to the loading shed brought Daniel P. O'Leary on the run. "Come with me, Dan," The Laird commanded, and started for the shingle mill. On the way down he stopped at the warehouse and selected a new double-bitted ax which he handed to Dirty Dan. Mr. O'Leary received the weapon in silence and trotted along at The Laird's heels like a faithful dog, until, upon arrival at the shingle mill the astute Hibernian took in the situation at a glance.

"Sure, 'tis no compliment you've paid me, sor, thinkin' I'll be afther needin' an ax to take that fella's measure," he protested.

"Your job is to keep those other animals off me while I take his measure," The Laird corrected him.

Without an instant's hesitation Dirty Dan swung his ax and charged the crowd. "Gower that, ye vagabones," he screeched. As he passed the Russian he seized the latter by the collar, swung him and threw him bodily toward old Hector, who received him greedily and drew him to his heart. The terrible O'Leary then stood over the battling pair, his ax poised, the while he hurled insult and anathema at the knee-bolters. A very large percentage of knee-bolters and shingle weavers are members of the I. W. W. and knowing this, Mr. O'Leary begged in dulcet tones, to be informed why in this and that nobody seemed willing to lift a hand to rescue the Little Comrade. He appeared to be keenly disappointed because nobody tried, albeit other axes were quite plentiful thereabouts.

Presently The Laird got up and dusted the splinters and sawdust from his clothing; the Red, battered terribly, lay weltering in his blood. "I feel better now," said The Laird. "This is just what I needed this morning to bring me out of myself. Help yourself, Dan," and he made a dive at the nearest striker, who fled, followed by his fellow-strikers, all hotly pursued by The Laird and the demon Daniel.

The Laird returned, puffing slightly, to his office and once more sat in at his own desk. As he remarked to Dirty Dan, he felt better now. All his resentment against Daney had fled but his resolution to pursue his contemplated course with reference to his son and the latter's wife had become firmer than ever. In some ways The Laird was a terrible old man.

XXXXII

NAN was not at all surprised when, upon responding to a peremptory knock at her front door she discovered Andrew Daney standing without. The general manager, after his stormy interview with The Laird had spent two hours in the sunny lee of a lumber pile, waiting for the alcoholic fogs to lift from his brain, for he had had sense enough left to realize that all was not well with him; he desired to have his tongue in order when he should meet the bride and groom.

"Good morning, Mr. Daney," Nan greeted him. "Do come in."

"Good morning, Mrs. McKaye. Thank you. I shall with pleasure."

He followed her down the little hallway to the living room where Donald sat with his great thin legs stretched out toward the fire.

"Don't rise, boy, don't rise," Mr. Daney protested. "I merely called to kiss the bride and shake your hand, my boy. The visit is entirely friendly and un-official."

"Mr. Daney, you're a dear," Nan cried, and presented her fair cheek for the tribute he claimed.

"Shake hands with a rebel, boy," Mr. Daney cried heartily to Donald. "God bless you and may you always be happier than you are this minute."

Donald wrung the Daney digits with a heartiness he would not have thought possible a month before.

"I've quarreled with your father, Donald," he

announced, seating himself. "Over you—and you," he
added, nodding brightly at both young people. "He
thinks he's fired me." He paused, glanced around,
coughed a couple of times and came out with it. "Well,
what are you going to do now to put tobacco in your
old tobacco box, Donald?"

Donald smiled sadly. "Oh, Nan still has a few dollars
left from that motor-boat swindle you perpetrated, Mr.
Daney. She'll take care of me for a couple of weeks
until I'm myself again; then, if my father still proves
recalcitrant and declines to have me connected with
the Tyee Lumber Company, I'll manage to make a
living for Nan and the boy somewhere else."

Briefly Mr. Daney outlined The Laird's expressed
course of action with regard to his son.

"He means it," Donald assured the general manager.
"He never bluffs. He gave me plenty of warning
and his decision has not been arrived at in a hurry.
He's through with me."

"I fear he is, my boy. Er-ah-ahem! Harumph-h-h!
Do you remember those bonds you sent me from New
York once—the proceeds of your deal in that Wiskah
river cedar?"

"Yes."

"Your father desires that you accept the entire two
hundred thousand dollars worth and accrued interest."

"Why?"

"Well, I suppose he thinks they'll come in handy
when you leave Port Agnew."

"Well, I'm not going to leave Port Agnew, Andrew."

"Your father instructed me to say to you that he
would take it kindly of you to do so—for obvious reasons."

"I appreciate his point of view, but since he has kicked me out he has no claim on my sympathies—at least not to the extent of forcing his point of view and causing me to abandon my own. Please say to my father that since I cannot have his forgiveness I do not want his bonds or his money. Tell him also, please, that I'm not going to leave Port Agnew, because that would predicate a sense of guilt on my part and lend some support to the popular assumption that my wife is not a virtuous woman. I could not possibly oblige my father on this point because to do so would be a violent discourtesy to my wife. I am not ashamed of her, you know."

Mr. Daney gnawed his thumb nail furiously. "'The wicked flee when no man pursueth'," he quoted. "However, Mr. Donald, you know as well as I do that if your father should forbid it, a dicky bird couldn't make a living in this town."

"There are no such restrictions in Darrow, Mr. Daney. The superintendent up there will give me a job on the river."

Mr. Daney could not forbear an expression of horror. "Hector McKaye's son a river hog!" he cried incredulously.

"Well, Donald McKaye's father was a river hog, wasn't he?"

"Oh, but times have changed since Hector was a pup, my boy. Why, this is dreadful."

"No, Mr. Daney. Merely unusual."

"Well, Donald, I think your father will raise the ante considerably in order to avoid that added disgrace and force you to listen to reason."

"If he does, sir, please spare yourself the trouble of

bearing his message. Neither Nan nor I is for sale, sir."

"I told him you'd decline the bonds. However, Mr. Donald, there is no reason in life why you shouldn't get money from me whenever you want it. Thanks to your father I'm worth more than a hundred thousand myself, although you'd never guess it. Your credit is A-1 with me."

"I shall be your debtor for life because of that speech, Mr. Daney. Any news from my mother and the girls?"

"None."

"Well, I'll stand by for results," Donald assured him gravely.

"Do not expect any."

"I don't."

Mr. Daney fidgeted and finally said he guessed he'd better be trotting along, and Donald and Nan, realizing it would be no kindness to him to be polite and assure him there was no need of hurry, permitted him to depart forthwith.

"I think, sweetheart," Donald announced with a pained little smile, as he returned from seeing Mr. Daney to the front gate, "that it wouldn't be a half bad idea for you to sit in at that old piano and play and sing for me. I think I'd like something light and lilting. What's that Kipling thing that's been set to music?

> So we went strolling,
> Down by the rolling, down by the rolling sea,
> You may keep your croak for other folk
> But you can't frighten me!

He lighted a cigarette and stretched himself out on the old divan. She watched him blowing smoke rings at the ceiling—and there was no music in her soul.

In the afternoon the McKaye limousine drew up at the front gate and Nan's heart fluttered violently in contemplation of a visit from her husband's mother and sisters. She need not have worried, however. The interior of the car was unoccupied save for Donald's clothing and personal effects which some thoughtful person at The Dreamerie had sent down to him. He hazarded a guess that the cool and practical Elizabeth had realized his needs.

XXXXIII

RETURNING to the mill office, Mr. Daney sat at his desk and started to look over the mail. The Laird heard his desk buzzer sounding frequently and rightly conjecturing that his general manager was back on the job, he came into the latter's office and glared at him.

"I thought I fired you?" he growled.

"I know. You thought you did," the rebel replied complacently. "I see by your knuckles you've been fighting. Hope it did you good."

"It did. Are you going to leave this office?"

"No, sir."

"I didn't think you would. Well, well! Out with it."

Mr. Daney drew a deal of pleasure from that invitation. "The boy directs me to inform you, sir, that he will not accept the bonds nor any monies you may desire to give him. He says he doesn't need them because he isn't going to leave Port Agnew."

"Nonsense, Andrew. He cannot remain in this town. He hasn't the courage to face his little world after marrying that girl. And he has to make a living for her."

"We shall see that which we shall se," Mr. Daney replied enigmatically.

"I wonder if it is possible he is trying to outgame me," old Hector mused aloud. "Andrew, go back and tell him that if he will go to California to live I will deed

335

him that Lassen county sugar and white pine and build
him the finest mill in the state."

"The terms are quite impossible," Daney retorted
and explained why.

"He shall get out of Port Agnew," The Laird threatened. "He shall get out or starve."

"You are forgetting something, sir."

"Forgetting what?"

"That I have more than a hundred thousand dollars
in bonds right in that vault and that I have not as yet
developed paralysis of the right hand. The boy shall
not starve and neither shall he crawl, like a beaten dog
currying favor with the one that has struck him."

"I am the one who has been struck—and he has
wounded me sorely," The Laird cried, his voice cracked
with anger.

"The mischief is done. What's the use of crying
over spilled milk? You're going to forgive the boy
sooner or later, so do it now and be graceful about it."

"I'll never forgive him, Andrew."

Mr. Daney walled his eyes toward the ceiling.
"Thank God," he murmured piously, "I'm pure. Hereafter, every time Reverend Mr. Tingley says the Lord's
prayer I'm going to cough out loud in church at the
line: 'Forgive us our trespasses as we forgive those
who trespass against us.' You'll hear that cough and
remember, Hector McKaye."

A deeper shadow of distress settled over The Laird's
stern features. "You're uncommon mean to me this
bitter day, Andrew," he complained wearily. "I take
it as most unkind of you to thwart my wishes like
this."

"I'm for true love!" Mr. Daney declared firmly.

"Ah come, come now! Don't be a stiff-necked old dodo. Forgive the boy."

"In time I may forgive him, Andrew. I'm not sure of myself where he is concerned, but we canna receive the girl. 'Tis not in reason that we should."

"I believe I'll cough twice," Daney murmured musingly.

And the following day being Sunday, he did! He sat two rows behind the McKaye family pew but across the aisle, and in a cold fury The Laird turned to squelch him with a look. What he saw in the Daney pew, however, chilled his fury and threw him into a veritable panic of embarrassment. For to the right of the incomprehensible general manager sat the young ex-laird of Port Agnew; at Daney's left the old Laird beheld his new daughter-in-law, while further down the pew as far as she could retreat, Mrs. Daney, with face aflame, sat rigid, her bovine countenance upraised and her somewhat vacuous glance fixed unblinkingly at a point some forty feet over Mr. Tingley's pious head. Donald intercepted the old man's amazed and troubled glance, and smiled at his father with his eyes—an affectionate overture that was not lost on The Laird ere he jerked his head and eyes once more to the front.

Mrs. McKaye and her two daughters were as yet unaware of the horror that impended. But not for long. When the congregation stood to sing the final hymn, Nan's wondrous mezzo-soprano rose clear and sweet over the indifferent-toned notes of every other woman present; to the most dull it would have been obvious that there was a trained singer present, and Mrs. McKaye and her daughters each cast a covert glance in the direction of the voice. However, since every other woman in the church was gazing at Nan, nobody observed the effect of her presence upon the senior branch of the McKaye family, for which small blessing the family in question was duly grateful.

At the conclusion of the service old Hector remained in his pew until the majority of the congregation had filed out; then, assuring himself by a quick glance, that his son and the latter's wife had preceded him, he followed with Mrs. McKaye and the girls. From the church steps he observed Donald and Nan walking home, while Mr. Daney and his outraged spouse followed some twenty feet behind them. Quickly The Laird and his family entered the waiting limousine; it was the first occasion that anybody could remember when he had not lingered to shake hands with Mr. Tingley and, perchance, congratulate him on the excellence of his sermon.

They were half way up the cliff road before anybody spoke. Then, with a long preliminary sigh, The Laird voiced the thought that obsessed them all.

"That damned mutton-head, Daney. I'd run him out of the Tyee employ if it would do a bit of good. I cannot run him out of town or out of church."

"The imbecile!" Elizabeth raged. Jane was dumb with shame and rage and Mrs. McKaye was sniffling a little. Presently she said:

"How dare he bring her right into church with him," she cried brokenly. "Right before everybody. Oh, dear, oh dear, is my son totally lacking in a sense of decency? This is terrible, terrible."

"I shall not risk such another awful Sunday morning," Elizabeth announced.

"Nor I," Jane cried with equal fervor.

"We shall have to leave Port Agnew now," Mrs. McKaye sobbed.

Old Hector patted her hand. "Yes, I think you'll have to, Nellie. Unfortunately, I cannot go with you. Daney doesn't appear to be quite sane of late and with Donald out of the business I'm chained to a desk for the remainder of my life. I fear, however," he added savagely, "I do not intend to let that woman run me out of my own church. Not by a damned sight!"

The instant they entered the house, rightly conjecturing that the Daneys had also reached their home, Mrs. McKaye went to the telephone and proceeded to inform Mr. Daney of the opinion which the McKaye family, jointly and severally, entertained for his idea of comedy. Daney listened respectfully to all she had to say touching his sanity, his intelligence, his sense of decency, and his loyalty to Hector and when, stung because he made no defense, she asked: "Have you no explanation to make us for your extraordinary behavior?" he replied:

"I am an usher of our church, Mrs. McKaye. When Donald and his wife entered the church the only vacant seats in it were in my pew; the only person in the church who would not have felt a sense of outrage at having your daughter-in-law seated with his or her family, was my self-sacrificing self. I could not be discourteous to Donald and I'm quite certain his wife has as much right in our church as you have. So I shooed them both up to my pew, to the great distress of Mrs. Daney."

"You should be ashamed of yourself, Andrew. You should!"

"I'm not ashamed of myself, Mrs. McKaye. I've been a pussy-foot all my life. I had to do something I knew would detract from my popularity, but since I had to do it I decided to do it promptly and as if I enjoyed it. Surely you would not have commended me had I met the young couple at the door and said to them: 'Get out of this church. It is not for such as you. However, if you insist upon staying, you'll have to stand up or else sit down on the floor. Nobody here wants to sit with you. They're afraid, too, they'll off'end the Chief Pooh-bah of this town'."

"You could have pretended you did not see them."

"My dear Mrs. McKaye," Daney retorted in even tones, "do you wish me to inform your husband of a certain long distance telephone conversation? If so——"

She hung up without waiting to say good-by, and the following day she left for Seattle, accompanied by her daughters.

Throughout the week The Laird forbore mentioning his son's name to Mr. Daney; indeed, he refrained from addressing the latter at all unless absolutely necessary to speak to him directly—wherefore Daney knew himself to be blacklisted. On the following Sunday The Laird sat alone in the family pew and Mr. Daney did not cough during the recital of the Lord's prayer, so old Hector managed to conquer a tremendous yearning to glance around for the reason. Also, as on the previous Sunday, he was in no hurry to leave his pew at the conclusion of the service, yet, to his profound irritation, when he did leave it and start down the central aisle of the church, he looked squarely into the faces of Donald and Nan as they emerged from the Daney

pew. Mrs. Daney was conspicuous by her absence.
Nan's baby boy had fallen asleep during the service
and Donald was carrying the cherub.

Old Hector's face went white; he gulped when his
son spoke to him.

"Hello, Dad. You looked lonely all by yourself in
that big pew. Suppose we come up and sit with you
next Sunday?"

Old Hector paused and bent upon his son and Nan
a terrible look. "Never speak to me again so long
as you live," he replied in a low voice, and passed out
of the church.

Donald gazed after his broad erect figure and shook
his head dolefully, as Mr. Daney fell into step beside
him. "I told you so," he whispered.

"Isn't it awful to be Scotch?" Nan inquired.

"It is awful—on the Scotch," her husband assured
her. "The dear old fraud gulped like a broken-hearted
boy when I spoke to him. He'd rather be wrong than
president."

As they were walking home to the Sawdust Pile, Nan
captured one of her husband's great fingers and swung
it childishly. "I wish you didn't insist upon our going
to church, sweetheart," she complained. "We're spoiling your father's Christianity."

"Can't help it," he replied doggedly. "We're going
to be thoroughbreds about this, no matter how much
it hurts."

She sighed. "And you're only half Scotch, Donald."

XXXXIV

BY noon of the following day, Port Agnew was astounded by news brought by the crew of one of the light draft launches used to tow log rafts down the river. Donald McKaye was working for Darrow. He was their raftsman; he had been seen out on the log boom, pike pole in hand, shoving logs in to the endless chain elevator that drew them up to the seas. As might be imagined, Mrs. Daney was among the first to glean this information, and to her husband she repeated it at luncheon with every evidence of pleasure.

"Tut, tut, woman," he replied carelessly, "this is no news to me. He told me yesterday after service that he had the job."

The familiar wrinkle appeared for an instant on the end of her nose before she continued: "I wonder what The Laird thinks of that, Andrew?"

"So do I," he parried skilfully.

"Does he know it?"

"There isn't a soul in Port Agnew with sufficient courage to tell him."

"Why do you not tell him?"

"None of my business. Besides, I do not hanker to see people squirm with suffering."

She wrinkled her nose once more and was silent.

As Mr. Daney had declared, there was none in Port Agnew possessed of sufficient hardihood to inform the Laird of his son's lowly status and it was three weeks before he discovered it for himself. He had gone up the river to one of his logging camps and the humor had seized him to make the trip in a fast little motor-boat he had given Donald at Christmas many years before. He was busy adjusting the carburetor, after months of disuse, as he passed the Darrow log boom in the morning, so he failed to see his big son leaping across the logs, balancing himself skilfully with the pike pole.

It was rather late when he started home and in the knowledge that darkness might find him well up the river he hurried.

Now, from the Bight of Tyee to a point some five miles above Darrow, the Skookum flows in almost a straight line; the few bends are wide and gradual, and when The Laird came to this home-stretch he urged the boat to its maximum speed of twenty-eight miles per hour. Many a time in happier days he had raced down this long stretch with Donald at the helm, and he knew the river thoroughly; as he sped along he steered mechanically, his mind occupied in a consideration of the dishonor that had come upon his clan.

The sun had already set as he came roaring down a wide deep stretch near Darrow's mill; in his preoccupa-tion he forgot that his competitor's log boom stretched across the river fully two-thirds of its width; that he should throttle down, swerve well to starboard and avoid the field of stored logs. The deep shadows cast by the sucker growth and old snags along the bank blended with the dark surface of the log boom and prevented him from observing that he was headed for the heart of it; the first intimation he had of his dan-

ger came to him in a warning shout from the left bank
—a shout that rose above the roar of the exhaust.

"Jump! Overboard! Quickly! The log boom!"

Old Hector awoke from his bitter reverie. He, who
had once been a river hog, had no need to be told of the
danger incident to abrupt precipitation into the heart
of that log boom, particularly when it would presently
be gently agitated by the long high "bone" the racing
boat carried in her teeth. When logs weighing twenty
tons come gently together—even when they barely rub
against each other, nothing living caught between them
may survive.

The unknown who warned him was right. He must
jump overboard and take his chance in the river, for
it was too late now to slow down and put his motor in
reverse. In the impending crash that was only a matter of seconds, The Laird would undoubtedly catapult
from the stern sheets into the water—and if he
should drift in under the logs, knew the river would
eventually give up his body somewhere out in the Bight
of Tyee. On the other hand, should he be thrown out
on the boom he would stand an equal chance of being
seriously injured by the impact or crushed to death
when his helpless body should fall between the logs.
In any event the boat would be telescoped down to the
cockpit and sink at the edge of the log field.

He was wearing a heavy overcoat, for it was late in
the fall, and he had no time to remove it; not even time
to stand up and dive clear. So he merely hurled his
big body against the starboard gunwale and toppled
overboard—and thirty feet further on the boat struck
with a crash that echoed up and down the river, telescoped and drove under the log boom. It was not in

sight when old Hector rose puffing to the surface and bellowed for help before starting to swim for the log boom.

The voice answered him instantly: "Coming! Hold on!"

Handicapped as he was with his overcoat, old Hector found it a prodigious task to reach the boom; as he clung to the boom-stick he could make out the figure of a man with a pike pole coming toward him in long leaps across the logs. And then old Hector noticed something else.

He had swum to the outer edge of the log boom and grasped the light boom-stick, dozens of which, chained end to end, formed the floating enclosure in which the log supply was stored. The moment he rested his weight on this boom-stick, however, one end of it submerged suddenly—wherefore The Laird knew that the impact of the motor-boat had broken a link of the boom and that this broken end was now sweeping outward and downward, with the current releasing the millions of feet of stored logs. Within a few minutes, provided he should keep afloat, he would be in the midst of these tremendous Juggernauts, for, clinging to the end of the broken boom he was gradually describing a circle on the outside of the log field, swinging from beyond the middle of the river in to the left-hand bank; presently, when the boom should have drifted its maximum distance he would be hung up stationary in deep water while the released logs bore down upon him with the current and gently shoulder him into eternity.

He clawed his way along the submerging boom-stick to its other end, where it was linked with its neighbor, and the combined buoyancy of both boom-sticks was sufficient to float him.

"Careful," he called to the man leaping over the log-field toward him. "The boom is broken! Careful, I tell you! The logs are moving out—they're slipping apart. Be careful."

Even as he spoke, The Laird realized that the approaching rescuer would not heed him. He *had* to make speed out to the edge of the moving logs; if he was to rescue the man clinging to the boom-sticks he must take a chance on those long leaps through the dusk; he *must* reach The Laird before too much open water developed between the moving logs.

Only a trained river man could have won to him in such a brief space of time; only an athlete could have made the last flying leap across six feet of dark water to a four-foot log that was bearing gently down, butt first, on the figure clinging to the boom-stick. His caulks bit far up the side of the log and the force of his impact started it rolling; yet even as he clawed his way to the top of the log and got it under control the iron head of his long pike pole drove into the boom-stick and fended The Laird out of harm's way; before the log the man rode could slip by, the iron had been released and the link of chain between the two boom-sticks had been snagged with the pike hook, and both men drifted side by side.

"Safe—o," his rescuer warned Old Hector quietly. "Hang on. I'll keep the logs away from you and when the field floats by I'll get you ashore. We're drifting gradually in toward the bank below the mill."

The Laird was too chilled, too exhausted and too lacking in breath to do more than gasp a brief word

of thanks. It seemed a long, long time that he clung
there, and it was quite dark when his rescuer spoke
again. "I think the last log has floated out of the
booming ground. I'll swim ashore with you now, as
soon as I can shuck my boots and mackinaw." A few
minutes later he cried reassuringly, "All set, old-timer,"
and slid into the water beside The Laird. "Relax yourself and do not struggle." His hands came up around
old Hector's jaws from the rear. "Let go," he commanded, and the hard tow commenced. It was all foot-
work and their progress was very slow, but eventually
they won through. As soon as he could stand erect
in the mud the rescuer unceremoniously seized The
Laird by the nape and dragged him high and dry up
the bank.

"Now, then," he gasped, "I guess you can take care
of yourself. Better go over to the mill and warm yourself in the furnace room. I've got to hurry away to
'phone the Tyee people to swing a dozen spare links of
their log boom across the river and stop those runaways before they escape into the Bight and go to sea
on the ebb."

He was gone on the instant, clambering up the bank
through the bushes that grew to the water's edge;
old Hector could hear his breath coming in great gasps
as he ran.

"Must know that chap, whoever he is," The Laird
soliloquized. "Think he's worked for me some time or
other. His voice sounds mighty familiar. Well—I'll
look him up in the morning."

He climbed after his rescuer and stumbled away
through the murk toward Darrow's mill. Arrived
here he found the fireman banking the fires in the fur-

nace room and while he warmed himself one of them summoned Bert Darrow from the mill office.

"Bert," The Laird explained, "I'd be obliged if you'd run me home in more or less of a hurry in your closed car. I've been in the drink," and he related the tale of his recent adventures. "Your raftsman saved my life," he concluded. "Who is he? It was so dark before he got to me I couldn't see his face distinctly, but I think he's a young fellow who used to work for me. I know because his voice sounds so very familiar."

"He's a new hand, I believe. Lives in Port Agnew. I believe your man Daney can tell you his name," Darrow replied evasively.

"I'll ask Daney. The man was gone before I could recover enough breath to thank him for my life. Sorry to have messed up your boom, Bert, but we'll stop the runaways at my boom and I'll have them towed back in the morning. And I'll have a man put in a new boom-stick and connect it up again."

Bert Darrow set him down at the Tyee Lumber Company's office, and wet and chilled as he was, The Laird went at once to Mr. Daney's office. The latter was just leaving it for the day when The Laird appeared.

"Andrew," the latter began briskly. "I drove that fast motor-boat at full speed into Darrow's boom on my way down river this evening; I've had a ducking and only for Darrow's raftsman you'd be closing down the mill to-morrow out of respect to my memory. Bert Darrow says their raftsman used to work for us; he's a new man with them and Bert says you know who he is."

"I think I know the man," Mr. Daney replied thoughtfully. "He's been with them about three weeks;

resigned our employ a couple of weeks before that. I was sorry to lose him. He's a good man."

"I grant it, Andrew. He's the fastest, coolest hand that ever balanced a pike pole or rode a log. We cannot afford to let men like that fellow get away from us for the sake of a little extra pay. Get him back on the payroll, Andrew, and don't be small with him. I'll remember him handsomely at Christmas, and see that I do not forget this, Andrew. What is his name?"

"Let me think." Mr. Daney bent his head, tipped back his hat and massaged his brow before replying. "I think that when he worked for the Tyee Lumber Company he was known as Donald McKaye."

He looked up. The old Laird's face was ashen. "Thank you, Andrew," he managed to murmur presently. "Perhaps you'd better let Darrow keep him for a while. G—g—good-night!"

Outside, his chauffeur waited with his car. "Home —and be quick about it," he mumbled and crawled into the tonneau slowly and weakly. As the car rolled briskly up the high cliff road to The Dreamerie, the old man looked far below him to the little light that twinkled on the Sawdust Pile.

"She'll have his dinner cooked for him now and be waiting and watching for him," he thought.

XXXXV

HECTOR McKAYE suffered that winter. He dwelt in Gethsemane, for he had incurred to his outcast son the greatest debt that one man can incur to another, and he could not publicly acknowledge the debt or hope to repay it in kind. By the time spring came his heart hunger was almost beyond control; there were times when, even against his will, he contemplated a reconciliation with Donald based on an acceptance of the latter's wife but with certain reservations. The Laird never quite got around to defining the reservation but in a vague way he felt that they should exist and that eventually Donald would come to a realization of the fact and help him define them.

Each Sunday during that period of wretchedness he saw his boy and Nan at church, although they no longer sat with Mr. Daney. From Reverend Tingley The Laird learned that Donald now had a pew of his own, and he wondered why. He knew his son had never been remotely religious and eventually he decided that, in his son's place, though he were the devil himself, he would do exactly as Donald had done. Damn a dog that carried a low head and a dead tail! It was the sign of the mongrel strain—curs always crept under the barn when beaten!

One Sunday in the latter part of May he observed that Nan came to church alone. He wondered if Donald was at home ill and a vague apprehension stabbed him; he longed to drop into step beside Nan as she left the church and ask her, but, of course, that was unthinkable. Nevertheless he wished he knew and that afternoon he spent the entire time on the terrace at The Dreamerie, searching the Sawdust Pile with his marine glasses, in the hope of seeing Donald moving about the little garden. But he did not see him, and that night his sleep was more troubled than usual.

On the following Sunday Nan was not accompanied by her husband either. The Laird decided, therefore, that Donald could not be very ill, otherwise Nan would not have left him home alone. This thought comforted him somewhat. During the week he thought frequently of telephoning up to Darrow and asking if they still had the same raftsman on the payroll, but his pride forbade this. So he drove up the river road one day and stopped his car among the trees on the bank of the river from the Darrow log boom. A tall, lively young fellow was leaping nimbly about on the logs, but so active was he that even at two hundred yards The Laird could not be certain this man was his son. He returned to Port Agnew more troubled and distressed than ever.

Mrs. McKaye and the girls had made three flying visits down to Port Agnew during the winter and The Laird had spent his week-ends in Seattle twice; otherwise, save for the servants, he was quite alone at The Dreamerie and this did not add to his happiness. Gradually the continued and inexplicable absence of Donald at Sunday service became an obsession with him; he could think of nothing else in his spare moments and even at times when it was imperative he should give all of his attention to important business matters, this eternal, damnable query continued to confront him. It went to bed with him and got up with him and under its steady relentless attrition he began to lose the look of robust health that set him off so well among men of his own age. His eyes took on a worried, restless gleam; he was irritable and in the mornings he frequently wore to the office the haggard appearance that speaks so accusingly of a sleepless night. He lost his appetite and in consequence he lost weight. Andrew Daney was greatly concerned about him, and one day, apropos of nothing, he demanded a bill of particulars.

"Oh, I daresay I'm getting old, Andrew," The Laird replied evasively.

"Worrying about the boy?"

It was a straight shot and old Hector was too inexpressibly weary to attempt to dodge it. He nodded sadly.

"Well, let us hope he'll come through all right, sir."

"Is he ill? What's wrong with him, Andrew? Man, I've been eating my heart out for months, wondering what it is, but you know the fix I'm in. I don't like to ask and not a soul in Port Agnew will discuss him with me."

"Why, there's nothing wrong with him that I'm aware of, sir. I spoke to Nan after services last Sunday and she read me a portion of his last letter. He was quite well at that time."

"W-wh-where is he, Andrew?"

"Somewhere in France. He's not allowed to tell."

"France? Good God, Andrew, not *France!*"

"Why not, may I ask? Of course he's in France,

He enlisted as a private shortly after war was declared. Dirty Dan quit his job and went with him. They went over with the Fifth Marines. Do you mean to tell me this is news to you?" he added, frankly amazed.

"I do," old Hector mumbled brokenly. "Oh, Andrew man, this is terrible, terrible. I canna stand it, man." He sat down and covered his face with his trembling old hands.

"Why can't you? You wouldn't want him to sit at home and be a slacker, would you? And you wouldn't have a son of yours wait until the draft board took him by the ear and showed him his duty, would you?"

"If he's killed I'll nae get over it." The Laird commenced to weep childishly.

"Well, better men or at least men as fine, are paying that price for citizenship, Hector McKaye."

"But his wife, man? He was married. 'Twas not expected of him——"

"I believe his wife is more or less proud of him, sir. Her people have always followed the flag in some capacity."

"But how does she exist? Andrew Daney, if you're giving her the money——"

"If I am you have no right to ask impertinent questions about it. But I'm not."

"I never knew it, I never knew it," the old man complained bitterly. "Nobody tells me anything about my own son. I'm alone; I sit in the darkness, stifling with money—oh, Andrew, Andrew, I didn't say good-by to him! I let him go in sorrow and in anger."

"You may have time to cure all that. Go down to the Sawdust Pile, take the girl to your heart like a good

father should and then cable the boy. That will square
things beautifully."

Even in his great distress the stubborn old head was
shaken emphatically. The Laird of Port Agnew was
not yet ready to surrender.

Spring lengthened into summer and summer into
fall. Quail piped in the logged-over lands and wild
ducks whistled down through the timber and rested on
the muddy bosom of the Skookum, but for the first time
in forty years The Laird's setters remained in their
kennels and his fowling pieces in their leather cases.
To him the wonderful red and gold of the great
Northern woods had lost the old allurement and he no
longer thrilled when a ship of his fleet, homeward
bound, dipped her house-flag far below him. He was
slowly disintegrating.

Of late he had observed that Nan no longer came
to church, so he assumed she had found the task of
facing her world bravely one somewhat beyond her
strength. A few months before, this realization would
have proved a source of savage satisfaction to him,
but time and suffering were working queer changes in
his point of view. Now, although he told himself it
served her right, he was sensible of a small feeling of
sympathy for her and a large feeling of resentment
against the conditions that had brought her into con-
flict with the world.

"I daresay," Andrew Daney remarked to him about
Christmas time, "you haven't forgotten your resolve
to do something handsome for that raftsman of Darrow's who saved your life last January. You told me
to remind you of him at Christmas."

"I have not forgotten the incident," old Hector answered savagely.

"I think it might be a nice thing to do if you would send word to Nan, by me, that it will please you if she will consent to have your grandchild born in the company hospital. Otherwise, I imagine she will go to a Seattle hospital, and with doctors and nurses away to the war there's a chance she may not get the best of care."

"Do as you see fit," The Laird answered. He longed to evade the issue—he realized that Daney was crowding him always, setting traps for him, driving him relentlessly toward a reconciliation that was abhorrent to him. "I have no objection. She cannot afford the expense of a Seattle hospital, I daresay, and I do not desire to oppress her."

The following day Mr. Daney reported that Nan had declined with thanks his permission to enter the Tyee Lumber Company's hospital. As a soldier's wife she would be cared for without expense in the Base Hospital at Camp Lewis, less than a day's journey distant.

The Laird actually quivered when Daney broke this news to him. He was hurt—terribly hurt—but he dared not admit it. In January he learned through Mr. Daney that he was a grandfather to a nine-pound boy and that Nan planned to call the baby Caleb, after her father. For the first time in his life then, The Laird felt a pang of jealousy. While the child could never, by any possibility, be aught to him, nevertheless he felt that in the case of a male child a certain polite deference toward the infant's paternal ancestors was always commendable. At any rate, Caleb was Yankee and hateful.

"I am the twelfth of my line to be named Hector," he said presently—and Andrew Daney with difficulty repressed a roar of maniac laughter. Instead he said soberly.

"The child's playing in hard luck as matters stand; it would be adding insult to injury to call him Hector McKaye, Thirteenth. Isn't that why you named your son Donald?"

The Laird pretended not to hear this. Having been fired on from ambush, as it were, he immediately started discussing an order for some ship timbers for the Emergency Fleet Corporation. When he retired to his own office, however, he locked the door and wept with sympathy for his son, so far away and in the shadow of death upon the occasion of the birth of his first son.

XXXXVI

SPRING came. Overhead the wild geese flew in long wedges, honking, into the North, and The Laird remembered how Donald, as a boy, used to shoot at them with a rifle as they passed over The Dreamerie. Their honking wakened echoes in his heart. With the winter's supply of logs now gone, logging operations commenced in the woods with renewed vigor, the river teemed with rafts, the shouts of the rivermen echoing from bank to bank. Both Tyee and Darrow were getting out spruce for the government and ship timbers for the wooden shipyards along San Francisco Bay.

Business had never been so brisk, and with the addition of the war duties that came to every community leader, The Laird found some surcease from his heart-hunger. Mrs. McKaye and the girls had returned to The Dreamerie, now that Donald's marriage had ceased to interest anybody but themselves, so old Hector was not so lonely. But—the flag was flying again at the Sawdust Pile, each day of toil for The Laird was never complete without an eager search of the casualty lists published in the Seattle papers.

Spring lengthened into summer. The Marine casualties at Belleau Wood and Château-Thierry appalled The Laird; he read that twenty survivors of a charge that started two hundred and fifty strong across the wheat field at Bouresches had taken Bouresches and held it against three hundred of the enemy—led by

357

Sergeant Daniel J. O'Leary, of Port Agnew, Washington! Good old Dirty Dan! At last he was finding a legitimate outlet for his talents! He would get the Distinguished Service Cross for that! The Laird wondered what Donald would receive. It would be terrible should Dirty Dan return with the Cross and Donald McKaye without it.

In September, Donald appeared in the Casualty List as slightly wounded. Also, he was a first lieutenant now. The Laird breathed easier, for his son would be out of it for a few months, no doubt. It was a severe punishment, however, not to be able to discuss his gallant son with anybody. At home his dignity and a firm adherence to his previous announcement that his son's name should never be mentioned in his presence, forbade a discussion with Mrs. McKaye and the girls; and when he weakly sparred for an opportunity with Andrew Daney, that stupid creature declined to rise to the bait, or even admit that he knew of Donald's commission. When told of it, he expressed neither surprise nor approval.

In November, the great influenza epidemic came to Port Agnew and took heavy toll. It brought to The Laird a newer, a more formidable depression. What if Donald's son should catch it and die, and Donald be deprived of the sight of his first-born? What if Nan should succumb to an attack of it while her husband was in France? In that event would Donald forgive and forget and come home to The Dreamerie? Somehow, old Hector had his doubts.

For a long time now, he had felt a great urge to see Donald's son. He had a curiosity to discover whether the child favored the McKayes or the Brents. If it favored the McKayes—well, perhaps he might make some provision for its future in his will, and in order to prove himself a good sport he would leave an equal sum to Nan's illegitimate child, which Donald had formally adopted a few days after his marriage to Nan. Why make fish of one and fowl of the other? he thought. They were both McKayes now, in the sight of the law, and for aught he knew to the contrary they were full brothers!

The child became an obsession with him. He longed to weigh it and compare its weight with that of Donald's at the same age—he had the ancient record in an old memorandum book at the office. He speculated on whether it had blue eyes or brown, whether it was a blond or a brunette. He wondered if Daney had seen it and wondering, at length he asked. Yes, Mr. Daney had seen the youngster several times, but beyond that statement he would not go and The Laird's dignity forbade too direct a probe. He longed to throttle Mr. Daney, who he now regarded as the most unsympathetic, prosaic, dull-witted old ass imaginable.

He wanted to see that child! The desire to do so never left him during his waking hours and he dreamed of the child at night. So in the end he yielded and went down to the Sawdust Pile, under cover of darkness, his intention being to sneak up to the little house and endeavor to catch a glimpse of the child through the window. He was enraged to discover, however, that Nan maintained a belligerent Airedale that refused, like all good Airedales, to waste his time and dignity in useless barking. He growled—once, and The Laird knew he meant it, so he got out of that yard in a hurry.

He was in a fine rage as he walked back to the mill office and got into his car. Curse the dog! Was he to be deprived of a glimpse of his grandson by an insensate brute of a dog? He'd be damned if he was! He'd shoot the animal first—no, that would never do. Nan would come out and he would be discovered. Moreover, what right had he to shoot anybody's dog until it attacked him? The thing to do would be to put some strychnine on a piece of meat—no, no, that would never do. The person who would poison a dog—any kind of a dog—

It was a good dog. The animal certainly was acting within its legal rights. Yes, he knew now where Nan had gotten it. The dog had belonged to First Sergeant Daniel J. O'Leary of the Fifth Marines; he had doubtless given it to Nan to keep for him when he went to the war; The Laird knew Dan thought a great deal of that dog. His name was Jerry and he had aided Dirty Dan in more than one bar-room battle.

Jerry, like his master, like the master of the woman he protected, was a Devil-dog, and one simply cannot kill a soldier's dog for doing a soldier's duty. Should Jerry charge there would be no stopping him until he was killed, so The Laird saw very clearly that there was but one course open to him. If he marched through that gate and straight to the door, as if he meant business, as if he had a moral and legal right to be there on business, Jerry would understand and permit him to pass. But if he snooped in, like a thief in the night, and peered in at a window—

"I wish I had a suit of Fifteenth Century armour,"

he thought. "Then Jerry, you could chew on my leg and be damned to you. You're a silent dog and I could have a good look while you were wrecking your teeth."

He went back to the Sawdust Pile at dusk the next evening, hoping Jerry would be absent upon some unlawful private business, but when he approached the gate slowly and noiselessly Jerry spoke up softly from within and practically said: "Get out or take the consequences."

The following night, however, The Laird was prepared for Jerry. He did not halt at the dog's preliminary warning but advanced and rattled the gate a little. Immediately Jerry came to the gate and stood just inside growling in his throat, so The Laird thrust an atomizer through the palings and deluged Jerry's hairy countenance with a fine cloud of spirits of ammonia. He had once tried that trick on a savage bulldog in which he desired to inculcate some respect for his person, and had succeeded beyond his most sanguine expectations. Therefore, since desperate circumstances always require desperate measures, the memory of that ancient victory had moved him to attempt a similar embarrassment of the dog Jerry.

But Jerry was a devil-dog. He had been raised and trained by Dirty Dan O'Leary and in company with that interesting anthropoid he had been through many stormy passages. Long before, he had learned that the offensive frequently wins—the defensive never. It is probable that he wept as he sniffed the awful stuff, but if he did they were tears of rage.

Jerry's first move was to stand on his head and cover his face with his paws. Then he did several back flips and wailed aloud in his misery and woe, his yelps of distress quite filling the empyrean. But only for the space of a few seconds. Recovering his customary aplomb he made a flying leap for the top of the gate, his yelps now succeeded by ambitious growls—and in self-defense The Laird was forced to spray him again as he clung momentarily on top of the palings. With a sob Jerry dropped back and buried his nose in the dust, while The Laird beat a hurried retreat into the darkness, for he had lost all confidence in his efforts to inculcate in Jerry an humble and contrite spirit.

He could hear rapid footsteps inside the little house; then the door opened and in the light that streamed from within he was indistinctly visible to Nan as she stood in the doorway.

"Jerry!" he heard her call. "Good dog! What's the matter? After him, Jerry. Go get him, Jerry!" She ran to the gate and opened it for the dog, who darted through, but paused again to run his afflicted nose in the dust and roll a couple of times. Apparently he felt that there was no great hurry; his quarry could not escape him. It is probable, also, that he was more or less confused and not quite certain which direction the enemy had taken, for Jerry's sense of smell was temporarily suspended and his eyes blinded by tears; certain his language was not at all what it should have been.

The Laird ran blindly, apprehensively, but for a very short distance. Suddenly he bumped into something quite solid, which closed around him viciously. "Halt, damn you," a commanding voice cried.

Despite his years, Hector McKaye was no weakling, and in the knowledge that he could not afford to be captured and discovered, seemingly he slipped forty years from his shoulders. Once more he was a lumberjack, the top dog of his district—and he proceeded to fight like one. His old arms rained punches on the midriff of the man who held him and he knew they stung cruelly, for at every punch the man grunted and strove to clinch him tighter and smother the next blow. "Let go me or I'll kill you," The Laird panted. "Man dinna drive me to it." He ceased his rain of blows, grasped his adversary and tried to wrestle him down. He succeeded, but the man would not stay down. He wriggled out with amazing ease and had old Hector with his shoulders touching before The Laird's heaving chest and two terrible thumbs closed down on each of The Laird's eyes, with four powerful fingers clasping his face like talons. "Quit, or I'll squeeze your eyeballs out," a voice warned him.

The Laird's hand beat the ground beside him. He had surrendered to a master of his style of fighting. With something of the air of an expert, his conqueror ran a quick hand over him, seeking for weapons, and finding none, he grasped The Laird by the collar and jerked him to his feet. "Now, then, my hearty, I'll have a look at you," he said. "You'll explain why you're skulking around here and abusing that dog!"

The Laird quivered as he found himself being dragged toward the stream of light, in the center of which Nan Brent stood silhouetted. He could not afford this and he was not yet defeated.

"A thousand dollars if you let me go now," he panted. "I have the money in my pocket. Ask yon lass if I've done aught wrong."

His captor paused and seemed to consider this.

"Make it ten thousand and I'll consider it," he whispered. "Leave it on the mail box just outside the Tyee Lumber Company's office at midnight to-morrow night."

"I'll do it—so help me God," The Laird promised frantically.

His son's voice spoke in his ear. "Dad! You low-down, worthless lovable old fraud!"

"My son! My son!" Old Hector's glad cry ended in a sob. "Oh, my sonny boy, my bonny lad! I canna stand it. I canna! Forgie me, lad, forgie me—and ask her to forgie me!" His old arms were around his son's neck and he was crying on Donald's shoulder, unashamed. "I was trying for a look at the bairn," he cried brokenly, "and 'twas a privilege God would nae gie me seeing that I came like a sneak and not like an honest man. The damned dog—he knew! Och, Donald, say ye forgie ye're auld faither. Say it, lad. Ma heart's breakin'."

"Why, bless your bare-shanked old Scotch soul, of course I forgive you. I never held any grudge, you know. I simply stood pat until you could see things through my eyes."

"Is that you, Donald?" Nan called.

"Aye, aye, sweetheart. Dad's here. He wants to know if you regard him as a particularly terrible old man. I think he's afraid you will refuse to let him look at Laird Hector, Thirteenth."

"Man, man," the old man urged, quite shocked at this casual greeting of a returned hero to his wife, "go to her, lad. She'll not relish favoritism."

"Oh, this isn't our first meeting, Dad. I got home yesterday. I have thirty days leave. They sent me home as an instructor in small arms practice and gave me a boost in rank. I was just up town for a beefsteak and I've lost the beefsteak battling with you."

The Laird wiped his eyes and got control of himself. Presently he said: "Keep that blessed dog off me," and started resolutely for the front gate. Without a moment's hesitation he folded Nan in his arms and kissed her. "Poor bairn," he whispered. "I've been cruel to you. Forgie me, daughter, if so be you can find it in your heart to be that generous. God knows, lass, I'll try to be worthy of you."

"Am I worthy of him?" she whispered, womanlike.

"Far more than his father is," he admitted humbly. "Damn the world and damn the people in it. You're a good girl, Nan. You always were a good girl——"

"But suppose she wasn't—always?" Donald queried gently. "Is that going to make any difference—to you?"

"I don't care what she was before you married her. I haven't thought about that for a long time the way I used to think about it. I built The Dreamerie for you and the girl you'd marry and I—I accept her unconditionally, my son, and thank God she has the charity to accept an old Pharisee like me for a father-in-law."

Donald slipped his arm around Nan's waist, and started with her toward the door. "Tag along, father," he suggested, "and Nan will show you a prize grandson."

At the door, Nan paused. "Do you think, father

McKaye," she queried, "that the remainder of the family will think as you do?"

"I fear not," he replied sadly. "But then, you haven't married the family. They'll accept you or keep out of Port Agnew; at any rate they'll never bother you, my dear. I think," he added grimly, "that I may find a way to make them treat you with civility at least."

"He's a pretty good old sport after all, isn't he, Nan?" her husband suggested.

"I'll tell the world he is," she answered archly, employing the A. E. F. slang she had already learned from Donald. She linked her arm in old Hector's and steered him down the hall to the living-room. "Your grandson is in there," she said, and opening the door she gently propelled him into the room.

NAN was right. His grandson was there, but strange to relate he was seated, as naked as Venus (save for a diaper) on his grandmother's lap.

Hector McKaye paused and glared at his wife.

"Damn it, Nellie," he roared, "what the devil do you mean by this?"

"I'm tired of being an old fool, Hector," she replied meekly, and held the baby up for his inspection.

"It's time you were," he growled. "Come here, you young rascal till I heft you. By the gods of war, he's a McKaye!" He hugged the squirming youngster to his heart and continued to glare at his wife as if she were a hardened criminal. "Why didn't you tell me you felt yourself slipping?" he demanded. "Out with it, Nellie."

"There will be no post-mortems," Nan interdicted. "Mother McKaye and Elizabeth and Jane and I patched up our difficulties when Donald came home yesterday. How we did it or what transpired before we did it, doesn't matter, you dear old snooper."

"What? Elizabeth and Jane? Unconditional surrender?"

She nodded smilingly and The Laird admitted his entire willingness to be—jiggered. Finally, having inspected his grandson, he turned for an equally minute inspection of his soldier son under the lamplight.

"Three service stripes and one wound stripe," he

murmured. "And you're not crippled, boy dear?"

"Do I fight like one? Hector, man, those punches of yours would have destroyed a battalion of cripples. Oh, you old false-alarm! Honestly, Dad, you're the most awful dub imaginable. And trying to bribe me into permitting you to escape—what the deuce have you been monkeying with? You reek of ammonia— here, go away from my son. You're poison."

The Laird ignored him. "What's that ribbon?" he demanded.

"Distinguished Service Cross."

"You must have bought it in a pawnshop. And that thing?"

"Croix de Guerre."

"And that red one?"

"Legion d'Honneur."

A pause. "What did Dirty Dan get, son?"

"The one thing in the world he thought he despised. The Congressional Medal of Honor for valor in saving the life of a British colonel, who, by the way, happens to be an Orangeman. When he discovered it he wanted to bayonet the colonel and I won the Croix de Guerre for stopping him."

"Oh, cease your nonsense, Donald," his wife urged, "and tell your father and mother something. I think they are entitled to the news now."

"Yes, Nan, I think they are. Listen, folks. Now that you've all been nice enough to be human beings and accept my wife at her face value, I have a surprise for you. On the day when Nan married the father of my adopted son, he waited until the officiating minister had signed the marriage license and attested that he had performed the ceremony; then while the minister's attention was on something else, he took possession of the license and put it in his overcoat pocket. Later he and Nan drove to a restaurant for luncheon and the overcoat with the license in the pocket was stolen, from the automobile. The thief pawned the coat later and the pawnbroker discovered the license in the pocket after the thief had departed. The following day the fellow was arrested in the act of stealing another overcoat; the pawnbroker read of the arrest and remembered he had loaned five dollars on an overcoat to a man who gave the same name this thief gave to the police. So the pawnbroker——"

"I am not interested, my son. I require no proofs."

"Thank you for that, father. But you're entitled to them and you're going to get them. The pawnbroker found on the inside lining of the inner breast pocket of the overcoat the tag which all tailors sew there when they make the garment. This tag bore the name of the owner of the overcoat, his address and the date of delivery of the overcoat."

"Now, the pawnbroker noticed that the man who owned the overcoat was not the person named in the marriage license. Also he noticed that the marriage license was attested by a minister but that it had not been recorded by the state board of health, as required by law—and the pawnbroker was aware that marriage licenses are not permitted, by law, to come into the possession of the contracting parties until the fact that they have been legally married has been duly recorded on the evidence of the marriage—which is, of course, the marriage license."

"Why didn't the idiot send the license back to the minister who had performed the ceremony?" The Laird demanded. "Then this tangle would never have occurred."

"He says he thought of that, but he was suspicious. It was barely possible that the officiating clergyman had connived at the theft of the license from his desk, so the pawnbroker, who doubtless possesses the instincts of an amateur detective, resolved to get the license into the hands of Nan Brent direct. Before doing so, however, he wrote to the man named in the license and sent his letter to the address therein given. In the course of time that letter was returned by the postoffice department with the notation that the location of the addressee was unknown. The pawnbroker then wrote to the man whose name appeared on the tailor's tag in the overcoat, and promptly received a reply. Yes, an overcoat had been stolen from his automobile on a certain date. He described the overcoat and stated that the marriage license of a friend of his might be found in the breast pocket, provided the thief had not removed it. If the license was there he would thank the pawnbroker to forward it to him. He enclosed a check to redeem the overcoat and pay the cost of forwarding it to him by parcel post, insured. The pawnbroker had that check photographed before cashing it and he forwarded the overcoat but retained the marriage license, for he was more than ever convinced that things were not as they should have been.

"His next move was to write Miss Nan Brent, at Port Agnew, Washington, informing her of the circumstances and advising her that he had her marriage certificate. This letter reached Port Agnew at the time Nan was living in San Francisco, and her father received it. He merely scratched out Port Agnew, Washington, and substituted for that address: 'Care of —— using Nan's married name, Altamont Apartments, San Francisco.'

"By the time that letter reached San Francisco Nan had left that address, but since she planned a brief absence only, she left no forwarding address for her mail. That was the time she came north to visit her father and in Seattle she discovered that her supposed husband was already married. I have told you, father, and you have doubtless told mother, Nan's reasons for refusing to disclose this man's identity at that time.

"Of course Nan did not return to San Francisco, but evidently her husband did and at their apartment he found this letter addressed to Nan. He opened it, and immediately set out for San Jose to call upon the pawnbroker and gain possession of the marriage license. Unknown to him, however, his lines were all tangled and the pawnbroker told him frankly he was a fraud and declined to give him the license. Finally the pawnbroker tried a bluff and declared that if the man did not get out of his place of business he would have him arrested as a bigamist—and the fellow fled.

"A month or two later the pawnbroker was in San Francisco so he called at the Altamont Apartments to deliver the license in person, only to discover that the person he sought had departed and that her address was unknown. So he wrote Nan again, using her married name and addressed her at Port Agnew, Washington. You will remember, of course, that at this time Nan's marriage was not known to Port Agnew, she had kept it secret. Naturally the postmaster here did not know anybody by that name, and in due course, when the letter remained unclaimed he did not bother to advertise it but returned it to the sender."

"It doesn't seem possible," Mrs. McKaye declared, quite pop-eyed with excitement.

"It was possible enough," her son continued drily. "Well, the bewildered pawnbroker thrust the license away in his desk, and awaited the next move of the man in the case. But he never moved, and after a while the pawnbroker forgot he had the license. And the minister was dead. One day, in cleaning out his desk he came across the accumulated papers in the case and it occurred to him to write the state board of health and explain the situation. Promptly he received a letter from the board informing him that inquiries had been made at the board of health office for a certified copy of the license, by Miss Nan Brent, of Port Agnew, Washington, and that the board had been unable to furnish such a certified copy. Immediately our obliging and intelligent pawnbroker, whose name, by the way, is Abraham Goldman, bundled up the marriage license, together with the carbon copy of the pawn ticket he had given the thief; a press clipping from the San Jose *Mercury* recounting the story of the capture of the thief; carbon copies of all his correspondence in the case, the original of all letters received, the photograph of the check—everything, in fact, to prove a most conclusive case through the medium of a well-ordered and amazing chain of optical and circumstantial evidence. This evidence he sent to Miss Brent, Port Agnew, Washington, and she received it about a week before I married her. Consequently, she was in position to prove to the most captious critic that she was a woman of undoubted virtue, the innocent victim of a scoundrel who had inveigled her into a bigamous marriage. Of course, in view of the fact that the man she went through a legal marriage ceremony with already had a wife living, Nan's marriage to him was illegal—how do you express it? Ipso facto or per se? In the eyes of the law she had never been married; the man in the case was legally debarred from contracting another marriage. The worst that could possibly be said of Nan was that she played in mighty hard luck."

"In the name of heaven, why did you not tell me this the day you married her?" The Laird demanded wrathfully.

"I didn't know it the day I married her. She was curious enough to want to see how game I was. She wanted to be certain I truly loved her, I think—and in view of her former experience I do not blame her for it. It pleased you a whole lot, didn't it, honey?" he added, turning to Nan, "when I married you on faith?"

"But why didn't you tell us after you had discovered it, Donald?" Mrs. McKaye interrupted. "That was not kind of you, my son."

"Well," he answered soberly, "in the case of you and the girls I didn't think you deserved it. I kept hoping you and the girls would confess to Dad that you telephoned Nan to come back to Port Agnew that time I was sick with typhoid——"

"Eh? What's that?" The Laird sat up bristling.

Mrs. McKaye flushed scarlet and seemed on the verge of tears. Donald went to her and took her in his arms. "Awfully sorry to have to peach on you, old dear," he continued. "Do not think Nan told on you, Mother. She didn't. I figured it all out by myself. However, as I started to remark, I expected you would confess and that your confession would start a family riot, in the midst of it I knew father would rise up and declare himself. I give you my word, Dad, that for two weeks before I went to work up at Darrow I watched and waited all day long for you to come down here and tell Nan it was a bet and that we'd play it as it lay."

Old Hector gritted his teeth and waged his head sorrowfully. "Nellie," he warned his trembling wife, "this is what comes of a lack of confidence between man and wife."

She flared up at that. "Hush, you hypocrite. At least I haven't snooped around here trying to poison dogs and kill people when I was discovered playing Peeping Tom. A pretty figure you've cut throughout this entire affair. Didn't I beg you not to be hard on our poor boy?"

"Yes, you had better lay low, Father," Donald warned him. "You've been married long enough to know that if you start anything with a woman she'll put it all over you. We will, therefore, forget Mother's error and concentrate on you. Remember the night I dragged you ashore at Darrow's log boom? Well, permit me to tell you that you're a pretty heavy tow and long before my feet struck bottom I figured on two Widows McKaye. If I'd had to swim twenty feet further I would have lost out. Really, I thought you'd come through after that."

"I would if you'd waited a bit," old Hector protested miserably. "You ought to know I never do things in a hurry."

"Well, I do, Dad, but all the same I grew weary waiting for you. Then I made up my mind I'd never tell you about Nan until you and Mother and the girls had completely reversed yourselves and taken Nan for the woman she is and not the woman you once thought she was."

"Well, you've won, haven't you?" The Laird's voice was very husky.

"Yes, I have; and it's a sweet victory, I assure you."

"Then shut up. Shut up, I tell you."

"All right! I'm through—forever."

The Laird bent his beetling brows upon Nan. "And you?" he demanded. "Have you finished?"

She came to him and laid her soft cheek against his. "You funny old man," she whispered. "Did you ever hear that I had begun?"

"Well, nae, I have not—now that you mention it. And, by the way, my dear! Referring to my grandson's half-brother?"

"Yes."

"I understand he's a McKaye."

"Yes, Donald has legally adopted him."

"Well, then, I'll accept him as an adopted grandson, my dear. I think there'll be money enough for everybody. But about this scalawag of a man that fathered him. I'll have to know who he is. We have a suit of zebra clothing waiting for him, my dear."

"No, you haven't, Father McKaye. My boy's father is never going to be a convict. That man has other children, too."

"I'm going to have a glass frame made and in it I'm going to arrange photographic reproductions of all the documents in Nan's case," Donald stated. "The history of the case will all be there, then, with the exception, of course, of the name of the man. In deference to Nan's desires I will omit that. Then I'll have that case screwed into the wall of the postoffice lobby where all Port Agnew can see and understand——"

"Nellie," The Laird interrupted, "please stop fiddling with that baby and dress him. Daughter, get my other grandson ready, and you, Donald, run over to the mill office. My car is standing there. Bring it here and we'll all go home to The Dreamerie—yes, and tell Daney to come up and help me empty a bottle to—to—to my additional family. He'll bring his wife, of course, but then we must endure the bitter with the sweet. Good old file, Daney. None better."

Donald put on his cap and departed. As the front gate closed behind him Hector McKaye sprang up and hurried out of the house after him. "Hey, there, son," he called into the darkness. "What was that you said about a glass case?"

Donald returned and repeated the statement of his plan.

"And you're going to the trouble of explaining to this sorry world," the old man cried sharply. "Man, the longest day she lives there'll be brutes that will say 'twas old man McKaye's money that framed an alibi for her.' Son, no man or woman was ever so pure that some hypocrite didn't tread 'em under foot like dust and regard them as such. Lad, your wife will always be dust to some folks, but—we're kindred to her—so what do we care? We understand. Do not explain to the damned Pharisees. They wouldn't understand. Hang that thing in the postoffice lobby and some superior person will quote Shakespeare, and say: 'Methinks the lady doth protest too much.' "

"Then you would advise me to tell the world to go to——"

"Exactly, sonny, exactly."